EMPIRES OF MOTH

EMPIRES OF MOTH

THE MOTH SAGA, BOOK TWO

DANIEL ARENSON

Copyright © 2013 by Daniel Arenson

All rights reserved.

This novel is a work of fiction. Names, characters, places and incidents are either the product of the author's imagination, or, if real, used fictitiously.

No part of this book may be reproduced or transmitted in any form or by an electronic or mechanical means, including photocopying, recording or by any information storage and retrieval system, without the express written permission of the author.

ISBN: 9781927601181

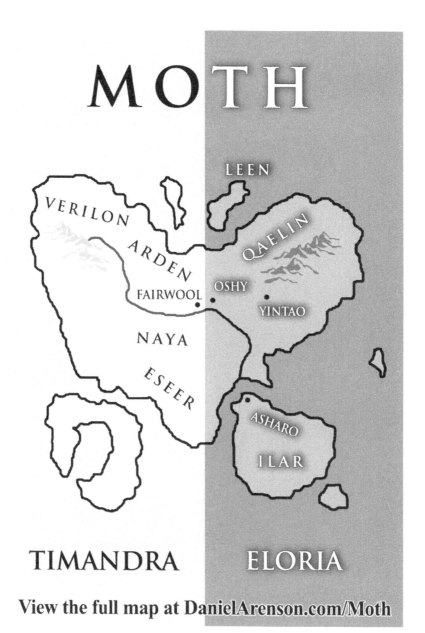

CHAPTER ONE
JIN

In the darkness of the new moon, another assassin tried to kill
Shenlai, the last dragon of the empire.

Jin felt so helpless, lying there, watching, shouting, unable
to move. He was Emperor of Qaelin, a vast land that stretched
across so much of the night, and yet as this enemy attacked, he
felt like no more than a crippled boy. How he wished for legs that
could run! How he prayed for arms and hands that could wield
weapons! He had none, but he had a mouth . . . and he screamed.

"Shenlai! Shenlai, fight him! Guards!"

Shenlai filled most of his bedchamber, his scaled body
coiling around the bed, pressing up against the walls, his blue
scales chinking. An ancient dragon, Shenlai was too large for this
chamber—he was meant to sleep in great caves, on mountaintops,
or even upon the moon itself—but Jin was always so scared to
sleep alone. Ten years old and limbless, even an emperor found
fear in loneliness and shadows. And so Shenlai entered his
bedchamber every hourglass turn, delicately looped himself
around the bed, and watched over Jin until he fell asleep.

Yet now . . . now would this kindness be the dragon's
death?

"Shenlai!" Jin called, tears in his eyes.

The assassin, clad in the dark silks of the dojai order, was
lashing a wavy dagger, slamming the blade repeatedly against
Shenlai's scales. The dragon tried to fight back. He raised his head
and lashed his tail, but he could barely move; the walls pressed
against him like a cocoon, and his horns kept clattering against the

ceiling. Perhaps the dragon could have fought better, Jin thought, were he not still carefully enveloping the bed, protecting his emperor.

Even as he bleeds, as the blade thrusts into him, he only thinks to protect me, Jin thought.

"Guards, please!" Jin cried, knowing they were dead. The only way a dojai assassin could reach his chamber, which lay deep within the palace, was to slay his defenders.

"Tell me your secret!" shouted the assassin, driving his dagger down against Shenlai. Blue scales cracked and blood seeped. "Feel your blood flow and reveal your secret, blue dragon of Qaelin."

Jin hopped upon the bed, trying to reach his friend, to leap onto the assailant and bite, but he only fell facedown onto the mattress. His bed was so large, a plain of silk, and he was so small, so weak. If he had limbs he could have leaped up, fought, and saved his friend. Born without them, he could simply lie and watch.

Like every other assassin, this robed man cared not to slay the boy emperor—only to hear Shenlai's dying words, for the last dragon of Qaelin held a secret, a great truth that could change the world, a knowledge for which armies had fought. Only with his dying breath could this ancient blue being reveal his secret. And so every year they tried to kill him—sometimes great hosts with a hundred thousand men and wolves, sometimes only lone killers. For five thousand years they had tried to slay Shenlai. For ten years, small Jin had loved his dearest—his only—friend.

I cannot see you die. But what can I do? His eyes burned. *I was born limbless, the child of siblings. How can I save you?*

The dagger sank again, driving between scales into the dragon's flesh, and Shenlai turned his head to look at Jin. His gleaming eyes, each as large as Jin's head, filled with sadness. He blinked, his lashes ruffling the blankets, and a tear streamed down into his white beard. Looking upon the dragon, Jin realized something that perhaps he should have seen years ago, that was so obvious his mind had never even considered it.

Shenlai has no limbs either. Jin took a shaky breath. *Yet he's the greatest being I know.*

"Reveal your secret, Shenlai," the assassin demanded, blood on his gloves. "You are dying. Your blood flows. Speak your words."

Shenlai opened his mouth, revealing sharp teeth, and Jin froze, tears in his eyes, wondering if this was it. After five thousand years, would Shenlai die here in this chamber, protecting him, and speak his mystery?

"No, Shenlai," Jin whispered, shoving his armless shoulders against the bed, pushing himself up. "I don't care what your secret is. You don't have to tell anyone. Please. *Please* don't die."

Dagger in hand, the assassin turned toward him. Jin couldn't see the man's face—a black scarf hid it—but he saw his eyes. Large, emerald eyes flecked with gold. The assassin stared, and those eyes narrowed.

"So the stories are true," the man said. "The Emperor of Qaelin is but a limbless boy, but a creature. Maybe after Shenlai bleeds out and I hear his secret, I will slay you too, and I will sleep upon your bed, and I will rule your empire."

Finally it seemed that rage filled Shenlai's blue eyes. The dragon bared his fangs and lunged toward the assassin, his horns scraping along the wall. The assassin leaped back, dodging the attack, and thrust his dagger again. The blade sparked across Shenlai's cheek.

"Still alive, old beast?" The man laughed. "Bleed out! Bleed for me. With your dying breath, you will reveal your truth. I will quicken the process."

He raised the dagger again, prepared to stab Shenlai in the neck.

I have no strength, Jin thought. *I have no speed. But this is my friend, and he's always protected me. Now I must save him.*

Jin narrowed his eyes, dipped his head down, and grabbed his silken sheet between his teeth. Most people were surprised Jin could move at all; they thought him capable of no more than lying like a pillow. But even without limbs, Jin would often roll across rugs, hop about, and even swim. Now he leaped higher and farther than ever. He flew from the bed, the sheet clutched in his teeth; it trailed behind him like a cape. He sailed over the assassin's head, then opened his mouth, letting the sheet fall upon the intruder.

The man grunted and slashed at the silk enveloping him.

Jin thudded against the corner and thumped to the ground.

He spun to see a figure like a ghost, a sheet spinning around, the dagger tearing through the fabric.

"Kill him, Shenlai!" Jin cried. He sat slumped in the corner, his body bruising. "Quickly."

The dragon hissed. His body began to constrict, crushing the bed frame. Splinters showered. If before Shenlai had to coil delicately around the bed, protecting Jin, now—with the emperor in the corner—the dragon could rise. The bed shattered as his serpentine body rose taller. The dragon's tail lashed. Scales clanked. The assassin finally tore the sheet off, but it was too late for him. Shenlai's body wrapped around him and squeezed, a python constricting his prey.

"Crush him, Shenlai!" Jin shouted. "Squeeze him dead."

Wrapping the assassin in his body, Shenlai looked upon Jin, and his eyes were sad. For the first time, the dragon spoke. His voice sounded both deep and high, rumbling and beautiful, a voice like water in the depths and clouds in the sky, like moonlight and dust upon rocky plains, like night and the memory of day.

Empires of Moth

"He will sleep in my grip," said Shenlai, the last dragon of Qaelin, "and we will deliver him to the guards of this palace, but we will not slay him. He came here to bring death; we will prove ourselves nobler, beings of life and compassion. One can only fight death with life. One can only fight cruelty with compassion. One can only light darkness with light. Here, he sleeps." Gently, Shenlai loosened his grip, letting the assassin drop unconscious onto the remains of the shattered bed. "He will sleep for a long time and dreams will fill him of your bravery, Jin."

Jin stared at the unconscious man, then raised his eyes to meet Shenlai's gaze.

"I wasn't brave," he said. "I only did what I had to. I was afraid."

Shenlai nodded, scales chinking. "That is what bravery is. Bravery is doing what you must even when you are afraid." He looked at the open window and the stars that shone outside. "Fly with me. Let us fly far and breathe the air that flows from the mountains."

Like a mother wolf lifting her cub, Shenlai grasped Jin's shirt between his teeth. The dragon lifted the young emperor and placed him upon his back. Jin slipped snugly into a small, golden saddle. He wriggled about, letting clasps snap into place. Sitting here in his harness, he felt safe and secure, no longer a limbless boy but part of a dragon.

Boots thudded outside the chamber. The voices of guards cried out; they had found their slain comrades. The door burst open. Defenders of the palace stood there, clad in scale armor. Their white hair was tied above their heads in knots, beards adorned their chins, and katanas gleamed in their hands. They looked down at the sleeping assassin and gasped, then raised their eyes to Jin.

"Are you safe, my emperor?" they asked, eyes wide.

9

Sitting in his harness upon his dragon, Jin nodded. "Take him. I never want to see him again." His eyes stung and he blinked furiously. "Now I will fly. Fly, Shenlai!"

The dragon turned to face the window. He coiled out like a snake emerging from a burrow, flying into the night sky.

The wind whipped Jin's face, cold and wet and sweet-scented, and he laughed. His hair fluttered. Beneath him, Shenlai let out a roar—a sound like thunder and joy itself, the sound of the night. They rose higher. The stars gleamed and the palace sprawled out below.

Jin looked down upon his home, the Eternal Palace. Inside that labyrinth of stone, he often felt like a queen ant trapped in a hive, never aware of the outside world, barely able to move. But here in the sky . . . from here his palace seemed a place of wonders—a walled complex of a hundred halls, towers, and courtyards. The buildings lay like blocks, each topped with slanting roofs of red tiles, their edges upturned like curling parchment. Here were barracks, temples, libraries, and armories, a city within a city. Cobbled roads spread between the structures, and countless guards marched back and forth, bedecked in scales and bearing spears and swords. In the center rose the Heavenly Hall—Jin's home—a great pagoda with seven tiers of roofs, their tiles red, their tips holding dragon statues.

"Thousand of soldiers live within the Eternal Palace," Jin said. "And yet a man entered my chamber. Perhaps there is no safety in the world."

Shenlai coiled beneath him, wingless, moving across the sky like a snake upon water. "There is always danger in the world, and even the greatest army cannot fight every shadow in the night."

They rose higher. The wind fluttered Shenlai's beard, sending it back to tickle Jin in his saddle. The dragon's blue scales clanked and shimmered. As they soared, Jin saw his city sprawl beyond the palace walls.

Empires of Moth

"Yintao," he whispered. "The wonder of the night."

Capital of Qaelin, the city was the greatest in his empire—
perhaps the greatest in all Eloria, the dark half of this world men
called Moth. It grew around the Eternal Palace like a field of
mushrooms around a lake. A million people lived in Yintao—it
was a city to dwarf all others, even the great Pahmey in the west.
Seven layers of walls rose here, squares within squares. Between
each level of fortifications, brick houses lined cobbled streets as
neatly as soldiers, their roofs tiled with adobe. Lanterns rose every
twenty yards, a painting of light and shadow. They said the
western cities were tangled hives, towers and homes and temples
all jumbled together, but not this place. The capital of Jin's empire
was as meticulous as a tapestry. From up here, it seemed to him a
clockwork, a city like an army, a wonder of light and life.

"Fly faster!" Jin cried upon the dragon's back. "Fly into the
wilderness of night."

The dragon flew faster, his serpentine body undulating.
Smoke puffed out from his mouth, and his beard and eyebrows
fluttered like banners. The city streamed below and Jin laughed,
for here was freedom greater than any in the palace. Here a
limbless, frightened boy who had grown up in stone halls could
feel the wind, taste the clouds, and be mightier and faster than any
hero.

They flew over the city's seventh wall, the outer layer, and
emerged into the open night.

The wilderness of Eloria spread out below, black plains that
rolled into the horizon. Only the Sage's Road broke the darkness,
a line of lights heading westward, small mushroom farms and
trading posts rising alongside; it stretched for many miles, all the
way to Pahmey in the west. Everywhere else Jin looked he saw
nothing but the night, rocky and black and empty. The lights
below grew smaller, and the stars brightened above, an endless
world of shine and shadow. Jin often wished they could fly to

11

those distant stars. He wondered if cities spread among them too and if other dragons flew there; only three dragons remained in Eloria, the dark half of the world, and only one in his empire of Qaelin.

"There is only you here, Shenlai," he said, the wind swallowing his words. "You are very old and very precious. You are my dearest friend." He blinked tears from his eyes. "I'm so glad you're still alive."

Flying through the night, leaving the city far behind, Shenlai turned his head and looked back at Jin. Sadness filled his eyes and he spoke in a low voice.

"We defeated danger in the palace, yet a greater danger rises in the west. A peril looms that could burn all the lands of night."

Jin shivered, suddenly feeling less safe in his harness. He looked around, seeking enemies. The city of Yintao lay upon the eastern horizon, a glowing smudge fading into the darkness. The Sage's Road sprawled beneath him, a mere thread from up here, its lights flickering upon each milestone. All else lay in shadow, for few people ventured far into the cold, dark wilderness of Eloria.

"What is the danger?" Jin asked in a small voice, scanning the darkness, seeking monsters or demons of the afterworld.

Shenlai's tufted eyebrows bunched together. His scales clattered.

"Hold on tight, little one," he said, an old joke of theirs. "We will fly faster than ever. I will show you."

Jin's heart sank. He didn't want to fly anywhere near danger.

"Are you sure, Shen—" he began, then gasped when Shenlai's body straightened and he flew faster than an arrow.

The lands blurred below. The stars trailed above. The wind whipped them and soon it seemed as if the earth below vanished, the hills and plains all falling into shadow, as if Eloria faded away, a mere bad dream like the ones that sometimes plagued him. All

Empires of Moth

creation was but the stars above, the soothing blackness, and the dragon beneath him. And it felt right. It felt like truth. As they flew and as the distance blurred, even dragon and rider seemed to fade, washing away until Jin was no longer a boy upon a dragon, until there was no more boy—he was thought itself. Then thought vanished too, leaving him only *being*, only *existing*, only consciousness among sky and darkness and stars and light and shadow. He was as a duskmoth. He was an ancient world, frozen in a cosmic ocean, one half light, one half dark, broken. Needing healing. There was fear here, deep and dark and sticky and cold, but also hope that stung, joy that would whisper if he could only find it.

The world had stopped like a dead heart. He—the world itself, the sky, the mind flowing through it—would have to fix it. He would have to uncover the shard inside and draw out the poison.

The world slowed.

The wind died.

He blinked and found himself within his body again, a small and limbless body in a harness, flying upon a dragon, gazing toward a horizon of fire.

"See them, Jin," said Shenlai. "See those who march from the sun."

They flew closer, and a gasp fled Jin's lips.

An army covered the horizon.

"An army of fire," he whispered.

A hundred thousand troops or more stood upon the edge of the night. They swarmed across the barren landscapes. They marched through a city of crystal towers. They raised banners and beat drums and howled for war.

"Who are they?" Jin whispered.

"They come from the land of sunlight," said Shenlai, voice soft. The dragon hovered, facing the distant light. "They come

13

here to burn, to conquer, to destroy. The city you see is Pahmey, the western jewel of your empire; it has fallen to their fire."

Jin's eyes stung. He had never seen Pahmey before, but he had read about this city in books and scrolls. Its hundred towers rose gleaming from the inferno of sunlit soldiers. The banners of the day—sunbursts upon white fields—rose from their crests.

"Timandrians," Jin whispered. "They're real."

He had read about Timandrians too, but he had always thought them legends, creatures no more real than cave spirits or river wisps. Many of his teachers claimed that Timandra, the sunlit half of Moth, was only a myth. Others claimed it was real but that no life could exist in a land of such heat and fire.

"This enemy will march across your empire, Jin," said Shenlai. "They will travel east. They will seek the capital and our palace. They will seek you too."

Jin stared, eyes wide and stinging, and his heart thudded. "Can you stop them, Shenlai? Can you stop them like you stopped the assassin in the palace?"

Shenlai lowered his head. "No, for I am but a teacher, not a warrior, not a leader. You will stop them." He turned his head toward Jin, his orbs gleaming with tears. "You will need all your strength and courage and wisdom. With them you can fight this enemy."

"But . . ." Jin swallowed and felt tears on his cheeks. "But I'm weak. I have no arms or legs. I was born crippled. The masters say I'm cursed because my parents were siblings, and now I must suffer for their sin. How can I fight this army?"

Shenlai moved his head closer, and the breath from his nostrils warmed Jin. "True strength is not of the body but of the soul. And your soul is strong. It is strong as mountains, as flowing rivers, as the night itself."

"I don't feel strong." Jin lowered his head. "Will you fight with me? Will you always stay near? Some whisper that you're very

Empires of Moth

old; I hear them. They say you'll die soon and reveal your secret." Jin's tears streamed. "Please don't die, Shenlai. Please always stay with me."

Shenlai smiled softly, the wind fluttering his beard and mustache. "I am very old, Jin. It's true. And yes, my time will soon come." Jin's tears flowed, but Shenlai kept speaking, his voice soothing. "Someday soon my soul will fly to the stars, leaving my body behind. And you'll have to carry on without me. You'll have to use all your strength and all the wisdom that I see in you."

Jin's chin pressed against his chest. "I don't want you to leave me. I love you, Shenlai."

The dragon's head moved closer, and his snout nuzzled Jin, tickling him with that bristly mustache.

"Death cannot kill love. Death cannot erase the joy of life. Good memories and love always stay inside you, a fire that burns forever and warms you even in the coldest, darkest night. That is why we have memories; they are a treasure loss cannot claim."

With that, Shenlai turned in the sky and began flying back east, back toward the distant capital of Yintao. They flew for a long time over the plains and under the stars, leaving the fires of war behind . . . fires Jin knew would spread. They flew until they saw the lights of Yintao on the horizon, the city he ruled.

"Shenlai, I don't want to return home." Jin lowered his head. "There is too much pain there . . . too many bad dreams. Can we sleep outside the city under the stars? I'm frightened and the starlight will soothe me."

Shenlai laughed softly, coiling upon the wind. "You are the emperor."

"I don't feel like one. I only feel like a boy. Not even a real boy. Please, Shenlai, let's sleep outside and I can lie upon your scales."

Shenlai began spiraling down. The wind whistled around them. Hills rolled below, smooth like polished onyx, and Shenlai

15

descended onto a hilltop. With gentle teeth, he pulled Jin out of his saddle and placed him upon his warm scales. The scales were hard as tiles but felt soothing to Jin, more so than his silken bed at home. Shenlai coiled up, enveloping Jin with warmth. The dragon's snowy beard draped over Jin like a blanket. His eyes, large orbs like crystal balls, gleamed as they watched him.

"Many people in the palace will worry about you and miss you," Shenlai said, "but you can fall asleep here, and when you are sleeping, I will carry you home."

Jin wiggled until he was comfortable and warm, but he did not feel safe. He was afraid of more assassins. He was afraid of the sunlit army in the west. And mostly he was afraid of his dearest friend dying.

"I hope you never die," he whispered. "And if you do, you don't have to tell me your secret. You don't have to tell anyone. I'll miss you when you're gone, Shenlai, but I promise to be strong and wise like you taught me. I love you."

His eyes closed and he slept, dreaming that he could fly on his own, a new dragon of the night, and reach the sun and the moon.

CHAPTER TWO
THE SUN AND THE MOON

"He's my half-brother."

Koyee stared into the mirror, the horror dancing in her eyes like yezyani upon a pleasure den's stage.

"Eelani . . . Ferius is my half-brother."

Several moons ago, Torin had taken her hand, stroked her hair, and revealed the secret to her, translating the words Ferius had spoken in Bluefeather Corner as she had lain wounded at his feet. She had laughed then, had shoved Torin back, had refused to believe . . . and every turn since, she had stood here in her chamber, staring at her reflection, those ghosts dancing.

"The demon of sunlight. Ferius the Cruel. The monk who nearly slew us in Bluefeather Corner. Eelani . . . he was born of my mother."

Her shoulder spirit was silent, and Koyee could barely feel the usual warmth on her shoulder, the weight—light as a feather—of her invisible friend. Since the battle, Eelani had been so quiet, so still, barely more than the hint of a whisper. Sometimes Koyee wondered if the spirit was crushed under the pain of this war.

And what of myself? Koyee stared at her reflection, seeking tears, pain, even a wince or grimace. Yet her face remained blank. A triangular face, her forehead too wide, her chin too small. Three scars—one across her brow, one along her cheek, and one tugging her lip into a half-smile. Long, smooth hair the color of snow. Her mother had died years ago, and many said that Koyee shared her features.

17

He has them too, she realized. Ferius too had the wide brow, the small chin. Her eyes were large and lavender, and Ferius had beady eyes—a relic of his Timandrian father—but Koyee had seen her mother in his face.

"His shame drives him," Torin had told her. "He's so ashamed of his mixed blood, of what he calls impurity, that now he seeks to slay all Elorians—a vengeance against your mother and what he believes was her sin."

Koyee turned away from the mirror. She stared at her chamber, the humble abode of a yezyana. Fur blankets topped a simple bed. A few silk dresses hung on pegs, dragons and stars embroidered upon them. Her flute and several books lay upon her bedside table. Her father's katana, the legendary blade Sheytusung, was hidden inside a rolled-up blanket under her bed. It was a simple place far from home. Perhaps this was her home now.

She looked out the window and saw them outside—the Timandrians troops, conquerors of her city. Somewhere out there, among them, he waited for her. Somewhere he was thinking of her, seeking her, dreaming of crushing her with his mace, of hushing all whispers of his shame.

"Ferius," she whispered. "We would've welcomed you into our family, even after Mother died. We would've given you a home with us—with me, my father, and Okado." She lowered her head and finally her eyes watered. "But you invaded our land. You slew our people. You would slay me, and you would slay all the children of the night if you could." She grimaced, reached for her sword, and drew the blade. "But I will not let you. I swear to you, my half-brother. I hide for now in shadow, a yezyana named Madori, but I do not forget you. I do not forget your sin. So long as I can wield this sword, deep within me I am still Koyee of Oshy . . . and I remember."

Shouts rose from downstairs in the common room.

Empires of Moth

"Madori! Madori Mai! You will play your flute now. Madori Mai!"

She blinked and squared her shoulders. She lifted her clay mask from her bed—the mask of Madori, a hidden musician, a living doll. She hid her scars behind it. She placed down her sword and lifted her flute. It was a costly silver instrument and it played beautifully, but she often thought it worth less than her old bone flute, which she kept hidden under her mattress. She had played that bone flute upon the streets, an urchin in rags, and it had saved her life; perhaps it was now too precious to play.

As she stepped downstairs and entered the smoky common room, men cheered and tossed coins her way. They were soldiers of Timandra seeking ale, song, and women to leer at. She stepped onto her stage, and she played her silver flute for these men, but behind her mask she thought of Ferius, and she thought of her sword.

* * * * *

Torin frowned at his book and struggled to form the words.

"*Ceshe—shee—*" he said, wincing.

"*Ceshuey!*" said Koyee, tapping the book with her fingernail. "Shuey . . . like . . . *seleshuey fen*, remember?" She frowned at him. "*Ceshuey.*"

Sitting on the bed beside her, Torin placed the book down on his lap, groaned, and shook his head. It seemed a remarkably complicated word for such a small, humble creature as a spider; he wondered when he'd even need to say 'spider' in Qaelish, the tongue of this city.

They sat in her bedchamber in The Green Geode, the pleasure den where she played her flute. From downstairs in the common room, Torin could hear the sounds of singers, musicians, and drunken crowds; Koyee herself had only finished

19

playing moments ago. It sounded like a good time, and Torin longed to step downstairs and join the fun, but Koyee glared at him and slapped the book again.

"Look at book!" She spoke in his tongue of Ardish, her accent heavy. "Try again. Or you never learn."

Torin sighed. "These words are too difficult to pronounce," he said, reverting to Ardish too, his tongue of sunlit lands. "Was Qaelish invented to break men's teeth?"

Koyee rolled her eyes and slapped his shoulder. "No! Qaelish is beautiful. Qaelish is . . . how you say . . . words of poem?"

"Poetic?" Torin suggested.

She nodded. "Poetic. In Qaelish we say *laerin*. Like . . ." She made a movement with her hand. "Like wind and water. *Laerin*. Like flute music."

Torin looked at her in wonder. Her accent was thick and her speech slow, but in only six months she had picked up a remarkable amount of his language. He had taught her some himself; she had learned the rest by simply keeping her ears open on the streets, listening to the soldiers occupying her home. Meanwhile, Torin had spent these six months struggling to learn her tongue—the language of this empire Torin found himself lost in.

"*Laerin*," he said hesitantly, struggling to wrap his tongue around the foreign word. "*Qaelish laerin tesinda*. Qaelish is a musical language."

She groaned and shook her head, hair swaying. "No! *Qaelish tesinda laerin*. Like that. Not like in Ardish. First the . . . how you say? The main word. Then the . . . other word."

"First the noun, then the adjective," he said, feeling rather clever now that he was speaking Ardish again. "I understand. In your tongue I would say: Qaelish language musical."

Empires of Moth

She nodded and finally allowed herself to smile. "Yes! You learn. Slowly. You little stupid. But I teach you."

Her words were sharp but her eyes were soft. As much as Torin marveled at her skill with languages, he marveled at everything else about her. Her lavender eyes gleamed, as large and oval as chicken eggs. Her skin was snowy white, her hair long and smooth like cascading milk. Three scars stretched along her face—one halved her eyebrow, the other trailed across her cheek, and the third raised the corner of her mouth. And yet Torin thought her beautiful; these lines did not mar her face, he thought, but made her seem more enchanting, fierce, and strong. Her body, clad in a blue silk dress, seemed just as alluring to him, lithe yet curved in just the right places, and—

"Torin!" She jabbed her finger against the book. "You look here. Not at me. Look at book."

He swallowed, nodded, and quickly returned his eyes to the book. He felt his cheeks flush. She had caught him admiring her too many times, and Torin cursed himself.

I'm a soldier of sunlight occupying her city of the night, he thought. *I cannot let myself think of her . . . like that.*

Yet by Idar's beard, for the past six months, he had barely been able to banish these thoughts from his mind.

He flipped a page in his book, cleared his throat, and tried to keep reading. This was only a children's book, full of myths of old philosophers who would wander the darkness of Eloria, yet Torin still struggled with the words. Ardish was written with a phonetic alphabet, left to right, but Qaelish utilized a complex system of runes inscribed top to bottom. He read out loud, speaking the story of Xen Qae, the wise founder of the Qaelish nation, who could communicate with animals and speak with the stars.

"*Fenea*—" he said, stumbling over a word. "*Fenaexe*—"

21

She leaned close, and her hair fell from behind her ear, grazing his arm. When she pointed at the book, her fingers brushed against his. He looked up at her and met her eyes, and he was struck by how close their faces were; he would only have to lean forward for their lips to meet. He felt the heat of her body, a warmth like embers during a winter snowfall. She stared back, then lowered her gaze shyly and withdrew her hand. A soft smile touched her lips.

"*Fenae xeluan*," she said. "A hundred kisses." Now her cheeks were those to flush. "This is story of how Xen Qae met his wife, the beautiful Madori. I am named after her when I play flute." She met his gaze again, then blushed deeper and looked away. "I must play flute again now. I must go downstairs."

She quickly rose from the bed, turned away from him, and left the chamber.

Torin remained sitting on the bed, and a sigh rolled through him. Six months ago, he had marched into this city with a host of a hundred thousand Timandrians, his people of sunlight. Six months ago, he had slain a man, watched thousands die around him, and brought the wounded Koyee to this very chamber for healing and safety. Since then, he had returned to this chamber every hourglass turn, seeking her company. He told her that he wanted to learn Qaelish, that she was the finest teacher he could find, but the truth he kept hidden.

I keep returning here to see you, Koyee, he thought, gazing at the door. *To look into your eyes. To feel your fingers when they accidentally brush against mine. To hear your jokes, talk to you about animals, and make you smile. Because I—*

He shook his head wildly. Again these thoughts had come unbidden to his mind. Koyee might be intelligent, beautiful, and kind, but she was also Elorian, a daughter of the night. He was Timandrian, a soldier occupying her land. She was forbidden to him, and he vowed he would never return to this chamber

Empires of Moth

again—the same vow he made every visit, the same vow he knew he'd break again.

He rose to his feet and cracked his neck. He wore the steel and colors of Arden, one of Timandra's eight kingdoms of daylight. His steel breastplate was engraved with a raven, sigil of his people, while vambraces and greaves covered his limbs. A checkered cloak of gold and black draped across his shoulders. His sword hung at his side; he had not parted from this weapon since invading the night, and he often thought of it as a fifth limb, a part of him he hated but could not rid himself of.

He had joined this army almost a year ago, and yet he still did not feel like a soldier, only a gardener. Often he missed his gardens back home—the rustling euonymus bushes, his flowerbeds of many colors, and the trees he grew from seed to sapling. But that was back in Timandra, the sunlit half of the world. No plants could grow here in Eloria, a land of eternal night. Often Torin wanted to run, to make his way upriver, to return to sunlight and start a new life away from this war. But always he stayed.

"For you, Koyee," he said, gazing out the window at the city of Pahmey, this great hive his people had conquered. Timandrian troops marched along the streets, swords drawn, thugs in steel puffing out their chests as Elorians cowered before them. "I promised to protect you. So long as danger marches along these streets, I will stay with you."

He left the chamber, walked down a hallway, and made his way downstairs into the common room.

When first arriving in The Green Geode, this pleasure den among the towers of Pahmey, he had found a lair full of bearded, frail spicers—men addicted to *hintan*, the purple dust they paid their fortunes for. Back then, the spicers had lain upon mattresses, smoking from hookahs, filling the room with green smoke. All that was gone. The city of Pahmey had new masters now, and The

Green Geode served new patrons. A hundred Timandrian soldiers sat at tables where once mattresses had lain. Where spicers had once smoked in stupor, soldiers now drank ale and wine and cried out lustfully at the women performing on stages.

The yezyani of The Green Geode wore flimsy silks, their faces painted, their jewels gaudy. Professional performers and flirts, they danced, sang, played music, and one—an impish little thing named Atana—made marionettes dance. Soldiers hooted from the tables, tossed empty mugs their way, and called for the women to sit on their laps or warm their beds. The yezyani laughed, batted their lashes, and winked at the crowd; promptly coins were tossed toward them.

All but Koyee, that was. She stood upon a pedestal, a single calm pillar in a storm. A clay mask hid her face, painted white, for men across the city still sought the Girl in the Black Dress, the one who had slain so many Timandrian soldiers. On her pedestal, however, Koyee became only a masked musician, a ghost of sound. She held a silver flute to her lips and played soft, sad music that nearly drowned under the roar of the crowd.

"Come here, little woman!" cried one soldier, a scruffy man with a yellow beard and red face. "Come play here on my lap."

Another Timandrian soldier guffawed. "He's a drunk! Ignore him and join me in my chamber. Elorian men are weak as boys; I'll show you a real man."

Other soldiers, cheeks red with booze, catcalled at Koyee and reached out toward her, but she ignored them. She kept playing, eyes closed, until the soldiers grunted and turned to call out toward more receptive yezyani.

"You don't belong in a place like this, Koyee," Torin said softly, his voice drowning in the din.

He had seen her fight against armies, a single woman with a sword. He had seen her courage and wisdom. And yet . . . a young orphan girl, only seventeen, unwed, the monks of Sailith hunting her . . . where else could she hide but here?

At the thought of Sailith, Torin grumbled and clutched the hilt of his sword. The monks of sunlight had almost killed him and Koyee during the invasion of this city. Since then, the Sailith Order had spread through Pahmey like rot. Their banners rose upon the old temples of starlight. Their monks presided in columned halls, judging Elorians to die for crimes as petty as busking on the streets or daring to meet a Timandrian's eyes.

"And they're hunting you, Koyee," Torin whispered. "Since you wounded Ferius, he hasn't stopped hunting you."

As if to answer his thoughts, the main door creaked open behind him.

Torin spun toward it and his heart sank.

"Speak of demons," he grumbled.

In the doorway, holding a lantern, stood the monk Ferius.

Short of frame and broad of shoulders, Ferius stared into the pleasure den, lip curling. His beady, far-set eyes narrowed in disgust, as if he were staring at a rotten carcass. His black hair was receding from a broad, thrusting brow, slicked back like some oily rag. He seemed to Torin like a hairless, rabid dog prepared to strike. In the past six months, the monk's superiors—aging preachers of hatred from the capital—had mysteriously fallen to Elorian daggers, rotten meat, and other accidental deaths. Though still a young man—not yet forty—Ferius now ruled the Sailith Order, a group of hundreds of monks and countless worshipers among the Timandrian host.

Ferius sniffed—a loud, dry sound like a bellows. "So this is a . . . *pleasure* den." He wrinkled his nose. "Looks more like a den of disease and debauchery."

Bringing a handkerchief to his nose, he took a step deeper into The Green Geode. He brushed his yellow robes as if trying to remove the smell of the place. With him came his bodyguards,

25

three men clad in crimson armor, sunbursts upon their breastplates, their faces hidden within helmets. Here were the bloodsuns, warriors of Sailith, a force Ferius had founded in the darkness after his battle with Koyee. Monks in armor, their faith forbade them to bear blades, and so they wielded flanged maces to crush bones. Rather than their old yellow robes, they wore mustard cloaks over steel plates. Since his injury, Ferius never traveled anywhere without these devout thugs at his side.

The cheering died across the den. The dancers froze upon their stages. Even Koyee, masked upon her pedestal, paused with her flute an inch from her lips.

"What are you doing here, Ferius?" Torin said, unable to curb his own sneer. He walked between tables toward the monk. "Return to your temple; this is a place for soldiers, not the Sailith."

Ferius's lips stretched into a cruel mockery of a grin, a twisted mask of small teeth and a darting tongue. His eyes blazed with amusement.

"You think you are safe, Torin the Gardener, child of sunlight who slithers in shadow." Ferius licked his chops like a snake about to swallow a mouse. "You think are safe, perhaps, thanks to that King Ceranor whom you serve as ward." Ferius leaned closer, breath hissing against Torin's face. "Yet you are not safe, child. Not here in the dark. Not under the light of Sailith. Your king cannot protect you forever. The fire of Sailith will burn you . . . and it will burn that girl you hide. Yes, gardener. I know that you hide her. I will find her. Perhaps the king protects your blood, but he will not protect the precious Girl in the Black Dress."

Torin shoved the monk back. "Stay away from me, snake. So long as Ceranor lives, you are nothing but his dog." He gripped his hilt and drew a foot of steel. "This is no lair for Sailith. Leave this place. Leave or I'll shove this steel into your belly of bile."

Empires of Moth

At his sides, Ferius's bodyguards raised their maces. The iron gleamed red in the lamplight as if already bloodied. Armor creaked, and Torin drew the rest of his blade. All sounds died; not a note wafted and not a man seemed to breathe.

With a snort, Ferius waved his bodyguards back. "No, my warriors. The boy is a pet of his king. I will let him live. Death would be a kindness to him." Ferius licked his teeth. "I want him to live to suffer. When we find this Girl in the Black Dress, the savage he was willing to die for, he will watch her burn." Ferius met Torin's gaze, and the monk's eyes blazed with fervor and bloodlust. "Yes, you will watch her suffer, boy. Her death will be slow. She will die not in a great pyre, no . . . but linger for ages of agony. And you will hear her every scream."

Torin sucked in his breath, remembering the Elorian— Koyee's father—whom Ferius had burned at the stake. The stench of smoldering bones still filled Torin's nightmares. To see Koyee burn too . . . it would fill Torin with a pain that would consume him. For a moment, he could only stare at the monk in horror; in Ferius's eyes, he saw visions of burning flesh, Koyee and thousands of her fellow Elorians screaming in the Sailith fire.

I won't let that happen, Torin thought, grinding his teeth.

"You have three guards with you," Torin said, refusing to break the stare. "Fifty soldiers loyal to King Ceranor sit behind me. You have five hundred monks in your halls, the Elorian temples you stole and converted to your twisted faith. My king commands a hundred thousand troops. I warn you now: Leave this blade or you will taste my blade again. Yes, Ferius. You've tasted my steel before. I see the scar on your cheek has not healed."

Ferius raised his hand to touch the white line; Torin had given him that wound last autumn, fighting in the square while Koyee lay bleeding at their feet. Torin wished he had finished the job then.

27

"A single monk of Sailith shines with more light than a million soldiers lost in darkness," Ferius said. Finally he broke the stare, turning to gaze across the room. "Dancers and singers perform upon these stages. Yet I think them closer to harlots. See how their silks barely cover that weak, sickly flesh of Elorian pallor. They disgust me." He brushed past Torin, moving closer to examine the yezyani who stood frozen upon their stages, watching him. "I wonder if one among them is the creature I seek."

Torin's heart thudded. Koyee no longer wore a black dress but blue silk. She no longer held a katana but a flute. A mask hid her face. And yet cold sweat trickled down Torin's back as Ferius moved from yezyana to yezyana, his eyes narrowed like a butcher scrutinizing fowls to choose one for beheading.

"Ferius, the king commanded you slay no civilians, and these women—"

Ferius snickered. "*Women*, are they? I call them *creatures*. The Elorians have no men, no women, no children. They are not human. They are not even animals. They are demons to be burned in our sunfire." The monk came so stand before Lilika, a tall and beautiful yezyana who sang for soldiers. "This one is too tall and fair." He turned toward Atana, the impish puppeteer. "This one is too short and scrawny, a pale little worm." He looked at two dancers next, then finally turned to stare at Koyee. "Ah . . . and what have we here? An Elorian of the right size, her face hidden behind a mask. I wonder . . . do three scars hide behind that mask?"

Koyee stood still upon her stage, flute in hand. Her mask was blank, but her body spoke of tense fear and anger; she seemed ready to pounce onto Ferius and attack with tooth and nail.

Visions of her father burning in his mind, Torin stomped between tables of soldiers, grabbed Ferius's shoulders, and tugged him back.

Empires of Moth

"Leave the yezyani alone," he said, clutching Ferius's collar.

Ferius sneered, spraying saliva. "Yezyani? You speak their tongue now, boy? Beware . . . for if I deem you a demon too, even your king could not protect you. Perhaps I will burn this creature upon her stage, and after you see her death, I will burn you too."

Torin shoved the monk.

Ferius stumbled backwards. His back hit a table, and mugs of ale fell and shattered.

Around the pleasure den, men leaned back and sucked in their breath. Ferius's bloodsuns advanced, maces in hand. Torin growled and raised his sword, placing himself between Koyee and the monks. Snarling, Ferius pushed himself off the table and lifted his own mace. Torin dared to hope his fellow soldiers in the den would fight with him, but the men only moved toward the walls, watching as Torin stood alone before the monks.

And so we fight again, Torin thought, heart pounding and breath quick. The four monks—Ferius in his yellow robes and his bloodsuns in crimson steel—advanced toward him. *I will not let them touch you, Koyee.*

He was prepared to swing his sword when the doors banged open again.

Cold wind blew into the pleasure den, extinguishing a lamp.

Three figures—one tall, one beefy, and one short—stood in the doorway, the street lamps bright behind them.

"I told you boys!" said the tall figure. "You had to turn left at the fish market."

The beefy figure whined. "I did turn left! This whole city is a labyrinth. Why did Torin have to pick a tavern so far away? Can we get something to eat now?"

The short figure groaned. "Hem, we could have eaten hours ago, if you hadn't—ow, Bailey!"

The tall figure grabbed the others by the ears and tugged, dragging them into The Green Geode. As they stepped inside, the

29

lamplight fell upon them. The glow illuminated Bailey Berin, a tall young woman with flashing brown eyes, two golden braids, and pale armor. Twisting their ears, she dragged forward Cam and Hem, two younger boys from her village, now soldiers in her service. When the three saw the monks ahead, their eyes widened.

"What in the name of Idar is going on here?" Bailey demanded. She released the boys and drew her sword. "Ferius! I told you that no monks are allowed in here." Her eyes moved to Torin, then widened further. "Winky! And I told *you*—stay away from these thugs. Do you really think you can fight them alone, a scrawny boy like you?"

Torin stood with his sword raised, not sure if he felt more relief or annoyance. The monks, who had been advancing toward him, grunted and spun between him and the new arrivals.

Within heartbeats, his three friends—his dearest, closest friends in the world—were standing beside him, their swords drawn. Bailey sneered and sliced the air with her blade. Even the lumbering Hem and the diminutive Cam, hardly the fiercest soldiers in this army, managed to look somewhat menacing as they brandished their weapons.

Ferius hissed at them like a snake. "So you cannot fight your own battles, boy." The monk spat; the glob landed near Torin's boot. "Still you hide behind the skirts of your gangly female friend." He sneered at Bailey. "The girl who fashions herself a warrior has not yet tasted pain. But she will. She will burn among the heathens."

Bailey growled. "Come and try to burn me, snake." She swung her sword, forcing the monks back a step. "We end this here."

Ferius's lip curled so far back it nearly touched his nose. With a grunt, the monk spun on his heel.

"Come, my paladins of sunlight," he said to his men. "We will not brawl in a tavern like lowly peasants." He looked over his

Empires of Moth

shoulder, giving Torin an evil glare. "We will deal them our justice, but not here in the shadows. All those who seek to protect the creatures will stand trial. They will confess their sins within our halls, and we will smell the sweetness of their flesh burning for Sailith."

"Yeah, you keep walking away!" Bailey called after him. "Go and hide, Ferius! If you ever set foot here again, I will show you no more mercy. Run, dog! Run with your tail between your legs."

"Bailey, don't goad him," Torin said, placing a hand on her shoulder, but he had to confess—the sight of the monks leaving the tavern, their pride wounded, swelled his chest.

For another moment, silence filled The Green Geode.

Then a soldier grumbled and gulped down his ale. Another began to sing a drunken song. Soon the yezyani were dancing and singing again, and the pleasure den returned to its former state of song, drink, smoke, and lights.

Bailey slammed her sword back into its scabbard and shook her fist at the door. "It's almost too bad he fled. I rather wanted to stick my sword into him."

Torin stared at the door grimly. "He'll be back with more of his thugs. Instead of three men, he'll return with a hundred." Belly sinking, he turned toward Koyee and gazed upon her. Through the holes in her mask, her eyes met his. "We have to get you out of here, Koyee. We're leaving. Now."

CHAPTER THREE
THE SISTERS OF HARMONY

As Torin dragged her down the street, Koyee tried to resist, planting her feet firmly on the ground.

"Torin!" she said, speaking in his tongue. "I no scared of him. If my half-brother come back, I fight him." The foreign words of Arden, his kingdom of sunlight, still felt awkward around her tongue, but she had mastered his language better than he spoke hers, and so she plowed on. "I wear mask in Green Geode and I have . . . how you say . . . little sword?"

She caressed her poniard, which she kept strapped to her thigh under her silken dress. Many a time, she had stroked that hidden blade, dreaming of shoving it into Ferius's throat. Her katana she kept inside a rolled-up blanket that now swung across her back. Should Timandrian soldiers catch her with a blade, they would place her against the wall and slice her throat. She had seen enough Elorians murdered on these streets to keep her weapons concealed.

And yet, while the streets were dangerous, she had always felt safe in The Green Geode. Since the enemy had conquered Pahmey with fire and steel, the pleasure den had served as an oasis of calm, a place of music and drink where even Timandrians—murderous soldiers who had slain so many—drank and sang and, for a few hours, could be nothing but boys who missed home, seeking distraction in the bottom of mugs and the beauty of yezyani.

"A poniard won't help if Ferius returns with a hundred monks," Torin said, leading her by the hand. "And he will. He's

Empires of Moth

been seeking you for six months—the Girl in the Black Dress, the one who wounded him. He now knows you play in The Green Geode . . . or suspects it, at least." He looked at her, his one eye green, the other black. "You can never return."

They walked down a cobbled street lined with braziers. He wore the armor of an Ardish soldier; she still wore her blue silk, her face hidden behind the clay mask yezyani often wore when performing plays or dances. If she walked alone along these streets, she knew that soldiers would harass her, rifle through her pack, leer and snicker, and might even attack. But with Torin at her side, all other Timandrians she passed—these tall, burly soldiers of sunlight, so much larger than slim Elorians—barely spared her a glance. It was not uncommon for Timandrian soldiers to walk with Elorian women on their arms, especially not yezyani, professional comforters of local and foreign men. Already some Elorian bellies were swelling with the children of Timandrian men.

"Torin!" she said again, trying to free her hand from his grip. "I no scared of him. Let him come back." She snarled. "I stabbed his leg last time. Next time, I stab his heart."

He stopped walking, though he still held her hand. In his eyes, she saw haunting memory and pain. It wiped the smile off her face and chilled her belly. She touched his cheek. His skin was still darker than hers, though with every moon in the endless night of Eloria, it grew paler.

"What wrong?" she whispered.

He lowered his head, took a deep breath, and looked around the street. A group of Timandrian soldiers stood outside a nearby pottery shop. A knight rode down the street upon his horse. Only three Elorians could be seen—young women rushing home from the market, mushrooms and fish in their baskets, quickening their steps as the Timandrians catcalled and jeered.

33

Koyee heard one soldier mumble, ". . . too scrawny, these savage girls are, but I'd take the short one to my barracks."

Eyes darkening, Torin led Koyee into an alleyway. The facades of a teahouse and a barbershop flanked them. Two stray cats—animals that had come unbidden aboard the Timandrian ships—hissed in the shadows and scurried deeper into the darkness.

"Koyee, Ferius is . . ." Torin began, and even though he spoke his own tongue now, she could tell the words pained him. "He is more dangerous than you know. Especially now that he rules the Sailith Order. He's capable of evil you cannot imagine." He squeezed her hand. "I told you that he's your half brother, but . . . I haven't told you everything. It hurt too much. Oh, merciful Idar."

She caressed his cheek. "What is it, Torin? You can tell me."

He clenched his jaw and could not meet her eyes. "I was there when he died. Your father." Finally he looked up and met her gaze, and she saw the ghosts within them. "I saw him burned at the stake. The man who judged him, who lit the fires, who murdered your father . . . was Ferius. And if he can, Koyee, he will murder you too. He will murder everyone in this city. Please don't goad him. *Hide.*"

Koyee felt as if the alley—no, the entire city—crumbled around her. All the lights of Pahmey, from the lanterns in the boulevard to the gleaming towers on the hilltop, seemed to vanish, and even the stars lost their shine.

Stars above, my father . . . I fought the man who killed him and . . .

A snarl rose deep inside her, fleeing her lips like steam. She ground her teeth. She reached into her rolled up blanket, grabbed the hilt of her sword, and shoved past Torin.

"I will kill him now," she said, eyes burning. "I will find him and . . . and . . ."

34

Empires of Moth

The rage and pain flowed over her. She no longer knew where she stood. She felt arms wrap around her, and she tried to free herself, but they held her firmly. She struggled. She kicked. But he kept holding her, her Torin, the boy who was her friend, the boy who had saved her, and she let him hold her. She let him stroke her hair. She trembled against him until she could see again.

"We will kill him someday," Torin said. "I promise you. You will be avenged. I will not rest until Ferius sees justice for his crimes, until my people are cleansed of his poison. But not now. Not in this city. Not like this. He's too strong now, and if we face him, we will die."

She snarled up at him, gripping his arms. "I will not spend my life hiding!"

"I don't ask you to." He held her waist and his eyes softened. "I just ask you to bide your time. That's all we can do now. This nightmare won't last forever. Help will come for Pahmey."

She gave a mirthless laugh and switched to speaking Qaelish, hoping he understood her words. "And who will help us? The Ilari Empire, our neighbors of the night? They hate Qaelin; they've raided our southern shores and butchered our people with us much relish as Timandra. The wise old Leen Empire in the northern darkness? No. Their people hide in forests of crystals, worship the stars, and care not for affairs beyond their island. We are alone, Torin. There is no help for us."

"The Emperor of Qaelin will help," he said, still speaking his own tongue. "They say he lives in a great city, that he commands an army as large as Arden's."

Koyee shook her head, hair swaying. "Then where is he? Where is this army of Emperor Jin?" She blew out her breath, blowing back strands of hair. "I don't know if this emperor even exists, if this great city of his—Yintao, they call it—is more than

35

some ancient myth. If we bide our time, we will fade into endless despair. Let us strike Ferius now! You and me. Your friends too. We will sneak into Ferius's temple and—"

"And find hundreds of monks in armor, all bearing maces," Torin finished for her. "Please, Koyee. You are hurt now, angry, and afraid. I am too. Now is not the time to strike. The tree cracks in the storm; the rushes bend and survive."

"We have neither trees nor rushes in Eloria," she replied; she was still speaking her own tongue while he spoke his.

"But you have me, and I swore to protect you. If I die, I will have failed. Please. Don't hide for the memory of your father. Don't hide for your people. Hide for me."

She tore off her clay mask and tossed it down; it clattered onto the alley floor.

"Look at my face, Torin. Look at my scars. The whole city knows what I look like. At The Green Geode, I could wear a mask. Hiding isn't very easy if it's outside a pleasure den."

Torin looked down at the discarded mask and took a deep breath. "There's one more place where your face can be hidden. You won't like it, but it's the safest place for you—a place where monks fear to tread, where no eyes will gaze upon you. Come with me. We go there now."

She nodded weakly, her belly roiling with fear and pain, and lifted her mask. They left the alley.

They walked along the streets of Pahmey, a soldier and yezyana, a son of sunlight and a daughter of the night. They walked through marketplaces where Elorians shopped, silent and quick as Timandrian soldiers watched from every corner. They passed by columned temples where Elorian philosophers had once worshiped the stars, where monks of Sailith now chanted for sunlight and sunburst banners waved. They passed the Night Castle, a pagoda of brick walls and five tiers of blue roofs, the place where soldiers of Pahmey had once trained . . . and where

36

Empires of Moth

hundreds of Timandrian soldiers now lived, including King Ceranor. Everywhere they walked, those sunlit soldiers marched and stood, sentinels of steel, occupiers of fire, ready to deal death to any who glanced their way.

After walking for what felt like miles, Koyee saw the building Torin was leading her to, and she stopped in her tracks.

"No, Torin," she said. "No. Not there."

"It's the only way." He stared ahead. "It's either stay here or leave this city and seek your luck in the wilderness."

"Then I choose wilderness."

He looked at her. "You will not survive on the dark, lifeless plains of the night. Not with hosts of Timandra sweeping across Eloria. Arden has conquered this city; the other seven sunlit kingdoms march across the rest of the night." His voice softened. "Come, Koyee. We'll step inside together."

She returned her eyes to the building and grimaced. The Hospice of Pahmey loomed above her like a mausoleum for giants. Upon a hundred pedestals, bronze incense burners scattered their scent, barely masking the stench of decay from within. Beyond the smoke, columns supported a roof of black tiles. Through tall windows, Koyee glimpsed healers moving to and fro. Each wore thick leather robes and a beak-shaped mask.

"The Sisters of Harmony wear beaks full of incense to protect themselves from disease." She shivered. "Torin, this place is full of illness."

"Which is why Ferius will never seek you here." He flashed her a rare smile.

Koyee had begun to roll her eyes when wails and chants rose behind her. She turned and covered her mouth. *Oh stars of Eloria . . .*

A group of women walked toward the hospice, clad in robes of boiled leather and iron bolts, their masks mockeries of beaks. True birds—wingless creatures as tall as horses—walked

37

among them, pulling a wagon. Twenty or more Elorians lay in the wagon, shivering and sallow, moaning with disease. Boils covered their skin, and their hair had fallen, revealing spotted scalps. They gazed at Koyee, whispering with toothless mouths, pleading, begging for death.

"They have the sunlit curse," she whispered.

The plague had come with the Timandrians, borne upon their ships like the feral cats. A decade ago, it had culled those of Timandra susceptible to its miasma. But in Eloria the disease was new, and it struck everywhere. Some Elorians never caught the illness, even when close to those infected; others fell at the first whiff of its stench.

"Bless you, my friends," Koyee whispered as the wagon rolled by. She raised her hand to the stars. "May Xen Qae heal you."

As they walked by, the robed women—the Sisters of Harmony—turned slowly, their suits creaking. Their leather beaks faced her, long and strange; the women seemed like vultures hungry for flesh. The masks spread across their faces; their eyes remained hidden behind smoky glass lenses. Wide hats topped their heads, and their robes trailed along the ground, clattering with iron bolts and buckles. Not a speck of their flesh was exposed; they could have been automatons of metal and leather, great toys with gears and springs inside.

"Beware the curse of light," one said, voice deep and eerie inside her mask. "Beware the wrath of boils, the raw gums, the blood that blackens. Leave this place, daughter of the night. This is a place of pain. Seek solace in the shadows, for the sun rises."

Koyee stared into those dusty lenses, those inhuman glass eyes, and shivered.

Here is a place, she realized, *that I must enter.*

She too would wear this mask, becoming a strange vulture of nightmares, and she too would watch so many perish.

Empires of Moth

The Sisters of Harmony turned back toward the hospice. They kept walking, taking their wagon of disease with them. The dying Elorians wailed, slumped together like discarded skins. The healers led their charges between the columns and into the great mausoleum.

"No one ever emerges from there alive," Koyee said.

"Those who catch the plague do not," Torin said. "But you will be a healer, not a patient. You will wear the beaked mask and none will hurt you." He squeezed her hand. "You've been with me for half a year now. I do not believe the sunlit plague favors you, or it would have struck already. But Ferius would kill you . . . and so here you must hide."

She shuddered and they stepped forward.

The incense burners crackled at their sides. Smoke wafted. They stepped between columns and into the darkness of the hospice. The stench of the dying flared, and the screams washed over them like waves.

CHAPTER FOUR
THE QUEEN OF SUNLIGHT

Linee the First of House Solira, Queen of Arden, arrived in the
dark city of Pahmey with a cavalcade of splendor—knights on
horseback, musicians in motley blowing trumpets, jesters juggling
silver balls, and Dalmatians running alongside her carriage with
silver bells ringing from their collars. Yet no fanfare could soothe
her now. She leaned toward the window, peered outside her
carriage, and wrinkled her nose.

"It absolutely *stinks*," she said. She cuddled her puppy to her
chest. "Doesn't it, Fluffy? Absolutely *stinks*."

She didn't understand how anyone could possibly live in
this place. The night was just . . . just *awful*. First of all, it was too
dark everywhere. Linee had known it was dark in Nightside—this
place the natives called Eloria—but, well . . . she had imagined
that at least the sun emerged *sometimes* to shine. As it was, she had
been traveling through Nightside for twenty hourglass turns now,
and she hadn't seen so much as a single sunbeam, only those
awful little spots people called stars and that hideous, bloated face
they called the moon. For so long, the wilderness of endless
darkness had spread around her, just shadows and rocks, and
every creak of a soldier's armor, and every bump on the road,
made her squeal with fright and imagine an army of demons.

And now, after so long in the dark wilderness, they finally
finally reached the city, they *finally* arrived in this fabled metropolis
called Pahmey, and it was just dreadful. Linee had expected to
find civilization in the darkness. Instead she found a place more
nightmarish than any she could have imagined.

Empires of Moth

"Look at them, Fluffy," she whispered, holding her puppy to her breast. The little terrier whimpered, pink ribbons in his fur. "They're . . . they're like naked cats or something."

The Elorians were everywhere. Once Linee had gone with her husband, the noble King Ceranor, on a hunt. While he'd run off spearing boars, she had tried to collect flowers for him, and insects flew everywhere, and not even nice ones like butterflies, but nasty things like bees and mosquitoes. She had cried and begged Ceranor to take her home, and this was even worse. This was the worst thing Linee had seen in all her twenty-one years. Thousands of the pale, thin nightfolk filled this city, staring at her carriage with those huge, weird eyes, their silvery hair flowing like shrouds, their skin white like corpses.

"Don't they know that Pahmey belongs to me now?" she said. "My husband, the brave king, conquered this place for *me*— for somebody pretty and *decent*, not for these weird creatures." She shivered and hugged her puppy as close as she could, even as Fluffy squirmed.

The royal procession kept advancing, the knights on horseback clearing the way, the trumpets blowing, the jugglers juggling, and the Dalmatians yipping. They moved along narrow, cobbled streets. Lanterns swung alongside upon poles, their tin shaped as ugly, mocking faces like the girls who used to torment Linee before she had married the king. Behind the lamps rose buildings of opaque glass bricks and sloping, tiled roofs whose edges curled up like wet parchment. When Linee stuck her head out the window, she could see towers rising ahead, not beautiful white towers like those back home, but weird things of crystal and glass like translucent bones. Pahmey didn't even seem like a city at all, more like a bad dream after eating something too spicy. It was still too dark and too cold, and Linee trembled.

"I hate it," she whispered into Fluffy's fur. "I wish we had never come here."

41

Her pup whimpered and licked her face.

Linee knew that she had only herself to blame. Ceranor did not want her here; when marching out to war last year, he had told her to stay in the palace back in sunlight, to play with her dolls, to pick her flowers, and to ask her seamstresses for as many new gowns as she pleased. She had done so for months, and it had become so *boring*. She missed her Cery, her dear old husband, a man thirty years older than her and so much wiser. She missed the boy Torin, the gardener who had spent a summer in the capital, playing boardgames with her and teaching her the names of flowers. In the long months alone in the palace, she had even begun to miss Bailey, that gangly girl she had once thought so horrible, what with her rough words, boy clothes, and angry brown eyes.

"And so I came here to find you all," she whispered as her carriage trundled along. She whimpered when she saw two Elorian children scuttle by, and she pressed herself deep into her seat and closed her eyes. "But now I'm afraid. Now I want to go home to sunlight."

This dreamscape city her husband had conquered for her sprawled for miles. Linee huddled in her seat, almost disappearing into the plush upholstery, and refused to look outside the window again, but she could still *hear* the city—a cackle of Elorians speaking their language, the caws of strange wingless birds as large as horses, and clinks and clatters of bones and metal and talons. And she could still smell the place too—a tang of seafood, spices, tallow, and oil. She tried to breathe through her mouth and cover her ears, but Fluffy kept sliding from her lap.

It seemed to take hours before her carriage finally halted and her knights knocked on her door.

"Your Highness!" said Sir Ogworth, peering through the window. He was a young knight with a handlebar mustache; she had thought him handsome in Dayside, but here in the night, their

Empires of Moth

oil lanterns painted everyone an ugly red like a baboon's backside. "We've arrived in the Night Castle, my queen."

When he opened the door, Linee whimpered. She had spent so long wishing she were here with her husband, yet now she couldn't bear the thought of actually setting foot in this place. She just wanted to go home. This city was nothing like what she had thought, and nobody would see how pretty she was here. In this lamplight, they would think her just a baboon's bottom too.

"I . . . I changed my mind, Sir Ogworth," she said in a small voice. "Turn the carriage around. We'll return back to Dayside."

The knight's eyes widened. "Your Highness! We've traveled for almost two months to arrive here."

Linee peeked outside the window and shuddered to see the darkness, the swinging lanterns with their faces, and the stars above. They could have traveled here much faster by boat; she knew that, and perhaps Ogworth would have been more willing to turn back then. But Linee had always feared the water, and so they had braved the rocky plains with horses and carriage; they would just have to spend another two months traveling home.

"This city is not what I thought," she said. "Please, Sir Ogworth. *Please.* Can we go home now?" Her eyes welled up with tears. "I'm your queen, and I'm very beautiful, and you *have* to do what I say. You *have* to."

His eyes softened and he opened the carriage door. Linee whimpered and pushed herself deeper into her seat, clutching her dog. Cold wind blew from outside—it was always so damned cold in Nightside—and she trembled.

"Your Highness," Sir Ogworth said, his voice kind, "I would be most honored to accompany you home. But before our journey, would you not like to see your husband? He has taken residence here in the Night Castle, right outside the carriage. Your friends Torin Greenmoat and Lady Berin are there too. Perhaps

43

you would like to play a round of board games with them before traveling back to Timandra?"

Linee swallowed and peered over the knight's head. The building that rose there looked nothing like a castle. Real castles had thin, white steeples with a hundred banners, ivy and roses that crawled over their walls, warrens with bunnies in their courtyards, and handsome knights in shining armor riding out their gates. *This* place looked like a demon's lair. Rather than sport steeples, it rose in five tiers, each one topped with a slanting roof—it looked to Linee more than five buildings stacked together. Golden statues of dragons perched upon those roofs, and stone dragons guarded its gates, roaring silently. Linee swallowed a lump in her throat.

"Cery . . . conquered this place for me?" she asked. "Did he kill all the demons inside?"

Sir Ogworth smiled and reached into the carriage, offering his hand. "King Ceranor killed all the Elorians for you, Your Highness. No more lurk here to frighten you. Come, Your Highness, let us step inside. If you're still scared inside the Night Castle, I promise to take you home right away."

Linee bit her lip and sniffed back her tears. "All right."

She reached out and held his hand. She let him escort her out of her carriage. She stood shaking on the cobbled street, clutching her pup, feeling very small and weak in this great darkness. Her soldiers moved at her sides. Her musicians blew their trumpets. Sir Ogworth led her by the hand.

Be brave, Linee, she told herself. *You are Queen of Arden. That means you are queen of this city too.*

She looked to the left where the streets sloped down to the river, lined with houses of glass bricks and ceramic tiles. She looked to the right where, beyond boulevards and columned manors, rose the crystal towers of the city's crest. She looked ahead where loomed the strange fortress, this black and twisted monolith like a demon of stone and metal.

Empires of Moth

Clutching her dog to her cheek, Queen Linee of Arden held
her breath and stepped toward her new castle.

* * * * *

Ceranor stood in the candlelit hall, leaning over a table and
studying the maps of Eloria.

Since conquering Pahmey, he had spent most of his time in
this hall, a shadowy cavern deep within the Night Castle. Its
domed ceiling displayed the constellations of the night, carved in
silver—running wolves, leaping fish, brave archers, coiling
dragons, and a hundred others. Its granite table stretched as wide
as a boat's deck, flecked with blue and silver like a second sky.
Columns rose on every side; bronze dragons wrapped around
them, gems bright in their eye sockets, incense burning in their
nostrils.

"We light only a corner of Eloria's great darkness," Ceranor
said, gesturing at the maps of the night. "Our lanterns have
brought civilization and order to Pahmey, but beyond this city, the
great wilderness of the night still awaits salvation. It too must be
liberated from shadow."

His lords crowded around him, barons and earls and other
nobles with pompous titles Ceranor barely bothered
remembering. He cared little for their bloodlines and titles, only
the troops they brought to battle. They wore breastplates
engraved with the raven of Arden, and cloaks of the kingdom's
colors—gold and black—draped across their shoulders. A few
wore sunburst pins; converts to the new Sailith religion.

"There are few lands left for Arden!" said one man, a beefy
brute with a walrus mustache. "The other seven kings have
become greedy."

Ceranor nodded, trailing his fingers across the map.
Wooden figurines, shaped as the sigils of all eight kingdoms of

45

daylight, stood upon the parchment map. The raven of Arden, his own kingdom, stood over a drawing of this city along the river. The bear of Verilon, carved from pine, was invading the northern shores of the Qaelish Empire. The orca of Orida was attacking the island of Leen north of Qaelin, a small kingdom of darkness. The scorpion of Eseer, the elephant of Sania, the tiger of Naya . . . all were attacking different locations. Some were nibbling at pieces of Qaelin, this sprawling empire, while others attacked the smaller kingdoms of the night.

The man speaks truth, Ceranor thought and frowned.

"Arden must advance," he agreed, "or we'll have the smallest slice of this pie. We must move. We must conquer more of the night." He slammed his fist against the map. "I will not see the other sunlit kings claim more than we do. Arden has led the charge into Nightside; it is Arden who must claim the greatest spoils of the night." His nobles nodded and slapped the table in approval, and Ceranor raised his voice. "All of western Eloria glows with the light of Timandra. But in the east, darkness still looms. We must advance into that darkness. We will march upon the city of Yintao, the distant capital of this wilderness they call the Qaelish Empire. We will bring Yintao to its knees!"

Some of his nobles cheered in approval; two even drew and brandished their swords. Others, however, bit their lips or tapped the table in concern.

"Your Highness," said one, a slim man with a wisp of a beard. "They say that a great army musters in Yintao. They say that a boy emperor rules there, that he commands fifty thousand Elorian savages, a host all in steel, bearing spears and swords. They say that a dragon fights with him." Laughter rose across the hall, but the slim man raised his chin and voice. "Your Highness, would it not be wiser to stay within Pahmey, to let this boy emperor march against us and perish against our walls?"

Ceranor stared at this skinny coward—more a worm than a warrior—in disgust.

This is what happens, he thought, *when men ascend to titles through bloodlines rather than proving themselves on the battlefield.*

"No," he said to the coward. "We will not cower here in one city. Not when we have an empire to conquer. Not as the seven other sunlit kings bite and peck at the carcass of the night." He raised his fist. "You may stay here among the savages. We true men will march to war! We—"

A high-pitched whine rose behind him, cutting off his words.

"Cery! Oh, Cery, my sweetling! I missed you, and oh . . . look! Dragon statues!"

Ceranor had faced barbarian hordes screaming for his blood, warships charging toward his navy, and the fire of cannons blazing . . . yet now, at the sound of that voice, his belly sank deeper than in any battle.

Oh, merciful Idar . . . she's here.

Grimacing, he turned toward the hall's doors and saw her there.

"Linee," he said, voice choked.

His young wife—thirty years his junior—ran toward him with open arms. Rather than simply embracing him, she leaped onto him, wrapped all four limbs around him like a squid, and clung. She showered him with kisses.

"Cery! Oh, Cery, I missed you, my little piglet."

Some of the nobles snickered behind him, and Ceranor groaned.

"Linee!" He tried to pry her off, but he'd have better luck freeing himself from iron shackles.

He sighed. He had married the girl two years ago, hoping to forge an alliance with her father who ruled some stone bridge Ceranor no longer cared about. At first, young Linee—barely more than a youth, a fey thing with golden elflocks and bright blue eyes—had been terrified of him, an old soldier with graying hair and battle scars. Yet quickly, her silly mind had filled with love for him, a love overpowering and clingy like a leech's love for blood.

I invaded the night for glory . . . and to escape her, he thought as she kissed him all over his face. *And now the little devil is back.*

Finally he managed to extricate himself. He turned toward his nobles, saw them snicker, and glowered at them.

"This council is over!" he barked, then grunted as Linee leaped onto his back and began kissing the top of his head. "Leave this place. We'll meet again in an hourglass turn."

The nobles left, hiding their snickers behind their palms. Ceranor fumed. He grabbed Linee's arms, pried her off his back, and placed her back down.

"Linee," he said, "what in the name of sanity are you doing here?"

She gave him a bright, toothy grin. Her golden locks cascaded across her face, and her blue eyes shone with love. She held on to his waist and hopped upon her toes, her grin growing only larger.

"I was so *bored* back in Arden," she said. "I was bored and lonely and . . . bored. There was nobody to play boardgames with. The bed was all cold. And I missed you. I know you missed me too." She kissed his cheek, held his hands, then jumped up and down. "But I'm here now! I told all my knights that they *had* to take me here, that I just *had* to see my Cery again. Aren't you happy to see me?"

Ceranor groaned inwardly. He vowed to find whatever knights had accompanied her here and have them whipped. In the same breath, he was shocked at his young wife's initiative. The girl who chased butterflies, cried when flowers wilted, and squeaked when kittens hissed had somehow managed to organize a journey

Empires of Moth

here. Linee would rarely leave her bed; to leave her entire kingdom was a feat he hadn't thought her capable of. She was vacuous, childlike, and endlessly silly, but perhaps there was some courage lurking within the pink ribbons of her heart.

"Linee, this isn't a place for you," he said. "It's dangerous in Eloria. We march to more warfare soon, and— Oh, damn it, Linee. Don't cry."

She sniffed, tears rolling down her cheeks. "I can't help it! You didn't miss me at all. You don't even love me. You . . ." She buried her face in her hands.

Rolling his eyes, Ceranor placed an arm around her. Truth was, he did love the young woman; he just couldn't bear to spend any time with her.

"Of course I missed you," he lied. "Of course I love you. It is because I love you that I want you safe. You understand, right?"

She peeked between her fingers. "You love me?"

He nodded. "I do."

A tremulous smile touched her lips and she wiped her tears away. "Do you want to take a nap?"

"No, Linee. I was in the middle of planning a campaign to conquer an empire's capital."

She pouted. "But I like naps and I'm sleepy. I'm hungry too. Is there nothing to eat here?"

He sighed and took her by the hand. "Come, I'll find you a warm meal. The dining hall is not far, and we've taught some Elorians to cook us Ardish meals. We'll get some food into you, and once I'm done with my work, we can nap."

She nodded, letting him lead her by the hand.

They walked down twisting halls that curved, rose up stairs, sloped down ramps, and still made Ceranor dizzy. Holes lined the walls and guards peered through them. The builders of the Night Castle had created a labyrinth to trap and slay invaders. Ceranor had lost three hundred men storming this castle. Their blood had

49

blessed the bricks of this place, and Ceranor vowed that Arden would forever rule here.

". . . and I saw fifteen butterflies since you left!" Linee was prattling as they walked. "Oh, and new puppies were born! I brought one with me. I named him Fluffy. And . . . and . . . once I saw a really blue bird, and . . ."

Ceranor tried to ignore her as she spoke of her adventures. Finally they reached bronze doors and entered the castle kitchens.

The scents of a feast filled Ceranor's nostrils. Pies and breads baked in a dozen ovens. Suckling pigs and slabs of beef roasted upon several fire pits. Pots simmered on stoves, full of stews and soups rich with meat, vegetables, and oats. Every turn, new ships arrived downriver from Timandra, bringing the richness of sunlit produce into the night. Every turn, this kitchen prepared meals from home. Ceranor had slain the enemy soldiers who had once guarded this castle, but he had kept its cooks. The Elorians stood in new livery—the black and gold wool of Arden rather than their old silken robes—as they tended to the meals. Their pale skin, oversized eyes, and large ears seemed comical in their sunlit clothes. Whenever he entered here, Ceranor felt tickled to see them; it was like seeing one of Linee's pups dressed in a miniature gown.

"Your Highness!" they said, accents thick. They bowed and curtsied as he'd taught them.

Ceranor nodded at them. "You may rise. My wife, Queen Linee, has arrived in the Night Castle. Prepare her a meal." He turned toward his wife. "Linee, what do you—"

Seeing her expression, he paused. Her face had blanched to near-Elorian pallor. She gaped at the servants, trembling.

"Are those . . . are those Elorians?" she whispered. "I've never seen Elorians so close before."

The cooks bowed toward her. "Your Highness." They knew little more Ardish than those two words.

50

Empires of Moth

"They're harmless," Ceranor said, feeling a rare smile tickling his lips. "These ones are loyal to their new masters. Here, sit!" He led her to a stone table. "Point at whatever you wish to eat, and they will serve it to you. I return now to my chambers upstairs; I have much work to do. When you're full, ask the servants to take you to me."

"Aren't you hungry too?" she asked, staring at him with huge, hurt eyes.

He kissed her forehead. "I hunger for power, for war, for conquest. Those are the meals of kings."

As Elorians brought forth plates of stewed vegetables, slabs of turkey, and chicken pies—proper Timandrian fare—Ceranor left his wife in the kitchen. He had not eaten in hours, but after only a short walk with his wife, he needed a break from her already. He had become antsy in this palace, and Linee felt like the last straw. Six months of idleness was fraying his nerves, and he longed to charge forth again, to discover new lands, to leap into battle and spray blood and taste glory.

"Yintao will be our next prize," he said to himself as he walked upstairs. "The greatest city in the night."

He walked down a hallway between braziers, approaching his chamber, the place where the castle's Elorian lord had once lived. He kept several books at his bedside; they were written in Qaelish, which Ceranor was only learning to read. Every time he opened those books, he learned more about this empire and its army. He read about Qaelin's battles with other Elorian clans— the cruel Ilari nation of the south, the renegade Chanku riders of the plains, and the mysterious Leen folk of the northern island. With every page Ceranor read, he learned about how Elorians fought—their code of honor, their battle formations, their weapons, their tactics. With every page, his hope to defeat the darkness grew brighter.

51

He reached his chamber doors, longing to delve into his reading, and stepped inside.

For the second time, his heart sank.

Inside his chamber, hunched over the books at his bedside table, stood Ferius.

A growl fled Ceranor's lips. "Why do you slither here, snake?"

Since taking over the Sailith Order, the monk had been intolerable—lurking in every shadow, slaying Elorians for sport, and spreading his twisted faith through the ranks. But this offense—entering the king's chamber—was taking things too far, even for the head of Timandra's most powerful religion.

Ferius smiled thinly. In his hands, he held not one of the Qaelish books Ceranor had been studying, but one of the letters Linee had written him several months ago. He read out loud.

"'To my sweet noble hero of sunlight!'" Ferius's hiss of a voice gave the words an eerie menace. "'How I long to see you again, my piglet. How sad I am that—'"

Ceranor marched forward, snatched the letter from Ferius, and glared.

"Leave," he said, voice strained. "Leave now if you wish to live."

Ferius licked his chops and his smile widened, showing small, sharp teeth. "Oh, I think I'll stay, noble hero of sunlight. I have entered your chamber to deliver tidings of peril, Your Highness. I will not depart without my warning."

Ceranor grabbed the monk's robes and snarled down at the shorter man. "I tire of your poisonous words. For too long, you have slunk in my shadow, spreading your hatred, whispering your fear mongering into the ears of soldiers. Too many dead bodies litter the streets, slain by the hatred you sowed. What is your warning? That Elorians are demons? That the darkness threatens the light? That Eloria must be cleansed of evil for Sailith to rise?"

Empires of Moth

Ceranor snickered. "I've heard all your sermons. They are useful for swaying the simple-minded, but I see through your lies. You are a tool, Ferius, nothing more. Remember that. I keep you alive so your words may serve me, not warn me. Save your doctrine for lowborn soldiers, not kings."

Ferius stared silently for a moment, eyes burning with unadulterated hatred, then began to laugh. It was a horrible sound, a sound like blood bubbling up from a wound.

"The danger lurks right under your nose, noble King Ceranor, and you are blind to it. In the city streets, more than corpses rot. An Elorian resistance rises against your rule. The uprising begins in tunnels, hovels, alleyways, and rooftops, a force of countless shadows. Already soldiers of your army lie dead, daggers in their backs and darts in their necks." Ferius hissed his laughter. "Do you truly feel safe in your palace, oh brave warrior?"

Ceranor tossed the monk back and turned toward the window. As infuriating as Linee could be, he suddenly missed her and regretted leaving her alone to eat. She was a silly thing, but her company was infinitely better than Ferius's. He stared outside the Night Castle upon the city he'd conquered. The streets snaked across the hillside, lined with lanterns and houses. The new Sailith stronghold—once a temple to Eloria's stars—rose a few blocks away, topped with the sunburst banners. Every time he stared outside, Ceranor saw more monks in yellow robes, their numbers swelling with new recruits. They were raising their own army now; their warrior-priests marched in crimson armor, guarding their temple and patrolling the streets.

This is the real threat, Ceranor thought, gazing outside at the distant monks. *Not some shadow resistance of Elorians, but the menace I brought here with me upon my own ships.*

His belly twisted. He had hoped to use the fanatics for his own gain, yet now they burned with a fire he could no longer control.

53

I have to eradicate them, he realized. *Their temple must fall.*

Before he could march against Yintao, he would have to face the enemy within.

"The Elorian resistance is but a whisper of a threat," he said, leaning against the windowsill and gazing upon the shadowy city.

Ferius snickered behind him. "Your Highness, do you remember the Fairwoolian girl, the orphan named Yana—the one I slew a year ago?"

Ceranor gripped the windowsill. "Of course. You murdered her and blamed the Elorians to spark this war. You—"

His breath died.

He gasped.

Pain bloomed from the center of his back, spreading across him. He tried to breathe. He could not.

A hand rested upon his shoulder, pale, its nails broken and yellow. A voice hissed in his ear.

"I will do the same with you," said Ferius, the stench of his breath wafting. "Your death too will be blamed upon the Elorians . . . and they will pay."

Ceranor reached for his sword. Before he could draw the blade, the monk behind him laughed, and the pain twisted through his back, cracking against his spine, and his blood stained his shirt and filled his mouth. He managed to spin around, tearing the shard from his flesh, and saw Ferius with a bloody dagger.

The blade thrust again. The dagger drove into Ceranor's neck.

He coughed blood. He couldn't breathe, couldn't scream. With his last strength, he drew his sword. Before he could swing the blade down, the dagger thrust a third time, entering his eye and driving deep, cold darkness into him.

But I promised her a nap, was his last thought. *I promised Linee that . . .*

Empires of Moth

He hit the ground, saw pools of blood, and heard laughter fading into silence.

* * * * *

Linee stood at the doorway, the plate of cake in her hands, staring with wide eyes.

I . . . I only came to bring you cake. I . . .

She watched as the monk Ferius twisted the blade. She watched as her husband fell into a puddle of his own blood. So much blood, red everywhere, flowing across the tiled floor toward her, and the scent of death, and her sweet Cery on the floor . . .

She wanted to scream. She wanted to cry for him. She opened her mouth and then froze.

Don't make a sound, she told herself. *You have to run. You have to escape!*

His back toward her, Ferius leaned over the body and laughed.

"For so long, you ruled over me with brute force," the monk said to the corpse. He spat upon the dead king. "Yet I am a being of light; I will always be victorious. Your kingdom is now mine. All that is yours belongs to me, from your castle to your armies to that pathetic little wife of yours. Oh yes, Ceranor. She will be mine too."

At the doorway, Linee gave a small whimper, barely audible.

Inside the chamber, Ferius stiffened.

The monk began to turn toward the doorway.

Linee leaped away and hid against the wall.

Run! spoke the voice inside her. *Run or he'll kill you too, or he'll force you to marry him, or he'll torture you, or—*

She shook her head mightily. If she ran, he would hear her footfalls. Breath held, her back to the wall, she inched along the hallway. She reached another door, grabbed the handle, and

55

twisted. She glimpsed Ferius's yellow robes enter the hallway, but before he could see her, she stepped backward into this new chamber.

She glanced around and nearly fainted. Soldiers of Arden lay here, clad in the raven armor, their necks slit. Blood stained Linee's slippers. She gasped and nearly squeaked, then saw a shadow in the hall.

Ferius.

She gulped, fear pounding through her. The monk had killed his king; he would kill his queen just as readily. She didn't know where to go. But she knew she had to flee.

Silent as a cat, Linee ducked behind a bed as Ferius entered the room. The oil lamps in the hallway cast orange light, framing the monk's squat form.

"Does a shadow lurk in this darkness?" he said, his voice like a snake's hiss.

Linee had to bite her lip to stop herself from crying. She wished she had a weapon. She wished she could disappear. She wished Ceranor were still alive and that she'd never come to this place, and—

Wishes are worth pebbles and earth. Her grandmother's voice filled Linee's mind; the old woman was fond of the saying. *Actions bring you gold.*

"Come out of your hiding, friend!" Ferius said, stepping deeper into the chamber. He still held his bloodied dagger. "Come and let us speak."

He came walking around the bed toward her.

Biting her lip so hard she tasted blood, Linee crept under the bed into the dusty darkness.

She could see Ferius's boots circling the bed. Somewhere outside, she heard men sing a song and laugh, and it seemed so strange to her that folk could find joy while her husband lay dead.

Empires of Moth

"Where are you, friend?" Ferius said. "Speak to me and you will not be harmed." His boots moved several paces away. She heard hinges creak. "Are you in the closet? No . . . Are you behind the table?"

Linee gritted her teeth and crawled.

Stay alive. Just stay silent and stay alive.

The voice rose behind her. "Are you . . . under the bed?"

His robes rustled.

Linee scurried out the other side of the bed, leaped toward the open door, and bolted outside.

"Friend!" rose his voice behind.

Linee ran. She leaped onto a stairway. She raced downstairs, heart thudding.

I have to find Sir Ogworth! I have to find his soldiers. I—

Across a hallway, she found herself entering the main hall of the Night Castle, the place where only moments ago, she had seen Ceranor meet his nobles.

Those nobles, all the dozens of them, lay dead in the hall, piled up upon the granite table. Their necks were split from ear to ear. Above their bodies hunched a host of Sailith monks, their yellow robes stained red. All raised their heads together to regard her, a flock of vultures turning from a carcass.

Tears filled Linee's eyes.

She turned away from the hall.

Through a labyrinth of stone and fire, Queen Linee of Arden ran, her heart pounding and blood staining the hem of her gown.

CHAPTER FIVE
DANCE OF DEATH AND LIFE

Koyee entered the Hall of Dying dressed like a vulture of metal, leather, and glass.

Her outfit creaked and clanked as she walked, hiding every part of her. Leather robes draped across her, stiff as armor, brushing the floor. A belt heavy with buckles and purses jangled around her waist, holding vials and spoons and scalpels. A wide-brimmed hat topped her head, and gloves encased her hands, ending with steel fingertips like thimbles. Worst of all was her mask; it wrapped around her head, laced up at the back. Its beak flared out, full of spices to stifle the miasma of disease. Even her eyes hid behind glass lenses that turned the world into a smoky, wavering dreamscape.

When she passed by a candlelit window, she gazed upon her reflection. She didn't see a girl; she didn't even look human. A gangly, creaking bird stared back, a creature of both nightmare and mercy.

"For I am a Sister of Harmony," she whispered, her voice muffled inside her beak. "I am here to guide souls into death."

And what of my own soul? she wondered. Hiding here from the monks of Sailith, would she scar whatever purity and hope remained inside her?

As if to answer her thoughts, the anguished screams of the dying echoed down the hall. Koyee tore herself away from the window and shuffled onward, her boots thumping and her outfit creaking and clanking. She made her way toward the doors, stepped into the Hall of Dying, and beheld a nightmare she knew would forever haunt her.

The hall was as large as a temple. Hundreds of beds stood in rows, and upon them lay the devastation of the Sunlit Curse.

Empires of Moth

Elorian men, women, and children lay writhing and moaning, their faces gray with fever, their bodies covered in oozing boils. Their teeth had fallen from bleeding gums, and their fingers had shriveled into black twigs. The plague had come upon the Timandrian ships, hidden inside rats, cats, and scurrying cockroaches; it had devastated Timandra ten years ago, the soldiers said, killing all those susceptible to its whispers. Now it tore through Pahmey, striking everywhere—from the towers of the wealthy to the huts of the poor.

"Sister," whispered the dying, hands reaching out toward her. "Mercy, sister. Prayer."

Koyee stood for a few breaths at the doorway, frozen. Several patients were no longer moving. The others were only moments from death, so frail they seemed like skeletons draped with skin. As strange as her costume appeared to her, the Sunlit Curse twisted these people into shapes far stranger, living death of pus and blood.

Koyee sucked in air, inhaling the scents of spices inside her beak, a thick and tangy breath that would protect her from the curse.

Yet they are no monsters, she thought. *They are my brothers and sisters, and they need me. The true monsters are those tall, fair Timandrians with their shining armor and endless cruelty.*

She stepped into the hall and walked among the beds. The hands of the dying reached out. Their fingernails, blackened with disease, scraped against her robes. Their bleeding mouths opened and closed, begging for prayer, and their boils oozed. At every bed, Koyee paused and held out a bottle of silverdream, a milky medicine of mushrooms in deep caves. It would not cure these people, for there was no cure for the Sunlit Curse, but it could ease their pain. She dripped two drops into every mouth and whispered a prayer.

59

"The stars of the night will bless you, child of Eloria. The moonlight will glow upon you. We are the night."

Her words and medicine sent them into shivering, feverish sleep, their eyes moving behind their lids, their gums smacking, their curling fingers reaching out to those stars, awaiting their journey to the world beyond.

More creaks and clanks rose in the hall. Other Sisters of Harmony, humanoid birds with their beaks and hats, moved between the beds. The sisters prayed, soothed, and poured their medicine. They moved like clattering marionettes, wheeling out the beds of those succumbed to the illness, angels of death escorting famished, rotted bodies into the darkness.

As Koyee stood above a young girl, praying as the child's breath faded into stillness, tears splashed her lenses. She missed The Green Geode. She even missed living in the alleyways, scrounging through trash to survive. But inside her beak, she tightened her lips and raised her chin.

In The Green Geode, I played music for those who brought this curse upon us, she thought. *Here I heal their victims. Here I suffer. Here I am noble.*

The Sunlit Curse killed Madori the yezyana; a Sister of Harmony rose from the ashes, a phoenix of leather and glass.

After passing by every bed, Koyee left the hall and walked down dark corridors, nodding her beak at those sisters she passed. She had been serving in the Sisterhood for twenty turns now—not yet a moon—though it seemed like a year. In all this time, she had not even seen the faces of her sisters, for they dared not remove their beaks unless alone in their chambers.

She reached bronze doors where two sisters stood, their robes and beaks black, and they held not medicine but halberds of cruel, twisting iron. As Koyee approached, they nodded, opened the doors, and watched her through their glass lenses as she passed. Twice since Koyee had joined the Sisterhood, patients had tried to leave the hospice's eastern wing. Twice had these guards, sisters trained not to heal but to kill, slain the dying.

"Bless you, my sisters," Koyee said.

"Bless you, Sister of Harmony," they replied in unison, voices muffled inside their beaks. "Seek solace in shadow, for the sun rises."

She repeated the chant—the words of the Sisterhood—and stepped into a second hall. The doors closed behind her, sealing the screams, the pain, and the miasma of death.

In this new chamber, bronze baths stood full of steaming water. Soaps and brushes hung from pegs. Slowly, buckle by buckle, Koyee removed her outfit. She placed her brimmed hat upon a peg. She unlaced the mask that enveloped her head, emptied the beak's spices into a bowl, and hung the device upon a rack. Finally she removed her thick robes and boots, remaining nude in the chamber of steam.

She stepped into a tub and scrubbed her skin raw, removing any hint of the disease that might have invaded her suit. She did not know what caused the illness, whether it was evil spirits, an invisible cloud of black magic, or a stench that invaded through the nostrils. Whatever the case, she would scrub every trace off, even as her skin turned raw and red. In wisps of steam and ripples in water, she thought she glimpsed Eelani bathing too, her invisible friend—no larger than her hand—scrubbing off the illness.

After toweling herself dry, Koyee dressed herself in the simple, white robes the sisters wore in their chambers. The silk caressed her skin, soothing the sting of the brushes.

She left the bathing chamber, walked upstairs, and entered her small chamber. It was no larger than her room in The Green Geode—a humble cube containing a bed, a table, and a chair, all forged of the same unadorned iron. A painting of Shenlai, the blue dragon of her empire, hung on a wall. Koyee sat on the bed, pressed her knees together, and trembled.

"Please, Shenlai the dragon," she prayed to that painting, "look after the ill in your kingdom. Please protect us from the sunlight."

She didn't know if Shenlai could hear. Perhaps dragons were simply myths, creatures for statues and paintings and unanswered prayers. And yet she prayed, for she was lost and afraid. She had lived on the streets of Pahmey, an urchin and thief. She had a chamber now and food and a sisterhood, but life in Pahmey was harder than ever, for the heel of Timandra was grinding them, and the skeletons of the curse forever danced in her mind.

She closed her eyes, and she saw them there: the dead and dying, skin draped over bones, cadaverous creatures dancing in a circle, holding hands, chanting to the sky, the dance macabre of the night.

How long before I dance with them?

A tap sounded on her window.

Koyee started and opened her eyes. For a heartbeat, she was sure those skeletons had arrived at her chamber, that they were knocking on her window, beckoning for her to join the dance. But then the tap sounded again—a pebble tossed against the glass.

The fear left Koyee like drawn curtains. A smile tingled her lips.

"Torin," she whispered, relief and love warming her like mulled wine.

He had been visiting her every hourglass turn, sneaking away from his barracks at the Night Castle. These visits were her shadow in the light, her dreams of joy in a world of death. Her smile spreading, she opened her window and leaned outside.

He stood below in the garden, disguised in the robes of an Elorian philosopher. When he pulled back his hood, he smiled at

Empires of Moth

her. Lavender mushrooms grew around him, as tall as his shoulders, glowing with inner light.

There was some hope in the sea of pain. There was her friend. There was Torin.

She grabbed the rope she'd woven from her sheets and tossed it out the window. He looked around the garden, perhaps fearing Sailith monks in the shadows, then grabbed the rope and climbed. He entered her chamber, smelling of the city, an aroma of spice, oil, and wine.

"Have you been practicing the new words?" she asked him, speaking Qaelish. "Will you be a better student this turn? If you're a bad student, I'll slap you."

He snorted, but the sound was more affectionate than offended. "I good student," he said in clumsy Qaelish. "You good student of Ardish?"

It was her turn to snort. She switched to his tongue. "I speak Ardish very well. Sit on bed! Sit. Open book. Let me hear you read."

They perhaps had to meet in secret now, but she would not let him abandon his lessons. She had started teaching him her tongue, and by the moonlight, she would make him fluent. And in truth . . . though it made her cheeks tingle, she had to admit she enjoyed these lessons. She liked his company—the way his hand sometimes accidentally touched hers, the way he tried not to laugh at her jokes, and the way she laughed at his.

He opened his book of stories, and he read slowly, stumbling over some words but plowing on. This time he read a story about the three dragons of Eloria, all born from the same brood, who flew to the three Dark Empires to watch over them. When he finished reading, he looked at her with his mismatched eyes.

"Better this time?" he asked.

She nodded. "Better."

63

Before she could resist, she did something that surprised her, that made her cheeks tingle. She leaned forward and kissed his cheek.

At once she pulled back and looked down, blinking and blushing.

He nudged her with his elbow. "I like your kisses more than when you slap me for making a mistake."

She spoke softly, staring at her lap. "You'll get more if you're a good student."

He nodded. "Good. Reward for success. I prefer that to punishment for failure."

She dared to look up at him. She found his face close to hers, and she looked down again at her lap, though a smile tingled her lips.

His fingers caressed her hair, making her tremble. "And you speak my language very well now, and you deserve a kiss too." He kissed her ear.

She turned toward him, surprised at his audacity, and his face was so close that her lips brushed against his. It was only an accident—it had to be—but somehow she was kissing him, not just a peck on the lips, but a real kiss, their mouths open, their tongues touching, and his fingers caressed her hair, and he held her close to him.

"You must have been a very good student," she whispered, pulling back from him only an inch.

"My Qaelish feel stronger alrea—"

She did not let him finish his sentence. She could not bear for her lips to be away from his. She kissed him again, and this time their kiss was deeper, a desperate kiss, a kiss for some goodness in this pain, for some hope and love in war. His arms wrapped around her, and she sat on his lap, her legs around him, her hair curtaining their faces in a white cocoon.

Empires of Moth

She had never kissed a man until now. She had never cared for such matters, for kisses or love, and yet she tugged at his tunic, and his hands slipped under her dress, moving up and down.

When she removed her silk, she worried that he'd think her too skinny, think her breasts too small, for she was only a slim Elorian, and she must have seemed so plain to him. And yet she saw the approval in his eyes, and she smiled softly and pulled his tunic off, then ran her hands across his chest.

"Look, Torin. Your skin is golden and mine is white like milk. We're like the sun and moon."

He kissed her again, and she lay on her back and closed her eyes, and he loved her, this boy from sunlit lands, this man who had saved her in the alleyways, this soldier who was supposed to be her enemy and whom she had taken into her bed.

They moved together, and this was a dance too, and this was a dance of life. She closed her eyes, holding him tight, and let the joy of him flood her until she cried out. After what seemed like the age of stars, she lay beside him in her bed, trailed her fingers across his chest, and laughed.

"Why are you laughing?" he asked, his hand caressing her, trailing from waist to hip and back again, an endless movement like a boat upon the waves.

"Because you're silly," she said. "Because I'm scared but happy too." She kissed his nose. "Now go back to your castle, soldier of sunlight, and don't return until you learn another tale."

He left her with tangled hair, her blanket wrapped around her naked body. She stared at the open window and laughed again.

"Oh, Eelani," she whispered to her invisible friend. "Did you really watch the whole thing?"

Her shoulder spirit hopped upon her shoulder, and Koyee sighed, though her lips would not stop smiling.

65

CHAPTER SIX
HIDDEN LIFE

As Torin walked back to the Night Castle, the Elorian fort where he was stationed, the smile wouldn't leave his face.

He was far from home. His enemies were growing stronger. The cruelty of conquest surrounded him. And yet as he walked down the street, passing between soldiers in steel, his heart fluttered and he felt more joyous than ever before.

"Koyee," he whispered, tasting the name.

The cobbled boulevard climbed the mountainside. Buildings rose along its sides, their walls built of glass bricks, and lanterns hung from their sloped roofs. Elorians rushed quickly between shops and homes, heads lowered, their silken robes fluttering and their hands tucked into their sleeves. When Torin had first invaded their city, the locals had worn elaborate sashes of embroidery and beads; now they merely wore white scarves around their waists, the color of their mourning. A few gathered around a towering, communal fireplace, its iron grill shaped as bats, its flames rising ten feet tall. When they saw Torin—wearing the armor of their enemy—they scattered into alleyways.

Other Timandrian troops—all of them Ardish, the people of his homeland—stood at every street corner, holding spears and swords. When first invading this land, they had worn ravens upon their breastplates, the sigil of their king. Now, however, many soldiers sported sunbursts upon their shields and armor, the symbol of Sailith. Seeing these soldiers—his own countrymen—Torin knew he should feel grief. But not now. Not this turn. Again her memory filled his mind.

Empires of Moth

"Koyee."

He could still feel her slim, naked body pressed against him. She had seemed so delicate, so lithe, a dainty creature of faerie. Her hair had cascaded between his fingers, white and soft as silk. Her eyes had stared into his, large lavender orbs, full of shyness and love. Torin felt his blood stir anew. He wished he could return to her now—forget his duty to his king, forget his fellow soldiers, and spend his life with her in the hospice.

Invading the night brought me pain, fear, and endless shame, but it also brought me you, Koyee, he thought. *Even in the greatest darkness some light shines.*

A spring in his step and a whistle between his lips, he rounded a corner and beheld the Night Castle.

The pagoda's five tiers loomed, each topped with a roof of blue tiles, its edged curving up to support bronze statues of dragons, snakes, fish, and other beasts. Arrowslits peppered walls of black bricks, and red lanterns shone within. Hundreds of Elorian soldiers had served and died here; some Timandrians now swore they could hear the ghosts of those old defenders, cursing them as they swept through the halls. Most of the Timandrian host, a horde of many thousands, camped outside the city in riverbank tents and huts. The king had taken residence here, and he had invited those closest to him to share his hall—his lords, his war heroes, and Torin.

I did not save King Ceranor's life like my father did, Torin thought, approaching the castle. *But if I can convince him to return home and end this madness, perhaps I can still save his soul.*

Torin tightened his lips and nodded. Yes. After half a year of occupying this city, the kingdoms of Timandra—eight old enemies—fought united. The goal of this war—internal peace in Timandra—had been achieved.

"Now I must convince you to return home," Torin whispered into the night.

67

King Ceranor was perhaps a conqueror, but he was no madman. He was no bloodthirsty killer like Ferius. He would listen to reason, Torin told himself. He would realize victory was achieved, that they could return home and leave Eloria to the Elorians.

Torin paused, a lump filling his throat.

And yet . . . if Torin returned home, would Koyee remain here? Would she agree to travel with him to sunlight? Torin's heart sank. Here was Koyee's home; could he truly ask her to abandon her people, to travel into the lands of her enemies?

Or . . . can I stay with her here in darkness?

Torin lowered his head and tightened his jaw.

"I must convince you, Ceranor, to return home, but I cannot go with you. I will stay with Koyee."

His mind decided, Torin pursed his lips, nodded, and kept walking.

Before he could reach the pagoda, a scream filled the street.

Torin's eyes widened.

A young Timandrian woman was running from the Night Castle, blood staining the hem of her blue gown.

Torin gasped. "Queen Linee?"

He had not seen the young queen, a woman only two years his senior, since invading the night. When spending the summer in Kingswall last year, preparing for this war, he had spent many hours playing board games with Linee, walking with her through the gardens and discussing types of flowers and birds. She had always seemed a happy, silly thing—naive perhaps, but good at heart, always smiling, her eyes bright and her golden hair flowing in perfect locks. She had reminded Torin of a butterfly, flighty and pretty and full of life.

Now she was weeping.

Empires of Moth

"Torin!" she cried, her hair in disarray, her eyes rimmed with red. "Torin, he killed him. Ferius the monk. He killed my Cery. He . . ."

Tears drowned her words.

Darkness covered Torin.

All his hope—of an end to violence, of a love with Koyee—vanished under a cold torrent.

Linee reached him, grabbed his shoulders, and clung to him.

"He's after me, Torin. He's after me!" She trembled. "He killed Cery and now he wants to kill—"

He wouldn't even let her finish her sentence. Torin grabbed her hand and tugged her along with him. They raced into an alleyway just as the Night Castle gates slammed open. Torin spun around in the shadows, peered toward the castle, and saw a swarm of monks spill into the boulevard.

Ferius marched at their lead, bloodied hands raised to the sky. Behind him, his fellow monks held aloft the body of King Ceranor. A dagger was embedded into the king's left eye. The right eye, still open, seemed to stare at Torin with pain.

"The Elorians have slain our king!" Ferius shouted, voice ringing across the boulevard. "Men of Timandra, the demons have struck! We will have vengeance! Soldiers of sunlight, hear my call, raise your swords, and march with me. Slay every demon you find!"

Torin watched, heart thudding and head spinning. He gripped his sword. Linee clung to him, trembling and still shedding tears.

"It wasn't the Elorians," she whispered and tugged Torin's arm. "It was Ferius who killed him. I saw him. He's lying. Please don't let him kill me too." She covered her face.

Torin held her, gritting his teeth and staring out to the boulevard. "I will keep you safe, Linee. I promise you. Now keep your voice low."

69

He pulled her deeper into the alley shadows. The monks kept marching down the boulevard. They raised their maces and roared for blood.

"Death to Elorians!" one shouted.

"Sunlight rises!" shouted another.

Soon all their voices morphed into a single cry, the rage of one beast of sunfire. They marched down the street, swung their maces, and smashed windows and shattered glass walls. What few Elorians walked along the boulevard fled into homes and alleyways.

"Let the blood fill the streets!" shouted Ferius as behind him his monks paraded the corpse of King Ceranor. "Vengeance!"

Soldiers began streaming out from the Night Castle. These were no monks—they wore the armor of Arden, ravens upon their breastplates, warriors of the fallen king. And yet they too followed the new Sailith faith; new converts, they sported the sunburst upon their shields. They too chanted for blood.

"Death to Elorians!" they shouted. "The sun rises!"

Hundreds flowed onto the street, not marching in formation, not following a commander, but swarming as a mob, blind with hatred.

They are no longer soldiers, Torin realized. He remembered the mob that had slain Koyee's father, mad with fear and hatred. These men were the same, but whereas a mob from Fairwool-by-Night had slain a single man, this force could massacre an entire city.

Linee tugged Torin's arm. "Please, Torin, *please.* I'm scared. I want to leave. Can we please leave?"

Torin nodded, throat tight. "I think that's a good idea."

Outside the alleyway, soldiers began breaking down the doors of homes and shops. Screams rose from inside. Elorians pleaded for mercy and blood spilled into the street. Torin glimpsed a dozen soldiers drag an elderly Elorian man out of his

Empires of Moth

shop; he recognized Old Meshu, a dyer of silks. The soldiers slashed his neck with a sword, then laughed as the blood sprayed their armor. They raised the corpse with cries of triumph.

"Vengeance! Vengeance! Death to Elorians!"

Torin turned away, nausea rising in him, and pulled Linee deeper into the shadows of the alley. They hurried around a few barrels, a stray cat, and laundry hanging on strings. Most other soldiers only knew the main streets of Pahmey, but Torin had spent many hours sneaking through the secret passages with Koyee.

"We have to find her," he said, heart thudding in his throat. "We have to find Koyee. Oh Idar . . . Ferius will tear down every building until he finds her."

They raced around a corner and down a narrow passageway, dusty glass walls at their sides and awnings forming a roof above. Rats scurried into holes. Linee stumbled along at his side, face pale and hair disarrayed.

"Who, Torin?" she said. "Who is that?"

"An . . ." He hesitated. "An Elorian woman. A friend of mine."

Linee gasped and tugged his arm. "By the light, Torin! There's no time to save . . . to save these creatures." Fresh tears welled up in her eyes.

Torin grunted. "We are the savages here, not the Elorians. Or, at least, Ferius and his thugs are." He glared at Linee. "The Elorians are humans like you and me, no different. We have to stop this . . . or at least save whomever we can."

She shook her head wildly. "We have to flee this city! We don't have time to be heroes. Please take me home. Take me back to Kingswall. Take me back to my palace where I'm the queen and none of this happens."

Torin stopped moving down the alley, turned toward her, and held her arms. From across the city, the chants of soldiers and the screams of Elorians rose in a din. The smell of blood wafted.

"Linee," he said, looking into her eyes, "there is no more home for you in Kingswall. The king is dead. This is a coup. If you return home you'll have no more palace there, and Sailith will seek you everywhere. Do you understand?"

She shivered but managed to nod, a tear on her nose. "But . . . maybe we can just . . . find a new palace? And a new garden?" She clung to him and placed her cheek against his shoulder. "What will we do, Torin? Oh, where will we go?"

He swallowed and sucked in breath between his teeth. He did not know.

"Somewhere safe," he said. "I promise you: You will be safe."

* * * * *

As they traveled through the labyrinth of alleyways, Torin's mind worked feverishly. He needed to find Koyee. He needed to find his friends: Bailey, Cam, and Hem. Koyee would still be at the hospice, but what about his friends? Were they still in the Night Castle in the thick of the Sailith uprising? Were they patrolling the streets or pleasure dens, and if so where would they head?

The hospice is where we must go, he decided. *Koyee is there, and if Bailey and the boys have any sense, they'll make their way there too.* Only a few hourglass turns ago, he had joked with Bailey how the hospice—with the plague raging inside its halls—was the safest place in the city, since Ferius dared not enter it. He had spoken those words in jest, but now they might be true. Would Bailey remember the conversation and head there now?

Torin kept moving, darting from alleyway to alleyway, avoiding the main streets. Stray cats fled before them and bats

Empires of Moth

fluttered above. Discarded scarves, broken pottery, and fish bones littered the cobblestones. Few people normally traveled these alleys, but as Torin and Linee raced here now, dozens of Elorians ran to and fro. One woman, clutching a gash upon her belly, stumbled into a house. An elderly man fell onto the cobblestones, his mouth smashed and bleeding.

"Please, sir!" An Elorian child faltered toward Torin, his arm a dripping mess. "Please, sir, mercy."

From the city streets, more screams rose, boots thumped, and swords whistled. When Torin peered out into a boulevard, he saw Timandrian soldiers laughing as they smashed windows and looted jewels within. Their boots stomped upon the corpse of the shopkeeper. Shards of glass lay strewn across the street like scattered diamonds.

"Please, sir, mercy," begged the Elorian child in the alley. He turned toward Linee. "Please, my lady, don't kill us."

Torin approached the cowering boy and held his hand. "Come with me. We'll get you somewhere safe." He turned toward Linee, who stood staring with wide eyes. "Linee, help the elder rise! Quickly. I know a safe place."

As Torin held the child's hand, Linee looked at the fallen elder. She shivered and grimaced, but approached the old man and helped him rise.

"What do I do, Torin?" she asked in a whisper.

"Help him walk. We're taking them to the city hospice. Few people dare enter that place; it's full of the plague."

Linee looked ready to burst into tears again. "And you want us to go there?"

He glared at her. "The plague is safer right now than these streets. Come on."

They hurried along the alleyways, a queen and soldier of sunlight, taking with them the two wounded Elorians. All the while, the screams rose across the city. Whenever they passed the

73

mouth of an alley, they witnessed the slaughter. Shattered glass, smashed doors, and corpses littered the streets. A discarded shoe lay in a corner. A basket lay fallen, its mushrooms scattered. Everywhere Torin looked, the monks led mobs of soldiers, smashing, killing, destroying.

Torin's eyes stung. Worry for Koyee and his friends burned within him. He forced himself to move on. Right now people depended on him. Right now he had to save as many as he could. He kept moving on through the shadows, holding the wounded child's hand, as behind him Linee helped the bleeding elder hobble forward.

It seemed ages before they reached an alley's end, peered around a bronze brazier shaped as a toothy spirit, and saw the Hospice of Pahmey loom across a square.

Koyee is in there, he thought, throat burning. *Stay safe. Stay put. I'm coming.*

"That is where we go," Torin said to his companions.

Linee stood at his side, her gown and hands splashed with blood. Her shivering had finally ended, and though red still rimmed her eyes, they were now dry. The wounded old Elorian leaned against her, his teeth knocked out; Linee held him wrapped in her arms.

"But . . . that means crossing this square." She winced. "It's lit with lanterns."

Torin stared, eyes narrowed, listening. The din of screams, cheers, and smashing glass still rose across the city, but no sound seemed to rise from the square ahead. When Torin peered around the brazier, he saw only a single cat scurry along the cobblestones. Across the shadows, the hospice rose like a tombstone for a god, its columns dark, its doors and windows closed. At his side, the wounded child whimpered and clung to Torin's leg.

"The Sunlit Curse," the boy whispered. "It dwells here."

Empires of Moth

Torin nodded. "The soldiers fear to walk near this place. We'll be safe inside." He took a step into the square. "Follow. We—"

Shouts rose.

Hooves thudded and light blazed.

Torin whipped his head to the left. From a boulevard, a dozen monks emerged, riding horses and brandishing lanterns. Ferius rode at their lead, the lamplight painting his face a demonic red. Ropes ran from the horses, dragging the mangled corpses of Elorians like mules tugging plows. As the procession rode forth, the corpses trailed along the square behind them, smearing the cobblestones with blood.

"Behold the justice of the sun!" Ferius cried; his horse dragged the corpse of a woman, her face crushed into a red pulp. "Behold the punishment of Eloria."

Torin cursed and leaped back into the alley, pulling the child with him; the boy wept and clung to him. Linee and the elder held each other, eyes closed. They waited in the shadows until the ghastly procession rode by and vanished down another street.

Like feral cats scuttling from hideout to hideout, they hurried into the square. Torin held the wounded child close; Linee held her hobbling charge. As they moved, Torin kept staring from side to side, breath held. Three roads led into this square, and in each one, he glimpsed the slaughter; hundreds of troops were now moving down the streets, tugging Elorians from their homes and slitting their throats. With every step, Torin expected more monks or soldiers to burst into the square and attack, plague or no plague. The hospice couldn't have been more than a hundred yards away, but that distance seemed endless now.

As they stepped over the trail of blood Ferius and his monks had left, the grisly ghost of their slaughter, Torin grimaced and Linee whimpered. Behind them, the chants of soldiers rose

75

louder. They quickened their pace. A few more steps and they reached the hospice steps.

Most of Pahmey was built of glass and crystal, but the hospice's stairs rose harsh, stony, and cruel as a dead mountainside. As they began to climb toward the columns that loomed above, Torin glanced over his shoulder back at the square. He cursed.

An Elorian family—seven or eight souls—burst out from a street and began running across the square. One of them, a grimacing woman, held a dripping wound on her belly; her children ran at her sides, and her husband shouted and urged them on. They had taken only several steps into the square when bowstrings thrummed behind. The Elorian family fell, pierced with arrows. Two children managed to rise and limp on, arrows in their shoulders; a second volley slammed them onto the cobblestones. In the road behind them, Timandrian troops laughed and pointed at the dead.

"The savages die like cockroaches!" one shouted.

His friend snickered. "Look, there are more on the hospice stairs."

The soldiers stared across the square. Torin stared back, holding the Elorian child with one hand, the hilt of his sword with the other. The murderous soldiers, still holding their bows, looked directly at him across the bloodied expanse.

"Get away from there!" the soldiers called to him, daring not leave the road. "Soldier of sunlight—that's the hospice there! The plague lives inside. Come here; join us."

Torin stared at them, frozen.

Join them? His eyes stung. He had joined this army a year ago. He had joined to . . . to what? To save his friend Bailey from the dungeon? To serve his king? To fight an invisible enemy, a demon that lived only in sermon and nightmare? He winced, feeling close to tears. Yes, he had joined them, and he had killed for them; the blood of battle still stained his hands.

But no more, he thought. *No more will I join you, my fellow soldiers of sunlight.* He breathed raggedly, each breath burning. *Now I am the night.*

Chest tight and eyes blurred, he spun away from the square. Leading his companions, he stepped between columns and into shadows.

Across a portico they reached towering stone doors. A Sister of Harmony stood here, clad in her robes of leather and metal, wide brimmed hat, and beaked mask. She stared through lenses, eyes nearly invisible behind the smoky glass. She blocked the doors, holding a spear.

"Open the doors!" Torin said. "These people need help."

The humanoid vulture of leather, glass, and metal stared at him, tilting her head. She looked at his side, seeming to regard the shivering queen, the wounded Elorian man, and the bleeding child.

"What happened?" she said, voice a ghostly whisper inside her mask.

Torin panted. "The Sailith monks have slain King Ceranor. They are slaughtering everyone they can find—Timandrian nobles and Elorians alike." His throat burned. "Please—protect these people behind your walls. The enemy fears this place. I bring with me Queen Linee of Timandra, hunted by the monks, and two wounded city folk. Please, Sister of Harmony, harbor them."

The Sister of Harmony stared at him a moment longer; he could hear her gasp, a hiss like steam, behind her beak. She turned toward the doors and shoved them; they creaked open on hinges the size of her head.

The sister reached out her arms; each hand ended with a leather glove tipped with metal thimbles, barriers against the diseased skin of patients.

"Come, children!" said the sister. "Enter the shadows. You will find safety here." The strange vulture looked over her shoulder into the shadows of the temple. "Sister Xia! Sister Jinyu! Patients arrive; we will heal them."

Two more Sisters of Harmony emerged from within, took hold of the wounded Elorians, and guided them inside. Seeing the blood on her gown, one sister tried to hold Linee's arm and guide her indoors; the young queen whimpered and leaped back.

"I'm scared," Linee said to Torin, her lips wobbling. "What are these creatures? They look like birds." She shivered wildly. "They're so ugly."

"They will help you," Torin said softly and touched her cheek. "Be brave. Not all those who are ugly are cruel. Not all who are fair of skin are fair of heart. The Sisters of Harmony will protect you. Enter their domain."

Tears rolled down to her quivering lips. "Aren't you coming with me?"

"I'll join you soon. First I must save more. I must save whoever I still can."

With another whimper, Linee allowed herself to be guided into the shadows of the hospice. The doors closed behind her, leaving only Torin and the spear-wielding sister outside.

Torin paused for a heartbeat, torn between seeking more Elorians to save and entering the hospice in search of Koyee. He took one step toward the stairs, meaning to race back into the streets, then looked over his shoulder at the sister who guarded the doors.

"One of your sisters is named Koyee," he said. "A young woman with lavender eyes. Is she safe?"

The sister regarded him through her smoky lenses. With her clawed glove, she reached behind her head. She pulled off the beaked contraption of glass, metal, and leather, revealing purple eyes, long white hair, and a scarred face.

Empires of Moth

She smiled at him tremulously. "Are any of us safe now, Torin?"

Torin's heart leaped. "Koyee."

A lump filled his throat and his eyes watered, but they were tears of joy and relief. He took several great steps toward her, pulled her into his arms, and held her tight. Her suit felt hard and cold against him, but when he touched her cheek, she was soft and warm. Before he could stop himself, he was kissing her, a deep kiss that tasted of fear and love and tears.

"Thank goodness you're safe," he said. "Koyee, it's madness out there. I'm going to find more people and bring them here."

She bit her lip. "Torin, be careful. Don't let them hurt you."

"I won't." He kissed her again; her lips tasted of the spices inside her mask. "I'll be back with more people. Goodbye, Koyee."

She nodded, eyes damp. Torin turned, raced downstairs, and left her there outside a house of disease—the only safe haven in this city of blood.

79

CHAPTER SEVEN
OF CLAY AND COURAGE

Bailey raced up the exterior stairs toward the hospice portico, dragging the boys behind her. She glared over her shoulder at them.

"Hurry!" She snarled at the pair. "Stop stumbling over your boots and climb faster. We have to find the babyface."

The boys stared back, eyes haunted and faces pale. Hem's lip wobbled; the beefy baker looked ready to burst into tears. Half his friend's side, Cam wrung his hands, his dark eyes darting from side to side. Bailey felt some of her rage seeping away. Despite their armor and swords, her friends from Fairwool-by-Night were no warriors, only frightened villagers. She let her voice soften.

"Just climb as fast as you can. Remember how we joked that the hospice is the only place Ferius would never slither into?" She looked back up toward its looming columns. "Torin will remember too. We'll find him there."

The three continued climbing the stairs, leaving the bloodied city streets behind. Bailey grimaced to remember the slaughter she had seen there. She had been patrolling outside the library as the convoy rode by, Ferius upon his horse, a hundred monks behind him. They had lifted the corpse of King Ceranor upon pikes, the moonstar of Qaelin etched across his bare torso.

"The Traitor King is dead!" Ferius had chanted, riding through the city, his thugs slaying any Elorian they came across. "Sailith rises and Eloria falls!"

Bailey kept climbing, dragging the two boys by the collar. For perhaps the first time in her life, she didn't know what to do.

Empires of Moth

She missed her grandfather and fear knotted her belly, but she would not show it. For now she just had to find Torin. She had to keep him safe.

At the thought of him, her eyes dampened. Since the plague had ripped through Fairwool-by-Night, killing so many, Torin had lived under her roof. A year younger, a little shorter, and nearly blind in one eye, the boy had seemed pitiful, a lost puppy she had brought into her home. Since then, he had grown into something else. In the shadows and blood of the night, she had watched him become a man. A friend. A brother at arms. Perhaps even . . .

She swallowed. Perhaps even what? A man she could love? Bailey laughed mirthlessly. Such thoughts had been filling her mind too often of late; again she shoved them out, snickering at herself.

"When I find you, Torin, I'm going to beat you up for making me worry so much about you."

She crested the last few steps, hurried between two columns, and stepped onto a shadowy portico. Flagstones spread toward a pair of stone doors.

Bailey froze.

He stood across the portico, maybe fifty feet ahead. Torin. In his arms, he was holding the young Elorian woman. Koyee. Their lips were locked in a kiss.

Bailey stared, feeling like the columns were crashing around her.

"I'll be back with more people," Torin was saying to the girl. "Goodbye, Koyee."

He parted from her, turned from the hospice doors, and hurried away. After a few steps, he saw Bailey and the boys standing between the columns. His eyes widened and relief swept across his face. He ran toward them, pulled all three into a great embrace, and squeezed them.

81

"Thank Idar!" he said. "Bailey! Boys! I'm glad to see you here. It's a damn nightmare out there. I brought two wounded Elorians into the hospice, but . . . by the light, they're killing so many."

When seeking Torin through the city, Bailey had imagined squeezing him in her embrace, kissing his cheek, mussing his hair, then slapping him a few times for making her worry, only to then smile and kiss him again. Now she only stood stiffly in his arms, and a strange coldness filled her, and the image of him kissing Koyee kept dancing in her mind.

This is no time for jealousy, you woolhead! she scolded herself. *The city is drenched in blood, and Torin is only a winky-eyed babyface besides. Stop acting like a stupid, lovestruck girl.*

She pulled away from the embrace. The four friends, once the Village Guard and now occupiers of the night, stood between the columns, faces pale, armor splashed with blood. For a moment, all four could only stare in silence. The three looked at her—Hem with his plump cheeks and wobbling lip; Cam with his sharp features, his normally mocking grin gone from his face; and Torin, once a soft youth, now a grim and silent soldier.

Bailey grimaced and looked at her feet.

They look at me for guidance, she thought. The oldest, loudest, tallest, and bravest one of the group, she had always been their leader. Back in the sunlight, she had run at their lead through the forests, swam ahead of them in the river, scolded them for torn clothes or dented armor, praised them for a song well sung or a tree well climbed, and even comforted them through the sadness of lost pets, wilted crops, or broken hearts. Here too, she knew, they wanted her leadership. They wanted the brazen Bailey Berin, daughter of their mayor, to lead them through the shadow.

But things were different here. She could perhaps lead the boys up trees, through fields, and across rivers, but how could she lead them through blood and darkness? This was too big for her.

Empires of Moth

She was the granddaughter of a mayor, destined to rule a village of five hundred souls. Here in Pahmey, hundreds of thousands were suffering, dying, desperate for aid; how could she be a leader here?

It's too big for me, she thought, throat tight.

"Bailey," Hem ventured, his voice meek and shaking. "What do we do now?"

She forced herself to swallow the lump in her throat. She tightened her lips, nodded, and glared at the three boys.

"What do you think we do?" she said, hands on her hips. "We do what Winky did. We sneak more Elorians into this hospice." She stared at the babyface. "You saved two? I bet I can save twenty."

He barked a mirthless laugh. "Everything is a contest with you, isn't it?"

She nodded and jabbed a finger against his chest. "You know it is. Now come on!" She grabbed his hand and began dragging him downstairs and away from the hospice. "We're going to save whoever we can. Boys! You too. Winky and I will head along the east road; you two lumps go west. Grab whoever you can and smuggle them here—under your cloaks, inside barrels, I don't care how, just get people into this hospice."

They clanked and clattered downstairs. Fire blazed inside Bailey, searing her fear. This was better. This was a plan. This would make her forget Torin kissing that . . . that . . .

No. She gnashed her teeth. *Don't you think about that now, Bailey Berin, or I'll slap myself right in the face.*

They hurried downstairs and into the square again. Blood smeared the cobblestones. An Elorian family lay dead, arrows in their backs. Emerging from a narrow road lined with shops, several Elorian children tried to race across the square toward the hospice; a Timandrian knight rode his horse in pursuit, cut the children down, then turned to ride back onto the road. Elorians fled before him.

83

Bailey snarled and gripped her sword. She tugged Torin's hand.

"Come *on*, Winky! Down that road." She turned toward a second road, this one lined with glass homes and mushroom gardens. "Boys! You head down that way. We meet back at the hospice doors."

She raced down the road, dragging Torin behind her. Cam and Hem hurried down the second path. As Bailey ran, nausea rose inside her. The corpses of Elorians littered the streets, slashed with swords, beaten with clubs, and trampled with hooves. The knight ahead was galloping down the road. Other Timandrians, these ones marching afoot, were smashing the doors and windows of shops. They laughed as they plundered, scattering pottery, hourglasses, musical instruments, and mushrooms across the street.

"The savages cower like rats!" one soldier said and smashed a window. He peered inside. "Nightfolk, nightfolk, come out to see the light!"

His companion, a soldier missing two teeth, laughed and kicked a stray cat. "Where are they? Have we killed them all? I want more to kill."

As Bailey and Torin approached, the soldiers—there were about a dozen of them—turned toward them. They laughed and gestured at the ruin of the street. Shattered glass and smashed goods lay everywhere. Several corpses bled.

"You're too late," said one soldier, laughing. "We killed them all, we did." He kicked a corpse. "Help us find more. I reckon these nightfolk are hiding in every house."

A few soldiers stepped into one shop and began to topple shelves. A creak sounded above, and Bailey looked up to see two Elorian children—they looked no older than five or six—peering down from a shop's attic. Their gleaming eyes widened with fear, and they retreated from the window.

Empires of Moth

Torin met her gaze; he had seen them too. The soldiers around them, however, were too busy ransacking, smashing, and biting into mushrooms.

"I saw a couple!" Bailey said. Torin gasped and she shot him a withering stare. "I saw two Elorians."

The soldiers turned toward her, blood on their weapons, their eyes thirsting for more. She pointed down the road.

"They went there, around the corner. Little sneaky ones."

The soldiers hooted and laughed, nudged one another, and turned to run in pursuit.

"More vermin to kill!" one called.

"More cockroaches to crush!"

Hooting and laughing, the soldiers raced around the corner, disappearing from view. Bailey let out a shaky breath. She grabbed Torin's hand again.

"Let's get them into the hospice; the attic won't hide them for much longer, not if they keep peering outside."

Torin looked around the street, face ashen. For a moment he only stood staring at the corpses; ten or more lay across the street. Finally he tightened his lips, nodded, and moved toward the shop.

They stepped into a room of torn parchment, smashed clay, and blood. This had once been a pottery shop; bowls, jugs, and mugs lay shattered across the floor. Two corpses, a man and woman in blue silk, lay with slit necks. Bailey clenched her jaw to stop from vomiting. The sound of weeping children rose from the attic, though Bailey was tempted to dart outside, race through the streets until she found Ferius, and stab him dead.

She sucked in breath between her teeth. Ferius rode with hundreds of soldiers; here two children needed her. Fists trembling, she waded through the broken pottery toward a staircase. Torin moved at her side, eyes dark and mouth a tight line.

85

They climbed a narrow stairway, opened a trapdoor, and emerged into an attic full of uncooked clay wrapped in cloth. The two children saw them and cowered into the corner, shivering and begging. Bailey couldn't understand all their words—Torin was better at Qaelish than her—but she didn't need to.

They're begging for their lives.

"We here for help," Bailey said, speaking in Qaelish, which she had only been studying for several months; the words felt stiff and clumsy in her mouth. Though her eyes stung, she smiled gently and reached out her hand. "We help. Come."

The children only cowered deeper into the shadows. Tears flowed from their violet eyes, large Elorian eyes for seeing in the darkness. Their lips shook. One was a boy, the other a girl; neither seemed older than six.

"Please," the girl begged, shivering as she hugged a rag doll shaped like a dragon. "Please, my dragon is scared. I want my mama. Where is my mama?"

Bailey lowered herself onto her hands and knees, crawled forward, and smiled.

"What doll's name?" she asked, hoping they could understand her accent.

"Shenlai," said the girl. "Like the real Shenlai in the east. He's scared and he wants our mama."

"Can I pat him?" Bailey asked. When the girl nodded, she reached out and patted the dragon's silken head.

From outside, the thud of boots and shouts of soldiers rose again. A distant scream of pain tore across the street. Torin stiffened beside her, armor clanking.

"Bailey, we have to go," he said.

She nodded and smiled again at the young children. "Shenlai be very brave. You two be brave too. Hold our backs, under . . ." She couldn't remember the Qaelish word for cloaks. " . . .under back blankets."

Empires of Moth

With a few more smiles and soothing words, she got the little girl to cling to her back, hidden under her cloak. The young boy piggybacked onto Torin, similarly hidden. When they stepped outside the shop, they saw an Elorian man race along the street, yowling with fear. Five Timandrian soldiers ran in pursuit, laughing, their swords drawn.

Bailey closed her eyes for just a moment, steeled herself with a deep breath, and began to walk across puddles of blood. Torin walked at her side. Under their cloaks, the children clung silently to their backs.

"Back to the hospice," she said. "Then back to the streets. Again and again." She growled and tasted tears on her lips. "Thousands will die, but we can save a few. We can save a few."

They made their way down the road. Around them, the screams and blood flowed across the city.

CHAPTER EIGHT
INTO DARKNESS

They kept arriving—two refugee children, then a family, then a pair of young women, then an elder hobbling on a cane. Every hour, Torin or one of his friends rushed into the hospice, sneaking an Elorian under a cloak, inside Timandrian robes of wool, or—in the case of one toddler—even wrapped inside a blanket.

Standing in the hospice cellar, Koyee had removed her Sisterhood mask. Clad in her leather robes, she rushed from person to person. She tended to wounds. She dried children's tears and whispered comforts. She stroked hair and prayed.

"Be strong, children of Eloria," she said, throat feeling so tight. "We are the night."

The cellar was cramped, a place for storing food, vinegar, and bandages, a place of shadow lit by only several candles. Fifty or more Elorians now hid here, bloodied, shivering, some weeping. Between shelves and chests, their eyes stared at her, gleaming in the dark. They repeated the words of their people—not just of this city, not just of their empire of Qaelin, but the words shared by all Elorians, dwellers Moth's dark half. "We are the night."

The door burst open. As she did every time, Koyee started and reached for her sword, sure that Ferius or his thugs had invaded the hospice and found them. But it was only Torin and Bailey, faces flushed, leading in three more Elorians—children in torn clothes who huddled together, splashed with blood. Koyee rushed forward and began tending to the wounds. Only moments later, Cam and Hem entered the chamber too, leading several more city folk. The cellar was full to the brim.

"It's bad out there," said Cam, the short and slim soldier— he stood barely taller than Koyee. "We were by the library and . . ." His face paled and his words trailed off.

Hem—the largest man Koyee had ever seen—covered his face. "Ferius was there. He's horrible. His yellow robes were all red with blood, and his warriors were with him, monks in crimson armor. They . . . they . . ." Hem too could no longer continue.

Koyee narrowed her eyes, stepped forward, and placed her hands on the boys' shoulders; Hem's shoulder was taller than her head.

"What?" she said. "Tell me."

Cam swallowed and wiped sweat off his brow. "At first, I thought Ferius and his followers only wanted to let out steam—to plunder, smash, and destroy for a turn—and then things would go back to normal. But . . . oh Idar. He stood upon the library steps and raised his hands, and he shouted to an army of soldiers. He ordered them to kill every Elorian in this city. Liquidation, he called it. 'Leave no Elorian alive!' he shouted, face all red, blood on his hands."

Hem whimpered at his friend's side. "And it gets worse. Ferius was shouting about how Elorians caused the plague, how he must cleanse the land of the disease. He's organizing an army of masked soldiers with torches. He will lead them into the hospice himself, he said—to burn everything and everyone inside."

Koyee felt as if her heart stopped.

She turned away and faced a shadowy wall. Her chest constricted.

"Does it end here?" she whispered. "Do we fall now?"

The Elorians across the cellar prayed. Some wept. Others called for fighting. Koyee balled her fists at her sides, looked up

89

through burning eyes, and saw Torin standing beside her. He gazed at her, eyes inscrutable.

"We will fight from here," he said, and she heard the fear in his voice. "We will fight and hold them back."

She shook her head. "For how long? How many hours can we resist, only a few defenders, until the mob breaks in, until they burn and slay us? This is no longer a war, Torin. This is genocide."

Around her, the people heard her words and wailed. Children clung to her legs. Elders mumbled prayers.

Koyee raised her voice. "People of Eloria! Do not despair. As fire burns, your hearts must strengthen. You are children of the night; you are stronger than mountains and wind." She raised her chin. "We will flee into the wilderness. Follow."

As she turned to leave, the tall Timandrian woman with the two braids—Bailey Berin, her name was—grabbed her arm. For an instant, the woman's eyes—so dark and small compared to the eyes of Elorians—blazed.

"The streets are swarming with soldiers," Bailey said. "We'd be slaughtered if we step outside."

Koyee narrowed her eyes, regarding the fair-haired woman. There was fear in Bailey and rage against the bloodshed, but . . . something else too. Hostility. After living on the streets of Pahmey, dealing with thieves and spicers, Koyee knew something of hostility.

This one holds no love for me, Bailey thought, tilting her head. *I must be careful around her.*

"That's why we're going to take a wagon," Koyee said and stifled a shudder. "When the Sisterhood's wagons of death move across the city, all flee before them. We will move like a leper through a ball; all will recoil from us." She grabbed her beaked mask, wide-brimmed hat, and steel-tipped gloves. "Follow, my friends! I will lead you to safety."

Empires of Moth

She began walking toward the door. The people followed—fifty Elorians and five Timandrians, all splashed with blood and caked with ash and grime. As Koyee walked, she placed on her mask, lacing it behind her head. Through the glass lenses, the world seemed hazy and twisted, a nightmare of shadows and ghosts. When she pulled on her leather gloves, each finger tipped with a steel claw, she felt less a woman than a bird, a great night vulture, a dancer of death. The Sisterhood of Harmony was created to lead this dance macabre, to escort the departed into the beyond, yet now Koyee would lead a different procession.

Now I lead life.

She led them up stairs and along halls of stone. The hospice seemed strangely deserted; she saw no other sisters. Her followers walked behind her; the Timandrians clanked in their armor and held drawn swords, while the fifty Elorians whispered and mumbled prayers. Their footfalls echoed in vaulted ceilings.

From outside, screams and chants rose. Ringing steel and thundering hooves pealed across the city. When they passed a window, Koyee glimpsed the slaughter; countless soldiers rushed through the city, smashing doors, slaying all they could find. Blood covered the streets of Pahmey. Already some soldiers were advancing across the square toward the hospice; they held swords and torches, and rage twisted their faces.

"Burn the diseased!" they shouted, marching forth, not an organized army but a seething mob. "Burn the twisted creatures who spread the plague."

Behind her, the Elorians she led whimpered and one wailed aloud. Koyee looked over her shoulder at them; their faces were flushed, their eyes wide with fear. They clutched their wounds and pointed at the slaughter outside.

"Hush now," she said. "Hurry. Quickly." She looked at Torin. "Help them along, Torin. We must move fast."

91

They walked beyond the window, down a narrow corridor, and through a tunnel. Finally they emerged into the hospice stables, a dusty chamber of exposed brick. Several bluefeathers—wingless birds the size of horses—stood here, cawing and scratching the ground with their talons. A wagon stood by the wall, built of leather stretched over a metal frame.

"Into that wagon!" Koyee said, turning toward the Elorians. "Lie upon it and play dead. The Sisterhood often takes the dead out of the city for burning. We'll smuggle you out as plague victims."

The people hesitated, staring at the wagon, and whispered among themselves.

Standing beside her, Torin grimaced. "Koyee, this wagon . . ." He lowered his voice. "Does the miasma of disease cling to it? How many dead have lain here?"

Koyee glared at him. "The wagon is clean. We scrub it with boiling vinegar after every delivery. You will be safe. Now move! Pile up! Children on top."

She began ushering them onto the wagon, tapping her foot, her eyes darting. The sounds of soldiers rose outside. Chants of "Burn the diseased!" and "Death to Elorians!" rose louder. Koyee grimaced. Would they even let her wagon pass, or would they attack her on the streets? She ground her teeth. She had to take this chance.

"Here, Grandpapa, into the wagon," she said, helping an elder climb.

They began to pile up, lying one atop the other. When Hem tried to climb in too, Koyee tugged him back. "Not you!"

Finally they all filled the wagon—fifty Elorians stacked together like a pile of diseased corpses. Their silken robes were already tattered and bloodied, but they lacked the telltale signs of the curse; they bore no boils, their fingertips had not rotted, and teeth still filled their mouths. Koyee rushed to a shelf, grabbed

92

Empires of Moth

homespun sheets, and pulled them over the people. She bit her lip. Like this, only limbs emerged from the under the sheet; the rest of the Elorians were but lumps under silk. It wouldn't fool a Sister of Harmony, but perhaps it would fool the enemy.

She tethered four bluefeathers to the wagon and climbed into the seat. "We move. Timandrians, you walk alongside. Guard this wagon."

They opened the stable doors and wheeled out, leaving the hospice, a hive of dying, and entering the city of Pahmey, a dreamscape of slaughter.

Torin and Bailey led the way, helms on their heads, swords drawn. Clad in her Sisterhood mask, Koyee drove the wagon behind them, the bluefeathers clacking, the refugees hidden under the sheet. Cam and Hem brought up the rear. Koyee's heart thrashed as they moved down a cobbled backstreet, narrow buildings at their sides. When they passed through an intersection, she could see into the square; troops were racing across it toward the hospice entrance, the place where only hours ago she had kissed Torin.

Several soldiers burst from around a corner, laughing, their swords stained with blood. When they saw the wagon, they froze and their eyes widened. One spat and raised a torch.

Koyee's heart thudded, and for an instant she was sure their escape would end here, that they would die in a shadowy street corner only steps away from the hospice.

Torin raised his voice and sword. "Stand back! The plague festers in this wagon. We will burn them outside the city. Make way!"

The soldiers stared, rabid beasts with bared teeth. Koyee stared back through her mask, sweat trickling beneath her leather suit. She reached down between her legs where lay her katana; she was ready to fight and die if she must.

93

"Go on, move!" shouted Bailey, taking a step toward the soldiers. "Or do you want to catch the disease too? Go!"

The soldiers cursed, glanced at one another, then spun around and fled.

Koyee breathed a shaky breath of relief. "Walk!" she said and the bluefeathers obeyed, dragging the wagon forward.

They kept moving through the city, road by road. Torin and Bailey walked ahead, banging swords against shields, crying out for all to move aside.

"Death festers!" they cried out in Ardish. "Plague corpses for burning. Make way!"

As they moved down the boulevards of Pahmey, all parted before them, scuttling into shadows. The wagon trundled down streets lined with looted shops, bodies strewn across the cobblestones. They passed under crystal towers, their light dimmed, corpses piled up around their bases. They moved through marketplaces, the stalls smashed, the peddlers slain upon their wares.

So many dead, Koyee thought, eyes stinging behind her lenses. Thousands of Elorians lay fallen here. Soldiers kept rushing about, rifling through homes and gutters and attics, seeking more to kill, more blood to fill their endless appetite. Tears filled Koyee's eyes and her lenses fogged, but she kept moving her wagon forward. Her city crumbled around her, but she could save a few. She could carry a flicker of life through the endless death.

"Make way!" Torin cried. "Plague wagon for burning— make way!"

They rolled by the city library, a domed building lined with columns. When Koyee looked toward its doors, she grimaced. She was tempted to leap off her wagon, charge up the marble stairs, and attack.

Empires of Moth

Ferius stood outside the library doors, hands raised to the sky. Blood stained his palms and dripped down his arms. He led a chant to Sailith, a hundred monks chanting around him, their yellow robes turned red. A hundred Elorian bodies hung behind them from the library roof, their necks stretched. Countless more corpses littered the stairway below their feet.

"For the glory of sunlight!" Ferius called, seeming in rapture. "We have vengeance. We purify the night. We light the darkness. Slay them all!"

Without realizing it, Koyee wheeled the wagon toward the library. Snarling behind her mask, she reached down and grabbed her sword. Torin had to block the bluefeathers, stare at Koyee, and direct her away.

"We have to run this time," he said, kindness and sadness mixing in his eyes. "We will fight him, Koyee. I promise you. But not here. Not now. Now we must flee."

His face was pale, and dark bags hung under his eyes. He seemed so tired to her, so haunted, that she wanted to embrace him. She nodded. They kept moving, leaving the library and entering the narrow streets of the dregs. Soon they rolled down the old market way, heading toward the city gates.

Fifty Timandrian soldiers waited there, clad from head to toe in steel, pikes in their hands.

Koyee tugged the reins, halting the wagon. Behind her, she heard one of the Elorian children whimper under the sheet.

Torin took a step forward toward the small army. "Make way! Open the gates. We have plague victims to burn, damn it."

The soldiers would not budge. Their lord, a burly man in dark steel, stepped forward. The sunburst of Sailith blazed upon his breastplate, the gold turned red in the torchlight. He spoke from within his barred visor, his voice gravelly.

95

"On orders of Lord Ferius, none may leave this city." The man pounded his chest with a gauntleted fist. "I serve Sailith. All will remain within these walls. All will die."

Koyee leaped off the wagon and marched forward. Torin tried to hold her back, but she whipped around him. She stomped up toward the burly soldier—she barely reached his shoulders—and glared up at him through her mask. He took a step back and cursed.

"Stand back, Sister of Harmony." He covered the mouth hole of his visor. "I know your kind. Diseased birds! Stand back or I'll slay you."

Koyee would not budge. She raised her beak toward him. "*You* will stand back. I carry fifty bodies rife with the plague. Their miasma fills this street as we linger. They are already dead. Unless you want to join them, you will open these gates. Now move!"

A few of the soldiers at the back shifted, their armor clanking. They glanced at one another and a few covered their mouths. Koyee leaped back onto the wagon, drove the bluefeathers a few feet forward, and shouted out.

"Move—now! Move or the plague will touch you too. Move so we may burn them in the wilderness."

The beefy lord all but fled backward, nodded at his soldiers, and the gates creaked open.

The night spread outside.

For the first time in moons, Koyee saw the Inaro River, a stream of silver in the moonlight. She saw the rolling black plains that sprawled into the horizon. She smelled the cold, fresh air, air that did not reek of death. Lips tight, she drove her wagon onward, her friends walking at her sides.

The wagon bumped over the last few cobblestones, and they passed under the archway . . . and emerged into the night.

They kept going. They rolled across the boardwalk, heading toward the river. The stars shone above and the river sang,

Empires of Moth

screams rose and echoed, and she could still hear the chants of the monks. Even though darkness folded around them, she could still see those hanging corpses, still see the blood on Ferius's hands, dripping, seeping, blood that would forever fill her nightmares.

Her eyes stung and the screams rose behind her, but she kept going. She had to keep leading these people away, into darkness, into hope, into a cold endless night that could never drown the fires. She looked over her shoulder only once, and she saw the city walls behind her. She remembered herself a year ago, a frightened girl in a fur tunic, seeing this city for the first time, a hub of light and wonder in the darkness.

Now she saw smoke and fire. Now she smelled blood. Now countless voices cried in agony . . . then fell silent . . . vanishing in the wind until only the chanting of monks and the cheers of soldiers remained. And Koyee Mai knew: They were gone. They were silenced forever.

Lips tight and eyes stinging, she drove her wagon toward the docks where a hundred vessels moored. The river would take them into darkness. She did not look back.

CHAPTER NINE
THE WATER SPIDER

Torin was loading refugees into a boat when he heard shouts behind him, turned around, and saw Ferius at the city gates.

Torin froze and stared across the boardwalk.

About a hundred yards away, Ferius stared back and smiled—the smile a snake gives a mouse.

The city gatehouse rose across the wide, cobbled boardwalk. Torin stood upon a stone pier that stretched into the Inaro River. Several refugees had already boarded the vessel, a rowboat named the *Water Spider*. It was the same vessel Torin had first rowed into this city six months ago, a landing craft that had once hung across the hull of a towering carrack. Eight oars rose along its sides like spider legs. Cam and Hem were already manning two oars, while Elorian refugees were grabbing the others. It was a small boat, and Torin had a good fifty people to save, but his heart had already been rising with hope . . . until he saw the monk.

For a few heartbeats, the two only stared at each other across the dark distance. An Elorian child in his arms, Torin could only stand, frozen and breathless.

Fifty more monks emerged around Ferius, filling the gateway; here were the bloodsuns, the warriors of Sailith, clad in crimson armor and bearing maces with flanged heads the size of skulls. Two of the city guards, soldiers of Arden, were bowing and groveling, pleading for mercy. Never tearing his gaze away from Torin, Ferius snapped his fingers; his bloodsuns stepped forward, clubbed the two guards, and sent them bleeding to the ground.

Empires of Moth

The monk pointed at the docks. "Stop that boat! Slay them!"

Torin could finally move. Heart lashing, he all but tossed the child he held into the *Water Spider*.

"Bailey, hold them back!" he shouted, grabbing another Elorian and guiding the elder into the boat.

Eyes narrowed, Bailey was already nocking an arrow into her bow. She tugged the bowstring back, whispered a prayer, and sent her arrow flying.

Torin helped a wounded woman into the boat, looked back at the monks, and sucked in his breath. The arrow narrowly missed Ferius, instead slamming into a bloodsun. The shaft snapped against the man's armor.

Torin cursed and helped the last few Elorians into the rowboat. The *Water Spider* was meant for twenty soldiers; fifty Elorians now filled it, pointing at the monks and praying to the stars.

"Slay them!" Ferius shouted.

His bloodsuns ran across the boardwalk, heading toward the pier. They held lanterns and maces, and their eyes blazed red. Bailey shot another arrow, and this one punched through a man's armor, sending him sprawling across the cobblestones.

"Bailey, Koyee, come on!" Torin shouted, climbing aboard. "Into the boat!"

Koyee was struggling to untether the boat from its peg, but the knot wouldn't loosen. She cursed, drew her sword, and sliced the rope. The boat began to drift away, and Koyee leaped inside, landing between the refugees.

"Bailey!" Torin shouted. His friend still stood upon the dock, firing arrows at the approaching monks; the enemy was only paces away. "Damn it, Bailey, into the boat."

99

Her back toward him, she fired another arrow, hitting a second man. The bloodsun fell, an arrow in his chest. The boat floated several feet away.

"Bailey!"

Finally she turned, ran several paces across the pier, and leaped. Her legs kicked and she landed in the boat, missing the water by inches. She wobbled, arms windmilling. Torin had to grab her and pull her forward.

Quarrels whistled around them.

Torin cursed, pulled Bailey down, and leaned across several Elorian children. Metal bolts whizzed above them. One slammed into his back, denting his armor; it felt like a horse kick. Torin winced, looked over his shoulder, and saw the bloodsuns upon the docks.

"They have crossbows," he muttered. "Lovely."

Another barrage flew toward the boat. Torin raised his shield, wincing. A bolt slammed into the wood. More flew overhead. Bailey stood with a raised shield beside him. Together, they protected the boat's stern. Their shields blocked most of the barrage, but one quarrel whisked between them. An Elorian woman—a weaver clad in the azure sash of her guild—clutched her chest and fell, a steel shard in her heart.

When Bailey lowered her shield to fire another arrow, the bloodsuns on the docks entered three rowboats. The vessels detached from the docks like leeches off flesh, bloated with red steel. The warrior-monks began rowing, lanterns held high. Ferius stood behind them upon the docks, and his roars rolled across the river.

"Bring them to me alive! They will confess their sins before they burn."

Cam and Hem were rowing madly at each side of the *Water Spider*. The vessel tilted toward Hem's side; the baker-turned-soldier was thrice his friend's size. Three more oars lined each

Empires of Moth

side, and Elorians manned them. They chanted for their stars as they rowed, pushing the boat on.

Standing at the stern, Bailey kept firing arrows, but her quiver was running low. Upon the docks, more monks came racing from the city, leaped into more boats, and joined the pursuit; two hundred warriors or more now rowed toward them.

Do we die in the water? Torin wondered. He drew his sword.

"If we go down, we go down fighting," he said.

Koyee came to stand beside him. She too drew her sword; the curved katana seemed slim beside Torin's wide longsword, but he knew the blade could cut through armor. Koyee nodded, tossed down her beaked mask, and snarled at the approaching enemy.

"We fight side by side, Torin." She raised her chin, teeth bared. "We die side by side."

Beside them, Bailey fired her last arrow. The projectile whistled across the water, dived toward a boat full of bloodsuns, and sent a man falling into the water. Her quiver empty, Bailey drew her double-edged longsword.

"You two can die," she said and spat at the enemy. "I'm going to kill all of these beasts myself then stomp upon their corpses."

Behind them, Cam raised his voice. "Nobody is dying or killing anyone! We row faster than a deer fleeing a wolf. Hem, damn it, row faster—keep up!"

Sweat dampening their faces, they rowed. The refugees pushed themselves low as more bolts flew above. Torin stood at the stern between Bailey and Koyee, staring as the enemy approached. Even Linee came to stand by them, shivering, and raised a dagger Bailey had given her. A dozen boats now followed, armed monks in each. Ferius, however, remained upon the pier, watching the pursuit.

101

The coward dares not fight, Torin thought, staring at the distant figure in disgust. *He spews bravado but still fears our blades.*

"We'll row to the southern riverbank." Torin adjusted the rudder. "We're floating targets in the water."

Bailey looked at him, eyes wide, her chest rising and falling as she panted. "And we won't be targets on the land?"

"Easier to hide there." Torin glanced behind him; the southern bank was still too far to see in the shadows. "The moonlight glows on the water. Hills and valleys roll in the south. We'll move in shadow. It's the only chance we have."

They rowed. The boat moved south, tilting, low in the water. The enemy pursued, a foot or two closer every stroke of the oars. The monks' lamps burned like demons, painting their faces red, and they shouted.

"We will slay the savages!"

"We will break the traitors!"

"Children of sunlight breed with demons; they will scream in our fire!"

Muttering curses, Torin unstrapped his breastplate and tossed it into the water. "We're too heavy! Toss off your armor." He threw his helmet overboard. "What we need now is speed; steel can no longer help us."

Bailey stared at him, eyebrows raised, lips curling in dismay. Finally she groaned, reached behind her back, and unstrapped her own breastplate. She sent pieces of armor flying overboard, remaining in a woolen tunic. She raised her shield just in time to block two more crossbow quarrels. Behind her, Koyee shrugged off the Sisterhood's clunky suit of leather and iron, remaining in a silk tunic; she tossed the heavy outfit overboard.

It seemed ages that they rowed across the river. The Sailith boats oared closer and closer; soon they were close enough that Torin could see the white in his enemies' eyes. One Sailith boat—

102

Empires of Moth

the first to have left the docks—cut through the water, closing the gap. They oared only ten feet away, then nine, then eight . . .

"Row faster!" Torin shouted.

Cam and Hem shouted back. "We are!"

The enemy boat moved closer; eight bloodsuns lined its sides, rowing like machines. Ten more stood upon the decks, maces raised. With another swipe of their oars, the Sailith boat rammed into the *Water Spider*.

The two vessels jerked and Torin swayed, nearly falling. Bloodsuns leaped onto the *Water Spider*, their lamplight reflecting against their red armor, their maces swinging.

Shouting, Torin raised his shield. A mace slammed into it, showering splinters. Torin thrust his sword, hitting the monk's breastplate. Sparks flew. The mace swung again, and Torin ducked, barely dodging the blow. He leaped forward, shield held before him, and slammed into the enemy. The bloodsun teetered, crashed into the water, and sank.

More monks fought around him, shouting and waving maces, clambering to climb aboard. The Elorian refugees, unarmed and clad in only silk, screamed; most cowered, but three began to slam their oars against the enemy.

"Don't fight—keep rowing!" Torin shouted; more Sailith boats were still driving toward them.

At his sides, Bailey and Koyee fought too, swinging their swords. Even Linee lashed her dagger, squealing in fright. Two more bloodsuns fell into the water. A third leaped at Torin, who sidestepped; the man crashed into the *Water Spider*, and Elorians leaped upon him, kicking and punching, tearing the man's helmet off and pounding his head against the bulwark.

Torin stared through sweat that dripped down his face. A dozen monks still stood upon the boat ramming them; they could not defeat them all. Holding his shield before him and cursing with every foul word he knew, he knelt, grabbed the rudder, and

103

tugged. The *Water Spider* turned. Several of the refugees swayed and fell. Torin tugged the rudder again, pressing the *Water Spider*'s starboard bow against the enemy's port side. Several bloodsuns rowers sat there, staring down at him. Catching a crossbow dart on his shield, Torin lashed his sword.

His blade sang and crashed into the enemy's oars. Wood shattered. An oar splintered and fell into the water. Koyee leaped up beside him, grinning savagely, and swung her katana, shattering more enemy oars.

"Keep rowing, boys!" Torin shouted, grabbed the rudder, and directed them south again. The *Water Spider* kept moving toward the dark riverbank, leaving the crippled enemy boat behind. Only one bloodsun remained upon their deck; Bailey drove her sword into his neck, sending him into the water with a spray of blood.

They kept rowing. The *Water Spider* drove through the river. The remaining enemy boats—each one laden with monks—kept pursuing.

When the *Water Spider* finally slammed against the southern riverbank, Torin exhaled shakily with relief, only for new fear to flood him. They had survived the water; how long would they last upon the plains?

"Out of the boat!" he cried, leaped onto the riverbank, and began helping refugees descend. "Follow—into the darkness."

Linee stood at his side, shivering but helping children and elders out of the boat. One young child leaped onto her back and clung. Torin helped a few others descend onto the bank, lifted an elderly woman, and held her in his arms. When everyone was off the boat, the strong holding the weak, Torin began to run.

"Follow!" he shouted. "Into shadow."

He ran, heart thrashing, teeth grinding, the old woman in his arms. His companions ran at his sides, leaving the water and racing up a rocky hill. The stars shone above. When Torin looked

104

Empires of Moth

over his shoulder, he saw the enemy boats reach the riverbank. The monks began to emerge; two hundred or more pursued, each armed and howling for blood.

Torin returned his eyes forward, cursed, and ran as fear flowed through him like poison.

CHAPTER TEN
THE FISHERMAN'S CHILDREN

He lay with Suntai under the stars, kissed her lips, and stroked her naked body. Lying on her back, she gazed up at him, eyes half-lidded, and smiled lazily.

"My stars in the night," she whispered, caressing his strands of white hair. "My alpha. My mate. My lantern in the dark."

Her hair flowed around her head, covering the black fur rug like strands of starlight, silvery and gleaming. Her eyes, large and indigo, reflected the true stars above. Okado touched the tattoos of lightning upon her high, pale cheeks, the marks of a warrior.

"And you are my fish," he said.

She gasped at him, eyebrows rising and eyes widening. She slapped his chest.

"How dare you call Suntai of Chanku, an alpha warrior, a fish." She wrinkled her nose.

He laughed softly, which was rare for him; as ruler of his pack, he could not show weakness around his followers, and joy, humor, and love were weaknesses to most warriors. Yet Okado found that with Suntai, they gave him strength.

"A fish is a noble animal," he said. "I rule a mighty pack of wolves, but once I dwelled in a village, and fish were life to us. Fish were light in the dark, the glow of their stalks filling our jars. Fish were oil to warm our fires. Fish were meat to fill our bellies. Fish were—"

Suntai grabbed his cheeks and snarled at him. "I am a she-wolf. I will prove this to you."

Empires of Moth

Smiling crookedly, she released his cheeks and kissed his lips. She tasted of wine and of her passion for him. He wrapped his arms around her, sharing her fur blanket, and caressed her body, raising goose bumps across her. She gasped, closed her eyes, and they kissed, a deep kiss like wells and endless sky. The rest of the camp lay around them, but Okado cared not, for there was no shame, nothing hidden among the wolfriders of Chanku. And so he loved her here, moving atop her, kissing her lips and neck, his hands in her hair. She scratched her fingers down his back as he loved her, and she bit his shoulder, and she cried to the night, and she did as she had vowed. She proved that she was as a wolf, wild and strong and his to ride, a being of flame and strength and ferocity. She was Suntai, his mate, and she was the spirit of the hunt, the glory of battle, the light and shadow of the night sky.

When their love was spent, he lay with her in his arms and stroked her hair.

"My mate," she whispered, and suddenly tears gleamed in her eyes. "I'm sorry. I'm so sorry. I pray that this time your child fills my belly."

"Suntai!" Okado shook his head and touched her hair. "Never apologize for that."

She lowered her eyes and clung to him. Her voice was soft. "Three years ago you chose me as a mate, and still I've given you no children. My womb is barren. I've failed you, my light in the dark, and I'm ashamed. You are our leader and I give you no heir." She placed a hand on her belly, then looked back at him and touched his cheek. "Perhaps you should seek another mate."

He gripped her arm. "You fought with me against the sunlit demons. You shed blood by my side, and you loved me under the light of our ancestors in the stars. Never feel ashamed, Suntai, and never feel sorry. Every turn I'm proud that you are mine. I want no other mate. We will forever ride together."

107

She nodded and closed her eyes. "Always I will fight at your side."

Even upon the fur rug, his warm mate in his arms, Okado felt a chill. *The sunlit demons.* It had been six moons since they had fought the enemy upon the plains. Still the battle haunted him. He had fought bravely, leading his pack to slay many of the creatures. Yet he had not won the war. He had returned into shadow, five thousand of his brothers and sisters slain. And still the fiery threat lurked north of the river, a demon army bloating and festering like a tumor, ruling his ancestral home of Pahmey.

They say the demons burned Oshy, he thought and grimaced. *The home of my father. Of my sister.*

His throat burned. So many times he had wanted to raise the remains of his army, five thousand wolfriders, hardened and true. He wanted to charge at the horde of Timandrians, a hundred thousand devils or more, to die in their flame, to reclaim his honor and slay many, to avenge his home even as he perished in the fire. Yet always he remained here in this crater, their home in the shadows. He remained to defend his people, to keep them safe—mothers, elders, children, a mate. And still that distant war called to him. Still that sunfire burned in his belly.

"Okado?" Suntai nestled against him and ran her long, pale fingers across his cheek. "You are troubled."

Okado tilted his head and looked across the crater. Thousands slept around him, wrapped in furs. Some lay within tents of leather, fur, and bone; others lay under the stars. Their nightwolves slept around them, beasts as large and fast as those sunlit creatures the Timandrians called horses. The nightwolves too were part of the clan; they were his siblings as much as their riders. Chests rose and fell in sleep. No eyes peered. Okado closed his own eyes.

"I can still smell the fire, Suntai," he said. "I can still smell the torches of the Timandrians, of the Naya clan that slew so many. I can still smell the blood. I can still see the red smoke that hid the stars."

He opened his eyes and stared upward, and there he saw it again. A crimson glow in the sky, painting the moon red, swirling around the stars like blood around stones.

"I see it too," Suntai whispered. "I see the smoke and I smell the fire." She frowned, propped herself up on her elbows, and sniffed. "Okado! Okado, my mate. I smell fire not in memory; flames burn." She sniffed again, eyes narrowed, and cocked her head. "Great fire and pain in the north."

Okado stiffened and sniffed too. Suntai spoke truth; this was no memory. He rose to his feet, stared toward the north, and a growl rose in his throat. Blood. Fire. A distant chant that rolled across the plains.

"The sunlit demons," he muttered, reached down, and gripped his katana. He slung the sword across his bare back. "Timandra boils over. Suntai, ride with me."

He tugged on a pair of breeches, walked across bare stone, and knelt by his wolf. Refir slept, curled up into a hillock of black fur, his breath frosting. Okado placed a hand upon the beast's head. Two yellow eyes opened, crescent and glowing, and the nightwolf's nose twitched. Refir rose so quickly he nearly knocked Okado down. His tongue lolled and his lip peeled back, revealing fangs like daggers. The nightwolf sensed the danger too. Okado climbed onto him.

At his side, Suntai mounted her own nightwolf, a white female named Misama. Her wolf was mated to his—one alpha couple to lead beasts, another to lead riders. Together they rode through the camp, leaping over the sleeping pack members. When Okado looked at Suntai, he no longer saw a lover but a fierce warrior, her lips locked in a snarl, her body clad in fur, her white hair streaming and her katana raised. Riding beside him, she seemed as feral as her wolf.

They reached the edge of their camp, rode out of the crater, and raced across the plains to crest a northern hill. Several of their camp guards stood here, sitting astride their wolves, gazing into the north. When Okado reached them, he halted his mount and stared with narrowed eyes.

"Sorcery," muttered one of the guards.

Okado spat. "Sunfire burns in Pahmey."

He could not see the city from here, but orange and red now glowed beyond that horizon, a bloodied scar. When Okado sniffed, he could smell it. The stench of death.

"The city burns," he said, turning toward Suntai. "We summon the Red Fang clan. We ride."

She met his gaze, eyes burning, then tossed back her head and howled to the sky. "We ride!" She turned her wolf around, looking back toward the camp. "Red Fang Riders! Arise! Grab armor and blade. We ride north!"

They mustered in the darkness, the Red Fang Riders, five hundred of the pack's finest warriors, their wolves bearing the blood of alphas. Refir and Misama themselves had sired many among them. Here were the fastest, strongest nightwolves in the pack, and their riders were strong and brave. Scale armor they wore, and their helms were shaped as wolf heads, the teeth painted red. Each rider bore a katana, its hilt wrapped in fur, and a round shield fringed with fangs. They howled to the sky, men and women of Chanku, the finest warriors in the empire of Qaelin, perhaps in all of Eloria.

Omegas rushed forth, lowly men and women with only weak wolves to ride, and handed Okado his armor. He donned his shirt of scales and hefted his shield. At his side, Suntai slammed her sword against her armored chest, shouting for glory and blood and triumph.

Okado spurred his wolf, and the animal reared and clawed the air.

Empires of Moth

"Chanku Pack!" Okado cried. "Fire burns in the north. The sunlit demons brew their curses. Raise your swords. We are the night!"

Five hundred blades rose, silver shards like a forest of lightning. Their voices rolled across the land. "We are the night!"

Okado leaned forward and rode across the rocky plains. Behind him, with clattering steel, his warriors followed.

They rode across the shadows of their banishment, the lifeless lands south of the Inaro. They chanted for their gods as they rode beneath Wolfjaw Mountain, its halved peak silently howling at the sky. They rode until the towers of Pahmey rose ahead, needles of crystal glass. When Okado had gazed upon Pahmey before, this city where the Chanku nobles had once ruled, he had seen a nexus of light and life in the dark.

Before him now he saw an inferno.

Crimson smoke unfurled from the city. Distant chants rolled across the distance. The smoke filled his nostrils, scented of seared flesh. Screams echoed. Before his eyes, one of the towers—a distant blade from here—shattered and crashed down, a broken bone.

"They're destroying the city," Suntai said, riding at his side. She raised her katana high. "The sunlit demons slay our brothers and sisters."

Okado growled. Brothers and sisters? The elders of Pahmey had banished the Chanku riders. The decadent masters, sitting idly in their towers, had doomed the Chanku to cold and darkness and exile.

The smell of blood and smoke swirled through him, and Okado closed his eyes, remembering his battle against the sunlit Naya tribe. His body still bore the scars. His mind still harbored the memories. His heart still grieved for his fallen riders. Those creatures of sunlit lands, of the fiery half of this world men called Moth, now slew more dwellers of the night. The people of

111

Pahmey were strangers to him, but they were still children of this Qaelish Empire, speaking his tongue, sharing his blood. They were still children of darkness. Suntai was right. All Elorians were now his brothers and sisters.

As he rode closer, lights caught his eye. Boats were oaring across the river, heading away from the city toward the southern bank. One boat reached the riverbank before the others; figures emerged and began to race southward, and their lanterns extinguished; they disappeared into the shadows. Behind them, several other boats reached the bank and more figures emerged, these ones bearing many bright lamps, and their cries rolled across the land. They spoke the harsh tongue of sunlight. Okado did not need to understand the words; those were the cries of hunters.

"A few escaped the city," he said, riding forth. "A group of Elorians flee the fire. The Timandrians pursue. You speak truth, Suntai; these are my brothers and sisters now." He raised shield and sword and roared for his warriors to hear. "Chanku Pack! Slay the demons!"

Their wolves increased speed, saliva flying from between their fangs. The warriors brandished their katanas and their cries rolled across the land, the roars of hardened men and the yipping battle cries of wild women. They thundered down the hillside, and Okado stood in the saddle, sword raised high.

The enemy stared up at them, two hundred soldiers or more. Okado had learned of these sunlit demons, capturing their scouts and studying their lore. These ones served the cruel god called Sailith, a deity of flame and light. They wore steel plates the color of blood, and yellow sunbursts shone upon their shields. The monks of Sailith were forbidden to bear blades, and so they wielded flanged maces; if they could not cut flesh, they could crush it. There were fewer than the Chanku riders, and they rode no beasts of their own, but they stood their ground. They raised their lamps and chanted in their tongue.

Empires of Moth

"Death to Elorians!" they cried. "For the light!"

Okado spoke no Ardish, but he had heard those words from the Timandrian scouts he'd captured and slain.

"You will find," he said softly, "that the riders of Chanku do not die so easily." He roared his battle cry as he rode toward him. "We are the night!"

The wolves raced toward the enemy; three hundred yards separated the forces, then two, then only a hundred. Below, the Sailith monks would not retreat; jeering, they raised contraptions of metal and wood. Okado recognized them. Crossbows. Machines of the sunlit world. With hundreds of twangs, the bolts flew toward his forces.

Wolves yelped and fell. Riders spilled from the saddle and rolled across the plains. Okado waved his sword.

"For Eloria!"

His riders howled around him. "For Eloria!"

At his side, Suntai raised her bow and shot an arrow. A hundred other Chanku arrows sailed through the night, only to clatter against the Sailith armor. More bolts flew from below, tearing into riders and wolves.

"For Eloria!" his warriors cried.

Okado narrowed his eyes, the world rising and falling around him. "For Oshy. For my father. For Koyee."

With screams and clashing steel, he slammed into the enemy.

His wolf leaped, driving his claws and fangs against the enemy, denting their armor. The warrior-monks charged into them, their steel thick, their maces swinging. Okado took one blow to the shield; the pain drove up his arm and into his shoulder. He slammed his katana down, driving his enemy's helmet into the skull.   A second mace slammed into Refir, denting the wolf's armor, but the beast's thick fur cushioned the

113

blow. Rearing, Refir bit and tore off the enemy's visor. Okado finished the job, driving his sword into flesh.

His riders fought around him, wolves clawing, swords lashing. Some fell to the maces. Most fought on, shouting, slaying the enemy. Blood and shattered weapons littered the riverbank. Across the water, the city burned and the banners of Sailith filled the sky. Death rolled over the night.

When the battle ended, Okado panted and gazed upon the slaughter. Hundreds lay dead around him, Timandrians and Elorians alike, men and women and wolves. Not one of the monks had fled. Not one had surrendered. They had fought to the last man, dying with smiles and prayers upon their lips; two hundred lay torn apart, steel and bodies shattered. Riders and wolves lay dead among them, blood soaking fur.

Suntai rode her wolf toward him. The blood of her enemies splattered her face. She licked it off her teeth, spat, and gazed at him.

"My mate," she said, "the city burns. I hear the cries from here. Thousands die."

Okado wheeled his wolf toward the river. He gazed across the water at Pahmey, his belly tightened, and he gnashed his teeth. A mace's wound drove into his leg, but he did not feel the pain. No more screams rose from the distant city; the cries of the dying now rose only in memory. He heard only the chants of Sailith, only their prayers.

"Death to Elorians! Death to Elorians!"

Okado's fist shook around his hilt, and his eyes burned. "A hundred thousand Timandrians or more fill that city. How can we fight them, Suntai? How can we avenge our fallen?"

A soft voice answered him, but it was not Suntai speaking. This voice was higher, fair and young, a voice like summer rain upon stone.

"We will raise the night. Eloria must fight as one."

Empires of Moth

Okado spun back toward the southern plains. He saw her there, standing among the corpses, blood staining her bare feet. She was no rider of Chanku; in the fashion of Pahmey, she wore a silk tunic and a sash around her waist, and a katana hung at her side. Her long, white hair flowed in the wind, and her lavender eyes gazed at him. Three scars rifted her face—the scars of nightwolf claws, old and white. She was only a youth, but her eyes seemed old. There was pain and wisdom and haunting ghosts in those eyes.

Okado dismounted his wolf, walked through the blood, and stood before her. Other riders surrounded her, trapping her in a ring of blades and fangs. Here stood a woman of Pahmey, their ancient enemy. Okado snapped his teeth at those riders and wolves who approached.

"Stand back, riders!"

He stared down at the young woman; she stood barely taller than his shoulder, and she was probably only half his weight. Yet she met his eyes with serene strength; hers were not fierce, flashing eyes like those of Suntai, but two pools of ancient water.

"I saw you flee the river with several others," Okado said. "Have they fallen in the battle?"

The young woman shook her head, curtains of hair swaying. "They hide in the darkness behind the hills. Fifty people of Pahmey are among them; most are wounded. Five Timandrians there are too." The riders growled at this, and the woman spoke louder. "They helped us flee the city where their monks butcher our people; these five turned against their rulers and joined the night. You will not harm them, riders of Chanku. Yes, I know your name. Many speak of the fierce outlaws who torment the plains, their riders no more noble than beasts." She smiled crookedly. "Here I see that both beasts and riders are as noble as dragons. I thank you."

115

Okado looked back at the distant city. Smoke plumed from its streets and the chants of soldiers rolled across the water. The banners of the enemy fluttered from towers.

"How many have died in the city?" he said, turning back toward the young woman.

She lowered her head. "Thousands. Perhaps all. King Ceranor, who led the sunlit kingdom of Arden, lies dead. He was a conqueror and cruel, but an even crueler tyrant usurped him. The demon Ferius rules now, commanding both monks and soldiers. He seeks to slay every child of the night. We fled him and come to seek aid."

"The sunlit demons are too many," Okado said. "Thousands lurk within that city. Countless more swarm across the lands of Eloria. All we can do in these times of fire, daughter of Pahmey, is retreat to our dens, defend them as we can, and survive in shadow."

Her eyes narrowed and finally some fire filled them. "There will be no more shadows, master of wolves. The sunlit demons will light the darkness." She drew her katana. "I have fled slaughter, but not the war. I will fight."

A few of the riders around her, even the women, sneered at this youth with her bold words and naked blade, a slight thing clad only in silk, no wolf between her legs. But Okado did not sneer. A gasp fled his lips, and his brow furrowed. He took a step closer to her, leaned down, and stared at her sword.

The smell of cooking crayfish filled his nostrils. The songs his mother would sing filled his ears. Ghosts danced before his eyes: a brazier crackling in a hut, a sister playing with clay dolls, and a father polishing an ancient blade he had carried to war against the Ilari Empire.

Okado stared at the sword the woman held, and he knew it; he had held it himself, dreaming of becoming a soldier someday, a hero like his father. Swirls and mottles coiled across the folded steel. Blue silk wrapped around its hilt. Upon its guard, he saw the old etchings of lighting and stars.

"Sheytusung," he whispered. "You bear a blade of legend." Rage filled him, emerging as a growl. "Where did you find this sword, girl? How dare you raise Sheytusung, the blade of a hero, a sword that slew many in Ilar, that . . ."

Seeing her eyes widen, his voice trailed off. The young woman tilted her head, and her brow furrowed, and she gasped. She took a frightened step back, still holding her sword, and mouthed silent words.

Okado stared at her and his own eyes widened. His breath died in his lungs.

"Okado, Okado!" a young girl had cried years ago. "Okado, come play in the water!"

His sister, a mere child of six years, had tugged him into the Inaro and swam with him. They collected river stones, gems of the water, blue and green and shimmering black. His sister had thought them jewels and collected them in her boxes at home.

"Okado, look, a blue one!" she had said, emerging from the water, laughter on her lips, stars in her eyes. "Here, for you."

He had left her that year. He had been sixteen, old enough to follow his own path, to seek his fortune in the east. He traveled for many hourglass turns across the plains. He hunted and lived wild in the night. He found the great Chanku Pack, warriors of legend, and joined their ranks, serving first as omega, scouring pots and skinning hunted game until he rose to command. Yet he had never forgotten her. He reached into his pocket now, a man and leader of men, and brought out the blue river stone she had gifted him.

When she saw the stone, the young woman gasped. Her eyes filled with tears.

"Okado?" she whispered.

The other riders be damned. Okado stepped toward her, pulled her into an embrace, and nearly crushed her. She clung to him, whispering his name, and he held her head and gazed upon her and laughed.

"My sister." Fire rose behind him and death crawled upon the land, but standing here in blood, Okado laughed. "My sister. Koyee."

CHAPTER ELEVEN
THE FIRE

The child huddled in the darkness, tugging the claws off living crayfish. He laughed as the animals squirmed and died upon the floor.

"You will suffer." The child licked his lips, brought a severed claw to his lips, and sucked the juice. "You will watch me feed upon you."

He laughed and grabbed another animal from the bucket. Crayfish were weak. Crayfish couldn't mock him, shove him, laugh at his small eyes. Their eyes were even smaller and beadier than his. The child snarled. He wanted to pluck off their eyes, to blind them, make sure they could never look at him. He hated eyes looking at him.

He tore off another claw, but now his fists shook, his teeth gnashed, and too much pain filled him for laughter. He tossed the mangled crayfish down, rose to his feet, and stepped on the animal, grinding his heel, snickering as the pathetic thing cracked.

"Ferius, Ferius!" rose the voices outside. "Come play, Ferius!"

The child froze.

"Ferius!" the other children cried outside the hut. "Come play with us."

The child sucked in his breath. The other children . . . wanted to play with him? With the half-demon, the child born of a sunlit father, his hair dark, his black eyes too small for the darkness?

119

"I . . ." Ferius swallowed. "I'm coming."

He rushed to the door, yanked it open, and burst outside. The village of Oshy spread before him, its round clay huts encircling a cobbled square, moonstar runes glowing upon their doors. The river flowed to the south, lined with docks and swaying boats. The Nighttower rose in the north, a sentinel watching the glow of dusk. In the west, that strip of orange blazed, an eternal scar across the land.

The border with the day. Ferius stared at the glow, his throat tightening. His father had come from within that light. His father had loved an Elorian woman of the night. Ferius's eyes—the small eyes of a Timandrian—burned with tears. *My father left me.*

"Ferius, do you want to play?"

He blinked, noticing the children for the first time. They held no lanterns, and Ferius's eyes were too small to see what others could. When he squinted, he could just make out five of them—children his age. Full-blooded Elorians, they had pale skin, white hair, and gleaming blue eyes twice the size of his.

"You . . ." Ferius could barely speak. "You really want to play with me?"

"Of course!" one child said, a girl named Sanira. She was twelve years old, a couple years older than Ferius, and she had never before spoken to him.

Hope welled within Ferius. The children's eyes gleamed, and Ferius felt a smile tickling the corners of his lips. It was true! For years, the other children had shunned him. His blood was impure; his father had been a demon of sunlight. For years they had mocked him, called him Fish Eyes, and tugged at his black, coarse hair—a tattered rug compared to their smooth, white hair like silk. But now they wanted his company!

His smile growing, Ferius took a step closer to them. He still could not see them well—only a few lanterns hung from poles across the courtyard, casting dim light—but he could see their smiles. It was enough for him.

"What game do you want to play?" he asked.

Their grins widened. "Swim-in-the-dark!" they announced as one and leaped toward him.

Confused, Ferius only stood frozen as the children grabbed his arms and legs. He only blinked, blinded and dizzy, as they hoisted him above their heads. They carried him across the square, chanting and laughing. "Swim-in-the-dark, swim-in-the-dark!"

Ferius didn't like this. Lifted above them, he felt much like the crayfish he had tormented. He imagined these children tormenting him the same way, ripping off his arms to feed upon them. His eyes stung.

"Put me down!" he said. "I don't like this game. I—"

His breath died when he saw the docks ahead. The children carried him along the boardwalk and onto a pier. Ferius struggled, but they were too many, and he was too weak—the shortest and weakest among them, a scrawny boy half-blind in the endless night.

"Swim-in-the-dark!" the children shouted, and tossed him into the river.

Ferius crashed into the icy water. Instinctively, he opened his mouth to scream and swallowed water. He thrashed madly, his head bobbed over the surface, and he coughed and gulped air.

"Help!" he shouted, floundering. "I can't swim."

The children raced along the boardwalk, laughing and pointing as the current tugged Ferius downriver.

"Swim away, Fish Eyes!" shouted one child.

"You are a half-demon!" said Sanira—beautiful, pale Sarina whom he had secretly loved. "You don't belong with us. Your blood is full of sunlight. Drown in the darkness!"

He gave her a last look, tears in his eyes, and his head sank underwater again. He could hear them laughing as he floated away.

For a mile or more, he sputtered, rising over the water and sinking again. Finally the river slammed him into a jutting boulder, and he cried in pain. He clung to the rock and climbed out of the water, shivering, his teeth chattering. The river flowed all around him, a mile wide.

The village was only a distant glow of lanterns now. All around him spread the darkness of endless night. The stars shone above. The water flowed silver in the moonlight. Everywhere else there was only the cold, black emptiness of Eloria.

Eyes stinging, Ferius rose to his shaky feet upon the boulder, his little island in the river. He turned toward the west, and he saw it there.

The orange shine of dusk.

As Ferius shivered, tears flowed down his cheeks.

"You came from there, Father," he whispered, lips trembling. "You are a Timandrian, a sunlit demon. A creature of the land of light and fire." He nearly slipped from the boulder, stretched out his arms, and righted himself. "You made me. You cursed me. You created a . . . a half-demon, a creature like a duskmoth, half light and half dark, torn." His chest heaved with sobs. "I will find you, Father. I will travel the lands of sunlight and find you. And I will kill you."

It was an hour or more before a fishing boat arrived, his mother rowing downriver and calling his name. When Ferius climbed into her boat, she tried to embrace him, and tears filled her eyes, but Ferius only shoved her back. *He* was there. *He* was in the boat, sleeping in his crib. His mother's new, pure-blooded son. The boy meant to replace Ferius. The babe Okado.

122

Empires of Moth

Someday I will kill you, you little worm, Ferius thought, staring at the babe, the child of his mother and her new, Elorian husband. *I will burn you dead, Okado.*

His mother was speaking to him, tears on her cheeks, but Ferius ignored her. He sat sullenly, refusing to look at her large, lavender eyes, at her white hair, at her milky skin. She had married another. She had given birth to a better child. Ferius hated her as much as he hated himself. His eyes stung and he hugged himself, staring away from her.

"Ferius." She touched his hair. "Oh, my sweet Ferius, what did—"

"Don't touch me!" he said. "Take me home. Do not speak to me." He dug his fingernails into his palms. "This is your fault."

Holding an oar in one hand, she tried to touch his hair again.

Ferius struck her.

His hand slammed into her cheek, and she whimpered and cowered. The babe Okado woke and wept.

"You made me!" Ferius screamed, tears flowing, voice shaking. "You bedded a sunlit demon! You gave birth to a freak. This is your fault. All your fault."

She wept and Ferius grabbed the oar from her. His arms shook as he steered the boat to the riverbanks. He climbed out, still wet and shivering in the cold, and glared at his mother, at a woman he hated.

"The people of Eloria call me a freak," he said. "You will suffer. Your lands will burn." He screamed hoarsely. "I will travel to sunlight . . . and I will return with the fire to burn you all."

He turned away.

He ran along the riverbank, heading toward the dusk.

"Ferius!" his mother cried behind him, still sitting in the boat. "Ferius, please!"

123

He ignored her. He ran as fast as he could, barely able to see through his tears. He ran past the village. He ran out of shadow. He ran into the dusk, a land of glimmering lights like a thousand lamps.

He ran until he emerged into the blinding, searing, all-consuming light of endless day.

He kept running.

He ran through sunlight that burned his skin and blazed in his eyes. He ran through landscapes of swaying colors, of growing things, of life everywhere—sprouting from the earth, flying in the sky, scurrying away from his boots. He ran through dreamscapes of fantasy—past towering creatures with thin brown bodies and feathery green hair, over rugs of emerald fur that spread across hills and valleys, and under a sky of blue emptiness with no star or moon.

And everywhere . . . everywhere the sun.

"God of light," he whispered, lying in the green, staring up at the great yellow eye. "My lord of heat and unforgiving justice."

It burned his eyes. It burned his skin. And Ferius lay, laughing, worshiping the inferno above, the eternal flame of Timandra.

The river flowed here too, not silver under moonlight, but blue under the blaze of that fiery sky lord. Ferius caught fish. He ate raw flesh. He laughed and drank and ran onward, moving ever away from darkness.

When the monks found him, their robes yellow like the sun, he was a frail, mad thing, a miserable wretch that lay tattered on the riverbanks, laughing and feasting upon the animals he caught. His skin was peeling, his bones jutting, but still he laughed and worshiped his lord.

"Child of sunlight," the monks said, kneeling around him. "Share our wine and bread."

Empires of Moth

He blinked at them and laughed again, for they looked like him. Their skin was darker, their frames taller, but they had his eyes. The small eyes of sunlit lands.

"I am Timandrian," he whispered between chafed lips.

The men nodded. "You are a child of light. Sailith will bless you."

They gave him food they called bread—a round thing like a mushroom, soft and filling and buttery.

"Who is Sailith?" he asked between mouthfuls, sitting on the riverbank.

The men in yellow robes smiled. "Sailith is light. Sailith is fire. Sailith is the dominion of daylight and the fall of night."

Ferius bolted upright. He leaped to his feet and snarled. "The night will burn. The savages of darkness will drown in light."

The monks looked at one another, then back to him, and their smiles vanished. They nodded. "The darkness will burn. Join us, child of sunlight. Join our temple . . . and help us fight the evil in the east."

I will not help you, Ferius thought, crushing the bread in his fist. He looked back toward the east, seeking the distant land of shadows, but it lay too far to see. The bread crumbled, and he drove his fingernails into his palms. *I will lead you.*

* * * * *

And he led them. Through light. Into darkness. To endless flame.

Twenty-five years ago, you found me starving on the riverbank, Sailith, he thought, inhaling the smoke. *You gave me life. And now I give you fire.*

He stood on the stairs outside Pahmey's library, gazing down upon the mountain of burning corpses. The blood of Eloria still coated his hands. He raised them high and shouted for his people to hear.

"Behold the light of Sailith! Behold the fire of the sun." He inhaled deeply, savoring the smell of burning flesh. "The day is victorious."

The fire rose as tall as a temple, searing the air, but Ferius welcomed the heat against his flesh. The sparks and smoke landed on him; he welcomed the pain as gifts from his lord. Thousands of corpses burned below in the square. Soldiers kept streaming in from the streets, shoving wheelbarrows with more bodies and dumping them into the flames. They cheered as every new savage burned. More soldiers kept moving up and down the stairs around Ferius, entering the shadowy halls and emerging with scrolls and books. They tossed these too into the fire, feeding this god of wrath and light and heat, stoking the endless glory. The ancient spells of the night, scrawled upon parchment, crackled and burned among the creatures who wrote them.

"All knowledge of Eloria will fade!" Ferius shouted. "All demons of darkness will burn. I vowed to you, my people, that we would light the night. The night burns!"

His followers surrounded the fire. They stood in the square, the flames painting their faces. They filled the streets. They covered the roofs, chanting for victory. No more darkness covered this city; the light banished all shadows. No more stars shone in the sky; red smoke and white ash covered that canopy now. No more Elorians infested Pahmey; they burned in his flames.

"And you will burn too, Torin the Gardener," Ferius said softly, words for only himself to hear. As men stepped downstairs around him, carrying more library scrolls to burn, Ferius clenched his fists. "You will not burn in a great fire; you will burn slowly, one inch of your body after another, and you will scream louder than this army."

He drove his fingernails into his palms, feeling his blood seep and mingle with the demon blood already staining his hands.

126

Empires of Moth

He bit down so harshly a tooth chipped. Yes, he had seen the boy flee upon the river. The girl Bailey had been with him, the pampered daughter of nobles; Ferius swore that he would slay her grandfather himself, for the highborn of Arden were as demons to him, little better than the creatures of the night.

"And you too fled me, my half-sister," he whispered, savoring the taste of her name. "Yes . . . you wore the mask of the Sisterhood, but I know it was you. I will catch you too, Koyee of Eloria. But you I will not burn. No. You I will keep alive." He licked his lips as if tasting her. "When all other Elorians have burned, you I will keep as my pet. I will place you in a cage, a starved and broken thing, and parade you around the lands of Timandra. I will take you from kingdom to kingdom, from city to village, and let all gaze upon you—the last Elorian of Moth." He laughed. "They will mock you and pity you, but I will show you no pity."

The wound in his leg—the one Koyee had given him— flared with pain. Even six months later, Ferius walked with a limp. The pain kept his mind sharp, his passion hot. It would guide him across the night until he found her. She lurked now among the wolves of the southern plains; Ferius knew of those beasts, savages the fallen King Ceranor had been too cowardly to fight. But Ferius was no coward; the Chanku too would burn in his glory.

He looked north toward the hill's crest. Minlao Palace had fallen; its stub rose like a broken bone, a monument to his victory. He returned his eyes to the crowd and shouted anew.

"Muster your weapons, soldiers of sunlight! Polish armor and sharpen swords. A city has fallen. An empire will burn!"

The soldiers chanted for the sun and raised their swords. Ferius tilted his head back, closed his eyes, and savored the scent of flesh.

CHAPTER TWELVE
THE DAUGHTER OF WOLVES

My father is fallen.

He stood alone in his tent—the wide, towering tent of an alpha, its poles silvered, its leather walls painted with leaping wolves. He stood with his head lowered, his heart clenched into a tight ball.

I have a half-brother.

Okado closed his eyes. No tears flowed, for he ruled a great pack, a warrior leading many warriors, the strongest of his people. Yet still the pain clawed inside him, dragging the memories through him.

My mother loved a Timandrian. She birthed a demon. Ferius slew my father.

At first, Okado had refused to believe Koyee . . . but he had seen the truth in her eyes. That truth now tore inside him like a wolf at flesh. If the stars themselves were falling and the sun rising, Okado would not feel as lost.

He could see his father again in the darkness—a wise soldier, his wars over, a fishing rod in his hand instead of a sword. Okado was young again, sitting upon the riverbanks of the Inaro River. The dusk glowed orange, casting the glimmers that brought bass and crayfish to breed and flourish and feed his family. His father sat at his side, showing Okado how to raise a lamp above the water, drawing the fish near.

"Tell me about the war, Father," the child had begged. "Tell me stories of heroes and swords and battles."

Empires of Moth

His father had only smiled sadly. "There is no glory in tales of war. There is more honor in a fishing rod than a sword. There is more courage in feeding your family than slaying a man."

Standing in his tent, a man himself now, Okado grimaced.

"I railed against you, Father." His fists shook. "I wanted to be a hero too, to ignore your words, to fight my own war—to find that honor in battle. So I left you. I'm sorry. I'm sorry. I should have been there with you at the end."

His sister had shared the news with him hours ago, and Okado had stormed into his tent. How could he ever emerge? He led many now, a fisherman's son grown into an alpha rider, and his people needed him, but Okado felt that he had less honor than the old man who had died upon the riverbank.

"What do I do now, Father? How do I protect Koyee? How do I protect all those who need me?"

He stared at the tent walls, praying for guidance, missing his father's wisdom. He was a grown man, and he had a mate of his own, yet now he felt very young, still a child needing the wisdom of men.

A voice spoke softly behind him. "You will lead them to hope. You will be the light to guide them."

Okado turned around. He saw Suntai there. She stood at the entrance to the tent, holding up a leather flap. The moonlight outlined her white, cascading hair and her tall, slender form. Her eyes gleamed like blue moons. She entered the tent, letting the flap drop behind her, and approached him.

She took his hand and touched his cheek. "I'm here for you, Okado. Through victory, through glory, through darkness and light, through death and hope, I ride by your side. Always. In this life and in the great sky beyond."

She kissed his lips, and he held her against him, her hair like snow against his cheek.

"Always, my mate," he said softly and kissed her forehead. "Always we ride together."

He held her for a long time. They stood in stillness, silence, and warmth.

I'm not wise like you, Father, he thought. *I'm not as strong, as noble, as humble. But I will lead them. I will fight for Koyee, for my pack, for all the people of the night.*

He held his mate's hand. She smiled sadly, eyes gleaming. Hand in hand, they left the tent and walked across the crater between their people—the proud riders of Chanku, the last survivors of Pahmey, and the children of sunlight who had joined their cause. Over the horizon, the smoke rose and the flame burned, but here in the shadows, his mate, his sister, and the memory of his father lit his way.

* * * * *

They stood upon Wolfjaw Mountain, the sacred ground where all great decisions of the pack were made. They stood around Suntai: her mate, the brave Okado; her mate's sister, the young Koyee; and the five Timandrians who had fled their own people, a young queen and four soldiers. All eyes gazed upon her—Suntai, queen of wolves. They stood between the mountain's jaws of stone. Below across the plains, the rest of her pack waited—thousands of riders upon thousands of wolves, her noble people, all awaiting her decree.

My mate leads us in battle, Suntai thought. *Yet I am the alpha female. When swords are sheathed, it is I who lead. And now I must decide.*

She took a deep breath, raised her chin, and spoke in a clear voice.

"The enemy will not rest. They saw us across the water; they will seek to burn us too. This I do not doubt. A beast of sunlight roams our land, and one city will not fill its belly. They will crave

Empires of Moth

the Chanku Pack, and they will crave all the lands of night—here in Qaelin and beyond our borders. Under these stars, as Pahmey burns on the horizon, we must choose our path."

She looked northward. Her clan spread across the first mile of the plains. Beyond them, shadows rolled across the night, leading to a great fire. Pahmey blazed there like a collapsing star fallen onto the earth. They would be mustering there—the creatures from the sunlit half of Moth. These demons were of the Ardish clan, she knew; the same clan as these Timandrians who had joined them, their sigil a black bird they called "raven." But other sunlit clans crawled elsewhere in Eloria—the Nayans she had fought last year, warriors of the tiger, and many others, a great horde some said was half a million strong.

It was Koyee, the slim youth with a warrior's eyes, who spoke the thoughts in Suntai's own heart.

"How can we defeat them?" Koyee gazed toward the distant fire. "The Timandrians are so many and we are few. How can the night stop the day?"

Suntai rested her palm upon her sword's hilt. "We in Chanku are few. The defenders of Pahmey were few. But others live in the night. The Emperor of Qaelin, they say, commands fifty thousand troops far in the east. And other empires rule in the night. The Ilari nation is mighty; my parents fought their bloodthirsty warriors in the Great Southern War. Leen too is strong; its elders are wise and its soldiers are many, though they have not left their northern isle in many years." Suntai looked east, south, and north, as if she could see these distant lands from here. "We must seek their aid. All three empires of darkness must join forces: Qaelin, Ilar, and Leen. No more must Elorians fight one another; now is our time to lay aside our grievances and fight the sun as one."

She looked at Okado and met his gaze. His eyes shone with approval and his lips rose in a rare smile. She saw the love and

131

pride in him, and it warmed her chest. He was strong in battle; she would prove herself just as strong in this council.

Koyee spoke again. "The Ilari are ruthless and cruel. My father fought them too; he spoke of them as of monsters. And the people of Leen? They say they care only for gazing at the stars, counting crystals, and chanting ancient prayers. How will we show them wisdom? How can we unite Elorians—scattered across distant lands, miles of darkness between us?"

"We will unite," said Suntai, "or we will fall. We will unite as the Timandrians do, different kingdoms and clans fighting as one, or we will perish. We have no choice." She inhaled through flared nostrils. "We must travel across the night, spreading the news. We must speak of the slaughter in Pahmey. We must make the emperor of Qaelin send his troops west. We must convince Leen and Ilar, our enemies of old, to fight alongside their siblings in darkness. Three quests lie before us, three paths to hope. We must take these three roads, or we will perish in the flame from the west."

Because I do not crave death in battle, she thought. *Because I am not like the riders I lead; they want to die young, to die upon their blades, to die as men and women of honor and strength. But not I. Not Suntai, mate of Okado. I would live to see my barren womb flower. I would die an elder, my grandchildren playing with pups at my feet.* She looked toward the northern light then closed her eyes. *We must live. We must banish this nemesis of fire. By my sword, my wolf, and the blood of my heart, I will fight for life and darkness.*

She opened her eyes and looked at her companions. Her husband, strong and noble, his shoulders broad and his blade sharp. His sister, short and slim and clad only in silk, yet displaying the same strength as her brother in her eyes. The Timandrians who had joined her pack: a trembling queen with golden locks, a somber youth with mismatched eyes, a warrior

Empires of Moth

woman with braided hair, and two friends—one short and the other wide—with fear in their eyes.

"We are only a few," Suntai said, "yet we must save the night."

They stared back at her, some of them frightened, the others strong. It was Okado who spoke first.

"I will lead the pack east." He gazed down the mountain toward them, thousands of men and women astride wolves. "The crater is no longer safe for them, not with Timandrian hosts so near. If this Ferius demon has slain all in Pahmey, he will seek to slay us next. The Chanku riders are strong and fierce; one of our warriors can defeat ten of them in battle. And yet they outnumber our warriors twenty to one. We cannot stay. I will take the pack east along the Sage's Road for many turns. We will seek Yintao, our capital; its walls are tall and thick, and its soldiers are many. We will join our wolves to their warriors; together we are strong."

Suntai nodded. "The pack will head east. We were nomads for many years before we found our crater; we've lingered in its shadows for too long, and it has weakened us. You will lead the pack to Yintao. Yet who will travel north and south, seeking aid from other empires of night?"

Koyee stepped forth. Her eyes shone and she raised her chin. She was a decade younger than Suntai, and she stood barely taller than Suntai's shoulder, but her stance was strong, her face fierce. *This one would have made a fine rider,* Suntai thought.

"I will travel south," Koyee said. "Torin and I have a boat— the *Water Spider,* which we oared when fleeing Pahmey. We both grew up along rivers; we both know the water. We will sail south along the Inaro. It will take us across Qaelin to the southern coast. There we will cross the sea to the Ilari Empire." She looked back at Okado, and her eyes softened. "I spent many years dreaming of seeing my brother again. Yet now our roads must part."

133

Okado stepped toward her, lowered his head, and touched her arm. "My sister, we can send another south. You can travel east with the pack—with me. Ilar is a land of great danger; its people are warlike and have no love for us Qaelish folk."

Koyee shook her head. "None in Chanku have ever been in a boat; your people fear the water unless you ride upon a swimming wolf, and no wolf can swim such a distance." She smiled crookedly. "Yet you and I, my brother, we grew up in boats." Tears filled her eyes and she embraced him. "I love you, Okado. I love you more than the stars love the sky. I will miss you until we meet again."

When the embrace ended, Torin came to stand beside Koyee. He spoke in broken Qaelish, his accent heavy.

"I look after her, Okado. I fight with her." The boy—younger, shorter, and slimmer than Okado—gripped his sword. "I keep Koyee safe."

Okado stared at the youth, and a smile tugged at his lips. He snorted. "Koyee is a daughter of the night, a warrior who slew many demons in Pahmey; hers is a heart of darkness. She does not need your protection, child of sunlight; she bears Sheytusung, a sword greater than yours. *She* will keep *you* safe." He patted the boy on the shoulder. "I think, Torin of Timandra, that she is taking you with her not for protection, but to prove to Ilar that you sunlit folk are not merely legends."

Young Torin bristled. He puffed out his chest, his cheeks reddened, and he opened his mouth—perhaps preparing to object or defend his honor. Suntai cleared her throat, drawing their attention. She felt it best to speak quickly; she did not wish to see her mate clash with this youth.

"Torin and Koyee will travel south," she said, interrupting the potential feud. "We will fill their boat with what supplies they'll need. In a few moons, they will join us in Yintao . . . alone or with an Ilari host."

Inwardly, Suntai smiled. She saw what Okado did not.

Koyee has already mated with Torin, she thought. Suntai saw that in their eyes. They were bound, yet Okado would never accept it. Okado valued strength. He valued only warriors, while Torin was different—weak of arm but strong in different ways, the strength of a scholar and stargazer.

Suntai looked north again, then balled her fists and lowered her head. She knew what she had to do, though it tore at her. Ice seemed to encase her heart. She spoke between stiff lips.

"And I will travel north. I will take with me a Timandrian as well—two if we can spare them. I will show these beings of sunlight to the elders of the Leen nation. No rivers lead north; we will travel upon wolves, fast and hidden upon the plains. We will rouse Leen to battle."

Okado sucked in his breath, approached Suntai, and gripped her hands. "You will leave your mate?"

She nodded. "You can lead the pack without me. This is my task. The elders of Leen are ancient, pompous folk; they care for bloodlines and old names. I am Suntai, a daughter of the Chanku nobles of old, those great warriors who ruled in Pahmey. I am an alpha of a great pack. I am highborn and strong, and Leen will heed my words." Her voice softened, and she touched Okado's cheek. "I must do this, my mate, though my heart will weep while we're apart. I will miss you."

His eyes softened, showing those rare moments of emotion that Suntai, proud she-wolf of the pack, loved and cherished. She embraced him and kissed his lips under the stars.

A throat cleared at her side, interrupting the kiss.

"And I . . . I go with you," said the short Timandrian boy— his name was Cam, she remembered. He spoke in Qaelish too, his accent even heavier than Torin's. "I go north with you."

135

Suntai turned to smile down at the sharp-featured young man. "The road will be long and dark, my friend. And you will have to ride upon a nightwolf."

The boy—he seemed no older than seventeen or eighteen—raised his chin. He stood shorter than Suntai and probably slimmer too, but puffed out his chest with all the bravado he could.

"I was . . . how you say in Qaelish?" He turned to his friends, whispered among them, and found the word. "I was *herder* in Timandra. I always fight small sunlit wolves. Now . . . now I want ride big wolf." His eyes lit up. "It be fun. And you need one Timandrian. I go to Leen too."

Suntai smiled; the boy was young and green, perhaps, but honest enough. She nodded. "I will take you with me. I—"

The young Timandrian queen began to speak loudly, interrupting Suntai. She spoke in Ardish, the tongue of her people, which Suntai could not understand. She wrung her hands, scolded Cam, then looked at Suntai and spoke again. The young woman seemed to Suntai like some spirit creature, her skin bronzed, her hair golden, her eyes bright blue.

"What does she say?" Suntai asked.

Cam rolled his eyes. "She says she come too. She also want go north to Leen. She says it sound like her name, so it best place for her." He sighed. "Her name is Linee. Place in north is Leen. She think is some . . . how you say in Qaelish? Sign."

At his side, Queen Linee grinned, crossed her arms, and nodded. "Leen!" she said happily. "Linee. Leen."

Cam groaned. "This be long trip now."

The wind blew from the north, scented of fire, ash, and burning corpses. Below the mountain, the pack rustled and lanterns glinted against armor. Suntai stood upon the mountaintop, this sacred ground of her people, and looked at her companions. Her throat constricted and her heart felt too tight.

Empires of Moth

And so I will part from my mate, from the pack that I love, and I will travel into darkness for long moons. She tightened her lips and nodded. *For the night.*

"Okado, leave with the pack before the moon rises," she said. "You cannot linger here." She turned toward his sister. "Koyee, take the boat and take Torin; travel south along the river to distant Ilar, and may the Leaping Fish—the stars of your home—guide your quest." She turned toward Cam and Linee; the boy rolled his eyes as the young queen leaned against him, her elbow on his shoulder. "And you two—you two come with me, and I will find you wolves. You ride fast or I truss you up and carry you as cargo."

They all stared back and nodded. Suntai smiled, though her eyes dampened and she had never felt more pain in her chest.

"Goodbye, my friends," she said. "May whatever gods you worship guide your way. We fight for darkness. We fight for peace. We are the night and we are the day." She turned away and began walking down the mountain. "Now come! Three paths await us. We begin our journeys."

CHAPTER THIRTEEN
LEAVETAKING

Bailey sat in the center of a storm, sharpening her sword, cursing with every stroke of stone against blade.

The crater bustled around her. Nightwolves prowled back and forth, shaggy beasts the size of horses, their saddles elaborate works of leather and steel, each scale in their armor engraved with a moonstar. Their riders moved among the animals, stuffing saddlebags with supplies—dried meats, fur pelts, water skins, and blades. These riders too seemed beastly to Bailey; unlike the people of Pahmey, gentle folk who wore silks and glowing jewels, these Elorians looked more like the bloodthirsty night-demons Ferius railed about. Helms shaped as snarling wolves encircled their heads, and tattoos of lightning, claws, and flames adorned their skin. Weapons hung across their backs—katanas, bows, arrows fletched with silk, and belts of many daggers. Back among her own people, Bailey had been a rarity—a female serving among male soldiers—but here half the warriors were wild women, their eyes as fierce as their men's.

Bailey thrust her sharpening stone against her blade, scattering sparks, and grumbled.

Yes, back among my own people. She grimaced. Her eyes stung and she cursed and blinked furiously. She had left her people. She had abandoned her village, her kingdom, her sunlit half of Moth. She had followed Torin on his quest, and now . . . who was she now, and could she ever return?

She looked up from her blade, peered between the wolves and riders, and saw him there. Torin. A growl rose in her throat.

Empires of Moth

"I gave up everything for you," she whispered. "I left my village. I left my people. I travel the darkness of night. And you only stand there with her."

She stood beside him, the little Elorian woman with the scarred face. Koyee. Bailey remembered seeing her kiss him upon the hospice stairs, not a kiss of friendship like the ones Bailey used to plant on Torin's cheek, but a deep kiss of passion and love.

Why do I care? Bailey forced herself to snort derisively, though she felt like crying. Torin was only . . . only a babyface! He was the frightened little orphan she had welcomed into her home. He was the slow, meek child she could always beat at climbing, swimming, and wrestling. She had come here to protect him, not . . . not love him.

And yet, looking at him now, she no longer saw that boy. She saw a young man in armor—no longer the steel plates of Timandra, but the scaled armor of Eloria, red in the light of fires. He had changed. He had grown from boy to man to warrior of the night, and Bailey no longer knew her friend.

"But I still love you," she whispered. "I love you always with all my heart. And yet you've chosen Koyee. It was her you kissed upon the stairs. It's her you stand with now. I fought for you, but you fight for Koyee."

He finally noticed Bailey staring, turned toward her, and smiled. He came walking her way across the camp, leaving Koyee behind to stuff her pack full of supplies. Bailey forced herself to smile back, even to wave. She would not show him the anger in her heart. She would not confess to that winky-eyed boy that he could pain her so.

When he reached her, Bailey rose and sheathed her sword. She looked across the camp. Most of the tents had been folded up and packed upon the wolves. The first riders were already climbing out of the crater, their belongings stuffed into saddlebags

139

and sacks. She spotted Suntai a hundred yards away; the alpha
female stood upon the northern rim of the crater, the starlight
behind her, speaking animatedly to Cam and Linee.

"We're almost ready to leave," Bailey said, adjusting the
helmet the riders had given her, it steel shaped as a silver wolf.
"How will you get your boat to the river?"

Torin stared from within his own helm; his visor was raised,
letting the steel wolf's teeth rest upon his forehead like bangs.
"The pack has large, flat wagons; they use them for hauling back
stonebeasts, animals they hunt. A few riders will help us wheel the
boat to the river—it lies not far—then return to the pack." He
touched her arm. "Bailey, come with us. With Koyee and me. We
could use your sword."

His words cut her. She couldn't help but wince.

He needed her sword. That was all he cared for, it seemed.
Her protection. All her life, she had been protecting him,
sheltering him, watching over him as he grew into a man. And
now he only wanted more.

*He does not want my friendship, my kisses, my love for him. He has
Koyee now, a petite, pretty thing to kiss under the stars, and he thinks I'm
only a gangly warrior. Would he have me guard them with my sword,
standing upon the prow of the boat as they make love behind me?*

A small part of Bailey—a little voice deep inside—cried out
that she was being petty, jealous, a foolish girl. All her life, Bailey
had derided the other girls in Fairwool-by-Night, thinking them
silly, cow-eyed things who fawned over farm boys. This small
voice cried out that she was behaving just like them, but Bailey
could barely hear these cries. Too much rage pounded in her ears,
drowning the warning.

She raised her chin and fixed him with her best stare.
"Okado already asked me to accompany him eastward," she lied.
"I'll be joining him on our journey to Yintao." She looked across
the camp, saw the alpha male by a group of other riders, and

Empires of Moth

sighed theatrically. "Damn, the man is handsome. That is what a warrior looks like, Torin. It's a shame you can't join us—he probably could have taught you a few things—but I suppose Koyee needs to parade somebody before the Ilari."

She looked back at Torin, chin firmly raised, and enjoyed seeing the pain in his eyes. She had hurt him. Good. She wished she could hurt him a thousand times more.

Like you hurt me when you kissed her upon the stairs, she thought.

His eyes narrowed and he shifted uncomfortably. "Are you sure?"

"Of course I am. I'm always sure of what I do. You'll be fine without me. And you have Koyee's sword to protect you."

He lowered his eyes, then looked back up at her. He embraced her awkwardly. "I'll miss you, Bails. I've never been apart from you for more than an hourglass turn or two. Now I won't see you for moons." He looked into her eyes. "I've never told you this, but . . . damn it, I love you, you lumbering beast. Be careful out there."

Damn you, Torin. Damn you, you winky-eyed, babyfaced, weakling little boy! He could always do this to her. Tears filled her eyes, and she crushed him in her arms.

"Hug me properly, you silly boy!" she said. "Go on, squeeze a little, damn you." She laughed through her tears, touched his cheek, and kissed his nose. "I love you too, you pink-cheeked gardener."

Before she could stop herself—by Idar, she never even meant to do it!—she kissed him full on the lips. She could tell he was shocked; his body stiffened, but she kept him wrapped in her arms, pressing herself against him. She kissed him deeply, her tongue seeking his, all her body going into the kiss. It was a kiss to knock his boots right off.

When she was done, she pinched his cheek and smiled crookedly. "Something for you to remember me by."

141

She looked over his shoulder and saw Koyee watching them. Bailey smiled at the Elorian woman and gave her a quick, cruel wink.

And something for you to remember, Koyee.

The Elorian woman stared back, and Bailey's smile grew, a mirthless grin like that of a nightwolf.

She turned, leaving Torin, and walked among wolves and riders until she reached Okado. Bailey had always been the tallest among her group of friends, even the boys, and yet Okado stood taller, his shoulders wide and his arms strong. She smiled at him, placed a hand on his chest, and nodded.

"Let's travel east. Find me a nightwolf, Okado, and I'll ride at your side."

* * * * *

Hemstad Baker was walking through the wolfriders' camp, carrying a sack of furs, when he saw the bullied girl.

They had not been in this crater long, and Hem was eager to leave. Wherever he walked here, he drew stares, laughter, and scornful words. Elorian riders paused as he walked by, gazing at him in wonder, eyebrows rising. Hem ignored them, muttering to himself and feeling his cheeks flush. It wasn't like this was any different than back with his own people. There too soldiers stared and mocked him, reaching out to pat his ample belly for luck, pinch his pink cheeks, or simply laugh at his girth. Standing as close to seven feet as to six, weighing more than any scale could measure, Hem stood out wherever he went, and the Chanku Pack was no exception.

"A stonebeast walks among us!" shouted one wolfrider, perhaps not knowing that Hem had spent the past six months studying their tongue and could understand every word.

142

Empires of Moth

"If he falls, he'll create another crater!" cried another rider, a tall and beautiful woman with braided white hair and twin katanas in her hands.

Cheeks hot, Hem walked on, moving past the gawkers, seeking Cam, Linee, and Suntai whom he'd be joining. He could not wait to leave. The journey along the Iron Road, heading toward the northern coast and the empire of Leen, would be long and quiet and dark. For most of the way, Suntai had warned, it would be only them. That suited Hem fine. Cam bullied him sometimes, but Hem was used to those taunts, and as for Suntai and Linee, well . . . they were only two people and neither seemed hostile. Hem thought that he could survive the trip. It would be a respite after the past year, a year spent among soldiers—first Timandrians, then Elorians—who saw him as nothing but a beast.

But I'm not a beast, he thought, eyes stinging. *I'm a good baker. And I'm a good singer. And I know a lot about animals, especially dogs.* He rubbed his eyes, cursing them for burning. *But I hate people sometimes, especially bullies.*

Perhaps that was why he noticed the young woman while others walked by, ignoring her.

"Please," the little thing said, her large Elorian eyes entreating her tormentors. "Please, tell me what to do."

She seemed a year or two younger than Hem's own eighteen winters. As much as Hem was tall and corpulent, she was short and slim, a wisp of a thing. She wore only a tattered fur tunic, not armor like the other riders. No helm topped her head, and her hair—brilliant white like snow—cascaded in a mess of tangles. Her damp, blue-gray eyes peered between the pale strands.

The other riders, however, seemed not to share his sentiment. One—a tall, muscular woman in armor—kicked a pot across the ground.

"Fetch it, omega!" the woman shouted, then laughed as the girl scuttled toward the pot.

143

Before the girl could reach it, an Elorian man—a tall rider with a wolf's head helm—kicked the pot again, sending it clattering away.

"We told you to pack our things, omega," the man said. "Fetch that pot before we lash you."

The young woman kept scurrying to and fro, moving on bare feet, trying to grab the pot. Twenty other pots and pans clattered across her back like armor. Whenever she approached the last pot, another rider kicked it, sending her scurrying again.

"Fetch, girl!" said one rider, this one a smirking woman with claws tattooed onto the shaved sides of her head. She kicked, catching the omega girl in the stomach. The young woman whelped and doubled over. All the pots and pans she carried on her back came loose, scattering across the ground in a clanking chorus. The riders surrounding her roared with laughter.

"Fetch them, omega, pack our things!" one man said, stepped forth, and prepared to deliver another kick.

Hem had seen enough.

Though fear almost froze his head, he leaped forward, placed himself before the girl, and took the kick into his own belly. He gasped, unable to breathe, but managed to growl and stare at the Elorian rider.

"Leave . . . her . . . alone!" he said through a stiff throat.

The girl's tormenters—there were five or six of them—stared with wide eyes.

"By the stars, a whale!" said the tall, tattooed woman. She burst out laughing. Her friends joined her, poking Hem and muttering in wonder.

Grumbling, Hem ignored them. He turned around and knelt by the young omega. She was on her knees, clutching her belly with one hand, reaching for the scattered pots with the other.

Empires of Moth

"Are you all right?" he asked, speaking Qaelish, a tongue he'd mastered faster and easier than his friends.

She blinked and nodded, not meeting his gaze. "I cannot speak," she whispered. "I am omega. I cannot speak to you. I must pack their things. Leave me."

He reached for a pan, ignoring the laughter around him, and handed it to her. "Let me help you."

She shivered and shook her head. "Please. They'll hurt me. I'm their omega and must serve them alone." She looked up at him, eyes welling with tears. "Please. You cannot help or they'll hurt me when you leave."

Hem gasped. When the young woman's hair fell back, it revealed a bruise across her cheek.

Hem was a gentle man, but now rage flooded him. He balled his fists. "I cannot let them hurt you!"

She sniffed, lowered her head to let her hair cover her face, and reached for another pan. "Then go now. Please. An omega cannot have friends or they will strike me again."

Reluctantly, Hem rose to his feet and kept walking. When he looked over his shoulder, he saw the riders laughing again, pointing at both him and the omega. He tried to meet her eyes again, but her hair covered her face, and she wouldn't look his way.

As he walked away, confusion tugged at Hem. Bailey was always talking about how the Elorians were noble folk, that Timandrians were cruel occupiers, that night was good and daylight evil. Suddenly Hem wasn't so sure. If that were true, why would these Elorians bully a woman? And why would Hem—a child of Dayside, the cruel half of Moth—try to protect her? Maybe the world was more complex than what Bailey believed. Hem didn't know. He had always simply followed Bailey around—sometimes out of loyalty, usually because she was

145

tugging his ear. Yet now she was heading east without him, and Hem felt lost and afraid.

"Hem!" rose a voice from across the camp. "Damn it, Hem, there you are. Come on, you lumpy loaf of bread!"

Blinking his stinging eyes, Hem turned and saw Cam standing on the edge of the crater. The slim shepherd was gesturing for him to come closer. Hem nodded, hitched at his belt, and hurried forward. His armor clanked and his helmet wobbled, but he managed to avoid any other hostile encounters until he reached the crater's edge. He climbed and stood upon the brim beside his friend.

"What were you doing down there, you great pillock?" Cam said, staring up from his meager height. "Don't you know we're heading north?" His voice dropped. "Suntai is getting angry and antsy to leave. Damn . . . that woman is scary when she's angry."

Wincing, the shepherd looked over his shoulder and shuddered. Hem followed his friend's gaze and felt his own spine tingle.

Suntai, the queen of the Chanku Pack, sat ahead upon a great white wolf. Her back was turned toward them, and her hair streamed in the wind, a white curtain strewn with slim braids. Her sword, bow, and quiver hung across her back, and several daggers hung at her side. Hem caught glimpses of her face in profile; it shone in the light of her lamp, white and hard like marble. Her face looked much like the face of her wolf, cold and pale and usually snarling. Hem would not be surprised if Suntai, in her rage, could rip out his throat with her own teeth. He gulped.

Linee walked up toward them, hugging herself and shivering. She still wore her old royal gown, an elaborate construction of cotton, embroidery, and about a thousand jewels.

"She wants us to ride wolves too!" Linee whispered, leaning toward Hem. "Can you believe it? I can't ride one of those stinky animals." Tears welled up in her eyes. "I want a carriage. I'm the

Empires of Moth

Queen of Arden, and I demand a carriage, but that Suntai won't listen. She's just as beastly as the nightwolves." The young woman covered her face and trembled.

Cam rolled his eyes. "Toughen up, lady! You're not a queen anymore, so forget about plush carriages and pampering. You're one of the Chanku riders now, so act like one, unless you want them to make you an omega. Have you seen what they do to omegas here? They're like the servants you had back in Arden, scrubbing pots and rubbing sore feet."

That only made Linee cry harder. "But I don't want to be a servant. I want to be a queen again. Please, Camlin, can I share a wolf with you at least? I won't be as scared if we ride together."

"Merciful Idar!" Cam said, raising his hands to the heavens.

The talk of omegas stabbed Hem's chest; he was still thinking about the young woman he had tried to help. He turned around, stared back into the crater, and saw her there. Her tormentors were now tossing her pack from one to another, laughing as the girl tried to catch it.

Hem winced. *You're going to regret this, you stupid oaf,* he told himself, his thoughts surprisingly speaking in Cam's voice. *You know you shouldn't do this, you lumpy loaf.* And yet he bit his lip and winced, and the words fled his mouth.

"I'm staying with the pack."

Cam was busy scolding Linee, saying something about how no, nightwolves did not have cute puppies, and no, she couldn't have one. When he heard Hem, he stopped in mid-sentence, turned away from Linee, and raised his eyebrows.

"You what?"

Hem looked at his feet. "I'm staying with the pack. I'm not going north with you." He looked over his shoulder again, seeking the omega, but she was gone, vanished into the crowd. "I'm going to go east with Bailey. She needs a friend. Torin's going south with Koyee, and you and Linee are going north, and . . . well, Bailey shouldn't be alone."

The lie made sense to him, and as he spoke, Hem convinced himself that it was true—that *this* was the reason he would go east. Not because of an omega girl with big, pretty eyes at all.

"Bailey—needing a friend?" Cam said, eyebrows rising so high they nearly fell off. "Bailey—the girl who'd twist our ears, kick our backsides, and wrestle us into the mud if we so much as sang a bad note at the pub?" Cam guffawed. "What's wrong with you? This is our chance to get *away* from Bailey."

"I know, it's just . . ." Hem wouldn't raise his eyes. "I think it's the right thing, all right?"

Cam's eyes widened. "You're serious, aren't you?" He shook his head, crossed his arms, and looked away. "Well, fine then. Choose Bailey."

Hem winced and reached toward his friend. "Cam, it doesn't mean that I don't want to go with you. I just—"

When Hem placed his hand on Cam's shoulder, the smaller boy shrugged it off and took a step away.

"I said go, all right?" Cam took two more steps away, turning his back toward Hem. "I don't care what you want."

"Well, all right then." Hem twisted his fingers uncomfortably. "I guess I'll leave."

"I guess so."

Biting his lip, Hem turned back toward the crater. The pack was beginning to ride out, heading east. Across the other side of the crater, Hem could see Torin and Koyee heading in another direction, several riders dragging their boat along the plains. He took one step away, then looked back toward his friend.

Cam was watching him, and Hem lost his breath. Tears shone in the young shepherd's eyes.

"Cam—" he began, reaching back toward him.

Empires of Moth

"Go!" Cam roared, face red. "Go, I said. Go to your friend Bailey. I don't care. You and I have only been best friends for . . . what, our entire lives? So fine. I guess it's time for you to grow up and find your own way." Cam glowered. "Just . . . damn it, be careful out there, all right? Just listen to Bailey. If I'm not there to get you out of trouble, she'll have to."

Suddenly tears filled Hem's eyes too. He pulled a handkerchief from his pocket and noisily blew into it. "I promise."

Cam looked ready to shout again, then stepped forward and grabbed him, squeezing Hem. "You're a dumb loaf, do you know that?"

Hem nodded. "That's what everyone tells me. Goodbye for now, Camlin old boy. It won't be too long and we'll meet again in the east."

He released his friend, then turned to Queen Linee; her eyes were damp too. He took her hand in his, kissed it like in the stories, and felt his cheeks flush. Mumbling under his breath, he turned and left them there, heading back into the crater.

The riders were all seated upon their wolves now, heading eastward. Hem spotted Bailey in the distance, riding at the head of the pack. Hoping they had a nightwolf to spare, Hem ran after her, his pack and blankets jumping across his back.

Goodbye, Cam, he thought as he ran. *Goodbye, Torin.* It hurt to say goodbye. But now a girl needed him. Now was his time to be a hero.

149

CHAPTER FOURTEEN
THE PAINTED BUFFALO

As Torin sat in the boat, watching Koyee sleep, he could not stop the memories.

It was peaceful here upon the river. Aside from the fish that glowed in the water, he and Koyee were the only living souls for miles around. Dark, silent plains spread left and right, rolling into shadows. The stars shone above, brilliantly white, blue, and lavender, a painting that sprawled across the firmaments. A cold breeze blew, scented of distant rain, ruffling his cloak. When first entering Eloria, Torin had found the place frightening, but now he thought the night beautiful.

And yet, even here in this silence and solitude, the blood danced before his eyes.

He saw it again: the corpses in the gutters, the soldiers driving swords into children, the thousands dying as he rushed from street to street, struggling to save whoever he could.

I wanted to save more, he thought. *I wanted to save a city. But I only saved fifty souls.* He closed his eyes. *I failed. Thousands perished.*

He took a shuddering breath, opened his eyes, and looked at Koyee. She slept peacefully on the boat floor, wrapped in furs, her cheek upon her palms. She was so frail, so pale, beautiful even with the scars across her face.

By Idar, how could she be half-sister to Ferius, that twisted beast? He sat beside her. *One child of light, one of darkness. A brother of evil, a sister of good.*

Looking at Koyee sleep, her chest rising and falling and her lips mumbling sleepy nonsense, Torin thought that in all the fire,

Empires of Moth

blood, and pain of the world, there was still some goodness. There was still some hope so long as Koyee—kind, outcast, brave Koyee—lived and fought.

"So long as you're with me," Torin whispered, "this is some good in the world, and there is some good in me. I took a life, but I saved life too; you will always be my beacon in the night."

And . . . was she more to him now? Torin's blood heated to remember the last time he'd visited her chamber in the hospice. An urge came upon him to lie beside Koyee again, here in this boat, to kiss her, undress her, make love to her with only the fish and stars to see.

While he contemplated her fair skin and silvery hair, the memory of Bailey's kiss came unbidden to his mind, and his blood boiled even hotter. While Koyee warmed him like a mug of mulled wine, comforting and intoxicating on a cold autumn, Bailey was fire. The memory of her lips blasted through him, powerful enough to make him shudder. While Koyee was slim and fair like a faery maiden, Bailey was all curves and mocking smiles, flashing eyes and full lips and—

Torin shut his mouth and shook his head wildly.

"What am I doing?" he wondered aloud.

Bailey was his friend! She had taken him into his home when they'd been only children; she was more foster-sister to him than . . . than . . . well, than whatever these thoughts were now making her out to be.

Torin slapped his head, vowing to banish such thoughts from his mind—of both Bailey *and* Koyee. Right now, with war raging across the night, he had to focus on his quest. He would think only of reaching the southern island-nation of Ilar, forging an alliance, and fighting against the bastard Ferius and his followers.

Koyee stirred and opened her eyes to slits. "Torin? Did you say something?"

"Sorry, Koyee. I was talking to myself."

She smiled sleepily and sat up, her hair in tangles. "I do that too. Well . . . I talk to my invisible friend, Eelani, though I think she's real. Not everyone believes it." She yawned, stretching out all four limbs, and checked the hourglass beside her. "Oh no! I slept for too long."

She rose to her feet, stretched, and hopped about upon the *Water Spider*. The rowboat was built for twenty soldiers; only the two of them now stood upon it. Most of the boat was taken up by their supplies. Their food and drink were a mix of Elorian and Timandrian goods—pouches of mushrooms alongside jars of strawberry preserves, packs of salted stonebeast meat alongside pork sausages, and jugs of mushroom wine alongside kegs of ale. Since they had left the Chanku Pack two turns ago, Koyee had seemed happy to eat nothing but mushrooms, whereas Torin didn't know how he'd survive once their sunlit supplies ran out. They had weapons and armor too: wolf helms and shirts of scales, a katana and a longsword, a bow and arrow, knives and throwing stars, and the oil and sharpening stones to maintain the blades.

"We have enough supplies for a small army," Torin said, gazing at the hill of food, drink, and weapons.

Koyee grinned. "Well, I've seen you Timandrians eat; you gobble up enough for an army, each man alone. No wonder you people are so big. And besides, it'll be a long journey." She reached into a pack, produced a scroll, and unrolled it, revealing a map. "We'll be spending a good moon on the water."

She sat down, placed the map on a bench, and secured its corners with an hourglass, a dagger, and two jars of pickled squid. Torin sat beside her, gazing at the inked rivers, mountains, and craters of Eloria.

"An entire month on the water," he said in a whisper. He could barely imagine such a distance.

Empires of Moth

A month alone with Koyee, he thought, raising his eyes and looking at her. That familiar tingling filled him. She was sitting cross-legged, leaning forward and admiring the map, a soft smile on her lips. Torin thought her hair looked very soft and smooth, and he longed to touch it, to kiss her lips again, to hold her in his arms like he had back in Pahmey.

Was that a single moment of passion? he wondered. *Or will she . . . be my woman?* The thought spun his head, almost comical. Torin had kissed a couple girls back home; he had shared a quick peck on the lips with Leeya, the rye farmer's daughter, and an awkward mess of a kiss—noses banging—with Perry Potter, an older woman who then went off and married somebody else. With Koyee it had felt different, infinitely more real and yet infinitely more mysterious and ephemeral.

She looked up at him, saw him staring, and tilted her head. Feeling his cheeks flush, Torin quickly returned his eyes to the map. He pointed at a strand of silver ink.

"Is this the Inaro River?" he said. "Where we sail now?"

She nodded and tapped a point on the strand. "We're about here, two hourglass turns south of the Chanku crater. We'll sail all the way south across the plains of Qaelin." She traced her finger down the map. "In under a moon, if we oar along with the current, we'll reach the southern Qaelish port of Sinyong." She smiled, revealing bright teeth. "I've heard traders speak of Sinyong. They say it's a great city of wonder, its towers more beautiful than those of Pahmey, its streets wide, its people learned and wise. They say that glowing birds fly between its pagodas, and that its philosophers study the stars."

Her eyes shone, but Torin didn't share her sense of adventure. He would be happy never seeing another city of wonders. More than anything, he wanted to return home to Fairwool-by-Night, to tend to his gardens, and to forget about this war and bloodshed. He'd be happier seeing his humble old

153

cottage than any fancy towers. In his dreams, Koyee returned home with him, and they lived together in Fairwool-by-Night. Flowers bloomed in the gardens, Cam's sheep grazed peacefully, and the smells of Hem's baking bread filled the village. Torin cared little for magical towers, glowing birds, or markets of wonder; he loved the peace of home, a warm fireplace, and a mug of mulled wine, ideally with Koyee snuggled up under a blanket at his side.

Yet he could not speak of these things to Koyee; he knew he'd only stutter and his cheeks would blush, and he worried that she'd mock him for his humble dreams. After living in Pahmey, a great city, would she find his village dull? Instead, he only traced his finger farther south along the map.

"And from Sinyong, we'll have to navigate the sea," he said. "It looks like . . . by Idar, the sea's as wide as the distance between Oshy and Pahmey. I hope we still have enough supplies." He looked at their pile of food, then back at the map. "And then . . . what's this city on the coast of Ilar?" He squinted; reading foreign words in Qaelish still stumped him sometimes. "Asharo?"

Koyee's eyes darkened, the smile left her lips, and she hugged herself.

"Asharo," she repeated in a whisper, the voice of a woman speaking of ancient evil. She reached across the bench and grabbed the hilt of her katana.

"I take it . . . not as pleasant a place as Sinyong," Torin said.

Koyee shook her head. "I've never been there, but my father fought there in the great war between Qaelin and Ilar." She looked up at him, eyes haunted. "Not all wars are between day and night. We in the darkness of Eloria have fought amongst ourselves—great, terrible wars that have claimed the lives of many. Too many times did the Ilari warriors raid the southern coasts of our empire. My father sailed south with Qaelin's army. They crossed the sea. They reached the walls of Asharo. A demon

Empires of Moth

world, my father called that city." She shuddered. "The walls were black. The towers behind them rose dark and jagged, endless battlements manned by endless warriors. The Ilari rode strange creatures of shadow, their teeth bright; like cats they were, but the size of nightwolves. The armor of the Ilari was just as black; they blended into the night, and they attacked by the thousands. Many of my father's friends died." She caressed the katana. "He slew many with Sheytusung, his sword. The Ilari will not have forgotten the blade that felled so many of their sons. I pray to the Leaping Fish and to all other constellations that we can make peace with Ilar." She stared deep into Torin's eyes as if peering into his soul. "The Ilari are horrible and mighty. With their help, we can defeat the sunlight. Yet they are just as likely to slay us before we dock our boat."

Torin couldn't suppress a shudder. "So . . . yes, definitely not as pleasant as Sinyong."

She slapped his chest. "Be quiet and go get our books. It's time to practice a new language."

Torin raised his eyebrow. "A new language?"

For the past six months, he'd been speaking with Koyee in Qaelish, her language, mixed with a good dose of Ardish, his mother tongue. They both knew just enough of each language to mix them into something they both understood. Torin jokingly called their speech "Qaelardish," and he was finally enjoying being able to converse freely with Koyee.

She nodded. "The Ilari speak their own tongue. It's similar to Qaelish and shares many words, but you'll have to learn the differences. My father taught me some; I need to learn too." She scuttled across the deck, reached into a chest, and produced a leather-bound book. "We have a long time on this boat. We will learn."

With a sigh, Torin settled down beside her, the book lying between them.

155

The boat flowed downriver.

The hourglass turned.

The stars moved above.

They ate, studied, slept holding each other for warmth, and watched the landscapes roll by.

They were five hourglass turns along the river when they saw the burning village.

* * * * *

More than the cawing crows, it was the smell of burning flesh that woke Torin.

He lay in the *Water Spider*, Koyee nestled against him for warmth. Fur blankets wrapped around them. It was always cold in Eloria; most days chunks of ice floated in the river, Torin's fingers felt numb, and his breath frosted. Yet as he woke now, the smoky scent in his nostrils, heat floated on the wind. Sweat clung to his skin and dampened his hair. He opened his eyes, blinked, and saw ash swirling in the sky.

"Fire," he whispered.

Arms wrapped around him, Koyee opened her eyes and raised her head from his chest. Lines from his tunic creased her cheek. She blinked, sniffed, and then leaped out of the blankets. She stood in the boat, stared off the port side, and blanched. Never removing her eyes from the eastern bank, she knelt, grabbed her katana, and drew the blade.

Heart leaping into a gallop, Torin rose from his bed of furs, followed Koyee's gaze, and felt his heart sink.

"Merciful Idar," he said, grabbing and drawing his own sword.

"Are they all dead?" Koyee whispered.

156

Empires of Moth

Torin walked toward the stern and grabbed the rudder. He began directing the boat toward the eastern bank. "We're going to find out."

A village nestled along the riverbank—or at least it had once been a village. The place now smoldered. Clay huts lay shattered, their roof tiles strewn across the ground. Charred corpses lay upon a boardwalk, and crows—birds Torin had only seen in Dayside before—feasted upon them. Lantern poles rose along the docks, but rather than holding lights, corpses now hung from them.

Koyee winced. "The enemy might still be here."

"I see none." Torin grabbed an oar. "The Timandrians came, burned, and moved on. This is no longer a war of conquest. It's mindless slaughter."

When they reached the docks and moored, the stench flared so powerfully Torin nearly gagged. He pulled on his shirt of steel scales, donned his helmet, and stepped onto the stone pier. Koyee joined him, tugging on her own armor. Leaving their boat behind, they walked into the village, swords and shields raised.

"By the light," Torin said, wincing as he stepped onto the main street.

Corpses lay charred upon the cobblestones, their bones curling inward like wet parchment. The skulls seemed to have bloated and cracked like sausage casings stuffed with too much meat. Only bits of skin clung to the remains. The shells of houses rose around them; beyond the crumbled walls Torin saw more skeletons, these ones of children. Some of the skeletons sprouted extra limbs. One child's skeleton had two skulls, while another's ribs flared outward, flipped backwards upon the torso.

"Who did this?" Koyee said, voice shaky. "Who would desecrate the dead like this, rearranging bones to form these . . . these shapes?" She stared at a skeleton at her feet, its femurs coiling like pig's tails.

157

Torin swallowed bile. "They did not deform the dead. They deformed the living." He could not stop his hands from shaking. "Magerians did this."

He pointed at the wall of a temple, its dome collapsed. A mural spread across it, painted in blood, forming a buffalo with long horns and red eyes.

"Magerians?" Koyee whispered. She stared at the painted animal and shivered. "Who are these demons?"

"Mageria is a kingdom in Timandra." Torin kept walking, heading around a fallen bronze statue of Xen Qae, founder of Qaelin. "It lies west of Arden, my own homeland. You remember how you told me that different Elorian nations have fought one another? The same has happened in Timandra. There are three empires in Eloria. We have eight kingdoms in the daylight, and Mageria is the most dangerous among them. They fight not with swords and arrows, but with dark magic. Their spells can twist bones like clay, burn flesh, and spread death like a farmer spreading seeds. They conquered Arden's capital city thirty years ago; they would have reached my village too, had King Ceranor not driven them off." Torin rounded a corner, saw a hundred skeletons stacked in a grotesque hill, and grimaced. "And now they're here in the night."

Koyee stared at the hill of bones, her eyes dampened, and she shivered.

"I want to leave this place." She looked at him. "All are dead here; we cannot help them. We must seek aid. We must." She turned and began walking back to the river. "I don't know if any in Eloria can fight such evil, such power. But if we have any hope, it lies south. Come, Torin. Let us oar. We must reach Ilar before all lie dead."

They returned to their boat in silence, ash raining upon them, hot and stinging and scented of charred meat. Torin grimaced to think that these pale flakes might be the remains of

158

Empires of Moth

the dead. When they were sailing downriver again, he did not look back.

The hourglass turned and turned.

The moon waxed and waned.

The stars rose and fell.

The world became only their boat floating upon an endless black sky. Fish lit the water, luminous bulbs growing upon stalks, spine ridges bright with running pins of light. They shone like stars below. Nothing but darkness and glowing beads surrounded them, and Torin barely knew water from sky, ground from air. Endless night. Endless, cold darkness.

And endless death.

Every turn or two, they sailed by them—the burning remains of a village, a town, or a humble riverside temple burned down. At every outpost they saw them—the dead. The twisted corpses hung from lantern poles, hundreds of the fallen lining the riverbanks. Their bones coiled like fingernails left to grow too long. Bits of flesh clung to their skulls, the mouths agape in silent screams. Upon the walls of their houses appeared the same sigil, again and again, a mark of damnation crawling downriver—the buffalo of Mageria, horns long, eyes red, a demon painted in blood.

At every settlement Torin and Koyee docked their boat. At every settlement they prayed to find survivors. They found only death, a hill of skeletons between burnt houses.

"When we reach the southern coast, what will we find?" Koyee whispered as they sailed away from another burnt village. "Is Sinyong, the great city at the edge of the river, but a graveyard for thousands—another Pahmey, its people trapped and burned?" She lowered her head and hugged herself. "Will we find the same in Ilar? Torin . . . what if all the lands of night are dead and gone, if only a handful of survivors still live, dwindling every hourglass turn?"

159

Torin grimaced, watching the latest village fade into the distance behind them, the corpses swinging upon the lamp posts. "I don't know how many more live. But so long as *we* live, we will seek life. We will sail past death so long as we breathe, even if we are the last." He turned toward her and held her hands. "But I don't believe that all are gone. Even in the deepest darkness a light shines. We will find life again."

A tear trailed down her cheek, and Torin lifted it on his finger. He found himself stroking her cheek as she gazed at him, her eyes twice the size of his, deep lavender that reflected the stars. Her lips parted in a shaky breath, and he kissed her.

He did not mean to kiss her, and yet he found himself holding her against him, his hands stroking her back. She wrapped her arms around him and her eyes closed, and her body was soft and warm under her silks.

"We will find life," she whispered.

They lay upon a fur blanket, pulled another blanket atop them, and moved in the soft warmth and shadows. His blood burned and his body ached as he tugged at her sash. Her silks came free, and her hands ran across him, pulling the lacing of his tunic and breeches, and soon they were naked under the furs, their lips trailing across skin, meeting in a clash of warmth, and parting to explore before meeting again. She lay atop him, their chests pressed together, and he closed his eyes and whispered her name as he loved her.

They clung together, warm in the cold night, desperate for each other as their boat moved downriver . . . heading deeper into shadow and the fires of war.

160

Empires of Moth

CHAPTER FIFTEEN
THE IRON ROAD

"Furry sheep droppings, she's scary when she does that, isn't she?" Sitting cross-legged on the rocky ground, Cam shuddered. "One of these turns, she's going to spin around and toss those things into our necks."

Sitting beside him, Linee gave a small whimper. "Don't say that. Please, Camlin. Suntai is scary enough without you saying these things." She glanced at the three nightwolves who stood nearby, feeding from bowls of meat and bones. "And it's bad enough we have to share the road with those . . . those hairy things."

They had been traveling the Iron Road for many turns now—Cam wasn't sure how many, because his hourglass kept falling over in his pocket. Judging by the waning moon, they'd left the crater half a month ago. During all that time, Suntai—their guide, their protector, and their terror—had barely said a word.

"Look at her sat up there," Cam whispered. "Does she even eat or sleep? I don't think I've seen her do either."

Linee stared down into her bowl of salted beef and boiled chickpeas, part of their dwindling supplies of Timandrian goods. "Of course she eats and sleeps. She has to. She's not . . . not a ghost." Linee shivered. "Right?"

Cam himself had no appetite and shoved aside his own bowl. He stared up at the Elorian woman. About twenty yards away, she perched upon a milestone, one of the tall boulders that marked distances along the Iron Road. Suntai. Alpha female of

161

the Chanku Pack. The most terrifying woman Cam had ever met—and he'd suffered Bailey's kicks about a hundred times.

But Suntai . . . this woman was even worse. Bailey would scold him, wrestle him, kick him, and one time—when he'd accidentally broken her childhood doll—she had given him a bloody lip. Cam had learned to tolerate Bailey's aggression, believing that deep down she was his friend, that she cared for him despite her outbursts. Suntai, however, was a different story. Suntai held him no love. If Suntai got upset, Cam felt that she wouldn't just smack him—she'd stick her throwing stars into his neck.

The tall, armor-clad woman was sharpening those throwing stars now, running their edges against a stone again and again. Each stroke gave a hiss like a dying man. Her white hair billowed in the breeze, a sheet like gossamer, and the moonlight reflected against her armor of steel scales. Her back was turned to Cam, for which he was grateful. Suntai was pretty enough, what with her large indigo eyes, high cheekbones, and pale skin, but whenever she gazed upon him, her face spoke only of scorn.

She thinks Linee and I are weak, Cam thought, watching her. *And maybe she's right. We're no warriors like her.*

It didn't help that Suntai—who was almost as tall as Bailey—towered above him and Linee. Standing a humble five feet and three inches, Cam had rather enjoyed his stay in Pahmey; many Elorians there had been his height, even some of the men. Back in Fairwool-by-Night, Cam had been the shortest man around—shorter than most of the women too. On the streets of Pahmey, he had almost begun to feel confident about his height.

Ferius just had to destroy the only place where I felt good, Cam thought with a sigh. *And now I'm stuck here with these two—one who terrifies me, the other who barely stops crying.*

As if to confirm his thoughts, Queen Linee began to weep again. Cam had lost count of how many times she had burst into

Empires of Moth

tears along the Iron Road. The wolves, hearing her whimpers, raised their heads from their bowls.

"I'm scared and I'm cold and I want to go home." Linee tugged at Cam's sleeve. "Please, Camlin, please can we go home? Can you take me back to Kingswall to my gardens and pet puppies and flowers? Please. This place is just . . . just horrible."

On their journey so far, Cam had rolled his eyes so often he was surprised they hadn't fallen out. He rolled them again. "First of all, I told you—nobody calls me Camlin but my mother. Call me Cam like everybody else. Secondly, you know we can't go back. You know we have to keep you hidden. What do you think would happen if you returned to Kingswall, your husband dead and Sailith running the show? Do you think they'd let you play with your puppies and flowers?"

Linee only cried harder. "They have to. I'm their queen, I—"

"You *were* their queen," Cam said. "And Ceranor was their king, and you saw what happened to him."

Linee stared up at him with huge, horrified eyes. "I . . . Camlin— I mean, Cam, how . . ." She covered her face and wept silently.

Cam cursed himself, guilt rising through him. Maybe he shouldn't have said those words. It couldn't have been too pleasant for Linee to see her husband slaughtered, after all, especially not with her so young and naive. Linee was perhaps two or three years older than Cam, but internally she was still a child. He awkwardly touched her shoulder.

"I'm sorry, Linee. Please stop crying. Look around you—it's not that bad out here. The stars are pretty once you get used to them, don't you think?"

Linee only shook her head and kept her face hidden. With a sigh, Cam looked around him. He himself had thought the Iron Road frightening at first, but he'd come to see its beauty. Black

163

plains of rock sprawled into all horizons, shining silver where the moonlight hit them. Hills rose in the east, nearly invisible in the shadows. The sky spread like a great bowl, strewn with millions of stars, some bright, others small and clustered like clouds of dust.

Between earth and stars stretched the Iron Road, the great south-to-north highway of the Qaelish Empire. When Cam had first heard of the Iron Road, he'd imagined a road like the ones back in Timandra, wide and smooth and cobbled, only maybe the cobbles would be forged of iron rather than stone. But in truth, it was barely a road at all, just a string of milestones running endlessly north and south. Each milestone rose several feet tall, smoothed and topped with a glowing blue rune. Suntai now sat upon the nearest milestone; others stretched beyond her. Cam could count seven stretching north; the eighth lay beyond the horizon, but Cam knew it would be there. They had passed many already. Each milestone they rode by, he would peer at the glowing rune, struggling to understand the source of its light.

"Magic," Suntai had once said—one of the only words she had spoken on the journey. Cam had tried to ask how the magic worked, but she had only shot him a withering glare, and he'd dared not ask questions since.

A falling star streaked across the sky, then another, then a third. Cam touched Linee's shoulder and spoke softly.

"Some stars are falling, Linlin. Want to see?"

She shook her head mightily and finally removed her hands from her face. "No! And I told *you*, don't call me Linlin. That's a stupid name for babies, and I'm not a baby." Her voice rose and her cheeks flushed. "My name is Queen Linee or Your Highness. I'm *still* your queen, Camlin Shepherd, and—"

Her voice died and she paled.

Cam turned to see Suntai stomping toward them.

Rage twisted the tall Elorian's face. She growled, revealing very white and very sharp-looking teeth; her canines almost looked like fangs. She seemed like a nightwolf, and she clutched the hilts of daggers.

"Lower your voices!" she said in her tongue; Cam spoke enough Qaelish by now to understand. "You disturb the nightwolves. When you cry, it makes them nervous." She glared at Cam. "Tell the little girl to be quiet, or I will cut her tongue from her mouth and feed it to the wolves."

Cam gulped and turned to look at the former queen. Linee perhaps did not speak Qaelish, but she seemed to need no translation. Face almost as pale as an Elorian's, she covered her mouth with her palms. She trembled and a tear streamed down her cheek, but she made not a sound.

"Good," Suntai said. "And keep quiet. Now stand up. We've rested long enough. Onto the wolves. We ride again."

Suntai spun away, stepped toward her white nightwolf, and stroked the beast's fur. She whispered soothing words into the animal's ear and then climbed into the saddle. She stared down at Cam and Linee, hand caressing her katana.

She thinks us weaker than pups, Cam thought, gulping. *And maybe she's right.* As strange as Suntai was to him—with her fierce ways, oversized eyes, and many weapons—they must have seemed just as strange to her, darker and weaker and prone to laughter and tears. *We must seem like children to her.*

Reluctantly, Cam rose to his feet and stuffed his emptied bowl into his pack. He approached his own nightwolf—or at least the one Suntai let him ride. It was a shaggy gray beast, its withers the height of Cam's head. It took several attempts—Linee pushing him—to climb into the saddle. He reached down, grabbed Linee's hand, and helped her climb into the saddle before him. She wriggled into place, and he placed his arms around her waist.

Looking over her shoulder at them, Suntai spat and shook her head sadly. "Like children you two ride." She spurred her nightwolf. "Now follow."

165

Daniel Arenson

* * * * *

The three nightwolves began to move—Suntai ahead upon her white wolf, Cam and Linee sharing the gray one, and the third animal bringing up the rear. This last beast, a scarred male with brown fur, carried sacks of their supplies. At first Suntai had insisted that nightwolves were not pack animals but noble beasts; the Elorian warrior had tried to place Linee upon the brown male, but the former queen kept squealing, weeping, and falling off. Finally, with a string of curses, Suntai had given up on ever teaching the young woman to ride. Since then, Cam and Linee had shared a mount.

For a while they rode in silence. Cam heard nothing but the wind and the occasional wolf's snort; their paws padded silently upon the rock. Cam had ridden a pony once and remembered bouncing in the saddle, but the nightwolf moved as steadily as a boat upon smooth waters. If not for Linee's hair which kept entering his mouth, he would have enjoyed the ride; the damned saddle was too small for two, and he could barely breathe with the back of her head pressed against his face. He tried to distract himself by looking up at the stars, counting the blue ones that shone among the silver specks.

"Camlin," Linee whispered, wriggling in the saddle; Suntai now rode too far ahead to hear. "Camlin? All right—*Cam*!"

"What?" He spat out a strand of her hair. "I can hear you."

She twisted in the saddle and looked at him. "Do you think . . ." She bit her lip, lowered her head, and twisted her fingers. "Do you think when we finally reach the kingdom of Leen, they'll let me be a queen there? I mean . . . not queen of the whole island. Maybe just . . . a small part of it?"

Cam's jaw dropped and he raised an eyebrow. "Are you serious?"

166

Empires of Moth

Her eyes watered for the thousandth time. "No! Well . . . maybe. I don't know. I guess I kind of thought that . . . well, that if I joined you on the journey to Leen, and if they learned that my name is Queen Linee—it sounds like their kingdom!—they'd . . . I don't know . . ." A teardrop hung from her nose. "I guess that's just stupid and it can never happen."

Cam gaped. "You didn't actually think that—" He blinked. "I mean, you really—"

She spun away from him and crossed her arms. "Forget it, *Camlin.* Just don't talk to me. Look at your stars."

He shook his head in bewilderment, sighed, and looked back up at the sky. Most turns upon the road, Cam didn't know who frustrated him more—Suntai with her glares and blades or Linee with her nonsense. He missed his friends. He wished Hem could have come with them—lumbering, stupid Hem with that ridiculous appetite of his, that mellifluous singing voice, and pockets full of treats. He missed Torin—quiet, wise Torin who could always make sense of things that confused the rest of their gang. He even missed Bailey . . . a little.

I hope I see you again, he thought, feeling alone and cold even with Linee pressed against him, her mane of hair tickling his face.

Loneliness in his belly, Cam was about to strike up another conversation with Linee when roars sounded ahead.

He tensed up, leaned around Linee, and stared north along the road.

"Camlin?" Linee began. "I—"

"Hush!"

The roars sounded again, deep and rolling across the plains, still distant but closer this time. Suntai had heard them too; riding a hundred yards ahead upon her nightwolf, she drew her katana. She looked back at them and gestured urgently, then doused her lantern, disappearing into the shadows.

"What—" Linee began again.

"Shh!" Cam reached forward, grabbed her lantern, and extinguished its flame.

Darkness fell.

Nothing but the stars and crescent moon lit the night.

Cam gave a tug to the reins, and his wolf fell still beneath him and Linee. He could no longer see or hear Suntai ahead. The night became a silent, black cloak wrapping around him. Linee began to shiver, and Cam wrapped his arms around her and held her close, not even minding her hair in his face now.

For a few long moments, he heard and saw nothing.

Then the roars rose again, inhuman and definitely closer now. Laughter and the language of men rose among them; the sound was still too low for Cam to make out the words. Lights gleamed ahead—torches, he thought. People were moving southward along the Iron Road toward him.

As the lights grew closer, the voices grew louder, deep and raspy. Cam frowned. He knew that language. These men were from Verilon, a sunlit kingdom north of his homeland of Arden. Torin's father had fought the Verilish in the war years ago; the man would often tell stories of barbarians riding upon bears, their bodies nearly as hairy as their mounts, wielding war hammers that could shatter steel like clay. Cam had even met a Verilish man once—a bearded peddler, clad in old furs, who'd come to Fairwool-by-Night to swap pelts for barley and wheat.

More enemies, he thought, clinging to Linee. *The northern invasion of the night.*

Something rustled to his left, maybe two feet away, and Cam nearly leaped and fell from the saddle. Two blue orbs glowed in the dark. For an instant, Cam was sure a ghost or spirit was lunging to rip out his innards, but it was only Suntai upon her wolf. He could make out nothing more than her eyes, the twin stare of her wolf, and her finger pointing east. Then she was riding off the road. Cam didn't even have to heel his wolf; the

Empires of Moth

beast followed its alpha. Behind them, their third nightwolf—Telshuan, the shaggy brown animal who bore their packs—followed silently.

Suntai led them to a group of boulders; Cam only saw them once they were a couple feet away, but Suntai's large eyes had always seen better in the darkness. They led their nightwolves around the boulders and stood still, waiting and watching the road.

The sounds of conversation grew louder, and another roar rose, pealing across the land. When Cam peered around the boulder, he saw them approach, and his heart sank.

There were five of them—Verilish warriors just as Torin's father used to describe them. Each rode a bear, beasts Cam had only seen in bestiaries; spiked armor hung around the animals' necks and helmets topped their shaggy heads. The five riders were almost as shaggy, their beards thick, their hair long and brown. Each held a lamp, and war hammers hung at their sides. Two were drinking from tankards of ale.

They conversed as they rode. Their language was similar to Cam's own. A thousand years ago, Verilon and Arden had been parts of Riyona, an empire stretching across the north of Dayside. Even now, so many generations after that empire's fall, the kingdoms of Old Riyona shared many words. Cam was able to understand most of what these men said. They were speaking of an attack on Eeshan—a port city in the north of Qaelin—and how many Elorian "savages" they had slain with their hammers.

"I killed three!" one man was boasting. "Cracked their skulls with my hammer, I did, and bedded their wives." His accent was thick and a couple words were different from Ardish, but Cam understood enough.

One of his friends roared with laughter. "Three? I killed fourteen of the little creatures—my bear ate one of their children."

169

An older rider, this one with grizzled eyebrows and a leathery face, glared at the two braggarts. "Hush! This road is swarming with Elorians. The bastards lurk in shadows. You don't see them till they leap right at you." He flipped and caught a dagger. "Men say there's a great city of them in the south; thrice the size of Eeshan, they say it is. The bloody Ardish conquered it, but Verilon will have a bite."

The bears and their riders rode close now; soon they would go south along the road. Hiding behind the boulders, Cam bit his lip, praying the men wouldn't hear or smell them. Cam could have perhaps convinced Ardish soldiers to ride on, but Verilon held his people no love, despite being a fellow kingdom of sunlight.

If they see me here with an Elorian, they will attack, Cam knew. *They will kill Suntai and me, and they will take Linee as their captive.*

The riders kept moving down the road; soon Cam could only see the backs of the men. He remained very still, holding Linee close in the saddle; she was trembling. Suntai waited at his side, eyes narrowed to slits.

The Verilish riders kept speaking as their bears headed south.

"I hear Arden's got a pretty little queen," one man said, contorting to scratch his back. "They say she got blond hair and green eyes and is all young and fresh."

One of his friends snorted. "I reckon if we find her here in the night, she's ours to keep. Would like to have me a queen, I would."

Linee's trembling grew more violent. A whimper rose from her, barely more than a squeak. Cam tensed and held her more tightly.

Hush, Linee, in Idar's name . . .

The bears kept rambling farther south, lanterns bobbing.

"I hear she's called . . . what was her name again?" one of the Verilish riders said. "Queen Linee! That's it. Queen Linee of

Empires of Moth

Arden." He barked a laugh. "I think I'll grab her right up—take her back home in chains. Could serve me ale and warm my bed, Queen Linee can."

This time Linee's whimper was louder—a plaintive sound like a flute that wafted across the night.

Cam cursed and covered her mouth with his palm.

The bear riders stiffened, their armor creaking. Heads spun around and a bear sniffed and grunted.

"I heard something," said one rider. "I heard—"

"Elorians on the road," said his companion, the older rider with the thick, grizzled brows. "Men, raise your hammers! Find them."

Cam's heart pounded as the five riders spurred their mounts. The bears came charging off the road, their riders readying their hammers. Lamplight cascaded across the land, falling upon Cam and his companions.

His heart seemed to freeze and shatter. Linee screamed. Cam reached for his sword, but his fingers fumbled. The five Verilish men stared at him, eyes wide. Their bears reared beneath them, clawed the air, and roared. Strings of saliva glistened between their teeth.

Cam drew his sword, gulped, and prepared to die.

A high-pitched yowl tore across the night.

White fur and steel flashed.

Shouting battle cries, Suntai raced past him upon her wolf, shield and katana raised in her hands.

With a yowl, her wolf leaped toward the five bears. Her blade lashed. Hammers swung her way.

Before Cam could even take a breath, his wolf reared beneath him and Linee. The gray beast leaped after his alpha, claws lashing.

Sitting ahead of him in the saddle, Linee screamed. Cam cursed and swung his sword blindly.

171

"Camlin!" Linee cried.

A bear came lolloping toward them. The rider atop the beast snarled, saliva spraying into his beard, and swung a hammer. Linee shrieked. Beneath them, their wolf clawed and bit. Unable to breathe, Cam raised his shield.

The hammer slammed down.

Cam cried out. The hammer drove into his shield, denting the metal; Cam thought his arm almost dislocated.

"Linee, duck!" he shouted.

When her head was lowered, he swung his sword, trying to hit the Verilish soldier. His blade only sliced the air. The bear and rider pulled back then leaped forward. Cam's wolf bucked beneath him. The two animals slammed together in a storm of fur, fang, and claw.

Shouting, Cam slipped from the saddle, slid across his wolf's back, and thudded onto the rocky earth. The air jolted out of his lungs. Before he could breathe again, Linee slammed down onto his chest.

"Linee, get off!" he said, struggling to rise from under her.

He managed to shove her off just in time to see a rider, burly and brutish, leaning down from his bear to swing a hammer. Cam winced and raised his shield again. The steel took another blow, bending around his arm; even with the shield, it felt like his arm had come close to snapping. The brute above laughed and raised his hammer again.

Cam grimaced, knowing he was going to die.

White fur flashed.

A nightwolf leaped.

Suntai yelped a battle cry, swung her sword from her saddle, and raced on. Blood flew in a curtain.

The Verilish rider's head drooped, revealing a cut that all but severed his head. The man collapsed upon the saddle, tugging

Empires of Moth

the reins and driving his bear sideways to smash into another one of the beasts.

Cam leaped to his feet and stood above Linee; the queen still lay on the ground, whimpering. He raised his dented shield and sword, prepared for more fighting, and gaped.

The battle raged on without him. The three nightwolves—Suntai atop one, the two others fighting riderless—were tearing into the enemy. Two bears and riders already lay dead, their blood trickling. As Cam watched, eyes wide, Suntai leaped from her wolf's saddle. She rose several feet in the air, then plunged, her sword pointing downward. She landed atop a bear, driving her blade into the poor beast. Her shield drove upward, crashing into the bear rider's neck, tearing open the flesh. As both rider and bear collapsed, Suntai leaped again and landed back upon her wolf.

"By Idar's beard," Cam whispered, standing with his sword raised, feeling rather unnecessary as Suntai tore into the enemy like a fox tearing through a chicken coop. Linee finally rose to her feet and stood beside him, gaping. She drew her dagger—the one Bailey had given her back in the city—and held the blade before her.

As they watched, Suntai drove her wolf into another bear. Blood sprayed. Her face splashed with her enemy's blood, Suntai turned toward the last surviving bear.

The shaggy Verilish beast was battling Telshuan, the brown nightwolf, pack animal of their expedition; sacks of food, rolled up blankets, and packages of oil and candles still covered the wolf's back. The bear was a towering thing, scarred and one-eyed, the largest of the beasts. Blood soaked the nightwolf's fur.

Suntai leaped from her saddle. She landed atop the one-eyed bear and swung her sword, slicing into the rider. Its master dead, the bear reared, howled, and slammed its paws into Telshuan's muzzle.

173

The brown nightwolf whimpered and fell, face lacerated. Suntai still stood atop the bear, driving her blade into its flesh. The beast fell atop Telshuan, biting at the nightwolf even as Suntai stabbed it again and again.

Both animals fell still.

Suntai stood upon the furry corpses, panting. She gazed around, eyes wild.

All her enemies lay dead around her.

"Telshuan . . ." Suntai whispered. She leaped off the bear and knelt. The brown nightwolf lay crushed under his enemy, only his head visible; no life filled his eyes.

"Telshuan!" Suntai cried, voice hoarse. She tossed back her head and howled at the moon.

Cam bit his lip, standing several yards away, daring not approach. Linee moved gripped his hand; her lips wobbled but she made not a sound.

"Suntai," Cam said softly; the woman was whispering and touching the dead wolf's face. "Suntai, I'm sorry. I—"

The wolfrider raised her head, and Cam took a step back, the breath leaving his lungs. Suntai's eyes blazed with rage. Her lips peeled back in a horrible snarl in her bloodied face. She leaped to her feet, drew a dagger, and came stomping forward.

Linee squealed and squeezed Cam's hand.

"Telshuan did not have to die," Suntai said when she reached them, voice strained. She stared at Cam, her eyes withering; Cam thought that they could burn through steel. "The girl made a noise. Now he is dead."

Linee did not speak more than a couple words in Qaelish, but she tried to stammer an apology, gesturing at the wolf. "I sorry, Suntai. I sorry. I—"

Suntai spat and thrust her blade.

A bloody line blazed to life on Linee's cheek.

Empires of Moth

Linee clutched the wound, stared for a moment in shock at her attacker, and burst into tears. She turned and ran into the darkness.

"Oh wormy sheep's livers," Cam whispered. He looked at Suntai, but the woman left him and returned to the fallen wolf. Cam stared at her for a moment longer, then spun around and began running after Linee.

He ran for a long time through the darkness, following the sound of her sobs. A thump sounded ahead, followed by a curse and whimper. A few more steps and Cam stumbled upon a lump in the darkness—Linee curled up on the ground, weeping.

Cam knelt beside her. "Linee, it's me." He touched her hair. "It's all right."

He expected her to hide her face, cower, or tremble. He gasped when she leaped up, wrapped her arms around him, and clung.

"I'm scared, Camlin," she whispered, squeezing him. "I'm so scared. I'm so sorry. You don't have to take me home anymore. You don't have to say I'm a queen. You can even call me Linlin if you want. Just please hold me. Hold me tight because I'm so scared."

He nodded and kissed her forehead. "Of course."

As the sound of Suntai praying rose behind them, he held Linee for a long time in the shadows.

175

CHAPTER SIXTEEN
THE GAUNTLET

After nearly a moon on the river, their supplies dwindling, Koyee and Torin reached the southern coast and beheld the buffalo banners.

Koyee stood at the prow, hand resting on her sword's pommel. Her breath left her lungs like a deflating bellows.

"Sinyong," she whispered into the wind, watching the port city grow nearer. "The southern jewel of Qaelin. The city burns."

The *Water Spider* still sailed several miles away, but it was close enough for Koyee to see the carnage. The hosts of sunlight surrounded the city. Their ships sailed upon the river ahead, pushing into Sinyong like worms up an artery. Their ground troops surrounded the city walls, sprawling across the plains— footmen, horsemen, and charioteers, thousands in all. Their banners rose high—not the raven banners that had flown in Pahmey, but ones sporting the crimson buffalo, its horns long.

"Mageria," Torin said, standing beside her. His eyes darkened. "We followed their path of rot to this pulsing heart."

"The city still fights." Koyee's hand trembled around the hilt of her sword. As their boat sailed closer, more details emerged. "There is still hope for Sinyong. Look, Torin! Elorians still stand upon the city walls."

Two halves formed Sinyong, semi-circles clasping the river between them. A hundred pagodas rose here, their tiled roofs topped with statues. Several towers crumbled before Koyee's eyes. As she watched, a catapult upon the plains hurled a boulder into a pagoda, sending statues, tiles, and bricks crashing down. Walls

Empires of Moth

surrounded the city's two halves, and upon them stood Elorians in armor, firing arrows and cannons. Lights blazed like lightning. Cannonballs crashed like thunder.

"How will we sail through?" Torin said. "Damn it. Is there another way to the sea?"

Koyee stared grimly. Their boat still sailed two or three miles away, but soon the river would take them through Sinyong and its raging battle. Where the river flowed between the city's halves, the combat blazed brightest. Fifty ships or more sailed there; a few were Elorian junks, but most were the carracks of Timandra, the crimson buffalo upon their sails. Walls and towers rose along the riverbanks, many soldiers upon them, forming a canyon. Arrows and cannonfire crashed down onto the enemy ships, a gauntlet of flame and steel and blood. Bolts of black fire blasted out from Mageria's vessels, dark magic that crashed into towers and sent them crumbling. Koyee couldn't even glimpse the sea beyond the port; the battle curtained the view.

"We'll have to sail through," Koyee said, feeling the blood drain from her face. "It's the only way to the sea. It's the only way we can row south to Ilar."

Torin winced. "It's a damn bloodbath in there. We'll wait until the battle ends at least." He pointed ahead. "Nothing can survive that gauntlet. Look at it. Every ship sailing through the city is being pelted with arrows, fire, and death from above."

Koyee raised her chin. "When the battle ends, Timandra will seize this city. They will inspect every boat that sails through." She gave Torin a wry smile. "Arrows, fire, death? The perfect distraction for a sneaky little boat like ours."

They sailed closer. The city loomed less than a mile away now. The smell of gunpowder, oil, and dust wafted on the wind. A dozen Magerian ships rose ahead, each boasting three masts, many sails, and hulls lined with men in dark robes. Elorian soldiers raced across towers above, clad in scales, firing from

177

silvery bows. Arrows pelted the enemy ships; several Magerians clutched their chests and fell. Others stretched out their hands, shouting words in a foreign tongue. Dark fumes blasted out from the men's fingers, shooting toward a stone tower. Where the smoke hit, bricks twisted like wet cloth. The tower creaked. The Elorian guards screamed between the battlements, and Koyee winced to see their breastplates shatter and their heads crack.

"The dark magic of Mageria," Torin said, his knuckles white as he clutched the oar. "Damn it, Koyee, this is too dangerous. We have to turn back. We'll find another way, even if we have to swim to Ilar."

She shook her head. "No. There is no other way south. We must find aid in Ilar. If we cannot, this war will not only destroy the cities along the Inaro River. It will destroy the night. We must sail on." She touched Torin's arm. "I won't ask you to come with me. We can oar the boat to the riverbank. You can try to join your people here; you are from Arden, an ally of Mageria. But I cannot stop here. I will sail through fire and magic to save my home."

He sighed. "You know that only convinces me to go with this crazy scheme."

She couldn't help but grin. She mussed his hair and kissed his cheek. "I know. Now put on your armor and helmet—and stay low. We're going to do some tricky rowing."

She pulled on her own helmet—the wolf-helm her brother had given her. She already wore her shirt of steel scales. Keeping her sword drawn in her left hand, she grabbed an oar with her right. Torin grabbed a second oar.

The *Water Spider* gained speed.

The city loomed ahead.

Wincing, they oared through a curtain of smoke and flame . . . and entered the gauntlet.

The world became an inferno of blood, steel, and fire.

"Keep oaring, Torin!" Koyee shouted. "Faster!"

Empires of Moth

"Really? I thought we'd just sail leisurely!"

Arrows whistled through smoke. They clattered against the hull of the *Water Spider*, and Koyee cursed and ducked. An arrow grazed her helmet, and another slammed into her side. She grunted as it dented a steel scale. Between the smoke and flame, she could just make out the walls at her sides; Elorian archers stood upon the battlements, firing on anything that moved. The shouting of men, the blasting of cannons, and the shrieks of magic flowed through the canyon, deafeningly loud.

"Around that ship!" Koyee shouted, pointing ahead; she could barely hear her own words.

The carrack rose ahead, lined with three stories of portholes. Rents filled its sails, its railings rose like shattered bones, and the crimson buffalo of Mageria reared upon its burning banners. Arrows peppered the ship, tearing down Magerians in dark robes. The black swirls of magic rose from the ship, flying toward the city's defenders like demons seeking flesh. Cannonballs flew down from the walls; one crashed into the ship's hull, tearing a hole. Sailors screamed and fell.

Koyee gritted her teeth as she rowed around the ship. The towering carrack dwarfed the small *Water Spider*. Torin cursed at her side, face red as he rowed. An arrow slammed into his arm and ricocheted off his vambrace, incurring a new stream of curses. A cannonball crashed into the water ahead, and the *Water Spider* jolted. Koyee yelped, nearly fell overboard, and managed to steady herself and keep rowing.

"Between those two ships!" she shouted at Torin.

Two junks rowed ahead, their hulls lined with oars, their battened sails painted blue and silver. Elorians stood upon the decks, shouting and firing arrows. A Magerian galley came charging toward them, its figurehead shaped as a buffalo.

"Between the junks!" Koyee shouted, grimacing as she oared.

179

They rowed. The *Water Spider* shot forward, rocking over waves, bumping Koyee and Torin in their seats. A bolt of magic shot over their heads; its tail grazed their boat, twisting its frame. They kept oaring until they were moving between the two junks. Arrows whistled overhead. The ships blurred at her sides, forming walls around her, squeezing tighter. Koyee screamed and kept oaring.

"Koyee!" Torin shouted. "To your right!"

She turned to see the Magerian ship loom. Its figurehead rammed into an Elorian junk. A great wave tossed the *Water Spider* into the air. The junk ship tilted, slamming into the smaller *Water Spider*, cracking its hull where Koyee sat.

She shouted and fell from her seat. Her oar shattered. The *Water Spider* crashed back into the river, tilting, its bulwark cracked and leaking. They spun, trapped between the larger ships. Elorians and Magerians leaped from deck to deck above them, fighting with magic and steel. The little *Water Spider*, cracked and leaking, swayed between them like a mouse caught in a room of battling cats.

Koyee grabbed another oar; designed for twenty soldiers, the boat had several to spare. She pressed the oar against the junk's hull, pushing the *Water Spider* away.

"Keep oaring!" she shouted at Torin. "We're almost there."

A second ship was pressing against Torin's side. He rose to his feet, shoved against the larger hull, and pushed them free. The *Water Spider* shot forward, popping out from between the larger ships like a creature emerging from the womb. They oared toward the sea again.

Koyee inhaled a shaky breath. Several ships were sinking ahead; masts rose like a forest from the water. The dark brick walls of Sinyong still soared at her sides. More arrows kept raining down, and cannonballs crashed into the water like comets, leaving trails of fire. Three Magerian ships still sailed ahead, the dark

wizards on their decks battering the walls. As Koyee and Torin
rowed on, several Magerians crowded together at the railing of a
caravel. Their voices chanted as one. Blasts of smoke left their
fingers, raced across the water, and climbed up the eastern wall.

Stone cracked.

Koyee winced.

With a sound like the shattering ribs of a god, the wall
collapsed.

Koyee screamed as bricks rained down. The soldiers on the
battlements plunged with the stones, crashing into the river.
Blood mixed in water. Several bricks buffeted the river just ahead
of the *Water Spider*, sending the boat into a spin. One brick grazed
Koyee's helmet and light flashed. She blinked, unable to see, only
vaguely aware of Torin shaking her and calling her name.

She shook her head wildly and gritted her teeth. She kept
rowing.

"I can see it, Torin! The sea. The sea lies ahead. Keep
going!"

Her vision was blurry. Smoke, blood, and fire curtained the
world. But she could see the black shadow ahead—the open
waters, the stillness that would lead them to Ilar, to hope. She
shouted as she kept sailing through death and pain, water
gathering around her feet.

Two towers rose ahead, one from each riverbank, framing
the exit to the sea. Archers stood atop them, raining down their
arrows. Koyee and Torin raised their shields, grimaced, and oared
as fast as they could.

Arrows flew down, slamming into their boat and shields.
One arrow drove into Koyee's oar. With three more strokes, they
leaped over a wave, crashed down, and cleared the towers.

The *Water Spider* shot into the open sea.

Koyee breathed out shakily. "We made it." Her eyes stung
and she blinked rapidly. "We survived. Tori—"

181

He shouted and leaped toward her.

"Down, Koyee!"

She spun around. She screamed.

She caught only a glimpse of the Magerian—a man clad in black robes, his face hidden under his hood—standing upon a pile of fallen bricks. Then the blast of dark magic flew from the man, driving toward Torin and her.

She raised her shield. The ghostly fumes slammed into the *Water Spider*. Pain blazed and she couldn't breathe. Smoke and iciness flowed across her, and the shield bent and cracked upon her arm. Torin writhed beside her, clawing at his armor; the steel was steaming.

Koyee's shield shattered into metal shards. Her arm blazed, the steel of her vambrace twisting, driving into her flesh, cracking and reaching out metal fingers. She cried out in pain, nearly blinded, as she yanked at the armor. Agony flared in white light as she tugged, pulling the metal free from her flesh. She smelled her blood. She tossed the twisted vambrace into the water. Through narrowed eyelids, she saw the black smoke clinging to her forearm, twisting and coiling like worms, crushing her; her bone felt ready to snap. The fumes began to race toward her chest, cracking her scale armor, crawling along her skin.

Tears of pain in her eyes, Koyee leaped off the boat. She crashed into the icy water, slapping at the tendrils of dark magic.

The curse left her with a hiss like a torch dunked into a bucket.

Just her face above the water, Koyee sputtered for air, eyes rolling back.

"Tor—" she began.

She couldn't move her arm.

She sank.

Blackness flowed across her, and her hair floated around her, and she was sinking—sinking into the sea, away from Torin,

Empires of Moth

away from hope, but at least the pain was gone now. She could see beads of starlight in the water above.

A hand reached down through the water.

Fingers closed around her wrist.

She swallowed water as she was tugged up. Her head breached the surface, and she coughed, gasping for breath. A second hand reached under her arm, and Torin pulled her back into the boat. She collapsed onto the floor, coughing out water.

Trembling, she sat up. She bit her lip so hard she tasted blood. She kept oaring. When she glanced at her arm, she winced. Black welts coiled around her flesh like a snake, oozing blood. She looked away.

They rowed on through the darkness. The stars shone above and the waters calmed. Blackness spread all around. When Koyee dared to look over her shoulder, see saw the city of Sinyong far behind. It was rising in flames. The screams of the dying rolled across the water.

"We made it," Torin finally whispered. "We made it out alive." He rummaged through the darkness and lit one of their lanterns. "Damn! We lost half our food into the river. But we still have the fishing gear. I—Koyee? Are you all right?"

She was shaking, tears on her cheeks. Her arm would not stop throbbing, and she felt it inside her—something dark, twisting, coiling through her veins, the smoke of magic, a worm seeking her heart.

"I'm fine," she whispered. "Torin . . . I'm fine. Can we stop rowing for a bit? Can you hold me?"

She had barely finished her sentence when he pulled her into an embrace. She held him with her right arm; the left tingled at her side, feeling too heavy. She laid her head against his shoulder, and he stroked her hair for a long time, whispering into her ear. She closed her eyes, shivering against him.

183

* * * * *

He stood outside the ruins of his victory. A moon had turned
since he had killed his king, slain the demons, and crushed their
lair, but the stench of burning flesh still clung to his robes and
filled his nostrils. The ruins of Pahmey still smoldered, a sun upon
the earth, a beacon of his glory in the vanishing darkness.

"The sun rises on the east!" he shouted from the hilltop,
sitting astride a white stallion. The wind whipped his yellow robes.
"The light of Timandra sears the demons of the night."

They mustered before him, the hosts of light, the greatest
army the world had known. All eight sunlit kingdoms gathered
upon the plains, the fires of their conquest blazing behind them.
Thousands of banners rose, revealing the beasts of their realms—
ravens, bears, scorpions, tigers, and more, all the tribes of
Timandra joined as one. Above them all, Ferius raised his own
banner—the sunburst of Sailith, a sigil to bind all others, a symbol
of his dominion. He was no longer a man of Arden—Arden was
but a kingdom of mortals, an invention of petty men. He was the
light of Sailith, an eternal flame. He was domination.

"We will cover the night with light!" he called out, hands
raised. Around him upon the hill stood his bloodsuns, warriors of
Sailith, their armor red, their breastplates blazing with golden suns
like external hearts of light. "We march to the wretched lair the
savages call Yintao. The demons call it the greatest city of the
night. I call it their graveyard!"

Bellow the hill, the multitudes cheered. Men raised swords,
spears, and hammers. Beasts roared—bears of the north, horses
of the plains, camels of the deserts, tigers of the rainforests, and
elephants of the southern isles. Chariots gleamed in the torchlight.
Siege towers and trebuchets rose like a city of iron and wood.
Warriors from across Timandra banged weapons against steel and
cried for sunlight—northerners wearing iron over fur, their beards

Empires of Moth

wild; plainsmen in plate armor stride horses; jungle dwellers in tiger pelts, spears in hand; desert warriors in robes, their blades curved; southern soldiers in armor of beads and shells, their elephants' tusks gilded and jeweled. From across the day they had gathered under his light; they would fight as one. Half a million strong, they sprawled across the dark plains, the mightiest army to have ever mustered.

"The old kings cared for thrones," Ferius hissed into the wind, his words too soft for any to hear. "I care only for annihilation."

He grinned and licked his teeth. His father, a weak worm, had bedded one of the Elorian savages. The dirty blood of the night flowed through Ferius's veins.

"But when all the night burns, my blood will be purified. When the shame of Eloria dies, so will my own impurity." His grin widened, hurting his cheeks. "I slew you, my sinful father. And I will slay all the demons that you loved." He inhaled deeply, nostrils flaring, savoring the scents of the smoldering city. He shouted for all to hear. "To the east! To war! To the blood of the night!"

His stallion reared, kicking the air. Ferius wheeled the horse around, grabbed the lantern that hung from his saddle, and raised the light. Ahead in the east, the road stretched through the darkness. Ferius spurred his mount, and the courser burst into a gallop. The wind shrieked. Ferius leaned forward in the saddle, racing into the shadows.

"You wait there too, Koyee." He licked his chops, imagining the taste of her blood. "My half-sister. You will be the only one left alive, my little savage. You will be the one to suffer most."

Behind him, his army chanted and shouted for victory. Hooves thudded. Elephants trumpeted and tigers roared. Horns blew and drums beat and endless voices rose in song.

185

"Death to Elorians!" they sang. "Sunlight rises!"

Like the fabled dawn of old, the hosts of sunlight spread across the darkness.

Empires of Moth

CHAPTER SEVENTEEN
SAGE'S ROAD

"Hem! Damn it, Hem, keep up." Riding ahead upon a silver nightwolf, Bailey gestured to him. "You're lagging behind."

Hem whimpered and dug his heels into his own wolf, but the poor beast only lumbered on slowly. He was now among the last stragglers of the pack. Twenty thousand men, women, and children rode ahead upon their nightwolves, heading east along the road toward the distant capital. Here at the back lingered the omegas—the elderly, the lame, and him. With a grumble, he goaded his poor mount again.

"Come on, boy. A little faster."

The wolf—a shaggy old thing called Zan—mewled.

"It's not my fault!" Hem cried out to Bailey. "They gave me the slowest wolf."

Riding several yards ahead, Bailey looked over her shoulder at him and rolled her eyes. "Your wolf is just as good as mine. I could have ridden at the vanguard if I wasn't always hanging behind here to wait for you. Come *on*!"

Hem gulped. It wasn't fair! Bailey's wolf was slim, silvery, and young, a noble female named Ayka, her fur bright and her eyes like molten gold. Poor Zan, meanwhile, was grizzled, scarred, and missing a fang. Not only did Bailey have a proper wolf, she looked a proper rider too. The pack had dressed her like one of their own. She now wore armor of scales over a white silken tunic. A wolf's helm topped her head, its visor lined with steel teeth. She still bore her old sword, the doubled-edged blade of a Timandrian,

187

but otherwise she looked to Hem like any of the Elorian riders ahead.

Hem himself wore his old woolen tunic, the same one he'd left Fairwool-by-Night with. The pack had no other riders his size; no armor would fit him. It was bad enough being larger than everyone else and riding the worst wolf; without proper attire, he stood out like a frog in a bowl of bread rolls.

"Bailey, please," he said. "Can we switch wolves?"

She groaned. "Hem! I swear. If you don't hurry up, I will clobber you to bits. The Timandrian army chases us, and if you can't keep up with everyone else, maybe you should just go join the Sailith monks. You won't have to ride any wolves then."

Hem lowered his gaze, blinking furiously. "It's not fair," he whispered, but his voice was too soft for anyone to hear.

Being here with Bailey was awful. Just awful. They had been traveling along Sage's Road for an entire month now—perhaps the worst month of his life—and they were barely halfway to the capital. The Elorian riders only gaped at or ignored him. Only Bailey talked to him, and when she did, her words were scornful.

I miss home, Hem thought, eyes stinging and nose sniffling. *I miss Cam and Torin. When Bailey would yell at all of us together, it wasn't so bad. But now it's only me here to soak up her anger.*

"That's *it*, Hem!" Bailey said, face twisted in disgust. "You're just sniffling like a pup. Man up! I'm riding ahead to be near Okado. Catch up when you learn how to ride."

Shaking her head sadly, she spurred her wolf. The silver beast burst into a run, racing between thousands of other nightwolves and disappearing into the crowd.

"Fine, go to your Okado!" Hem shouted after her. "Forget your friend, why don't you? I've only known you all my life."

At least, he had meant to shout those words. In actuality, they came out barely a whisper; he doubted even his wolf heard him.

Empires of Moth

Hem sighed, reached down from the saddle, and patted the animal's fluffy flank. "At least you're still my friend."

The wolf twisted his head around and licked Hem's fingers. It warmed Hem's heart until he noticed that the movement caused the wolf to walk in circles.

"No, boy, no! Forward." Hem pointed ahead at the pack, which was moving farther away. "Go!"

As the poor beast resumed trudging forward, Hem gazed around him at Sage's Road. The highway stretched eastward across the Qaelish Empire; the riders called it the longest road in all Eloria. Most of the way was unpaved—here the road was nothing but milestones spread across dark, lifeless plains. Some hourglass turns, the road was smooth and flat, coiling around hills and through rocky fields. They had passed several villages along those stretches, humble communities built around wells and caves. Most of the time they simply traveled through hilly darkness, and there was nothing for Hem to see but the stars.

Snorts rose behind him.

Hem turned and sucked in his breath.

Another scout was returning from the west. This Elorian wore no armor; he rode bare-chested and barebacked for speed. His wolf panted, eyes narrowed as his paws raced across the plains. With a gust that fluttered Hem's hair, the wolf raced by him and toward the vanguard of the pack.

Hem gulped. He hated when scouts returned from the west. Every time they did, they spoke dire news. The last rider had reported a huge host—hundreds of thousands strong—heading east along the road behind them. They bore the raven flags of Arden, but many other sigils too. Burly men astride bears rode there, dark wizards who could snap bones from afar, and armies bearing the sigils of strange animals the Elorians did not recognize.

189

"All the kingdoms of Timandra are marching behind us," Hem said and shuddered. "How can we stop them?"

He wished they were in Yintao already. The riders said that Yintao, capital of Qaelin, had high walls and many soldiers. Perhaps Hem would feel safer there. He wouldn't have to ride his wolf any longer. And maybe even Bailey, secure behind the walls, would calm down and treat him kindly. The road to Yintao still stretched for many miles—it would take another month to reach that city—and Hem wondered if he'd die of fright and loneliness by then.

His joints were aching and his belly rumbling when horns blared, calling to set camp. Hem breathed out a shaky breath of relief. Riding was painful, and it was often a whole hourglass turn between their times of rest. The riders ahead halted, dismounted, and began to unpack their supplies. Tents rose and men lit braziers. Soon the smells of roasting meats and mushrooms filled the camp. Riders sat down with their families to eat, pray, and sleep.

Hem found a flat boulder for himself. He dismounted his wolf and sat down with a groan. He wanted to find Bailey and share a meal with her but decided against it. These past few turns, it seemed Bailey only wanted to spend time with Okado; the two could talk for hours about wars and battles and other things that scared Hem. Right now he preferred being alone. Being lonely wasn't much fun, but it was better than sitting next to Bailey and Okado and feeling ignored.

He looked around him. Thousands of Elorians spread across the field, talking with their families and friends, eating from the cooking meat. Some were warriors of the pack, clad in steel, weapons across their backs. Others were children, nursing mothers, and elders; they wore only furs and leathers. Hem felt too shy to approach any of the campfires; whenever he had tried to join a group, he ended up stammering and forgetting most of

Empires of Moth

the Qaelish he'd learned. Instead, he reached into his pack and rummaged around for his own food.

He produced salted sausages, a wheel of cheese, a few limes, a pack of crackers, and a jar of figs—Timandrian goods that ships would regularly bring into Pahmey before the monks had destroyed the city. Hem didn't have much of the stuff left, and once it was gone, it would be Elorian food or starving. He was determined to enjoy his last few meals of home. He was biting into his first fig when he saw her, lost his breath, and nearly choked.

"It's her," he whispered, juice dripping down his chin.

He had seen the omega girl—the reason he had joined this exodus in the first place—only twice since leaving the crater, always at a distance. He had almost approached both times, but had felt too shy. Now she was bustling about only a few yards away, carrying a pile of bowls and mugs. As always, her snowy hair lay in tangles across her face, and holes filled her fur tunic.

And as before, her fellow riders—the same old group— were tormenting her.

"Here, omega!" called one, the tall woman from before. "Come here, dog. Serve me my meal."

As the girl rushed toward the woman, a man from behind cried out, "How dare you serve her first? You know I outrank her. Come, omega! Come here before I lash you."

The poor girl rushed from rider to rider, not knowing who to serve first. Drops of stew flew from the bowls she carried, only enraging her tormentors further. One woman rose to her feet, drew her sword, and lashed the poor girl across the legs with the back of her blade.

Hem had seen enough. An enraged cry left his throat with bits of half-chewed fig, sounding like something between a growl and a yelp. He rose to his feet, leaving his meal upon the boulder, and rushed toward the omega.

191

"Leave her alone!" he said, turning from one rider to another. "She's not your slave. Come get your food if you like, but don't force her to race around like . . . like . . ."

He gulped. In his initial burst of rage, courage had come easily enough. Now, with all eyes upon him, Hem felt his fear rise. The words would no longer come. A hundred riders or more stared at him—the five or six tormentors and many riders behind them. They were all silent, staring incredulously.

At his side, the omega—hair still hiding her face—gave a squeak. She rushed from rider to rider, quickly setting down her bowls of stew. The riders were too busy gaping at Hem to torment her. With another squeak, the young woman raced away into the shadows.

Hem bit his lip, wiped sweat off his brow, and hurried back toward his boulder. He quickly snatched his food, stuffed it back into his pack, and lolloped after the omega. Soon she disappeared into the crowd. Hem wanted to call her name but didn't know it. Many riders crowded around him, and most Elorians—with their pale skin, large eyes, and white hair—looked the same to him.

"Omega!" he called out, wishing he knew her true name, feeling rather silly as soon as the word left his mouth.

Finally he caught a glimpse of her ahead. With a flutter of hair and fur, she disappeared behind a few tall boulders.

Sweat on his brow, his heart pounding, Hem lumbered after her. He was panting when he made it around the boulders, and as his pack bounced upon his back, he was sure he'd smashed every cracker inside.

He saw the omega there. She stood beside a short, frail nightwolf that looked in even worse condition than Hem's; it seemed to badly need a good meal. The young woman was hugging the animal and whispering into its ear.

"I . . ." Hem panted and wiped his brow. "I'm sorry, I didn't mean to scare you off."

192

Empires of Moth

The young woman looked at him, her hair falling back from her face. For the first time, Hem got a good look at her.

He lost his breath.

She was beautiful.

Maybe not beautiful like Bailey, who had full lips and golden hair, and not beautiful like Suntai, who had those wise indigo eyes and high cheekbones. This young woman looked mousy; her nose was thin and upturned, her mouth was very small, and her eyes were close-set and blinked too much. But Hem thought her beautiful nonetheless, a special kind of beauty he suspected others wouldn't appreciate, but a beauty that pierced his heart and sent it galloping.

"You're not scary," the young woman said, her voice barely more than a whisper. "The others are. But you're not. At least, not that I can tell. My eyesight isn't very good, but you seem friendly."

Hem couldn't help but smile—a smile he suspected looked too big and goofy. He took another step toward her.

"I'm Hemstad Baker. Most people just call me Hem. What's your name?"

She blinked several times as if trying to bring him into focus. "My name is Kira. And this is my wolf, Yuan. She is very old and her eyesight is bad too." Kira kissed the wolf. "We're both omegas—me among the riders, she among the nightwolves. She's my only friend."

Hem thought he knew something about having few friends. "Well, maybe I can be your friend." He reached into his pack and pulled out the crackers; they had indeed crumbled. "Would you like something to eat? Yuan can have some too. I also have figs and other food from Timandra."

Kira gasped and took a step back. "You . . . you are from Timandra?" She began to shiver.

Hem reached out to her. "Don't be scared! Don't run again. Please. I thought . . . I thought you saw. I mean, my hair is dark

193

and my skin isn't pale. I look nothing like an Elorian. I— oh, your eyesight. I'm sorry. I didn't realize you couldn't see me that well. Can I step a little closer and maybe you'll get a better look?"

She shuddered but nodded. Hem stepped closer until they stood only a foot apart. She looked up at him, barely a third his size, her head no taller than his shoulders. Slowly a smile trembled across her lips, and she reached up to touch his cheek.

"I think you're handsome," she said.

Joy burst through Hem like figs inside his mouth. Handsome! No woman had ever called him handsome before. Back in Timandra, most women mocked him whenever he approached; even his mother would always call him a clumsy ox. He felt his cheeks flush, and his tongue felt too heavy for words. Unable to speak, he reached into his pack and began pulling out more food.

"Here, let's eat," he said.

She smiled and nodded. "Okay. Can we sit down first?"

He nodded. "Okay."

They sat down cross-legged, and Hem set out a spread. He'd been hoarding these treats from home, knowing they wouldn't last long, but couldn't bear to see Kira and her wolf go hungry—both looked far too thin.

"These are figs," Hem said, pointing at the fruit. "And these are pork sausages. I don't think you have pork here in the night. And oh! This is a jar of strawberry jam; it's good on the crackers, see?"

As he kept pointing at item after item, talking faster and faster, Kira simply looked at him and smiled silently. It felt good to have somebody just listen. Back home, whenever he started discussing food, Bailey would groan, Cam would mock his girth, and even Torin wouldn't pay attention. When Bailey spoke of her adventures in the countryside or Torin talked about his gardens, that was all fine, but they never paid attention to the things Hem

Empires of Moth

loved. Having Kira sit here beside him, leaning gently in his direction, listening raptly and smiling at him . . . well, that felt even better than being back in the tavern at Fairwool-by-Night. Maybe this journey wasn't so bad after all.

He was about to explain about honey, and he was working at unscrewing the jar, when the snorts sounded behind him.

Kira saw them first, gasped, and scuttled several feet back on her bottom. Hem turned, saw the girl's tormentors, and the food turned to ash in his mouth.

"We didn't say you could leave," said one of the group, a broad man with large blue eyes. "Come back here, omega, and clean our bowls." He raised a leather strap. "Now! Or I'll beat you and your wolf, you dirty little cockroach."

Kira only cowered, raising her arms over her face. The man stepped forward and brought the lash down. Leather cracked against flesh.

Hem placed his jar of honey down.

He rose to his feet.

Very calmly, he walked toward the man and tapped him on the shoulder.

"What do you want, whale?" the man said with a sneer.

Hem's fist drove into the rider's face.

The man collapsed, squealing and clutching his face. Blood spurted between his fingers. Several of his friends rushed forth, cursing and shouting. Hem spun toward them, fists raised.

"Stand back!" he shouted, hating that his voice sounded so high-pitched, that his knees shook. "Stand back or I'll punch you too. I'm bigger than you and can beat you all." He punched the air a few times. "Leave Kira alone."

Kira leaped to her feet at his side. She rushed toward the man who'd whipped her and kicked him, driving her foot into his belly. The man doubled over and Kira kicked him again, then froze, covered her mouth, and fled behind her wolf.

195

Hem stood with fists raised. His knees shook but he wouldn't back down. For an instant, he was sure the group would attack him, and he was prepared to die defending the woman he loved—and at that moment, Hemstad Baker did love her, and he felt rather like a hero from the old stories Bailey would tell in the tavern, a noble knight defending a damsel.

He punched the air again, and the fallen man—blood leaking from his nose—ran away, calling for his friends to follow. Spitting Hem's way, the villains turned to leave. They vanished into the crowd of riders and wolves.

Hem collapsed onto the ground.

His heart beat madly, threatening to burst from his chest, and his hands wouldn't stop shaking.

"Moldy bread rolls, that was a close one." He turned toward Kira. "Are you all right? Did he hurt you badly?"

Kira shook her head, her hair falling over her face again. She twisted her toes, bit her lip, then stepped toward him. Blushing, she leaned down, kissed his cheek, then squeaked in fright. With a few leaps, she fled into the shadows.

That kiss sent more trembles, excitement, and terror into Hem's heart than the fight. He fell onto his back, stretched out his arms, and stared up at the stars. A grin spread across his face. At that moment, Hemstad Baker loved the night more than all the jars of honey and mugs of ale in the world.

* * * * *

She stood in the camp, sweat dampening her hair, and swiped her sword again and again. With every swing, she grunted and imagined the blade tearing into Ferius.

"I already slew several of your monks with this blade, Ferius," she said and swung again; the blade whistled through the air. "You're next on its list."

Empires of Moth

Her arms were tired and sweat soaked her brow, but she kept swinging. She vowed to train with her blade every time the Chanku Pack set camp. When she met Ferius again—and she knew the monk was following them—she would be ready.

"Torin only wounded you." Bailey growled as she sliced the air. "I'm not as friendly."

She wore Chanku armor—scales over a silk tunic, vambraces and greaves, and a wolf's head helm. She had tossed her old armor into the Inaro River when fleeing on the boat, hoping to lighten the load, and only now she realized how important that move had been. She had left the old Bailey to drown in those waters. The girl she had been—a naive child of sunlight—was as gone as that steel. Here she was a warrior of the night.

"You swing well." The voice rose behind her. "You will be a warrior yet."

Braids swinging, Bailey spun around to see Okado watching her. She sneered at him, blade raised, and blinked sweat out of her eyes.

"I am a warrior already. I slew many enemies with this blade."

Okado only smiled, the smile of a carpenter seeing the whittling of a child. Bailey fumed. She had spent her life among the boys of Fairwool-by-Night, a group of bakers and shepherds and gardeners. She had led them easily enough, always the tallest, strongest, and bravest among them. Yet Okado would not be as easy to impress. He stood taller than her, his shoulders wide, his face exuding relaxed confidence. He wore armor similar to hers, and two katanas hung from his belt. Something about his large eyes, thin lips, and good looks—damn it, Bailey had to admit that was part of it—unnerved her.

197

"Your sword is crude." He sounded more amused than scolding. "A hunk of metal with no elegance or speed. You swing it as if you're hacking meat, not battling a warrior."

She sliced the air. Her blade swung only inches away from him, but he didn't flinch.

"This blade has shed the blood of Sailith," she said. "Its thirst is not yet quenched. I'm as much a warrior as you, rider."

Okado's smile widened. He unhooked one katana from his belt. He tossed her the sheathed blade. She caught it in one hand and glared at him.

"A katana is the blade of a warrior." He drew his second sword, and the moonlight gleamed upon the curved blade. "This is the weapon of an artist, a weapon of water, wind, and spirits."

Bailey spat, holding both swords. "Your katanas are puny; weapons for girls. My doubled-edged longsword is longer, wider, and heavier. It has twice the steel for shedding twice the blood."

"A bluefeather is larger than a nighthawk, yet none would dispute that the smaller bird is mightier. Place down your sunlit blade. Draw the weapon of the night. I will teach you to become a swordswoman."

Rage exploded through Bailey, shooting fire through her limbs. She roared. How dare he insult her sword? How dare he imply she was a child? She tossed his katana aside; it flew toward a group of riders, scattering them. She raised her old longsword, a blade larger than his.

"Fight me." She spat. "My blade against yours. We both wear armor. Fight me!"

Not waiting for a reply, she charged toward him, longsword swinging.

Okado sidestepped and raised his katana. The blades clashed together.

Shouting, Bailey stepped back and lashed her sword again. The katana once more blocked the blow and then swung toward

Empires of Moth

her. The blade drove across her armor, showering scales. The bits of steel flew through the air.

"I could have cut your flesh," Okado said. "I—"

She howled and lunged toward him, blade swinging down. He parried one blow, but Bailey attacked with fury, slamming her sword again and again. Finally one blow crashed against his armor. It did nothing but dent a scale.

Okado reached out, grabbed her wrist, and twisted.

She screamed; it felt like he'd snap her bone. Her longsword clanged to the ground.

"You could have killed me," he said, twisting her wrist, staring at her sternly.

She yowled, struggling to free herself but only bending her wrist further. "You . . . taunted me. That would qualify as suicide."

He stared at her a moment longer, eyes wide, then burst into laughter. He kicked her fallen longsword aside and released her wrist.

"Clumsy with the sword," he said, "yet brave like a wolf."

She shook her wrist, wincing at the pain. She feigned a smile. "And I bite like one too."

Before her words could sink in, she leaped onto him—just as she'd leap onto Torin back at home before wrestling him to the ground. Okado grunted in surprise. He did not fall down like Torin always had, but he reacted too slowly. Bailey grabbed his arm and bit down hard, driving her teeth into his wrist. He cursed and his fingers uncurled. His sword too clanged to the ground. Bailey gave another shove, tangling her leg between his—one of the moves she'd learned back with the boys at home.

This time Okado fell.

His breath left his lungs. He groaned and tried to shove her off, but Bailey grew up wrestling boys in the fields of Fairwool-by-Night. She drove her knee into his belly and pinned him down.

199

Lying on his back, Bailey atop him, he stared up with wide eyes.

"Is this how you Timandrians fight?" he asked.

Her face an inch from his, she gave him a crooked smile. "This is how farm girls fight."

"I tried to show you how to fight with elegance, with grace, with intelligence," he said.

She nodded. "Aye. And you lost."

As he stared up at her, their bodies pressed together, Bailey realized that she'd only need to lean down another two inches— she could almost do it accidentally!—for their lips to touch. She wondered what it would be like to kiss him . . . the way she had kissed Torin. Kissing Torin had been a thing of jealousy, and it had sent no warmth through her body; it had felt more like patting a beloved dog. But Okado . . . with him, she thought that it would feel different. Strange. Intoxicating. Somehow wrong and right at the same time.

"Get off me," he said.

She shook her head. "I defeated you in battle. By the laws of your people, I rule your pack now." She winked. "Maybe I will banish you into the wilderness. Maybe I will make you an omega. Or maybe . . . maybe I will forget your lessons, and you will forget that you thought me weak."

She patted his cheek, leaped off him, and lifted her fallen sword. As she walked away, she felt his eyes on her back, and a thin smile stretched across her lips.

Around her, the riders were gathering their supplies and mounting their wolves. Bailey joined them, her old sword hanging from her belt. The journey east to Yintao continued.

Empires of Moth

CHAPTER EIGHTEEN
THE HALL OF THE DARK EMPRESS

She stood at the prow, biting her lip and trying to ignore the stinging on her arm.

The sea surrounded them, a blackness spreading into the horizons, rising and falling, whispering. Clouds hid the stars. For many turns, they had sailed through this void, cold and alone, their lantern a single light in the night. Koyee felt like a fly trapped in the stomach of some great, dark creature, forever floating and swimming in circles, forever imprisoned in the beast.

The boat creaked and swayed. She had patched its cracks with clay, but some water always found its way in. Torin came to stand beside her, holding a half-eaten fish.

"How do you feel?" he said softly. "Does it still hurt? Do you want to eat some—"

She spun toward him, lips peeling back. "I told you I'm fine!" She shoved the fish away. "And I told you: I'm not hungry."

He recoiled, pain in his eyes. That only infuriated Koyee further. "I'm sorry—" he began.

"Stop apologizing!" She glared. "Why do you always apologize? What kind of man are you? Be a little stronger, damn it."

His eyes narrowed and his mouth closed, forming a small line. He turned away and trudged to the stern, yet it was only a few feet away. He was always only a few feet away.

"This damn boat is too small," she muttered and tugged her hair. "It's too damn small! You're always so near me. Damn!"

He did not reply, only sat there, and Koyee wanted to pummel him. Why wouldn't he fight back, stand up to her like a man? Why wouldn't he just leap overboard and drown? She hated him. She hated his small, mismatched eyes, and his breath always on her shoulder, and—

She groaned, sat down, and clenched her fists. She forced herself to take deep breaths, to close her eyes, to clear her mind. She had spent a moon with him upon this boat, maybe longer— and for the past few turns, it had been here at sea, nothing but blackness around them. Her arm had not stopped burning since the battle at Sinyong upon the southern Qaelish coast, and as much as the oppression of this tiny boat, the pain constantly nettled her, endless hooks driving into her flesh. Whenever she looked at her arm, the wound seemed worse, the welts ticker and darker, wrapping around her like a snake. After a while she had stopped looking, keeping the wound always under her sleeve. Even Eelani, her dearest companion, dared not approach her most turns; Koyee only rarely felt the warmth of her shoulder spirit.

It will be better once we reach Ilar, she thought, eyes stinging. *They'll have healers for my arm. Eelani will want to sit on my shoulder again. And maybe, once I can breathe away from him for a while, I can love Torin again.*

That thought surprised her. Love Torin again? Had she ever loved him? She turned around and looked at him. He sat with his back to her, staring into the sea, his shoulders pushed inward. Koyee sighed. The foolish, silly boy.

She stood up, tottered across the boat, and knelt behind him. She wrapped her arms around him and kissed his ear.

"I'm sorry," she whispered. "I've spent too long in this boat, and my arm still hurts, and I'm sorry." She closed her eyes and squeezed him, remembering that night he had carried her to The

Empires of Moth

Green Geode, the night her city had fallen. "I love you, Torin Greenmoat. You know that, right?"

He turned toward her. She was about to kiss his cheek, to undress him, to make love to him to forget the pain and darkness, but his eyes widened. He gasped.

She pulled back. "Are my words so shocking to you?"

So there it was—she had confessed her love, and he would not return it, would not say he loved her too, only gasp. She felt her rage flare anew, and she was about to slap him, and then she saw the light in his eyes.

He pointed over her shoulder. "Behind you, Koyee. In the south. Lights."

She spun around and exhaled slowly. A tremble seized her. Though she had spent so long on this boat, dreaming of finally reaching this place, now those distant lights shot fear through her, and her arm stung with new vigor.

"Ilar," she whispered.

The lights were still distant, a mere line along the horizon— the northern coast of a southern empire. Koyee gripped her sword. Her father's stories returned to her. He had fought with this sword upon this coast. The Qaelish Empire had clashed against these southern warriors; her father had borne the scars until his last breath. He had spoken to Koyee of killers in black armor, of dark beasts greater than nightwolves, of a people warlike and cruel who drank blood from the skulls of their enemies. Ilar—the land that had tormented Qaelin for many generations, the land of blood and steel . . . the land that could now save all Eloria from daylight.

"We're here," Torin said. "Thank Idar, we're here."

She turned to look at him and held his arm. "Be careful in this land, Torin. Keep your sword loose in your scabbard. Remember all the words I taught you. And stay near me. Whatever happens, stay near me. The Ilari hold no love for

203

Qaelish folk, but I'm still a fellow Elorian; they might slay *you* on sight."

He cleared his throat. "Blimey, aren't you a cheery one." He nodded. "I've been to a few dangerous places this past year. I know how to watch over myself."

"Not here." She shook her head. "Not in Ilar. We sail toward the darkest, most dangerous corner of the night. They say the world used to turn, Torin, that day would follow night in an endless dance. If that's true, the place we sail to is midnight."

They rowed the rest of the way in silence.

With every mile, more details emerged. The lights belonged to torches, Koyee saw. Thousands burned upon black walls that lined the coast. The firelight glinted on armor; soldiers manned the battlements, their steel as dark as the walls. Behind them rose towers, not thin and glowing like the towers of Pahmey, but cruel and jagged like broken, blackened femurs rising from a tar pit. Here lurked Asharo, the great port of the Ilari Empire, a factory for warships and warriors who had so many times tormented the Qaelish coast. Distant booms rose from the city—the drums of war. Men shouted and metal clanged.

"Does a battle rage here too?" Torin asked, leaning forward and squinting.

Koyee narrowed her eyes, staring ahead as the city grew closer; she could see better in the darkness than him. "I see no cannon fire, no arrows flying, and the guards upon the walls stand still." She shook her head. "No, there is no battle. But I don't like the sound of those drums or the screaming. Hope may lie here, but death too."

"Well, I'm not turning back now." Torin smiled wanly. "After a month with you in a boat, I could use a rest in a nightmarish city of pain like this."

She rolled her eyes then winced as fire shot through her arm. She ground her teeth, pushing the pain down, ignoring the

Empires of Moth

thought that had been rattling through her mind since the battle: that her arm was getting worse, that an infection was crawling up to her shoulder and coiling onto her chest. For now, she had no time to contemplate her wound; the night was dying and she had to save it before she died too.

As they rowed closer, Koyee saw a port nestled between two jagged breakwaters. She narrowed her eyes. Several ships in the port were listing, and a few were sunken down to the tips of their masts. Holes gaped open in the city walls behind the docks, and a guard tower lay fallen upon the shore. The city gates were smashed, and many guards stood before them.

"A battle was fought here," she said. "And not long ago. I can still smell the fire and blood. Yet the city still stands. The banners of Ilar still fly."

She pointed at those banners now. The streamers fluttered from the remaining guard towers, sporting the red flame of Ilar. *The flame and moonstar must join*, she thought, gazing upon that sigil. *Ilar and Qaelin—no longer enemies but fighting together for the night.*

"A flame sigil?" Torin asked, staring at the banners. "A flame emits light and we're in Eloria."

She gave him a wry smile. "Have you learned nothing in the night? Fire is life in the darkness. And for the Ilari, fire also means the burning death of their enemies."

They rowed toward the port. The ships of Ilar were different from the junks of Qaelin—these vessels were larger, lined with many oars, floating fortresses with several tiers of decks. Their hulls were painted black and red, and iron figureheads, shaped of dragons, jutted out from their prows. The red flame danced upon their black sails. As the *Water Spider* entered the port, navigating between the breakwaters, Koyee gasped. Torin covered his mouth and emitted a strangled sound.

"Oh bloody Idar's vomit," he said.

205

Koyee winced, staring ahead. "They're slaves," she whispered. "Slaves of war."

Outside the city walls, a hundred or more Timandrians toiled upon the sand. They were stripped naked even in the cold of night, and iron collars encircled their necks. Ilari soldiers stood as masters, whips in hand, landing blows upon the Timandrians' backs. At first, Koyee thought the prisoners were building a hill of sand. When she rowed closer and understood their task, she nearly gagged.

The Timandrian prisoners, naked and chained, were piling up a hill of bodies.

"You're lucky you're not with your brothers!" one Ilari soldier shouted and laughed. A tall man in black plate armor, he lashed his whip, bloodying the back of a Timandrian. "Go on, faster, you sunlit worm. Stack up the bodies of your slain brothers. Cold, are you? They'll burn soon and warm you." He cracked his whip again, hitting a second man. "Be thankful we don't burn you with them."

Koyee had to look away, wincing. Torin grimaced and covered his face.

"Koyee, I don't like this," he said. "They're . . . torturing Timandrians."

She nodded. "Prisoners of war. Look at the sunken ships. I see banners of Timandra."

Torin nodded, looking at the banners that still hung from sinking masts. "A scorpion for Eseer—desert warriors. The elephant is Sania, a southern island, and the crocodile is Daenor from the western coast of Dayside."

Koyee tugged the rudder of the *Water Spider*, guiding the boat around one of the sunken ships. They moved closer toward the smashed gates.

"A army of three Timandrian kingdoms attacked," she said. "They smashed the gates and shattered a tower and nearly broke the walls, but they lost this battle." She looked back at the beach where the chained prisoners toiled. "Now they stack up their own dead for burning."

Torin loosened his collar, his face pale in the lamplight. "I don't think they like Timandrians much in this place. I know I said I wanted to visit, but . . . maybe I should just wait in the boat."

Koyee grabbed a rope from the floor. She raised it and smiled crookedly at Torin. "You're still coming with me. I'm not leaving you alone anywhere in this place. If they catch you, you'll be stacking bodies with the rest of them." She began to form a knot. "So long as we're in Ilar, you're my prisoner of war."

When she slung the rope around his wrists, he gasped and tugged himself free. "Koyee! You're not going to . . . to tie me up and drag me around like your dog, are you?"

She glared, hands on her hips. "Of course not. I'm going to tie you up and drag you around like my *slave*. Torin, look around you." She gestured at the Ilari soldiers on the coast; they were busy whipping more prisoners. "Do you think the Ilari will understand that you're a renegade, that you're here to help them fight? Of course not. But they understand slaves. They understand brutality. So I'll be a little brutal to you here." She grinned and mussed his hair. "It'll just be an act . . . mostly."

He groaned, but he dutifully let her tie his wrists.

They navigated around several more ships—some sinking ruins, others the proud ships of the Ilari fleet. A chorus of whips and screams followed them toward the docks outside the smashed gates. Guards stood upon flagstones, staring at them, hands on their bows and hilts.

Koyee moored, secured her boat with what roped remained, and made a show of dragging Torin onto the docks.

"Move, maggot!" she shouted at him. "Damn it, move or I'll toss you into that pile of bodies on the beach."

Torin winced, bit his lip, and climbed out of the boat. Koyee began to walk toward the gates, not sparing him another glance. She held the rope in her left hand; it ran several feet and connected to Torin's wrists. She tugged him toward the shattered gates, clad in her armor, her katana hanging from her belt. Torin's armor and sword remained hidden upon their boat. After so long at sea, her legs wobbled and her head spun, and her arm still blazed, but she forced herself to march onward.

"Faster, worm!" she shouted over her shoulder.

The soldiers at the gates—there were about fifty—stared at her. Koyee raised her chin and stared back, refusing to slow down or look away. She had to display nothing but cruel strength here. It was the language the Ilari spoke, and she would speak it fluently. While she wore the silvery scales of her empire, these soldiers donned bulky armor of black, lacquered plates engraved with red runes. Jagged horns rose from their flaring helms; the visors were pulled down, shaped as snarling faces complete with bushy mustaches of fur. Koyee could see only their eyes peering from within—deep, mistrustful eyes that gleamed red in the torchlight. They held bows in their armored hands, and tasseled katanas hung from their belts.

Koyee came to a stop before them. They stood quite a lot taller than her, but Koyee squared her shoulders and raised her chin.

"Soldiers of Ilar! I am Koyee of Qaelin, a princess of the Chanku nobles." She figured that with her brother being the alpha, that was close enough to the truth. "I come to your empress in peace, bearing tidings of the war against sunlight. And I bear this worm." She gave the rope a tug, pulling Torin closer. "This one is a prince of daylight; I will make him scream for the empress."

Torin gave a little squeak, and Koyee shot him a glare.

208

Empires of Moth

The guards stared at her from head to toes, taking in her armor and sword. They stared at Torin, then back at her. Finally a tall man stepped forward; his lacquered armor shone a deep crimson, and his visor was shaped as sneering old face, its mustache and brows bristly, its nose bulbous.

"Timandrians are worms; Qaelish are maggots. You are no better than the hosts of the day."

Koyee growled. "That is not for you to decide, sentry of broken gates. I am an emissary of an empire. I will speak to your mistress. Take me to the empress! If you do not, fight me here, and your empress can thank you for stealing my tidings from her."

Her legs still shook from the journey, her arm burned, and her insides roiled, but she forced herself to stare back forcefully, struggling to sound as strong and noble as her brother.

The guard grunted, then turned and walked through the shattered gates, heading into the city. Koyee took that as an invitation to follow. Tugging Torin behind her, she climbed over bricks and smashed metal, following the guard into Asharo, capital of Ilar.

* * * * *

Koyee did not know if the Timandrians had managed to enter this city, but if they had, they had done it little damage. While outside the walls she had seen fallen bricks, sunken ships, and piles of corpses, the inside of Asharo seemed untouched by war—which, Koyee thought, did not make it any more pleasant than the ruined port.

While Pahmey had been a city of light and color—its roofs tiled green and red, its statues golden and bronzed, its towers a glowing array of greens, blues, and silvers—this city was a painting all in black and red. Black were the cobblestones that formed its twisting roads. Black loomed the buildings along the

209

roadsides—square structures like barracks, their roofs spiky with battlements. Black was the armor of the countless soldiers who patrolled the streets, their helms hiding their faces, their boots thudding. Red shone the sigils on their breastplates, and red fluttered the standards from every roof.

Walking down the boulevard, following the city guard, Koyee at first thought that she was walking among fortresses. Yet some buildings were shops; she could see blades, herbs, and painted pottery in their windows. Others were homes; scrolls hung from their doors, displaying red runes that named the family dwelling within. Yet every building here looked like a castle— shops and homes alike sported crowns of jagged crenellations, and soldiers stood upon every roof, arrows and spears in hand. Guard towers rose at every intersection—some were elaborate pagodas, their bricks black and their roofs crimson, while others were simple minarets holding a single archer. The banners of Ilar draped walls and flew from towers everywhere, hundreds of them—a red flame upon a black field, proud and horrible to behold.

There is almost no distinction here between civilians and soldiers, Koyee thought. *Barely any shade between peace and bloodshed.*

It was a city built for a single purpose: warfare. That both chilled her and kindled hope within her breast.

A growl sounded ahead, and Koyee nearly stopped in her tracks. She drew in breath with a hiss and clutched her sword. Behind her, she heard Torin curse.

"A shadow panther," she whispered.

The beast prowled ahead, crossing the road. Koyee had seen the stray cats that had come upon the Timandrian ships, slinking creatures that lurked in shadows. The creature ahead looked like a black cat the size of a nightwolf. Its eyes gleamed, two golden plates, and its fangs shone. It moved with the grace of wafting smoke. Upon its back rode a soldier, a whip in his hand.

Empires of Moth

Both beast and rider turned to stare at Koyee, and her heart nearly stopped. She was sure the creature would lunge and tear out her neck; its claws were like swords. She was about to draw her own blade when the rider cracked his whip. The panther hissed and bristled, then padded onto another road.

Koyee let out a breath of relief and released her hilt. They kept moving through the city.

They walked for two or three miles, moving up and down the sloping streets. Finally they reached a long, wide road lined with torches in iron sconces. It coiled up a hill like a rotten tongue, leading toward a castle upon the hilltop. A pagoda of black bricks, the castle rose six tiers tall, its roofs tiled blood-red. A great flame burned upon its crest, taller than a man, shrieking in the wind. Koyee had seen the fabled palaces of Pahmey, yet this castle dwarfed them; it was the largest structure she had ever seen, a monument more befitting a god than an empress.

"It looks like a demon's lair," Torin said, walking behind her.

She glared over her shoulder at him. "Hush!"

She gave the rope a tug. Grumbling, he followed silently.

They began to climb the road. Troops lined the roadsides, standing between the torches. Their armor seemed so bulky and heavy—lacquered plates like the shells of beetles—that Koyee wondered how they remained standing. Their helmets, shaped as twisted iron masks, all seemed to leer. Leashed panthers growled at their sides, eyes golden like more torches, fangs bared and black fur bristling.

It was a long climb to the castle. The road alternated between stairs and cobblestones. Koyee's knees ached and her breath burned when they finally reached the gates of Asharo Castle, Hall of Ilar's Dark Empress.

Two panthers framed the gates, clawing the flagstones beneath them. A dozen guards stood between the cats, swords

211

drawn. The gatekeeper who had led Koyee here spoke with them. Koyee expected to be turned aside, ushered into an antechamber for moons of waiting, or even slain on the spot. In Pahmey she had waited for moons to speak to city elders, and here she came seeking an empress. To her surprise, the guards nodded grimly, and the towering doors of the palace—carved of stone and inlaid with golden flame sigils—opened.

As Koyee entered the castle, she thought, *Who would have imagined that a village girl would someday enter the hall of an empress?*

She found herself in a dark chamber full of soldiers, their helmets the twisted masks of mocking spirits. Banners hung from the walls and torches crackled. A mosaic of a chained, beaten man sprawled across the floor; the figure's mouth was open in anguish and arrows and blades tore into his flesh. Living prisoners stood chained to columns, stripped down to their underclothes, the sigils of their Timandrian kingdoms—scorpions, elephants, and crocodiles—etched into their chests with bleeding cuts. Leashed panthers growled at the prisoners, close enough to claw at skin. The smell of blood, burnt flesh, and embers filled the hall.

Koyee took several steps forward, moving through the smoke of the torches and braziers. When she saw the throne of the empress, she gasped and had to struggle not to draw her blade.

"Stars of my home . . ." she said.

A dragon slithered ahead—not a statue like the thousands across Eloria, but a living beast of black scales, red eyes like smelters, and white fangs as long as her sword. The great serpent regarded her, smoke pluming from his mouth. His red beard and mustache crackled, the tips lit with fire, and his grin spoke of hunger for flesh.

"Tianlong," Koyee whispered. "The last dragon of Ilar."

The dragon coiled around a dais like a snake around an egg. Upon the block of stone rose a throne, all jagged black spikes like

Empires of Moth

blades, its rubies glittering like droplets of blood. It seemed to
Koyee more like a torture device than a seat. Upon this hunk of
steel and gems sat Empress Hikari, Mistress of Ilar. She was long-
limbed and powerfully built, a woman not unlike the panthers
who prowled her hall. She wore plate armor, the steel lacquered
black, gleaming with crimson gems and bristly with tassels. A
mane of white hair cascaded across her shoulders, and her eyes
gleamed red, two lanterns in her feline face. A crown of gilded
bones sat atop her head, and steel claws grew from her fingers.

Koyee came to stand before the empress and her dragon.
She knelt, tugging down Torin to kneel behind her.

"Your Highness, Empress Hikari, Mistress of Night!"
Koyee called out. "Tianlong, great beast of fire! I am Koyee, a
daughter of Qaelin. I bring with me a prisoner from our war . . .
and the allegiance of my people."

Of course, Koyee could not speak for all of Qaelin—
perhaps not even for the Chanku Pack, only one of her empire's
peoples. Yet the empress did not need to know that.

Empress Hikari stared down at her, fingering a drawn
katana that lay upon her lap; fresh blood stained the blade. She
slung one leg across the throne's armrest and snickered.

"Qaelin!" said the empress, voice thick with mockery. The
word echoed across her hall, and sneers rose among her guards.
Even Tianlong the dragon snickered, smoke blasting from his
nostrils.

Koyee nodded and rose to her feet. "Qaelin is your ally.
Qaelin too fights against the day. Qaeli—"

"Kneel before me, Qaelish worm!" shrieked the empress.
"Kneel lest my dragon bites off your soft head. Down!"

Stifling a growl, Koyee knelt again. She stared up at the
empress. "You've seen the threat of the day. Let our two empires
fight together. Let—"

213

The empress laughed, the sound of a demon laughing before a meal of man-flesh. "Two empires? Last I heard, the miserable backwater your folk call Qaelin cannot even protect its borders. Tianlong has flown over your darkness, and he saw cities in ruin, soldiers lying torn apart, piles of dead and dying. Qaelin? It is no empire; it is a graveyard for the weak. You could not defeat Ilar with your cowardly assault thirty years ago; now you cannot defeat the day. Yet Ilar still stands strong, proud, and noble." The empress rose to her feet and raised her sword. "We are fire!"

Across the hall, her guards raised their own swords, shouting out the cry. "We are fire!"

Koyee remained kneeling, but she dared to stare at the empress. "Fire? We are *the night*! Those are the words of all Elorians. We are one people. We are—"

The empress howled and sliced the air with her sword. "You will not spew your poison here! Tianlong will enjoy feasting upon you. One people? We share none of your Qaelish blood. The Ilari are strong, proud, and cruel. Your people are weak and decadent, crumbling into shadow." Hikari thrust her sword into a burning torch, then brought the blade to her mouth and licked the bubbling blood. "But our fire will always burn."

Koyee would not remove her eyes from the empress. "I walked outside your city. I saw the ruins of several sunlit ships. I saw a few hundred Timandrians dead, a few hundred more enslaved. Yes, Ilar defeated a small force in a small skirmish." She clenched her fists. "Half a million Timandrians now march to Yintao, capital of Qaelin. If they sack that city, they will turn their eyes south. Ilar will follow. You won one battle—can you defeat the entire horde of sunlight?"

The empress stared down at Koyee—a stare of loathing, of mockery, of bloodlust. She nodded once then left her throne. The dragon coiling around her dais loosened his grip, allowing the

Empires of Moth

empress to walk down a flight of steps. She stepped onto the mosaic and came to stand before Koyee.

"A skirmish?" the empress said softly. "Rise, child. Stand and follow. I will show you the most beautiful thing your eyes have seen . . . before I gouge them out."

The empress spun and began walking to the back of her hall, moving around the throne. Her armor clattered and her boots thumped.

Koyee looked over her shoulder at Torin. He stared back, eyes dark.

I will get you out of here alive, Torin, she swore to him silently. *We will not fail. We cannot.*

She rose to her feet. Dragging Torin with her, she followed the empress. As she walked around the throne, Tianlong the dragon reared above her, chuckling. Smoke blasted between his teeth down onto Koyee, and his saliva dripped. Grimacing, Koyee walked beneath the black dragon, climbed over his tail, and reached the empress at the back of the hall.

A strange light in her eyes, Empress Hikari grabbed a sliding door and pulled.

Firelight flooded the throne room.

"Come, Qaelish worm," said Hikari. "Come see the might of Ilar's flame."

The empress stepped through the doorway and into the red light. Koyee followed, holding Torin's tether. She found herself upon a balcony overlooking a waking nightmare. Her breath died.

A river flowed south of the castle, its waters red with firelight and blood. A dam of stone and steel rose like a fortress. In the shallow waters, thousands of slaves toiled—naked, chained, their backs whipped, their bodies bloodied. Most were Timandrians, beaten into wretches. They hauled metal, clay, and tallow, bustling in the water like flies in blood. Metal ribs rose around them, tall as houses.

215

"It's a shipyard," Koyee whispered. "They're building ships."

Empress Hikari smiled thinly. "And forging swords and armor." She pointed to the river's southern bank where slaves toiled over cauldrons and anvils. "And serving as archery targets." She pointed to a hill where slaves stood chained to posts, pierced with arrows as Ilari archers stood before them. "A skirmish, you said? Twenty thousand Timandrians attacked our coast. Some lie dead. The others are building Ilar the greatest army it's ever known. That, child, is why we are strong and you are weak. When the Qaelish meet an enemy, they flee, die, or beg for aid. When the enemy attacks me . . ." She clenched her fist. "I crush it."

Koyee turned toward the taller, older woman. "Then fight the enemy in the north. If Qaelin is truly but a backwater, let it be a battleground for your might. Show the enemy that Ilar will not cower on its island, content to fight behind its walls. Use these ships! Sail north along the Yin River and join the great battle at Yintao. It will be the greatest battle in the history of the night. Let your flame burn there."

The empress raised an eyebrow. "You speak well for a Qaelish worm. You have either learned to mimic our customs, or some Ilari blood burns within your veins. There is fire in you." The empress tapped her chin. "My soldiers have often raided the Qaelish coast, planting their seed in the wombs of your women; perhaps some ended up in you."

Koyee swallowed down the rage those words kindled within her. "Fight with us, Empress Hikari. The enemy marches along Sage's Road to Yintao. Fight at our side."

Hikari turned to regard Torin. She stepped toward him, reached out, and trailed a steel claw across his cheek. Blood beaded. Torin winced but did not move. The empress brought the claw to her lips and tasted the blood.

"He tastes of fear." She spat. "This one is weak. His flesh would serve to test swords and arrows."

Empires of Moth

Koyee shook her head. "That one is mine, not yours to claim. He is my prisoner of war. You will not take him."

The empress laughed, turning back toward her. "Fire indeed! I will offer you this, Koyee of Qaelin. You've proven that you can speak our words. Yet can you fight with our strength? I will test your might. You'll fight a champion I choose. If you win the battle, you'll have proven yourself a warrior, and I will fight by your side. Yet if you fail . . ." The empress smiled. "I will cut out your heart and feed it to my dragon, and your prisoner will feed the fires of our forges."

Koyee stared back, chin raised, and though her innards trembled and her arm blazed with renewed pain, she managed to speak in a steady voice. "Send me your champion. Flame or death."

217

CHAPTER NINETEEN
THE BEAR MASQUERADE

Cam and Linee wandered the streets of Eeshan, dressed in furs, war hammers hanging across their backs.

"Camlin . . . I . . ." Linee wobbled at his side. "This hammer is too heavy and this fur *stinks*."

He turned to glare at her. "Hush! Don't speak Ardish here." He glanced around nervously at the countless Verilish soldiers, broad and bearded, who wandered the streets, tankards of ale in hand, belches fluttering their lips. "Just try to blend in."

She blinked, looking ready for tears. "How can I blend into this place?" Her voice rose louder. "Am I to grow a beard and belch like a barbarian? I'm a queen and—"

Cam grabbed her arm and leaned in closer. "Linee! Be quiet! Like it or not, the forces of Verilon occupy this city. They might be fellow people of sunlight, but I doubt they love the Queen of Arden very much. Our kingdom did after all burn down half their forests a generation ago."

Tears filled her eyes. In her oversized Verilish disguise— crude iron plates strapped over patches of fur and leather—she seemed like a child drowning in her father's clothes. The cut Suntai had given her had faded into a pale, pink line on her cheek; tears now streamed down the groove.

"I didn't burn anything," she said. "I wasn't even *born* then. Please, Camlin, can we go back to Suntai and the wolves? I promise I'll be good. I won't cry anymore or be afraid. But please can we go back? It wasn't as bad outside on the plains."

Empires of Moth

Suntai, along with their two remaining nightwolves, was hiding outside the city; these streets were too dangerous for them. At first, Cam had wanted to leave Linee in the dark too, but— after her altercation with Suntai—the dethroned queen had insisted on donning a disguise and joining Cam.

He shook his head. "Too late; you're already here. We'll go back to Suntai once we hire a ship. You know we have to sail north to Leen and find aid."

She nodded and lowered her head, lip wobbling. "I don't even want to go to Leen anymore."

"It was never about what you wanted, don't you get it?" Cam wanted to throttle her. "Leen has an army. They can help Qaelin fight."

She rubbed her eyes. "Who's this Qaelin person anyway?"

Cam groaned. "Linee! By Idar's beard! It's not a person. How could you not know this by now?" He stamped his foot. "*This* is Qaelin—the Elorian empire we're in. The one you've been traveling across for a month."

She pouted. "I don't know all these names. This whole place is just Nightside to me. As far as I'm concerned, all the dark places are the same."

"As far as I'm concerned, your brain is the same as a rock. Now please be quiet and don't draw attention."

Grumbling under his breath, Cam looked around the street again, hoping nobody heard the argument. Fortunately, the Verilish soldiers who walked here all seemed too drunken to pay Linee and him any heed. Cam was thankful. Linee and he wore Verilish furs and armor—relics of their battle along the road—but they stood a good foot shorter than everyone else. The Verilish, dwellers of the snowy pine forests north of Arden, were a towering folk, their shoulders broad and their bellies ample. They wore breastplates over fur, and their wooden shields bore paintings of bears. Most were men, their beards brown and bushy,

219

but women moved among them too, nearly as broad and powerful, their cheeks round and red, their laughter raucous. Like the men, these bear-maidens drank from tankards of ale, and war hammers hung across their backs; they too towered over Cam.

"Sheep's droppings, it's a wonder Torin's father ever survived a war against these people," he mumbled under his breath. He had heard the old soldier speak of Arden's invasion of Verilon; Cam had always thought the stories of giants riding bears mere tall tales for the fireside.

A bear lolloped down the street ahead, grunting with every step. The rider atop the beast—a woman with hair as brown and shaggy as her mount's—shouted down at him.

"Move, dwarves! Out of my way."

Cam and Linee leaped aside, landing in a puddle. The bear rambled on.

"Come on, Linee," Cam said softly. "Let's keep walking. The port must be around here somewhere."

They made their way through the crowd of soldiers, stepping between wandering bears, drunken warriors boasting of their kills, and the odd pile of bear droppings. The city of Eeshan, located on the northern coast of Qaelin, bore little resemblance to the fallen city of Pahmey. Cam saw no crystal towers here, only rows of squat brick homes, their green roofs curling up at the corners like sneering lips. Lanterns lined the cobbled streets, the tin shaped as fish. A few pagodas rose here and there, and public fireplaces belched out heat and light, but he saw no grand castles or temples. This seemed to have once been a city of traders and merchants; he saw many workshops with pottery, candles, silks, and other goods in the windows.

It was a smaller city than Pahmey—Cam guessed that perhaps twenty thousand people lived here—though he saw few of its denizens. The Elorians hid inside their homes; Cam caught only brief glimpses of their large, bright eyes peering from

Empires of Moth

windows before disappearing into shadows. Only once did he see an Elorian outside on the street; the poor man was a prisoner of war, naked and chained, a Verilish soldier tugging him along.

From the drunken boasting of soldiers, Cam could piece together the story. Verilon had invaded the place a few months ago, it seemed, and the city had fallen after only an hourglass turn of battle. Since then, most of the Verilish troops had left the city, streaming toward some eastern campaign.

"It's the capital we sack next!" one Verilish soldier shouted, standing at a street corner and waving his hammer. "The sun will rise on Yintao."

Cam grumbled. Yintao. Capital of Qaelin.

It's there that we must bring aid, he thought and swallowed. *It's there that I'll meet my friends again. It's there that the fate of the night will be sealed.*

He shuddered, remembering the great Battle of Pahmey last year. Thousands had died fighting for that city, the forces of Arden clashing with the city defenders. Nightmares of the blood and fire still filled Cam's sleep. But that battle would seem like a mere wrestle with Bailey compared to war at Yintao. If Cam and his friends could bring aid to that city, empires would clash. Hundreds of thousands, maybe even millions of troops would kill and die for the night. Cam felt faint and his knees wobbled. More blood would spill. More cannons would fire. More soldiers would die around him, armor cleaved open, innards leaking, and—

"Look!" Linee pointed down the street. Cold wind ruffled her stolen furs and clanked her crude, iron armor. "I see masts. The port!"

Cam shook his head wildly, clearing it of thoughts. He squinted and peered along the street. The cobbled road sloped downward, lined with brick homes, pagodas, and swinging lanterns. Beyond a crowd of Verilish revelers astride bears, he

221

could just make out the tips of masts. He counted a dozen. Beyond them loomed shadows.

"Let's go." Cam tugged on Linee's hand. "Do you still have your jewels?"

She sniffed, bit her lip, and nodded. "You promise to buy me more jewels once the war's over, right?" She reached into her pocket and produced chains glittering with diamonds, rubies, emeralds, and sapphires. "My Cery gave me these, and—"

"Not here!" Cam hurriedly pulled her hand down, glancing around and hoping no one saw. "We're supposed to just be Verilish soldiers. Verilish soldiers don't have the jewels of a queen."

"But I *am* a queen—" she began. "Oh." A sly look spread across her face. "Now I finally understand! I was wondering why we were dressed in furs and armor and carrying hammers." She giggled. "It's a *disguise*! Like at the masquerades back home."

Cam's jaw hung open and his eyebrows rose. "You just now . . ." He shook his head again and sighed. "Come on. And keep your jewels in your pocket."

They made their way down the road. A stone archway rose ahead, topped with bronze statues of leaping fish and whales, candles inside their eyes. Linee pointed upward, gaping at the statues, as they walked under the archway and emerged into the port of Eeshan.

A boardwalk stretched along the coast. Piers drove into the sea, topped with lighthouses. Fifty-odd boats docked here, while further out in the ocean, Cam could make out the lamps of anchored carracks, vessels too large to moor at the piers. Two breakwaters engulfed the port like wings of stone. Most of the ships had wooden hulls, canvas sails, and bear figureheads— Timandrian ships. Others were Elorian junks, their hulls smaller, their sails battened, but they too now bore the bear banner—ships captured in battle, Cam surmised.

Empires of Moth

"We're looking for a civilian ship," he said to Linee, walking along the boardwalk. "A merchant would do nicely, even a mercenary or smuggler."

"I don't like any of these boats," Linee said. "I *hate* water, unless it's a warm bubble bath. Can we just look at the boats, then walk the rest of the way?"

Cam held out his hands, exasperated. "How can we walk to Leen, an *island*?"

"The same way we walked here!" She tapped his helmet. "Think, Camlin."

He groaned. "Linee, do you even know what an island is?" When she shook her head, Cam covered his face with his palm. "Oh thorny sheep hooves . . . just . . . just be quiet then and let me choose a ship myself."

He returned his eyes to the ships. Right away, he ruled out most of them; they bore the banners of Verilon's navy, and soldiers in armor guarded their decks. Cam and Linee walked along the boardwalk, scanning the piers. Hundreds of people moved around them. Most were soldiers of Verilon, their wide breastplates snug atop their fur tunics; they sang between gulps of ale, their tankards as large as their hammerheads. But Cam saw other Verilish folk too: bearded peddlers hawking food from the homeland; ladies in fur-trimmed gowns, golden bear-paw amulets hanging from their necks; and every sort of tradesman from engineer to doctor to haberdasher. Even a few Elorians stood on the boardwalk, seemingly unperturbed by the forces occupying their city: yezyani batting their eyelashes and giggling at soldiers' jokes, buskers playing flutes and juggling torches for coins, and— Cam cringed to see it—three Elorian prisoners in stocks.

"What about that one?" Linee tugged his sleeve and pointed. "I like that ship. There's a nice puppy painted on it."

223

Cam looked and groaned. "That's a military vessel. See the soldiers on deck? And that's a *bear* on the hull, not a puppy. We can't travel with Verilon's navy."

She pouted. "Why not? I like that ship. It's painted nicely and it's the biggest one."

"Linee! For pity's sake, a Verilish warship isn't going to give us a lift to recruit Leen to fight them. Think! Ah . . . here we go. This one is more like it."

He began leading them toward a creaky old cog with a single mast. The unpainted hull bristled with barnacles. A ragged Verilish man stood on the deck, his head bald but his beard thick, sorting through piles of furs.

Linee froze, planting her feet firmly on the ground. "That ship stinks! I can smell it from here. And the sailor looks like a disgusting gutter rat."

"He looks like a disgusting fur trapper." Cam smiled. "Just the sort of chap we need. If he's not a soldier, he might take us north to Leen for your jewels."

Linee looked ready to burst into tears. "I'm not giving my jewels to *him*! I'll only give them to a nice, beautiful lady like me."

A growl fled Cam's throat. "If you don't come with me to this ship right now, I'm going to tell you another ghost story."

Her bottom lip wobbled. "But I'm scared of ghost stories."

"I know. And I've got a cracker of a story for you. It's about a ghost who was haunting a young queen, and—"

"All right!" She stamped her feet. "You don't have to be so mean. You're worse than Suntai when you try to scare me."

Three bears rumbled by, soldiers waving tankards upon their backs. When the beasts had passed them, Cam and Linee walked along the docks toward the old fur trapper's cog. Linee gave a little squeak, and even Cam wrinkled his nose; she was right, this boat did stink, a sickening aroma of sweat, rotten food, and dried blood.

224

Empires of Moth

"Ahoy!" Cam shouted up to the man on deck, deciding it was a good nautical greeting. "Ahoy, friend!"

The bald, bearded man leaned across the railing and squinted down at Cam. He hawked and spat noisily, narrowing missing Linee; the exiled queen whimpered and hid behind Cam.

"Bit short for soldiers, you two are." The man scratched his backside. "Show me your coin before I sell you fur. I got deer hides, rabbit slippers, squirrel tails, fox scarves, raccoon cloa—"

"We're not looking for fur," Cam said. "We're looking to book passage north. We'd like to hire your ship."

Linee whispered behind him, "I'd like a scarf."

Cam shushed her and looked back up at the fur trapper.

The bearded man snorted. "I don't sail back to Verilon for another month. Got me plenty more furs to sell round here."

"We're not going to Verilon!" Linee said, stepping from behind Cam. "We're going north to a magical, beautiful kingdom called Leen. It sounds like my name! They say it's full of crystal forests and wise sages in silken robes, and maybe there are butterflies there too. Will you take us?"

The fur trapper gaped at her, hands dropping to his sides. He blinked, then burst into laughter, a hideous sound like a strangled animal.

"You two are drunker than half the navy!" he bellowed. "Get lost, you two, before I skin you and sell your own hides back to you. Go on, get lost!"

The two turned to leave, Cam grumbling and Linee sniffling. As they walked along the boardwalk, searching for another ship, Cam spoke in a low voice.

"Next time, you might try to break the news about Leen a little more gradually. And try not to sound like an empty-headed fairytale queen."

"But that's who I am!" She covered her face with her palms. "I can't do this. I can't pretend anymore. I can't wear this stupid,

225

stinky fur and armor, traveling around the night like this." Tears streamed down her cheeks and dampened her fur cloak; Cam didn't understand how eyes could even produce so many tears. "I thought I could do it, but . . . you're right. I'm just an empty-headed fairytale queen, and I'm not strong. I'm not smart. I'm not brave. I'm not like you, Camlin."

A few soldiers, rambling along the docks, noticed her tears and began to mutter among themselves. Heart sinking, Cam took Linee by the arm and guided her toward the awning of a fish shop. Her lips trembled as she wept.

"Linee," he said softly. "Linee, look at me. Do you see me?" She nodded, blinking tears away.

"Good," he continued. "I'm no hero. I'm not strong or smart or brave either. I'm only a shepherd's boy from a village. I'm short. I'm just as lost and scared in this huge, dark land as you are."

She gasped. "Really?"

He nodded. "Really. Being brave and strong and smart . . . that's not just for people like Suntai or Bailey or Okado. It's just about . . . doing the right thing. Fighting on. Moving forward step by step. You can do this. I know you can. I believe in you."

A smile trembled on her face. She embraced him and squeezed.

"All right. But I think you *are* a hero." She grinned. "Even if you're short and stupid and stinky."

He rolled his eyes. "Great. Now let's look for another ship."

* * * * *

They passed several more ships along the docks: three military carracks, a fisherman's dinghy too small to navigate the ocean, and a mercenary's galley whose tattooed, scarred, sneering sailors sent Cam and Linee scurrying away. It was at the edge of the

226

Empires of Moth

boardwalk, right by the eastern breakwater, that they found the creaky caravel. A vessel with two triangular sails, it bore a figurehead shaped as a woman with a bear's head. Words scrawled across the hull in Verilish script; it used the same alphabet Cam spoke in his homeland, spelling out "The Bear Maiden."

"Aye, I'll ferry you north to Leen," said the ship's captain when Cam and Linee stepped on board. "Came here all the way from Verilon to sell ale to soldiers. They drank the lot and now are marching south. Off to fight in Yintao, they are, some great alliance of the eight sunlit kings." The man gulped down ale from a tankard of his own. "Got no business left but ferrying you miserable two."

Cam placed a few jewels on the table. Emeralds, sapphires, and rubies glimmered upon the scarred wood. "You get these now and the rest when we arrive in Leen. It'll be Linee and I joining you, our Elorian prisoner, and two nightwolves too—beasts as large as horses. You ask questions, we take our business elsewhere."

They sat in the captain's chamber, the ship anchored in the port. Candles burned in an iron holder. Casks, rolled-up scrolls, and bundles of canvas lay upon a dozen shelves. The captain, an aging Verilish man, sported a mane of wild auburn hair and an even wilder, redder beard. He scratched his veined nose and picked his teeth.

"No questions?" He sloshed his ale, dribbling some into his beard. "I see here two Ardish youths dressed in Verilon's furs, their disguises as pathetic as their fake accents. They got an Elorian stashed outside the city and two bloody nightwolves—them's illegal beasts in these parts. And you want to sail to an enemy empire." He chortled, spraying ale onto the table—and some onto Linee, who squealed. "No questions will cost you extra. Toss in another emerald and might be I'll keep mum."

227

Cam grumbled, reached into his pouch, and rummaged around. Ignoring Linee's whimpers, he placed another emerald on the table. "There's more where those came from. You'll get them once you drop us off at Leen." He managed a crooked grin. "You'll be the first Timandrian sailor to see the mystic island."

The captain brought the emerald near his eye, squinted, and pocketed the stone with an approving grunt. "First Timandrian? You've been on the road too long. Orida's been raiding Leen's coast for months now. Bloody barbarians probably burned the entire island down by now. You might want me to just ferry you back home to sunlight."

Cam groaned. He had heard of Orida, a Timandrian island far north in the arctic, their banners bearing the orca—killer of the sea. Folk spoke of great warriors, seven feet tall, with golden hair and thick mustaches, their swords wide, their oared galleys the fastest ships on the seas. He had never seen the warriors of Orida, but stories of their cruelty had reached south all the way to Fairwool-by-Night. If these men were attacking Leen, would Cam find only death and destruction, more conquered realms like here in Qaelin?

He cleared his throat. "Our journey leads to Leen. We sail on. We leave now. Our Elorian companion—that is, prisoner—and her wolves await us two miles east along the coast. When we pass by, she'll swim to join us."

The captain croaked a laugh—a hideous sound. "A prisoner willing to wait in darkness, then swim toward her captors? Aye, sounds very much like a prisoner indeed." He roared with laughter, revealing yellow teeth. "Ah! Wipe the shock off your faces. I don't care if you're marrying the damn savage, so long as you pay me. Aye. We set sail. I just got one rule." He pointed a finger at Cam; it ended with a scarred nub, the tip missing. "You stay away from my crew. They're not just my sailors—they're my daughters. You lay a hand on them, I cut it off."

Empires of Moth

Cam nodded and reached out his hand. "You got a deal, old man.

The captain spat into his hand before shaking Cam's. "My name's Captain Olor, boy. And you definitely got yourself a deal."

Cam winced, pulled his hand free, and wiped it against his pants. Linee stuck out her tongue in disgust, then giggled and elbowed Cam's stomach.

They set sail that very turn.

As the *Bear Maiden* sailed out of port, Cam stood upon the deck and watched the city of Eeshan grow smaller. Its pagodas, cobbled streets, and lamps faded into a smudge of light in the endless darkness. Beyond the city Cam could see a trail of more lights flowing south—the forces of Verilon traveling down the Iron Road.

"They will join with Ferius's army," Cam said softly into the wind, leaning over the railing. "All across Moth, armies muster to join him. And they will march east." He turned to look at Linee who stood at his side. "They will fight against Yintao, the greatest city in Nightside. It is there that Eloria will survive or fall. We must bring aid. We must succeed."

Linee nodded and took his hand. "We will." She spoke softly, the wind billowing her hair. "When I first came into the night, I was very scared. I thought the Elorians were monsters— their eyes so large, their skin so pale, their clothes so foreign. But . . . they're not monsters, are they? We are the monsters." She sniffed and lowered her head. "I see that now. I still see it in my dreams—Ferius killing him. He just . . . just stabbed my husband in the back, and . . . he killed so many others." For once she shed no tears; she squared her jaw and stared at the lights on the coast. "And so I will fight him. You were right, Camlin. Heroes don't need to be tall or strong or wise. They just need to keep going. And that's what I'll do."

229

They sailed two miles along the coast, the captain's daughters—dour women, their red hair as shaggy as their fur tunics—tugging ropes and rudder as they cursed and spat. When they saw the light upon the coast, flickering between a clump of boulders, Cam signaled with his own lamp.

Suntai and her nightwolves swam across the dark waters and joined them on board. The two canines, almost as large as the bears of Verilon, shook their fur upon the deck, spraying water everywhere. Suntai smiled thinly, her tall body clad in scales, her katanas and daggers at her sides. Seeing the strange companions, the sailors' daughters cursed with new vigor and grumbled under their breath.

"Now let's head north," Cam said. "North into the cold darkness. North to Leen."

The *Bear Maiden* turned in the water. They sailed into the shadows, leaving the empire of Qaelin behind.

CHAPTER TWENTY
Tianlong

They sat in the shadowy chamber, a single candle lighting a dusty floor and brick walls.

"Koyee, you don't have to do this," Torin said, eyes pained. "We can leave this place . . . sneak out in shadow, make our way to the docks, and sail back north."

She sat on the bench, staring at the sword on her lap. The candlelight played across the mottles and swirls in the steel. Sheytusung. Sword of her father. *Her* sword. The blade she had killed with. The blade that could, here in this pit, save the land of night.

"I will not turn back," she said, speaking more to the blade than to Torin. "I gazed upon the strength and cruelty of the Ilari Empire. How can I sail home without their might at my back? I must tame this creature of darkness. I must make the beast of Ilar my own." She raised her eyes and looked at Torin. "I must win this fight, or the empress will not help us. We need Ilar or the lands of darkness will fall."

"Not like this!" Torin shook his head mightily. "There must be another way to convince the empress. We will wait. The war will come here again. Empress Hikari will see reason. If we only—"

"We cannot wait. Ferius and his army march east along Sage's Road. Perhaps they are in Yintao already. We cannot wait." The curse on her left arm twisted and tightened, squeezing her like a vise, and she winced. "This is the only way."

231

The muffled cheering rose behind the door, a sound like a storm. They chanted for her death. They cried for her blood. They would see her torn apart upon the dust of the arena, and they would cheer the loudest if the creature tore out her heart.

So I cannot fail. For the memory of my village. For my family. For Eloria.

She rose to her feet and stepped toward the door. "I hear them calling. It's time."

Torin leaped toward her and grabbed her good arm. Pain twisted his face. His wrists were still bound, but his fingers clutched at her.

"Please, Koyee. If you go out there, you will die."

She touched his bristly, dusty cheek. "If I stay here, we all die." She stood on her tiptoes and kissed his lips. "Goodbye, Torin."

She turned to leave, but he held her fast, tugging her toward him, and she found herself pressed against him, kissing him deeply. He whispered into her ear, voice hoarse, almost drowning under the din from outside.

"I love you too, Koyee."

She kissed his forehead, opened the door, and stepped outside into the light, sand, and roars of the arena.

Fifty thousand souls howled. A ring of stone surrounded her, rising many tiers tall, crowded with the chanting people of the city. There were soldiers and priests, commoners and traders, men and women and even children. All shouted for her blood, waving the banners of their empire. The empress herself sat among them, her seat gilded, a canopy of red silk rising above her.

Koyee's head spun. The roars pounded into her like waves. She took several steps deeper into the arena, a sandy circle two hundred feet in diameter. Iron spikes surrounded the circle, pointing inward, their tips gleaming with poison; Koyee felt as though she stood in the mouth of a great beast, its teeth ready to

Empires of Moth

snap shut. She looked over her shoulder, hoping to see Torin one last time, but the chamber door had closed, sealing him inside. She stood here alone.

"Death to Qaelin!" shouted the people around her, their voices consolidating into a single chant. "Death to Qaelin! Death to Qaelin!"

Koyee lowered her helm's visor, hefted her shield, and raised her katana.

"Be with me, Sheytusung," she whispered. "Be with me, Father."

She stared across the arena at the second doorway; it was identical to the one she had stepped through. Her opponent waited there. The crowd chanted around her, fists pounding chests.

Suddenly laughter rose in her.

"Look at us, Eelani," she said, eyes stinging. "Koyee and Eelani—dragonslayers."

She had to grind her teeth to stop from shaking.

The door across the arena opened.

The crowd's roar swelled, pounding against Koyee's ears and chest, aching against her ribs.

Like a snake emerging from a lair, Tianlong the dragon, black beast of Ilar, burst into the arena.

"Death to Qaelin! Death to Qaelin!"

Koyee bared her teeth.

Stand your ground, Koyee. Focus. Breathe. Figh—

The dragon soared and came swooping down toward her, mouth opened wide enough to swallow her.

Koyee yelped and raised her shield.

The great serpent crashed against her with a force like a falling mountain. Screaming, Koyee dropped to one knee. The beast snapped at her shield, teeth lashing around the metal. Koyee strained to shove the shield upward, to keep the dragon away; she felt like Tianlong could push her into the earth.

"Death to Qaelin!" the crowd chanted. "Tianlong, Tianlong!"

Koyee sucked in her breath, growled, and swung her sword. The blade reached around her shield and slammed into Tianlong's black scales.

The dragon shrieked and pulled back.

Koyee leaped to her feet, facing the beast.

Fifty feet long, the reptile hissed. Though he had no wings, he hovered above the ground. His tail swayed. Sand filled his red beard, and his eyes gleamed, red orbs the size of Koyee's fists. In paintings and drawings, Shenlai—the blue dragon of Koyee's homeland—appeared long and limbless like a snake. But Tianlong, the black dragon of Ilar, had diminutive arms that ended with claws. They were no larger than Koyee's own arms, so disproportionately small that despite the fear of battle and roaring crowd, she laughed.

"Tianlong!" she said and raised her blade. "This sword slew many of your people. Come taste it again."

The dragon bellowed, shot skyward, and came plummeting down a second time.

Koyee leaped sideways.

Tianlong's fangs drove into the dust, and Koyee jumped and landed on his head.

The dragon shrieked and bucked. Koyee flew into the air. She reached out and grabbed Tianlong's horn, but her hand slipped. She tumbled and thumped into the sand. The breath was knocked out of her. The dragon's tail lashed, slamming into her side. Koyee flew again.

The crowd howled. In midair, Koyee held out her shield. The metal slammed into the spikes surrounding the arena. One

234

Empires of Moth

spike pierced the shield, emerging rusty and dripping poison an inch from Koyee's face.

She let go of the shield.

She slumped to the ground in time to see Tianlong race toward her, his beard dragging through the sand, his maw open.

She ran, skirted his head, and slammed her sword down. The blade hit the dragon's neck, but the beast's scales were hard as armor, sparking under her blade.

Her arm blazed with pain. She felt the curse crawling across her, driving down to the bone, and she screamed, nearly fainting from the agony. She tried to strike again, but the pain dulled her reflexes. Tianlong lashed his tail, hitting her chest. She slammed into the sand.

The dragon rose and swooped again, and this time Koyee had no shield. She held her sword upward, hoping to skewer the beast's maw as he tried to bite. But Tianlong dodged the attack, grabbed the blade between his teeth, and tugged.

The sword came free from her hand.

"Sheytusung!" she shouted.

The dragon spat the blade out like a man spitting out a toothpick. Blood trickled from Tianlong's gums, but he managed to grin and hiss, leering down at her in the sand. Koyee wanted to rise. She wanted to chase her sword, to keep fighting with tooth and nail if she had to. But her arm kept blazing; it felt like a swarm of insects scuttling across her, and her sleeve bulged.

The dragon drove in to bite.

Nearly blind with pain, Koyee rolled aside, and the fangs drove into the sand. Her body pressed against her wounded arm, and she screamed in agony, tears budding in her eyes. The heat of battle stoked the curse like oil on flame. She felt the black welts rise to her shoulder, her neck, flowing down her back, creaking her bones, and—

235

Tianlong came plunging down toward her, an asp striking at a rat. Koyee's eyes rolled back. She managed to roll aside and the crowd chanted around her, an endless sea like the one she had navigated with Torin, and she wept because she missed him and she was sorry.

I'm sorry, Torin. I'm sorry I failed you, that I failed the night. I love you.

The dragon bit. Fangs drove into her armor, bending the scales, reaching toward her flesh. She was vaguely aware of the beast lifting her. She hung many feet above the ground, caught in his maw, her armor bending between his teeth, and she knew that she had only a few heartbeats left.

Her arm rustled. Her eyes fluttered open. And she saw him there. He was running across the arena, wrists bound. The crowd jeered. Torin leaped and landed onto the dragon, kicking and biting at the scales.

Koyee in his mouth, Tianlong snorted and laughed.

His amusement loosened his teeth.

Nearly fainting with pain, Koyee kicked, driving her feet into the beast's palate. The mouth opened. Koyee leaped out, grabbed a fang, and swung as if around a pole. She leaped into the air and landed on the dragon's head, a good fifty feet above the arena.

She had no shield. She had no sword. All she had was her pain. She tore off her sleeve, exposing her arm.

The black welts covered her completely, hiding her skin— the arm looked like a burnt log rustling with insects, searing hot and stinking. Tianlong bucked beneath her, shaking his head. Koyee held on tight and shoved her arm down, placing the festering limb across the dragon's eyes.

Pain blazed through her like a thousand suns.

The dragon shrieked—a sound of shattering glass, of crashing stars, of falling empires.

Empires of Moth

Koyee rubbed her arm against his eyes, driving it against the orbs, nearly passing out from the pain, unable to breathe. Through the fog of tears, she was just able to see the curse spread, the tendrils crawling into the beast's eyes.

Her grip on the dragon's horn loosened.

She rolled down Tianlong's scaly neck, fell through the air, and thumped into the sand.

Blinded, the dragon flailed. His head lashed from side to side, enraged, the dark magic in his eyes. He cried for his empire. He cried for his mistress.

Arm wobbling, Koyee rose to her feet. She trudged through the sand and lifted her fallen sword.

"Tianlong!" she cried hoarsely.

Hearing her cry, the blind dragon lashed his head toward her, still trying to bite.

Koyee sidestepped, grabbed the beast's horn, and placed the tip of her sword against his ear.

"Do not move, Tianlong!" she shouted. "Move and my blade will enter your skull."

The dragon froze, the curse rustling in his eyes like cockroaches inside two bowls.

Koyee was vaguely aware of Torin lying several feet away, moaning, his chest rising and falling. She dared not approach him. Holding the sword to the dragon's head, she raised her eyes and sought the empress.

Hikari was standing under her canopy, gazing down from above. Their eyes met—a Qaelish girl and the mistress of a southern empire. All across the amphitheater, the thousands of spectators stared, silent.

"Fight with me," Koyee said, chin raised. "Fight with Qaelin. I will spare Tianlong's life, for he is a noble beast and a true warrior. Let Tianlong fly north with us. We will roar together! We will slay sunlit demons."

237

The empress looked down at her, silent.

"Fight with me . . ." Koyee said, arm rustling. "Sail north. We must . . ."

Her eyes rolled back.

She thought that Torin caught her, but she wasn't sure.

She thought the empress was shouting, that soldiers were rushing forth, that the sun was rising. She closed her eyes and let her body glide through dark oceans.

Empires of Moth

CHAPTER TWENTY-ONE
THE HALLS OF ETERNAL HARMONY

As the full moon rose, Bailey beheld the distant city of Yintao, capital of Qaelin.

Riders around her murmured in awe. She heard phrases like "the heart of the empire" and "city of harmony" and "the halls of the undying" and other fancy words. Sitting atop her nightwolf, Bailey found it harder to be impressed.

"I expected something more . . . grand," she said to Okado; the tall warrior rode at her side. "Crystal towers of light like in Pahmey. Hot air balloons by the thousands. Fireworks and trumpets and fanfare. Jugglers and dancers and majestic animals with names I can't pronounce. But I only see brick walls."

Her nightwolf panted beneath her, the silvery female Ayka. Stroking the animal, Bailey stared ahead, trying to seek some grandeur she had missed. The walls stretched ahead across the land; they seemed miles long. Every hundred yards, a pagoda rose from the walls—guard towers, she surmised. Lanterns lined the battlements like orderly soldiers. Behind these defenses, she saw nothing—no hot air balloons, no glass steeples, no domes of light. Brick walls and shadows—that was how Yintao greeted them.

Okado shifted upon his nightwolf, turning to face Bailey. "Might is not judged by lights and fanfare. Would you judge the Chanku Pack by the crater that was our home? Pahmey shone with lights for many miles; it fell within two hourglass turns. Yintao is no center of beauty or pleasure; it is a fortress of stone and steel." He gave Bailey a mirthless smile. "I would choose no other place for Eloria to make its final stand."

239

Bailey patted her bow. "So long as I can slay Sailith monks from these walls, I suppose the place will serve."

The pack kept moving, thousands of warriors in armor upon their wolves, their elders and children within their protective ring. No stars shone this night; a shadow covered the sky like an omen of death. When the moon broke through the cover, it fell upon a silver river to her east and mountains ahead. Between water and stone, the city loomed.

As the pack drew closer, Bailey began to realize how tall these walls rose. Tiny figures stood atop them, armor and spearheads glinting in the light of lanterns. Judging by the sentries' size, the walls of Yintao must have risen a hundred feet tall. Lining them like a spine ridge, the pagodas rose even taller, their tiers of roofs tiled red. Not a sound seemed to rise from the city. Pahmey had always hummed, a blend of distant song, chatter, and footfalls. Yintao stood like a silent graveyard.

This city will be a graveyard, she thought and grimaced. *Thousands will die upon these walls. Here we stand or fall.* She looked into the northern darkness. *Hurry, Cam, and return with aid.* She turned to stare southward. *Hurry, Torin. Come back to me.*

She touched her lips, remembering their kiss, and winced with the pain of missing him. *Come back soon, Torin, so I can smack you for making me feel like a doe-eyed farm girl. I'm going to smack you so hard you cry.*

The Sage's Road led them toward the city gatehouse. An archway loomed between two guard towers, its keystone sporting a dragon of blue tiles. Iron doors stood closed within, their facades engraved with soldiers battling beasts under the constellations. Fifty living soldiers stood upon the gatehouse battlements, arrows nocked and aiming at the pack. Across the walls, many more troops stared down silently, bows in hand. They wore shirts of scales and curving helms. Broad men, their faces were hard and cold, and white mustaches adorned their upper lips.

Empires of Moth

Their banners flapped in the wind, hiding and showing the moonstar of Qaelin.

"Fire rises behind us!" Okado shouted, standing in his stirrups. "Hail, guards of Yintao. We bring aid!"

For long moments, the guards atop the walls merely stood silently, staring down, not lowering the bows. The pack stirred and grumbled. Voices rose, demanding entrance, vowing to attack the city should the doors not open. While the soldiers upon the walls were like automatons of steel, the pack was a wild thing, a horde thirsty for the fight. Okado turned around in the saddle, glaring at his riders.

"Silence!" He turned back toward the walls. "Chanku rides to aid Yintao. All armies of Qaelin must now fight united. A great enemy follows along Sage's Road. Timandra crawls upon the land. I am Okado, ruler of Chanku; I will speak to your emperor."

For another long moment, not a guard stirred, and even the banners drooped and would not flap. Bailey held her breath, staring, wondering if they had come all this way in vain.

Then, with wails like a mournful ghost, the iron doors of Yintao began to open.

The wolves yipped and clawed the earth. Bailey leaned forward in the saddle and a gasp fled her lips. She clutched the hilt of her sword.

"By Idar's flea-ridden beard," she muttered. "Civilization in the wilderness."

The opening doors revealed a boulevard as wide as most towns. Polished flagstones formed its surface, and columns rose in palisades, lining the road, lanterns flaring out from their marble like mushrooms upon trees. Between every column stood a guard in scales, a spear and shield in hand, so stiff Bailey thought they might be statues. The road stretched for miles; Bailey saw it pass through several other gates. Far in the distance, rising from shadow, stood a great pagoda with seven tiers of red roofs. A

241

golden idol stood atop the uppermost roof—the ancient sage Xen Qae, clad in robes, his hands pressed together in meditation.

Bailey turned to look at Okado. He gave her a wry smile before heeling his wolf and riding forth. A heartbeat later, Bailey joined him. With creaking armor, frosting breath, and snorting nightwolves, the Chanku Pack rode into the capital of their empire.

Bailey looked from side to side as she rode. The silence unnerved her. The soldiers of Yintao stared from the roadsides, still and grim. Beyond them, she saw many streets spreading away from the main boulevard like veins from an artery. Houses lined them, each one the same as its neighbors—their walls formed of adobe bricks, their curling roofs tiled red. Pahmey had been a jumbled hive—a place of rickety workshops, crystal towers, dirty alleyways, and magnificent pagodas of gold and silver. While that fallen city had celebrated color and life, Yintao was built with an austere, clockwork efficiency, every cobblestone perfectly aligned, every brick identical to its brethren, every doorway displaying the same moonstar rune. Bailey was willing to wager that every roof bore the same number of tiles, and that every guard stood the exact same height; they certainly all seemed identical to her. She wondered what had happened to the shorter or taller guards, then gulped and decided it was a mystery best not dwelled upon.

Huffing and moaning sounded behind her. She turned to see Hem racing forward upon his shaggy old wolf. The young man's cheeks were flushed red, and sweat glistened upon his brow even in the cold of night. His wolf panted beneath him. With a clatter of armor, he reached her and wiped his brow.

"Bailey!" he said. "Idar's bottom, don't you ever wait up?" He gestured around him. "We're here! We're in Yintao."

"Yes, Hem, I noticed."

He offered a shaky smile, reached over, and patted her wolf. "We'll be all right now, Bails. We'll be safe behind these walls."

Empires of Moth

Suddenly he was blinking too much. "Cam and Tor will join us here soon. I know they will. Maybe they're here already." He lowered his head. "I miss them."

Bailey sighed. Perhaps she had been too harsh on the boy along the road. He was, after all, the only one here from her home, and who knew when she'd see Cam and Torin again? She tightened her lips and nodded.

"Hush now, Hem. I'm not even sure we're supposed to talk in this city. It's so silent here."

The pack kept riding, stretching across the boulevard. They must have walked for a mile before they reached another layer of walls, identical to ones before them, and passed through a second gateway. As they kept riding, they passed through seven gates and walls, cities within cities. When they entered the seventh layer, Bailey gasped and covered her mouth. Her heart nearly stopped and she heard the pack whisper behind her. Tears filled her eyes.

"Hope," she whispered, voice trembling. "There is hope in the night."

The innermost city was a bastion of might. A square sprawled out, larger than ten Fairwools. Countless soldiers stood here in perfect formations, line by line, men and women alike. Each wore scale armor, greaves, vambraces, and a helm. Each bore a shield, tasseled katana, and spear. Every soldier stared ahead, face blank, eyes expressionless. Not a breath stirred. Beyond their lines rose a hundred halls or more, their roofs wide, their walls sporting arrowslits—barracks for the troops.

Behind the army loomed the great pagoda Bailey had seen from the first gateway. Seven tiers tall it rose, wide enough to house thousands; it was easily the largest structure Bailey had ever seen, even larger than the palace of Arden. This was a castle like a city. Braziers surrounded its columns. Gold lined its many roofs of red tiles. The golden idol stared down from above, wise and horrible.

243

"Behold the Eternal Palace," Okado said at her side. "For over a thousand years have the emperors of Qaelin ruled from this place. Here is the heart of our empire."

"This is no heart," she whispered. "This is the empire's sword."

She dug her heels into Ayka. The white nightwolf bolted forward.

For the first time, the soldiers of Yintao moved.

Thousands turned together, a machine of perfect precision, and slammed spears against shields. The shafts crisscrossed like an iron fence. All eyes stared at Bailey. Beneath her, her wolf snarled but stopped in her tracks.

For long moments, the two forces stood facing each other—the soldiers of Yintao in the square, an army of steel and silk and silence; and the Chanku Pack, a horde of fur and fang and fury. A cold wind blew and Bailey wondered whether they had passed through the seven layers of Yintao only to die at its center.

A trumpet blew.

As one, the soldiers parted, forming a path.

Bailey narrowed her eyes. In the darkness ahead, several men came walking down a stairway from the pagoda gates. After descending the last step, they walked across the square until they reached the wolf pack. The men sported flowing white mustaches, silken robes embroidered with moonstars, and golden sashes around their waists. They bowed, hands pressed together.

"Welcome to Yintao, riders of Chanku," said one, the oldest among them, face wrinkled and gums toothless. "We've heard many tales of the western riders; your forebears were honorable nobles, tracing their ancestry back to Xen Qae himself. We bring you the gifts of light." They held out floating silk lanterns on strings. "Who among you leads?"

Upon his wolf, Okado nodded down toward the men. "I am Okado, leader of this pack." He accepted one of the lanterns, its

244

Empires of Moth

silk painted with birds and fish. "With me is Bailey Berin, an emissary of Timandra."

As the men turned toward Bailey, she removed her helm, revealing her small brown eyes and golden braids. The Elorian elders—of white hair, pale skin, and large blue eyes—gasped and mumbled amongst themselves. Bailey stared down at them; if any here mocked her ancestry, she felt ready to slice through this entire army. She looked over at Hem, who sat upon his wolf behind her, and gestured for him to remove his helm too. He shook his head wildly and moved his wolf several feet back.

Finally the elders returned their eyes to Okado. "We've heard much about the Timandrians, the sunlit enemy. Emperor Jin the Blessed would much like to speak with . . ." He struggled to form the words. ". . . Bai-ley Be-rin. You would be most welcome in his hall. Your riders may rest in this square until we find them better accommodations. You and your Timandrian companion will follow me; I will lead you into the hall of the emperor."

* * * * *

The sages led them up the stairway, past statues of dragons with embers in their mouths, and through a golden doorway bejeweled with rubies. Leaving their wolves outside, Bailey and Okado entered the palace of Qaelin's emperor.

A towering hall awaited them, lined with columns of red and gold. Bailey gasped. She had never seen a chamber this large; all of Fairwool-by-Night could have fit in here with room to spare. A mosaic sprawled across the floor, depicting blue dragons coiling around silver stars, their eyes jeweled. Braziers rose every few feet, shaped as every animal known in the night, their bronze skin inlaid with gold and silver, their maws holding fire that filled the room with light and sweetly scented smoke. Guards stood

245

between the columns, more finely dressed than the army outside; gems glowed upon their armor, trapping the lures of anglerfish, and silken robes hung across their shoulders, embroidered with crescent moons.

A beacon of light shone across the hall, so bright it blinded Bailey. She leaned forward and squinted, but saw only a glow like the moon. The mustached sages stopped, stepped sideways, and bowed. They gestured ahead, inviting their guests to approach the light.

Bailey glanced at Okado. Strangely, despite the splendor of this place, she felt uneasy, almost afraid. The sight of Okado—a rougher sort of man, his armor dusty from the journey, his face rugged—comforted her. He met her eyes and nodded, the thinnest of smiles upon his lips. She nodded back and faced forward again. They began to walk, crossing the hall.

They moved between the columns, braziers, and guards. Some of these palace warriors frowned to see Bailey, a foreigner in their hall; one even raised his spear and seemed ready to strike before his comrade stopped him.

A high, young voice rose from across the hall, emerging from the light. "Come forth, guests! I've waited long to see you."

Bailey and Okado kept walking, boots thumping against the mosaic, and the throne of Qaelin came into view.

Bailey's jaw unhinged.

Red stairs led up to a dais. Between whorled columns rose a throne of gold and rubies. A great statue of a dragon coiled around the throne, its scales formed of blue tiles; it seemed so lifelike Bailey half expected the statue to rise and blow fire.

A child sat here, gazing upon her. His eyes were large and blue, his white hair was held up in a bun, and he wore a blue silken robe. At first Bailey thought his limbs were encased in gold, but then she let out a slow breath, and her heart softened. The boy bore four prosthetics, legs and arms of precious metal. Pity

Empires of Moth

filled Bailey at the sight, and she let out a wordless whisper, longing to climb onto the throne and embrace this damaged child.

Seeing Okado kneel at her side, she stopped herself. Coated with the dust and sweat of her journey, feeling like a beggar at a banquet, she knelt too with a clatter of armor.

"My emperor," said Okado, lowering his head. "I bow before you, Jin, Holy Lord of Harmony. I am Okado of Chanku. With me is Bailey of Timandra. We've come to bring aid, Your Highness, and warnings of evil in the west."

Bailey looked up and saw the child examining her. Their eyes met, and Bailey gave him a small smile. He might have been an emperor, but he was still only a hurt boy.

Our fate lies in the hands of a child, she thought. *A child whose hands are made of gold and cannot move.*

"I've heard of Timandrians," the emperor said, his voice high and beautiful and far too young for a hall this grand. "For many years, my sages told me they were but legends. But here one kneels before me. And many gather in the west. Tidings of this invasion have reached the capital. Tidings of Pahmey's occupation—and then its fall—have come here too. I grieve for the souls who died."

Sudden rage flared in Bailey, burning across her pity. She leaped to her feet.

"You knew of the invasion?" she said, voice echoing across the hall. If before she had wanted to hug this child, now she wanted to shake him. "You knew of Pahmey's fall? You have an army! Why didn't your soldiers march west? Why didn't you help us as Timandra murdered, as the towers crashed, as—"

Okado placed a hand on her shoulder, hushing her. She wheeled toward him, panting with rage, and spun back toward the emperor. Her chest rose and fell, and her fists clenched and unclenched.

247

The boy stared down at her, haunting sadness in his eyes. "Help *us*? Are you not one of the sunlit?"

Bailey pounded her armor of scales. "See my armor! I am a soldier of the night. I was born in sunlight, but I fight for darkness. Why don't you?" She took a step forward, ignoring the guards who shifted and raised their spears. "Why didn't you help Pahmey?"

"I could hear their screams in my dreams," Emperor Jin said, and a tear flowed down his cheek. "Many times I wanted to march west with the hosts, and yet I would not. Too many Timandrians gather; we could not have stopped them. Our army would have crashed against the walls of occupied Pahmey. And so we stay behind the walls of Yintao, sharpening our swords, waiting for the sun to rise upon us. The enemy marches across Sage's Road, the same path you took. Half a million warriors swarm toward us. We are forging blades and armor as the hourglass turns, and we are drafting men across the city and countryside, yet still the hosts of sunlight greatly outnumber us." The boy shivered. "They will be here soon."

Bailey's eyes stung. "Is there any hope?"

"There is always hope, child of sunlight," said the dragon statue.

Bailey nearly fell onto her backside.

She gasped, clutched the hilt of her sword, and drew a foot of steel. At her side, she heard Okado gasp.

"You're . . ." She sputtered, barely able to form the words. "You're real?"

The dragon of blue tiles uncoiled from around the throne, rising in the chamber. Bailey took several steps back, unable to breathe.

"Shenlai!" said Okado, voice hushed with awe, and knelt again. "Shenlai, dragon of Qaelin!"

248

Empires of Moth

Bailey stood before the beast, sword still half-drawn. Shenlai rose like a snake from a basket. His scales, which Bailey had mistaken for blue tiles, chinked like a purse full of coins. His eyes, orbs like crystal balls, gleamed as they gazed upon her. His beard and mustache flowed long and snowy, and his eyelashes—each as long as a peacock feather—fanned the air as he blinked.

"Shenlai," Bailey whispered, tears in her eyes. "I've seen your statues across the empire, though I didn't know you were real." She drew her sword, knelt before him, and placed the tip of her blade against the floor. "My sword is yours."

It seemed to her that the dragon smiled, a smile of warmth, wisdom, and ancient secrets.

"That gives me hope, child of sunlight," said the dragon. "The greatest hope is found not in armies or castles, but in the hearts of honest people. I see hope in your eyes and your soul. Rise, Bailey and Okado, warriors of the night."

They rose and stood before the dragon. Bailey wiped tears from her eyes and whispered, "My heart is strong, Shenlai . . . though it beats stronger with an army at my back." She returned her eyes to the emperor. "We bring an army of wolves! They are noble and strong. We've sent travelers south to Ilar and north to Leen, requesting aid. There is help for Yintao."

Jin looked at his dragon, then back at Bailey, and she realized: Shenlai was true master of the empire, sage and councilor and friend to the child upon the throne.

"Shenlai is not the only dragon in Eloria," said Jin. "Two more live, coiling around the thrones of Ilar and Leen. Shenlai has flown to meet them, yet they will not send aid. We are alone, Bailey of Sunlight. We must be strong."

She lowered her head and bit her lip. *As there are two more dragons, I have two friends in distant lands. Come back soon, Torin and Cam. Come back even if no aid is to be found. Stand with me here.*

249

Daniel Arenson

The next hourglass turn was a blur of lights, scents, and dreams to Bailey. Servants took her to chambers where she bathed, ate and drank, and donned robes of silk. Young women tried to unbraid and brush her hair, and she sent them fleeing with a glower and curse.

Finally they let her be, and she rejoined the pack, which camped outside upon the square, tents raised and nightwolves sleeping curled up into balls. Soldiers of Yintao patrolled outside the palace, and warriors of Chanku stood guard among their tents. Bailey found her own tent and wolf, but she couldn't sleep, even when she pretended to lie in her old bed at home.

Finally she rose from her fur blankets, her tent walls dark around her, and drew her sword. She tightened her lips until they shook. She swung her blade, up and down, again and again, and with every stroke she imagined cutting into her enemy's flesh, saving all those who had died around her.

250

Empires of Moth

CHAPTER TWENTY-TWO
THE CLOCKWORK KING

Cam was losing yet another meal over the ship's railing—the latest in a sad string of them—when he saw the distant glow.

"Camlin, Camlin!" Linee said, tugging his sleeve. "Land!"

Cam moaned and staggered back, wiping his mouth.

"Land!" Linee cried and danced a jig. "Leen. My kind of country."

Queasy and feeling weaker than a newborn lamb, Cam reached for his skin of spirits, sloshed the rye in his mouth, and spat. Sailing downriver into Pahmey last year had been bad enough, but this was worse. For long turns they had been sailing north through roiling, wavy, bouncy, swaying, and lurching ocean.

"My country," Linee said, hands pressed together against her cheek.

"Hope for the night," said Suntai, coming to stand beside them.

When Cam looked ahead, he thought of no hope for Eloria, no armies, no aid. He cared about only one thing.

"Solid ground at last."

The captain and his daughters cried out and pointed. One of the daughters, a stocky woman who normally laughed and sang, scowled and muttered curses. Her sisters worked in silence, staring at the lights and whispering.

"This place is cursed," said the eldest daughter, a doughy sailor with red cheeks. "That glow is unnatural. That is the glow of ghosts."

251

Cam felt more of his latest meal rising and swallowed it down. "I'll take ghosts over this ship. Keep sailing."

The *Bear Maiden*'s sails billowed. The ship made way toward the lights, bouncing atop every wave and making Cam cover his mouth and struggle not to gag. He tried to focus on the land ahead, watching the lights grow nearer. The entire horizon glowed. Was this a single city, miles and miles wide, straddling the whole southern coast of Leen?

"What do you know of this island, Suntai?" he asked the tall, pale woman.

Suntai narrowed her eyes. "I told you. I know nothing of this land." She stared ahead toward the lights and loosened her katana in its scabbard. "Few in Qaelin do. The people of Leen appear in our old legends. They are philosophers and stargazers, wise men with flowing robes and flowing beards. Some say that Xen Qae, founder of Qaelin, was born in Leen—that all Eloria began on this island." She spat overboard. "Old stories. Soon you will know. But be careful . . . and stay near me."

Ignoring the dire warning, Linee twirled around on the deck. "Oh, it'll be a beautiful country. I'm sure of it. There will be glowing butterflies, forests of purple mushrooms, fluffy unicorns, and castles." She grinned and ran her fingers through her hair. "And they'll appreciate somebody as beautiful as me, a real queen. Camlin, do you think they'll have cakes there?"

"I think you have cake between your ears." He held his belly. "I'm going to be sick again. Please don't talk about food, and please stop dancing around."

She stuck her tongue out, grabbed his arm, and made a point of dancing while tugging his arm and singing about plum pies. He groaned.

The coast of Leen grew closer, and Cam squinted and leaned forward. What he had mistaken for a sprawling coastline

Empires of Moth

city was . . . He rubbed his eyes, refusing to believe, but his eyes insisted it was true.

"Crystals," he said. "A whole damn forest of glowing crystals."

Linee nodded. "I *told* you. I told you they'd have magical forests."

Cam wasn't so sure the place was magical. To him the glow seemed ghostly, an eerie light. At first he thought the crystals silvery like a moon behind thin clouds, but as they sailed closer, he discerned tints of green and blue. Wisps floated above the land like haunting spirits. Cam reached down his collar and fished out his half-sun amulet, symbol of Idar; he clutched it so tightly it stung his fingers.

"Inagon," whispered the sailor's oldest daughter. She had no amulet of her own, but she made the sign of Idar, a half circle across her chest. "The land of the dead."

Her sisters cursed and grumbled. The youngest, a demure girl with a cleft lip, began to insist they turned back now. The captain emerged upon the deck, stared at the pale lights, and grew just as pale. He cursed and prayed and grabbed salt from his pockets to toss into the water.

"There is no such place as Inagon," Cam said, turning from one sailor to another. "A cursed land that punishes sinners after death? That's just a story they tell children to scare them into obedience. We have the same story in Arden. We're in Eloria, the land of night. They don't even know Idarism here." He turned back toward the coast. "It's not haunted. It's . . . pretty."

He heard the lie in his own voice. The closer they sailed, the odder this place seemed. The crystals jutted along the coast, reminding him of tombstones. Cam loosened his collar.

He turned toward Suntai and whispered to her, "The sailors call this the land of the dead. What do you think, Suntai? What do your people say of the afterworld? Does it . . . look like this?"

253

"In some stories it is so." Suntai stared ahead grimly, then turned to him and gave a rare grin, revealing her canines. "If this is the land of the dead, we will raise them to fight our war. We sail on."

They anchored offshore and the companions climbed into a rowboat. The captain grabbed the oars, but his daughters refused to board, speaking of curses and ghosts.

"We will stay until the moon is full," Cam said to the captain as they rowed toward the ghostly shore. He hoped that would give him time to find someone—anyone—who could help. "Wait for us, and you'll have more jewels as payment for the journey back south."

The captain patted his pocket where his latest payment chinked. "Sometimes I think my daughters run this ship, and they're a foolish lot. Scared of ghosts and old stories, they are." He hawked and spat into the sea. "But they'll wait. They like jewels as much as the next woman, despite their sordid appearance and abundance of body hair." He barked a laugh—a jarring sound like a rusty nail against a board.

They oared on—a rowboat with a grizzled captain, an Ardish soldier and his dethroned queen, and an Elorian warrior. Their two nightwolves swam alongside the vessel, eyes reflecting the crystals ahead. Cold wind shrieked as they reached the shores of Leen.

Cam stepped onto a beach of coarse black sand. The crystals rose before him, taller than they'd seemed from afar; they stood as large as pines, silver and blue and cruel as blades. It was very cold. He shivered and wrapped his cloak tightly around him, and when the nightwolves emerged from the water and shook, ice clung to their fur. Linee's teeth chattered and even Suntai, used to the cold night, grunted as her breath frosted.

As fast as he'd dropped them off, the captain began to row back to his caravel, not bothering to set a single foot ashore.

254

Empires of Moth

"Do you think he'll wait for us?" Suntai asked, smiling grimly.

Cam sighed. "Not for an instant." He looked around him at the crystal forest. "We sail back with aid or we're stuck here. So I suppose there's only one thing to do now." He grinned, teeth chattering. "Roam around aimlessly and hope we stumble across an army."

"If we don't freeze to death first," Suntai said, mounting her nightwolf.

The companions left the shore, heading into the crystal forest.

Cam walked in silence, letting Linee ride the second nightwolf alone. After so long at sea, he needed to keep his feet on the ground. As they walked, he kept craning his neck back, gazing up at the crystals. Their surfaces were smooth and cold, and when Cam leaned close to a few, he could see the source of their glow. Tiny creatures floated within them, no larger than specks of dust. When he squinted, he saw that they were all different—some creatures had wings, and some were wreathed with spinning rings, while others simply looked like snakes with glowing eyes. Each shone a light like the lanternfish in the Inaro River. Thousands filled each crystal, maybe millions, trapped inside and spending their lives floating up and down and casting their glow.

"Camlin," Linee whispered from her wolf, "where are all the palaces?" She kicked the air with both feet. "I want to find a palace already."

"We've only been walking for moments. Be patient. And stop kicking. You know the wolves hate that. And for the millionth time, stop calling me Camlin like you're my mother."

They kept walking. Moments turned into hours. Hours turned into an hourglass turn, and soon Cam and Linee were both yawning. As much as weariness, hunger gnawed on Cam; he had

255

eaten little on the journey at sea, and with his belly settling, he ached for a meal and a good sleep.

"I want to make camp!" Linee said, arms crossed. "Tell Suntai I want to stop."

Suntai growled over her shoulder. "Be silent! This place is . . ." She looked around her, contemplating. "Holy."

"It's a holy bunch of boring." Linee tugged the reins, climbed off her wolf, and stood among the soaring crystals. "I'm not going another step until I rest."

Suntai shrugged and kept riding onward. Linee squealed and climbed back into the saddle.

Yet after another couple hours, even Suntai slowed down and finally stopped. They spent a cold, miserable few moments huddled between the wolves, eating what supplies they had: dry crackers, sausages, and mushrooms. After their meal, they lay down upon a fur blanket, pulled a second pelt over them, and nestled together. Cam lay in the middle, his companions clung to his sides, and the nightwolves curled up around them, providing some protection from the wind. Even with the fur blankets, both women holding him, and the shaggy nightwolves, Cam shivered and could barely sleep for the cold.

I miss home, he thought. He tried to imagine that he lay in his bed back in Fairwool-by-Night, a simple wooden thing his father had built, the mattress stuffed with straw, the woolen blankets soft and warm. He even missed staying in the Night Castle in Pahmey, his friends at his side: silly Hem who wheezed as he slept, Torin who always read some book before bed, and even Bailey . . . crazy, angry Bailey who always knew what to do, who always reminded him of home.

Does that home even still exist? Cam wondered. Ferius ruled Arden now; with the Sailith Order spreading, perhaps the monk would rule all of Mythimna, this world they called Moth. Would

256

Empires of Moth

the monk burn Fairwool-by-Night to the ground as revenge against his enemies?

Linee mumbled in her sleep and nestled closer to him. Again her hair filled his mouth, but this time Cam didn't mind as much. Suntai shifted at his other side, pressing against him, breathing deeply in her sleep. Slowly their warmth drove the chill from Cam, and he slept.

* * * * *

They sat around their campfire, burning the last of their tallow and eating the last of their mushrooms.

Have I led them to death in the cold? Suntai thought, staring into the flames, her swords in her hands. *Have I abandoned my mate, his sister, and all our people to ruin?*

This had been a fool's quest. She had failed. She had arrived in this land with no map, no plan, nothing but . . . but what? Her courage? Her strength? The pride of an alpha female?

Suntai snorted, eyes stinging. What were those worth in a northern hinterland of ice and stone and no life?

"How long has it been?" the girl Linee whispered, shivering. A fur cloak wrapped around her shoulders, and she sipped from her bowl—the last bowl of food she would eat.

Wrapped in his own pelt, Cam looked at the hourglass that stood by the fire, its sand trickling away like their life, like their hope. "Seven hourglass turns."

By the eighth we will die, Suntai thought.

She rose to her feet. "We move on."

Cam and Linee looked up at her, eyes weary and sunken, two lost pups. She had brought them here as proof of Timandra, living demons of sunlight, but now Suntai saw them as her children, as innocents to protect. Suntai—taller, older, stronger, wiser—had thought that she could save them, guide them to

257

hope. She had thought she could lead a pack of wolves. The pack was gone; her children were freezing and starving.

My womb is barren, and I have given no babes to my mate, she thought. *Let these ones be as my children. I will keep leading them. We will keep moving until we freeze, starve, die . . . or find life.*

"Up, Cam!" she said. "Up. Get Linee onto her wolf. We move."

Cam looked at her, face pale, and whispered, "Can we just warm ourselves for a little lon—"

"No!" She glared. "We move. On your feet."

We cannot linger, she thought. *Lingering is slow death.*

She mounted her wolf—the animal was thinner and wearier than Suntai had ever known her—and rode on, moving between the towering crystals. They had left the coast far behind—so far Suntai did not know if they would ever see it again. Silently, the two Timandrians mounted their own wolf, holding each other for warmth.

They kept traveling, moving north every turn. The crystals here grew taller than at the coast, obelisks like soaring towers, shining with inner light. The moon and stars moved above.

Wait for me, my mate, my Okado, Suntai thought. *I will not forget you.*

She rode for a long time among the crystal landscape, riding up and down hills, along bridges of glowing stones, and under natural archways carved by wind and rivers. She remembered riding with Okado and the pack, and she remembered her parents whom Yorashi had slain, and Suntai began to believe that her home was lost to her. She would remain here, frozen in the wild. She wondered if these crystals had once been travelers like her, lost and frozen, awaiting more lost pilgrims. As she rode, it seemed to Suntai that the crystals became people, men and women wandering the hinterlands, clad in white robes, their souls shining within translucent skin—the people of Leen rising from the earth.

Snow began to fall, coating her hair and cloak. When she looked over her shoulder, she saw Cam and Linee riding behind, their hair and clothes icy, their breath frosting. They held each other for warmth, but they were fading fast.

"We are like snowflakes ourselves," Suntai whispered, "buried under a storm."

She turned forward again. She gripped the reins with numb fingers. She kept riding. She was alpha, and she was a leader of a pack, even if her pack was now only them. She would lead them onward—to hope or into the great realms of afterlife.

The snow was burying her wolf's paws when Suntai saw the woman ahead.

At first Suntai thought the figure another one of the crystals, slender and snowy, an apparition from a feverish dream. The woman stared at her, eyes large and violet, pearly hair flowing down to her waist. She wore robes of pale silk and held a silver lantern. A diamond necklace shone around her neck.

"Welcome, travelers of foreign lands, to snow and ice, to crystal and silver, to wisdom and riddle." The woman nodded, a small smile on her lips. "I have seen your ship upon our sea, and I have followed your journey through the lights."

Suntai blinked, still not sure she was seeing a true person— the woman ahead seemed little more solid than a daydream. But when she heard Cam and Linee gasp, she realized that the woman truly stood before her.

"Who are you?" Suntai said, clutching her sword's hilt. "Why did you let us travel alone, lost and cold and hungry?"

The woman bowed her head. "I am a greeter. I am snow upon stone. I am young and not yet wise. I was sent to see, to learn." Her eyes darkened. "Many have attacked our lands, beings like those behind you." Her eyes turned toward Cam and Linee,

259

and pain filled the violet orbs. "I danced upon the stone and watched from darkness, my dagger in my hand, until wisdom grew within me. You are friends. You may follow, and I will lead you to halls of light and questions."

With that, the woman turned and began to walk north—or *flow* north, Suntai thought, for she heard or saw no footfalls in the snow. The woman seemed to float like breeze.

"A ghost," Linee whispered.

Suntai stared at the spectral figure. "We follow."

They rode for a long time through the snow, following the robed woman. They crossed a bridge over a frozen river. Frosted hills bristly with stone obelisks rolled at their sides, and mountains soared ahead, their surfaces gleaming with ice.

Through snowy wind, Suntai saw a great archway rising ahead, carved of glass or perhaps ice. It soared hundreds of feet tall; Suntai gasped to see it. She thought that the great structure could arch across the entire fallen city of Pahmey, never touching even its loftiest towers. They traveled through this gateway—a ghostly woman and two wolves bearing their riders, tiny figures in a land of giants.

The clouds parted, the snow curtains cleared, and the moon gleamed above. Suntai beheld a city in a valley below. She halted her wolf and stared, eyes dampening. Cam and Linee rode up to her side, stared down, and whispered prayers.

"It's beautiful," Linee said, eyes gleaming with tears.

Suntai smiled softly. "It's hope. We stand before Taenori, the fabled Light of the North."

The city of snow and glass sprawled for miles. Pahmey had been a place of color, but here lay a painting all in silver and white. Roads curled like filigree, lined with houses of pale bricks and frosted glass. The roofs of pagodas glittered with snow. Across the valley, a castle rose upon a hill, its towers white, a palace that seemed carved out of the mountain itself, a place of

Empires of Moth

smooth stone, icy paths, and coiling bridges, as natural and flowing as snow upon rock. Thousands of lanterns glowed below; light filled the valley like a second moon.

The robed woman led them through the city, and Suntai saw many other silent figures, their hair as pale and flowing as their robes. They passed by many houses, icicles hanging from their roofs; halls lined with columns, sages burning incense and chanting prayers within; and great braziers that crackled with blue flame and heat, melting the snow around them. Suntai and her companions moved silently, for Taenori was a city of song—a song of fire, of harps in temples, of wind in gardens of hanging gems. Even the nightwolves did not grunt or drool in this place; they gazed around with large, gleaming eyes.

Snow coating their hair and cloaks, they climbed the hill toward the castle. Guards stood at the gatehouse, silver breastplates clasped atop their white robes. Curved helms topped their heads, and they held spears and tall shields emblazoned with a painted diamond, sigil of Leen. Their alabaster hair spilled across their shoulders like frozen waterfalls.

The robed woman bowed and spoke softly in her tongue, a language like wind on water and melting ice in summer, and the castle gates opened. A hall loomed beyond, lit with silver light.

"I will take your wolves to a warm house," said the robed woman. "It is a place where we feed snowy bears and other beasts in need. They will be tended to. There is food and rest for you here too, travelers from distant lands, but first you may enter the hall of our king. We have sensed great need in you, and he much desires to hear your tidings." The woman bowed her head. "Pirilin too will speak with you, for she is wisest in our land."

Suntai hesitated, for she rarely parted from Misama; her dear nightwolf was as a part of her. When she dismounted, she held Misama's head, kissed her brow, and whispered to her in the wordless language they shared.

261

They entered the hall of Leen, three travelers weary and thin: a tall rider in steel scales, bow and blades across her back; a young, exiled queen, her cheeks pink and her golden hair tangled and dusted with snow; and a shepherd of sunlight joined to the night, slim and quick and staring with wide, dark eyes. Suntai thought they must have been the strangest trio to have ever entered this hall of majesty.

Marble columns stood in rows, supporting a vaulted ceiling painted with stars and moons. Many guards stood here, pale and frozen as statues, their eyes large and blue, their spears long and their shields bright. A ticking echoed across the chamber, a repeated chant like a tiny metal drum. *Tick. Tock. Tick. Tock.* A sound like a beating heart.

Across a tiled floor rose a throne of twisting silver strands, and here sat an old king, his hair flowing into his hoary beard, his ivory robes embroidered with silver strands. Wrinkles lined his face, spots marred his hands, and his fingernails curled like tails. His eyes were closed; he seemed asleep. At his feet coiled a great beast that sent Suntai's heart into a gallop.

"Pirilin," she whispered. "The fabled dragon of Leen."

The beast raised her head and blinked at her, violet eyes sad. Silvery scales chinked across her long body, gleaming like mother-of-pearl; as the dragon moved, the scales turned purple, green, blue, and finally white again. Seeing the dragon, Cam emitted a shocked, strangled sound, and Linee whispered in awe. Their eyes widened further when the dragon spoke.

"Three travelers come before you, my king," said Pirilin, speaking to the ancient man upon the throne. The dragon's voice was high and feminine and clear, sounding both youthful and ancient. She spoke in Qaelish, perhaps for Suntai's benefit, or perhaps some magic in this hall translated the dragon's words. "Here stands Suntai, a rider of wolves, a warrior of the night. With her enter Linee of House Solira, a usurped queen of sunlight, and her soldier, Camlin Shepherd." The white dragon blinked and her maw seemed to twist into a smile, revealing her fangs. "They come to you, my lord, with great need and weariness, for sunlight rises upon their lands."

The king still did not wake. Suntai narrowed her eyes, staring at the old man. He lay slumped, nearly falling from his seat, his shoulders stooped.

By the stars of the night . . .

Suntai covered her mouth.

"He's dead," she whispered. "The King of Leen, he's . . . embalmed."

The king was not just pale; he was lacquered and gleaming, frozen like a creature caught in ice. Finally Suntai saw the source of the ticking. At first, from the distance, she had mistaken it for an embroidered sigil. Now she saw that a hole filled the king's chest, larger than her fist. A mechanical heart filled the cavity, made of bronze gears, springs, and sprockets. The gears turned, ticking with a metallic heartbeat. *Tick. Tock. Tick. Tock.* Yet still the king slept, his chin resting against his chest, his limbs splayed. *Tick tock*, beat his heart, a rhythm like pattering rain and the life of dreams.

"The King of Leen cannot die, child of night," said Pirilin the dragon. "His sons have fallen; all heirs lie beneath the sea. I have given him life, crafting a device of all my cunning. For five hundred winters has the king sat upon his throne, and my gift of a heart still beats within him. I guard him still."

Suntai slowly exhaled, staring at this lingering mockery of life, this creature half-machine and half-man. She returned her eyes to the dragon.

"It is Pirilin, then, whom I must speak to. It is Pirilin whom I will ask for aid. Timandra attacks!" Suntai gestured at the two she had brought with her. "I bring before you two Timandrians, two who've joined the darkness of night. An army of their kind crawls across the Qaelish plains. Join us in this fight."

Pirilin blinked, her great lashes—each as long as a human arm—fanning the air. She shook her body, letting her scales clatter and gleam.

"These are not the first Timandrians I've seen." Her voice was low like cold wind over pebbles. "The sunlit sailors have brought their fire, their swords, and their arrows to our lands. From the island of Orida they sail, a sunlit twin to Leen, and they bring death. Our ports burned. Our fleet battled theirs and sunk their ships. We cast the enemy back, yet already more of their galleys sail toward us. I have seen them upon the wind."

Behind her, Suntai heard Cam translating the words into Ardish for Linee, his voice hushed. Suntai stepped away from the two, moving closer to the dragon, so close that she could feel the beast's hot breath against her.

"Then you have seen the terror in Qaelin," she said to the dragon. "Half a million Timandrians now crawl across the plains toward Yintao. The demon Ferius leads them, and he seeks to burn all the lands of night—our empire and yours. I have come, Pirilin, to unite our strength. If your king sleeps and you speak for him, speak the words of war. Fight with me!"

She stared at that sleeping king and his ticking heart. Her chest rose and fell, and her fingers tingled. More than the warmth of a bed, the taste of meat, or the sweetness of wine, she longed for songs of war, for spears banging against shields, for drums and horns and thudding boots. She was Suntai of Chanku, raised to crave the glory of blood, yet here in this hall she craved no glory—only the strength to protect her people.

"Our soldiers are strong and wise," said Pirilin. "Yet never have we meddled in the affairs of Qaelin or Ilar. For thousands of years, we in Leen have remained upon our island, gazing at the

Empires of Moth

stars, studying the wisdom of the skies." She shook her scaly head. "The night is large and dark, and we have built a city of light."

Suntai sneered, resisting the urge to draw her sword. Her voice echoed across the hall. "You cannot stay on your island forever! You cannot ignore the world beyond your shores. That world came to you in ships—enemy galleys that burned your western coast . . . and a southern caravel bearing a warning." Her fists shook. "If Ferius the Demon conquers Yintao, he will set his sights on Leen next. He distinguishes not between Elorian to Elorian; we are all equal kindling for his fire. For thousands of years you lingered here, yet you cannot ignore this fire. Sail south with me, Pirilin! Face the enemy upon the mainland! Do not speak of Orida, Leen, or Qaelin; those are old names, and this is a new war. This is a war between day and night."

She stood, chest rising and falling as she panted. Even in the cold air, sweat beaded on her brow. For long moments, only the ticking of the mechanical heart filled the chamber. *Tick. Tock. Tick. Tock.* The guards stood still. The dragon said nothing, and Suntai wanted to charge forward, grab the beast's horns, and shake them.

"Will you not fight?" she cried, turning from dragon to guards and back again. "Will you wait in your hall until the demons burst into it? You spoke of commanding ships. Soldiers fill your city. Send them south! Roar your battle cry and fight with—"

"Leen does not take orders from Suntai the rider," said Pirilin, interrupting the speech. "You are a warrior, Suntai, and you are strong and brave, yet we in Leen value other qualities." The dragon's fangs gleamed. She uncoiled and rose to hover above the tiles, flowing toward Suntai like a snake upon the water. "We value wisdom above all else. You are strong, rider of wolves, but are you wise?"

265

Pirilin's scaly head hovered only a foot away now. Her toothy mouth opened. She could have swallowed Suntai whole.

"All great warriors are wise," Suntai replied, staring into the dragon's eyes, each one as large as her head.

The beast grinned, and it reminded Suntai of the grin her wolf made before tearing into living flesh. "We shall see." The dragon licked her chops with a purple tongue. "I will test your wisdom, Suntai of Qaelin, and the wisdom of the Timandrians you bring into my hall. My brother Shenlai, the blue dragon of Qaelin, is a keeper of secrets. My brother Tianlong, the black dragon of Ilar, is a warrior. Yet I am Pirilin the White, a riddler." The dragon's eyes gleamed, and her tail rose behind her like a scorpion's stinger about to strike. "Three riddles will I ask you. If you answer all three, I will judge you wise, and Leen will join its strength to yours."

"And if I cannot answer?" Suntai said. "You will cast us out?"

Pirilin laughed. "If you fail to answer, you are foolish, and I have only one use for fools. You will remain here as my playthings . . . until I grow hungry, and then you will become my meals." The dragon licked the drool off her chin. "Are you ready?"

The heart ticked. Suntai looked to the king, praying silently for him to wake, as if prayers could end a sleep of centuries, undoing the clockwork of an ancient dragon.

"Do not look at him!" Pirilin demanded, moving to block the view. "You speak with a dragon now, not a king. Do you accept my challenge? If you do not, leave this court."

Suntai growled. Was this a game to Pirilin? Her people were dying, and the dragon would play with riddles? She looked over at Cam and Linee. They stared back, faces pale and bodies stiff.

"I say we play," the shepherd whispered to her. "I'm good at riddles. Or at least I used to be at The Shadowed Firkin, our

Empires of Moth

tavern back home. Hem would tell riddles sometimes and I used to solve most of them."

Linee nodded, hair flouncing; she spoke in mix of Ardish and broken Qaelish. "I'm good at riddles too! We had a book of them back at the palace. I mostly read books about animals, but sometimes I read the riddles one." She twisted her foot and lowered her gaze. "I mostly cheated and just read the answers, but . . . I remember a lot. Maybe Pirilin will ask a riddle I already know."

Suntai grunted. She was wise at tracking stonebeasts, reciting histories of battles, and fighting with the blade, yet riddles were a strange craft to her. But what other option did she have? She would not leave this palace empty-handed. Not as Okado needed her.

She returned her eyes to Pirilin. "Very well, Pirilin the White, dragon of Leen. Ask us your three riddles. We will answer them truly, and then . . . then we will sail to war."

"Or I will enjoy a meal," said Pirilin with a hungry smile. "We begin."

* * * * *

Cam took a deep breath, struggling to calm his frayed nerves. Linee took his hand and squeezed it, but the warm gesture offered little comfort.

We should have brought Torin with us, he thought. Torin had always been the best at riddles. Instead he had Suntai, a woman who knew every way to kill a man but had probably never read a book, and Linee, a woman who had owned many books and probably only looked at the pictures. As Pirilin the dragon licked her lips and cleared her throat, Cam gulped.

I'll have to rely on myself, he thought. *It'll be just like a game back at The Shadowed Firkin.*

267

The dragon's tongue darted, and the beast spoke her first riddle, her voice carrying across the hall. She uttered it first in Qaelish for Suntai, then in Ardish for Cam and Linee.

"Lives in dungeons
And dead men's eyes
Dwells in holes
And beyond the skies
Fills a killer's heart
And the weary's yawn
Yet come to meet me
And find me gone"

Cam frowned, took another deep breath, and searched his thoughts for an answer. At his sides, he saw Suntai and Linee mumble to themselves, brows furrowed.

Come on, just pretend you're Torin and answer! Cam told himself. He tried to remember the dragon's words, but already they were slipping from his mind.

What lived in dungeons? Rats? Prisoners? A rat would disappear if you came to meet it, but . . . how could rats live beyond the skies? Cam clenched and unclenched his fists. How could *anything* exist beyond the skies?

"Well, foreigners," said the dragon. The beast emitted a hissing laughter, and her tongue darted. "Will you not answer?"

"Give us some time!" Cam said.

The dragon's teeth gleamed. "Answer, strangers, for I grow hungry."

Despite the cold air, sweat trickled down Cam's back. He glanced at Linee and saw her chewing her lip and wringing her hands. When he glanced at Suntai, however, he saw no nervousness. The wolfrider lowered her head, and her arms hung loosely at her sides. She seemed almost sad.

Empires of Moth

"Answer!" demanded the dragon. "Answer or I feast."

Cam wracked his brains. The riddle had said something about filling hearts and eyes. Cruelty? Joy? Why would those disappear if you visited them?

He opened his mouth to request—to beg for!—more time. Before he could speak, Suntai raised her head. She spoke in a soft voice, a voice full of sadness and frailty that Cam had never heard in the proud warrior.

"I know something of this thing," said the wolfrider and placed a hand on her belly. "The answer is: emptiness."

Pirilin seemed to pout—if it were possible for a dragon to pout. "Pity. I was hoping to eat you already. You answered truly."

Cam took a deep, shuddering breath, but his relief was short lived. The dragon rose higher, hovering several feet above the floor, and spoke her second riddle.

"Topples mountains
Cuts through stone
Mightier than crown and throne
Strangles men
And crumbles lead
Yet without him
All lie dead"

The companions stood before the dragon, frowning and mumbling to themselves. Cam bit his lip and twisted his fingers. Topples mountains and stone and lead? What kind of weapon could do that . . . yet foster life?

He glanced at Suntai, but she seemed just as stumped; she winced and twisted her brow, deep in thought. Cam cursed under his breath, and a shiver ran through him. A cannon? An army? One could claim that an army protected life, but how could even an army cut stone and topple mountains?

269

"It looks like I'll be enjoying a meal," said Pirilin. Saliva dripped between her teeth. "I do believe I'll eat the boy first; he is small as an appetizer."

Cam held up his hand. "Wait! Give us a moment."

At his side, Linee whimpered and covered her eyes, and Suntai cursed. Cam tapped his foot, thinking back to the war. What had been the greatest danger he'd faced? Arrows? Swords? Fire? None seemed to fit.

He snickered. It often seemed to him that more than weapons, it was the journey at sea that had crippled him; he had gagged overboard so often that—

Cam froze, mouth hanging open.

"Time to feast," said the dragon and hovered toward him, maw opening wide. Her hot breath blasted him, and strings of saliva quivered between her teeth like harp strings.

"Water!" Cam shouted. "The answer is: water!" He laughed. "Of course."

The dragon hissed, pulled back, and closed her mouth. She glared at Cam and whipped her tail. Her scales clinked like a sack of coins. With a growl, the dragon spoke her third riddle.

"Both question and answer
Both darkness and light
In the minds of the wise
And the stars of the night
I guard the paths to wisdom
I hide the greatest treasure
Name what lies behind my door
And you'll lose me forever"

For a long moment, the three companions stood silently.

Cam clutched his head, tapped his foot, and bit his lip, but no answer came to him. At his side, Suntai was balling her fists

Empires of Moth

and whispering, her eyes closed, but seemed no closer to finding an answer. Pirilin the dragon laughed, a sickening sound, and snapped her teeth.

Oh muddy sheepskins, Cam thought with a grimace. *I don't know this one. I don't know. We're dragon food. Oh Idar . . .*

Linee's voice rose beside him. "It's a riddle."

Cam groaned. "Yes, Linee, I know it's a riddle. Let me think."

She tugged his sleeve. "But Camlin! It's a riddle."

"I *know*, Linee!" He glared at her. "I know it's a riddle. Please be quiet and let me think of the answer."

Linee groaned, crossed her arms, and stomped her feet. "The answer *is* 'a riddle', you foolish boy. 'A riddle' is both the question and answer." She turned toward the dragon, puffed out her chest, and grinned. "The answer is: a riddle."

Cam turned toward the dragon, expecting the beast to lunge and feast upon him. But Pirilin only stared, her violent eyes gleaming. A smile stretched across the dragon's face, but this time it was not hungry, but a smile of kindness and wisdom.

"The riddles are solved," she said. "Your wisdom is deep."

Linee hopped up and down, clapped excitedly, and hugged Cam. He pried her off and stepped closer to Pirilin.

"Will you fight with us?" he said, chest rising and falling. He looked across the hall at the embalmed king upon his throne, clockwork heart ticking; at the guards between the columns, faces hidden behind silver helmets; and back again at the white dragon with the lilac eyes. "Will you sail south with us? Will you fight Ferius and his hosts?"

They were all silent. Cam panted, staring from side to side, and drew his sword. He raised the blade, eyes stinging.

"Will you not answer?" Cam walked from soldier to soldier and then back to Pirilin. Heart thrashing, he touched the dragon's

271

scales; they were ice-cold. "I've answered your riddles. Now answer mine! Will you fight?"

Pirilin blinked her crystal orbs. For a moment, the only sound was the sleeping king's clockwork heart. Cam stared at the dragon. Suntai and Linee came to stand at his side.

Tick. Tock. Tick. Tock.

Slowly, Pirilin rose like a snake from a basket, like smoke from a flame, until her head nearly touched the vaulted ceiling fifty feet above. Her body swayed and chinked. She looked down upon the companions and cried in a voice that shook the hall.

"Leen will fight!"

Linee hopped and squealed with joy, and Suntai raised her sword and cried for battle. Cam, however, could feel no joy, not even relief. He only closed his eyes, lowered his head, and squared his jaw.

I avoided starvation and a dragon's wrath. His eyes stung. *Now I will sail with an army. Now blood will spill, fire will burn, and death will cover the night.*

The cry echoed in the chamber, and the soldiers of Leen repeated the cry. "Leen will fight! Leen will fight!"

The chants rose. The heart ticked on.

CHAPTER TWENTY-THREE
THE SHIPS OF ILAR

"No," she whispered, thrashing her head. "Please, no, don't . . ."

She tried to pull back but could not. She begged, but the beast would not listen. Still the nightwolf fed, digging its teeth into her arm, ripping flesh, shaking its head and tugging and clawing, tearing tendons, cracking bone. Koyee wept, her ruin of an arm trapped within the beast's mouth, and she screamed as it ate her.

"He's eating me . . . please, stars, please . . . he's eating me alive . . ."

But the wolf was gone; it had never been a wolf at all. Her arm lay within a pile of smoking bones, not a beastly mouth. Bits of charred flesh still clung to the pile, hot, searing her. She recognized these remains. Here were the bones of her father, stacked in a wheelbarrow, and Koyee screamed again, trying to pull her arm loose, lost in the darkness. The bones were so hot, crackling with flame, and she watched her arm wither until it too was only a bone, only a smooth shaft coated with burnt skin. She wept.

"Help . . . help me, please . . ."

A hand touched her forehead. "I'm here, Koyee. I'm here. You're safe."

She knew that voice. It was Torin! Torin the demon, the creature with the mismatched eyes! He stood behind the wheelbarrow, pushing it forward, bringing this death into her land.

"Go away," she begged him. "Go back into the dusk. Leave Oshy. I don't want to leave. I don't want to go to Pahmey. Please . . . Torin, go away."

Yet he would still not release her. He still kept his hand on her forehead, only it wasn't Torin after all; why had she thought it was Torin? She tried to toss off the warty hand, but he only laughed—Old Snaggletooth, his gums stained with the spice, his strands of hair swaying. He reached into her pockets, seeking, rifling, stealing her money, her life, her memories of home.

Home . . .

Oshy . . .

She had to keep that memory alive. She kicked wildly, shoving him off. She had to remember Oshy. Her home had burned. They had killed her people . . . Yinlan, the elderly bead-maker who had once sewn her fur mittens . . . little Linshani who played the flute so well . . . all gone . . .

"I miss you," she whispered, tears in her eyes. "I miss you, Father. I miss you, Mother."

The hand caressed her forehead. "I'm here, Koyee. I'm always with you."

She blinked weakly. She seemed to lie in a hammock, the room swaying around her. A ship. She was in the belly of a ship or perhaps a whale. A figure knelt above her, whispering, and she thought that it was Torin again, but gentle light fell, and she knew her. She remembered.

"Mother," she whispered. "Mother, how can you be here? You died. You died when I was a baby."

And yet the gentle woman stared down at her, smoothing her hair. She looked like Koyee. She too had lavender eyes, smooth white hair, and a triangular face, only her mother was beautiful, for no scars marred her.

"I'm here, Koyee," she said, speaking in Torin's voice. "I'm always with you."

Empires of Moth

Koyee reached out to hold her mother's hand, to feel her warmth, to be a child again . . . but her mother withdrew. The woman's face twisted in agony and her belly bulged, and Koyee realized that her mother was pregnant, that the baby was coming.

"Mother!"

Her mother fell back, belly bulging and contracting, and the babe emerged, a twisted creature, biting and clawing, a child with beady eyes and yellow robes and sharp teeth.

"Ferius . . ."

The monk emerged from the womb, a parasite with bloody gums, and leaped onto her mother, not feeding at the breast but ripping into flesh, eating, killing, and Koyee screamed and reached out, trying to grab Ferius, to pull him off her mother, but she couldn't . . . she couldn't! He was her brother. He was linked to her. He was . . .

The whale swayed.

She rocked in her hammock.

Her eyes fluttered back.

"She's not getting better," said her mother.

A demonic hiss answered. "We've rubbed her arm with our herbs. We've used the ancient magic of Ilar. If she screams, that is good. That means the curse is leaving her. Stay with her, Torin, even as she shouts and weeps. She will be cured."

Her eyes fluttered. She saw a monk leave the chamber, not a monk of Sailith in yellow robes, but an Elorian all in black, a flame sigil upon his breast, and Torin stood in the room again, and she clutched his hand.

"Stay with me, Torin. Stay with me."

He squeezed her hand and wiped the sweat off her brow. "Always."

She spent a long time in the hull of this ship. An hourglass turned upon her table, but she was only vaguely aware of the time passing. Torin fed her, talked to her, and changed the damp cloth

275

upon her forehead, and it seemed that every turn that strange, robed monk returned to chant spells, to rub herbs onto her arm, to nod even as she screamed, even as the feverish dreams tore through her, making her thrash and weep.

The hourglass turned.

She closed her eyes.

She slept.

* * * * *

After half a moon of fever, Koyee emerged onto the deck of the ship, her limbs thin and her fingers trembling. Wrapped in a silk cloak, she beheld a starry sky, a smooth sea, and hundreds of lamp-lit ships.

Koyee gasped and her eyes dampened. "The navy of Ilar." She turned to Torin, and a smile trembled on her lips. "Ilar sails to war."

Torin nodded. He wore the armor the Chanku Pack had given him, and his sword hung at his side. "We've been sailing for turns as you slept. We'll see the coast of Qaelin before another turn passes."

She looked around her, eyes wide. Koyee had seen fleets before. She had stood upon the walls of Pahmey, firing arrows as the Ardish navy crashed into her city's flotilla. The fleet around her, sailing north through the night, dwarfed that memory. Hundreds of Ilari ships covered the sea, their banners sporting the red flame upon a black field.

Many were *panokseon* vessels, tall ships with three tiers of decks: one for rowers, one for dragon-shaped bronze cannons, and finally a roofed deck for warriors in black armor. Other ships were *geobukseons*—turtle ships—a hundred feet long, their sails tall, their decks crowded with soldiers. Their dragon figureheads puffed sulfur smoke, all but hiding the decks; when wind blew,

Empires of Moth

clearing the smoke, Koyee saw cannons lurking inside the dragons' mouths like tongues. Above them all loomed great *atakebune* ships, floating fortresses. Clad in iron, their hulls bristled with many oars. Cannons lined their railings, manned by armored soldiers. Pagodas rose upon their decks, full of archers, and figureheads of iron panthers loomed off their prows, ready to ram into enemy ships.

When Koyee examined her own ship, she found a vast deck of polished metal. A hundred soldiers or more moved across it. They wore armor of black, lacquered plates, and their helms—shaped as demonic faces with bristly fur mustaches—frowned at her. Three masts towered, their sails wide.

"This is a fleet greater than any in Qaelin," Koyee whispered, tears of awe in her eyes. "This fleet can save the night."

Torin looked at her, eyes soft. "How is your arm?"

She pulled up her sleeve, exposing a pale twig of a limb. Faded scars coiled around her arm like a snake around a pole, rising from wrist to shoulder. But the poison was out; the curse was gone. Where black, swollen welts had risen only pale scars remained. Koyee opened and closed her fist.

"It tingles," she said. "But the black magic of Mageria is gone. This arm can fight. The scars are ugly, but . . . I already have ugly scars on my face. What are a few more?"

"I don't think they're ugly." Torin touched her cheek. "Not the scars on your arm or your face. Scars are marks of survival. Scars are tattoos of strength."

She laughed. "Then you're weak, because your skin is as smooth as a baby's behind." She kissed his cheek. "But you're kind. And you stayed with me, even as I screamed and thrashed. You tended to me as I healed." Her eyes watered again. "Even in my worst dreams, through nightmares of blood and death, a white pillar always shone, piercing the darkness . . . sometimes only a distant needle, other times a warm, comforting light. I know now that you shone that light, Torin. That you were always there." She embraced him. "Thank you."

He cleared his throat, seeming uncomfortable. "Well, technically I'm still your prisoner, even if they let me wear armor and fight. I couldn't let you die; they'd toss me into the slave pits."

She tapped his nose. "That . . . and because you love me. I know you do. I heard you say so. So don't deny it!"

She walked across the deck, her knees still wobbly, and reached the prow. A dragon figurehead thrust out ahead, forged of iron. Ahead across the water, she saw a true dragon fly above the ships, a warrior upon his back. Tianlong was healed too, and when the dragon flew closer, roaring his cry, Koyee saw that the empress rode him, a banner in her hand.

Ilar's might is horrible to behold, Koyee thought, *but now it gives me hope. Now the enemy will taste the true wrath of the night.*

She leaned across the prow, staring north. Qaelin lay there . . . her homeland. The largest empire in Eloria. The land of her forebears, the land she had killed for, nearly died in . . . the land where the fate of the night would be sealed.

"The empress says we will sail up the Yin River," said Torin, coming to stand at her side. "It will lead us through dark plains to the capital."

Koyee nodded. "I've never sailed upon the Yin, for it lies far east of the Inaro. But when I lived on the streets of Pahmey, I heard songs of it. The Inaro is the left vein of Qaelin, buskers would sing—the Yin is its right."

Lights gleamed ahead. Koyee gasped. Were those the lights of Qaelin? But as she stared, she narrowed her eyes.

"Torin . . . does half the Ilari fleet sail ahead?"

He stared at the lights with her, face ashen. "We stand upon the *Red Flame*, the flagship of Ilar—we are the vanguard."

Empires of Moth

Koyee turned away. "A hundred ships sail ahead. Where is my armor and sword?"

Around them across the deck, soldiers rushed back and forth, grabbing bows and drawing flaming arrows. Horns blared across the Ilari fleet. One man, only feet away from Koyee, began to bang on a war drum. Distant drums answered. Koyee made to race back down into the hull, to find her father's sword, to find her armor and helm.

"Koyee!" Torin said, running after her, moving between the rushing soldiers. "You're still weak. You can't fight this battle."

She nearly crashed into a running soldier—a spirit of steel, his crimson pauldrons flaring out—and reached the stairs plunging into the hull. "I'm fine, Torin."

"You are not!" He climbed downstairs behind her. "You look thinner than a chicken bone. You must rest."

She glared over her shoulder at him. "I'll rest when I'm dead."

"If you fight in this shape, that might not be far off."

She ignored him, reached her chamber, and found her tunic of scales. She pulled the armor over her head, grabbed her helmet from a table, and found her sword hanging upon the wall. All the while, Torin objected, insisting that tens of thousands of Ilari soldiers could fight, that she should get back to bed.

"Torin, if you don't be quiet, I'm going to toss you overboard." She shoved past him. "Now, you can either hope you know how to swim in your armor, or you can come with me and fight some Timandrians."

He groaned but he followed.

When they emerged back onto the deck, the enemy fleet was close. Koyee inhaled sharply and drew her sword. A hundred ships or more sailed toward them, their masts high, their banners sporting green reptiles upon golden fields. In the distance behind

279

them, Koyee could make out the coast of Qaelin, a dark line rising from the water into the starry sky.

"Do you know their banners, Torin?"

He nodded grimly. "The fleet of Daenor sails against us. This kingdom lies upon the western coast of Timandra, a distant land where lizards grow as large as horses." Torin drew his sword. "Bards sing that Daenor's fleet is the greatest in the lands of sunlight."

Koyee grinned savagely. "Luckily we're not in the lands of sunlight."

The drums beat. The war horns blared. The two fleets sailed forward and lights lit the darkness.

Cannons fired across the Ilari fleet. Rockets blasted forward, leaving trails of fire that reflected in the black waters. From the Timandrian fleet, ten thousand flaming arrows flew like comets, crossed the sky, and rained down.

With screams and flame and blood, the dance began.

Koyee and Torin stood with raised shields as arrows slammed against them. Smoke blasted as cannons fired. Around them, men shouted, oars splashed, and the ships drove forward. The dragon figureheads blazed, embers bright within their maws, their smoke rising in clouds. The drums beat steady as a heart, a thud for every stroke of the oars. Above the battle, Empress Hikari chanted for the night, and her dragon roared.

"Last time, Torin, we fought against each other." Koyee flashed him a grin. "Let's see how we fight side by side."

Through smoke and raining fire, the two fleets smashed together.

Ironclad *atakebune* ships smashed into Timandra's carracks, snapping their wooden hulls. Masts tilted and men screamed. Galleons rowed forward, and their figureheads—shaped as the crocodiles of Daenor—drove into Elorian vessels. Masts fell and sails caught flame. Everywhere Koyee looked, arrows flew, cannons blazed, and fire spread. She lifted her sword and snarled as a Timandrian ship—a towering carrack with three masts—slammed against them.

The railing shattered before her. Smoke plumed, fire crackled, and water sprayed. Through the inferno, a horde of Timandrian troops leaped onto the *Red Flame*'s deck. Their helmets, shaped as reptile heads, gleamed in the firelight. Metal claws rose from their boots and gauntlets. The soldiers shrieked, inhuman sounds, and raised sabers—curved blades longer and wider than katanas, the steel gleaming with green poison.

Koyee and Torin raised their swords together. With a hundred Ilari troops, they rushed toward the enemy.

The ship rocked. Men fell and died. The sabers of Daenor swung. Katanas slammed into chain mail. Corpses littered the deck of the *Red Flame*, and all around across the sea, hundreds of ships crashed together, burned, sank, and bristled with fighting soldiers. The ring of steel, the screams of the dying, and the roars of cannons filled the night, an eternal song.

Koyee fought in a daze, weak after her long disease but shouting, never slowing, slashing her sword into the enemies. It had been a year since the Battle of Pahmey, since she had stood upon that city's walls, leaped across its roofs, and slain men on its streets. Yet she had never forgotten the smell of blood, the sight of the dying, the thirst of her blade. She had been a mere girl then, frightened and alone but fighting as thousands died around her. She was still frightened, she was still too thin, but now . . . now she fought as a killer.

Blood filled the sea.

The *Red Flame* sailed on.

Across the water, a hundred ships blazed. Tianlong, the black dragon of Ilar, howled overhead, dipping to crush men between his jaws. For miles across the water, soldiers splashed and drowned, and masts vanished like bones into bogs.

281

It was an hourglass turn, maybe two, before the Ilari fleet reached the coast of Qaelin.

Koyee fell upon the deck of the *Red Flame*, panting, her chest blazing where a saber had chipped her armor. Torin fell by her side, wheezing, his sword gripped in his bloody hand. Dents covered his armor, a scratch stretched across his arm, and blood stained his leg. They lay among the corpses of fallen soldiers. They reached across the sticky deck and grasped each other's hands.

"Ilar lives," Koyee said, voice hoarse. "There is hope for the night."

Devastation filled the water behind them. Two hundred ships of Ilar had sailed north, bearing the red flame banners; dozens now lay beneath the sea. A hundred other ships, the smashed fleet of Daenor, would be their company in the watery halls. Above the surviving ships, Tianlong sounded his cry, and the soldiers of Ilar repeated the words.

"We are the night!"

When Koyee tilted her head, she saw Torin mouth the prayer too, the ancient cry of her people, for he too was a son of Eloria now, born in sunlight but of a starlit heart. She squeezed his hand.

"They battle on the sea has ended," she said. "When we reach Yintao, the battle for the night will begin."

CHAPTER TWENTY-FOUR
THE HORNS OF YINTAO

Hem swung his sword, sweat trickling from his brow, his lips a thin line. Bailey parried the blow and riposted. With a grunt, Hem caught her blade on his shield and swung again.

"Good!" Bailey said. "You're faster now."

Hem didn't feel any faster. He still felt so heavy, so clumsy, his sword always close to slipping from his sweaty hand. Bailey, however, fought like a rabid wolf, her blade swinging again and again. Hem raised his shield, catching the blows; her sword had left a dozen dents in the metal disk. He stepped back across the dusty courtyard, step by step, retreating from her onslaught. When his back hit the wall, he attempted a desperate thrust. She parried the blow, then smacked her blade against his helm.

"That's a kill!" Bailey announced. She spat. "Good fight."

Hem blinked, barely able to see. His ears rang. He wore a thick helm of steel, its inside padded with fur, and Bailey was only swinging a dull, tin training sword, not a real blade. Still, she was strong enough that her blows hurt. He dropped his own training sword, pulled off his helmet, and sucked in a breath.

"Bloody Idar, Bails," he said. "Go easy on me. I'm still learning."

She jabbed her finger against his breastplate. "When I'm tough on you, that is how you learn." She grinned and patted his cheek. "You're getting better, old boy. The new beard helps you look tough too."

"Really?" Hem squeaked, then cleared his throat, squared his shoulders, and spoke in a deep growl. "I mean . . . thank you."

Bailey sighed and shook her head. "Don't do that voice again. It's not helping. Just keep training and she'll learn to love you back."

Hem sputtered and nearly choked. He glanced around the courtyard, hoping nobody heard, but only a few soldiers of Yintao stood by a distant wall, conversing amongst themselves. Feeling his cheeks flush, Hem turned back to Bailey.

"I don't know what you're talking about," he said.

"Of course you do!" Bailey stretched out her arms and raised her voice. "The girl you fancy! The omega named . . . what was it? Kira?"

"Bailey, hush!" His cheeks burned. "She can't know. All right? Just . . ." He glanced around again and lowered his voice. "Just keep practicing with me until I'm strong enough. I want to . . . you know . . . protect her and all that." His cheeks wouldn't stop burning.

"You could start by not blushing," Bailey said. "Here— pretend that I'm her and act tough."

She pressed her legs together, clasped her hands behind her back, and leaned forward on her toes. She planted a kiss right on Hem's cheek.

"Well, it's easy when *you* do it," Hem said. "You're just . . . Bailey."

She growled and grabbed her training sword. "Watch it! Now pick up your sword. I'm not done with you."

Hem wiped the sweat off his brow, lifted his sword, and their training continued.

He was puffing, his legs rubbery, when he finally left the courtyard. He walked along a street, moving between lantern poles and patrolling guards. When he glanced at the moon, it was nearly full, and Hem felt his heart sink.

We've been in Yintao for three months, he thought. *He must be near now . . . Ferius.*

Empires of Moth

Fresh sweat beaded on his brow. Hem didn't want to think about that. He had ridden here upon a nightwolf, moving fast across the plains, while Ferius led a slow, cumbersome army. They would be inching along Sage's Road, dragging siege engines yard by yard, but Hem knew they would be here soon. Training with Bailey, it was easy to imagine he was practicing to impress Kira . . . not to fight in a battle.

Yet that battle will come. And we will all have to fight. He looked at the northern stars, then the southern ones.

"Where are you, Torin? Where are you, Cam?" Hem sighed. "Damn it . . . come here soon with aid."

Holding his lantern, he made his way back to the hall he was staying in, one of many buildings in the palace complex. They called this place—the inner level of the city—the Eternal Palace, but rather than one building, it was a town unto itself. Barracks, squares, pagodas, and temples filled this center of Yintao, all protected by towering square walls. Beyond those walls, six more levels of the city spread out, squares within squares, each protected by more walls and towers.

Even if Ferius attacks, Hem thought, *he can't reach me here.* The monk's army would break through the first wall, perhaps. Maybe the second or even the third. But seven walls lay between the Eternal Palace and the dark plains. Hem nodded, telling himself this city was the safest place in Eloria . . . yet still his hands shook when he grabbed the doorknob to his hall.

It was a small building, its adobe bricks unadorned, its roof tiled red and topped with a statue of Xen Qae. A hundred Chanku riders shared the building; all were sleeping when Hem entered. He made his way to his chamber—as one of only two Timandrians in the city, they had given him a room of his own—and stepped inside.

A small, cozy space greeted him. A table topped with ceramic dishes, a bed with clawed legs, and a bronze mirror stood

285

along the walls. Hem placed down his lantern and examined his reflection. He did look different, he thought. The beard aged him, and since leaving Dayside—by Idar, it had been a year already!—he was down three notches on his belt. When he sucked in his gut and puffed out his chest, Hem could almost imagine that he was a true warrior, a man who could protect Kira . . . maybe even be her mate.

"And there it is," he said to himself. "Blushing again, damn it."

A knock sounded on his door.

Hem's heart burst into a gallop.

She was here! She was early! He had hoped to remove his armor, don one of the embroidered robes Emperor Jin had given him, mentally prepare himself, and—

The knock sounded again.

Hurriedly, Hem dabbed his brow, brushed back his hair, and gulped. He opened the door and saw her there.

While Bailey always walked tall and proud, chest thrust out and chin raised, every inch a warrior, Kira was the opposite. She stood small and short, hugging herself and staring at her feet. She nearly drowned in a great, shaggy fur cloak, and her hair all but hid her face. She peered up at him between the white strands, her eyes huge and blue, then back at her toes. She twisted those toes as if wishing the ground could swallow her.

"*Sen sen*, Hem," she said in a meek voice.

He instantly felt better. He was always nervous about meeting her, but Kira seemed just as shy. Moving a little too quickly, his fingers trembling just slightly, he gestured for her to enter his chamber.

When she sat on his bed, she bit her lip, kept staring at her feet, and hugged herself. Hem sat beside her, thrice her size and feeling as graceless as a bear on a dancer's stage. For a moment they only sat in awkward silence.

286

Empires of Moth

"I like your beard," she finally said, and a soft smile touched her face. Hurriedly, she looked back at her feet, her cheeks flushing behind her strands of wild hair.

"I like your . . ." Hem racked his mind for something to say; he liked all of her and didn't know which part to choose. "Your necklace."

She touched the string of clay beads. "Thank you. I'm not allowed to wear a necklace of wolf claws yet, since I'm still just an omega, but . . . maybe if I kick people a few more times, I can move up the ranks." She giggled and covered her mouth.

Her laughter was beautiful, and Hem's spirits soared. "That was a mighty kick!" he said. "I think he's still feeling it."

She looked up at him and smiled—not a nervous smile but a true one, a beautiful smile, a smile that showed her large white teeth and lit up her eyes. Before Hem realized what he was doing, he was pulling back strands of her hair and tucking them behind her ears. She stared at him, hands in her lap.

"You're pretty when I can see your face," he said softly.

Her lips parted and she placed a hand on his cheek. "You're pretty too."

Hem laughed. "No I'm not. I'm . . . I'm fat. And I'm awkward. And—"

"You're pretty," she whispered.

Hem remembered how Bailey had kissed his cheek—she had done it only mockingly, only trying to embarrass him, but now Hem wondered what it would be like to kiss Kira's cheek . . . and for her to kiss him. He shifted a little closer to her and—

Horns blared outside.

Hem froze.

Kira leaped to her feet.

"The silver horns of Yintao," she whispered.

The sound keened across the city, rising and falling, a sound like ghosts in the deep, like the death of a nation. Hem stumbled

287

toward the door and raced outside into the courtyard. Thousands were spilling out from their halls, pulling on armor and buckling swords to their belts. The horns blared from every guard tower, a sound that shook the city.

Kira clutched Hem's hand. "War."

Eye stinging, Hem reached down, raised her chin, and kissed her cheek—perhaps the last time he could.

He whispered, "Ferius is here."

* * * * *

He stood upon the city's outer walls, a sword in his hand, gazing at the dark plains as the horizon burned.

He marches there, Okado thought. *My half-brother.*

The wind smelled of smoke and metal. Firelight rose in the distance like the dusk back in Oshy, the village of his childhood. Standing here on the walls of Yintao, staring upon shadows leading to light, Okado could almost imagine that he stood in Oshy again, gazing at the dusk, imagining the demons that lived in the land of sunfire.

My mother loved a sunlit demon, he thought, lips twitching. His hand tightened around his hilt. *My mother gave birth to his child, a boy of both sunlight and darkness. Ferius.*

He realized his sword was shaking, rage pounding through him. This had happened a decade before his birth—his mother had been only a youth—but still Okado raged. How could his mother have loved the enemy? How could she have carried this child within her, kept it secret, lied to him and Koyee until she took that secret to her grave?

Okado found himself snarling, and his anger overflowed, emerging in a howl. He raised his sword high.

Now that child of sin, his mother's secret, came back to crush the lands of night. Now he, Okado, born of the same

288

Empires of Moth

woman but a different father, would have to send this shame back into daylight, to kill the cursed spawn of—

"Okado, I fight with you," Bailey said, interrupting his thoughts. Standing beside him upon the battlements, she raised her sword with his. "We will slay them."

Breathing heavily, he turned toward her. Bailey met his gaze, her eyes strong, her lips tightened. She wore the armor of his people, steel scales and a wolf's head helm. Though she still carried her double-edged blade of Timandra, not the curved katana of the night, she was part of his pack. She was strong and noble like Suntai, and Okado felt his rage lower to a simmer.

Not all Timandrians are demons, he thought, gazing into Bailey's brown eyes. *Perhaps my mother was not a sinner.* He turned his eyes to the western horizon. *Yet her son was born a monster. And I must kill him.*

"You are strong, Bailey Berin of the Arden clan," he said. "If we survive this war, I will name you a great rider in my pack, a beta warrior of Chanku."

She snickered. "I don't need no titles. I just want to stick my sword in Ferius's gut."

The fire grew brighter ahead, a red puddle oozing toward them. Individual soldiers were still too far to see; Okado could only make out rustling black specks under the flame and smoke. Their drums beat in the distance, and their own horns keened. When the wind gusted, Okado thought that he could hear a distant chant, a song for blood and victory. According to their scouts, all eight sunlit kingdoms marched there, soldiers and beasts, siege towers and chariots, monks and soldiers, death and destruction. It was the greatest army to have ever moved across Moth.

Okado looked around him at the walls of Yintao. He stood upon the outer wall, one of seven squares enclosing the city. Thousands of soldiers manned the battlements. Most were

289

soldiers of Yintao, helms hiding their faces. They held bows, spears hung across their backs, and swords hung at their sides. Guard towers rose at regular intervals, more archers upon them; the banners of Qaelin fluttered there, showing a moon within a star.

When Okado looked down into the streets behind him, he could see his own warriors—the riders of Chanku astride their wolves, their armor dusty, their fur pelts rustling in the wind. The civilians of Yintao had evacuated from the first level of the city; they now hunkered deeper in. Along the streets and upon the roofs, the Chanku Pack stood ready for battle. Should the enemy break through the first layer of walls, they would meet Okado's clan; thousands of wolves and riders would die before letting Ferius reach the city's second level.

"Seven walls," he said softly. "Five thousand warriors of Chanku. Fifty thousand soldiers of Yintao. Against half a million Timandrians."

He looked toward the northern darkness. Only shadows spread into that horizon. *Where are you, Suntai?* He turned toward the south, seeing only darkness there too. *Where are you, Koyee, my sister?*

Bailey touched his arm. "They will return with aid. Leen and Ilar will not abandon us."

Okado stared back to the west. The fire burned brighter now. He could make out glints on armor and distant spikes— siege towers as high as these walls. "The siege might end before our friends arrive. This battle will be ours to fight—we stand alone."

"Then we stand alone." Bailey drew an arrow from her quiver. "We will defeat the enemy—with or without our friends."

They stood side by side, silent, waiting. All across the walls, the thousands of defenders stared. The horns still blew from the city towers. The enemy trumpets and drums answered the call.

290

Empires of Moth

They swarmed across the land, spreading forward like wildfire. Okado could see the enemy clearly now, and he drew an arrow of his own.

They covered the land, a moving city of bloodlust. Eight armies marched side by side, eight hordes of flesh and steel. Their banners rose, billowing in the wind, showing their sigils—ravens and tigers, scorpions and bears, and other beasts of sunlight. Above them all rose the banners of the Sailith Order, the new emblem uniting the daylight—a golden sunburst upon a red field.

Lines and lines of troops marched, clad in the armor of their kingdoms. Some wore steel plates, others wore chain mail, while some wore suits of boiled leather strewn with iron bolts. They raised their weapons—swords, spears, pikes, bows. Not only men moved below; thousands of beasts approached too, creatures Okado recognized from Bailey's stories. Tigers tugged at leashes, roaring at the sight of the city. Some warriors rode upon horses, fast animals as large as nightwolves; others rode shaggy bears, humped camels, and even elephants with painted tusks. Alongside men and animals, the machines of war rolled forth: chariots with scythed wheels, siege towers topped with archers, wheeled battering rams hanging from chains, catapults and trebuchets, and ballistae loaded with bolts the size of men. From these hosts of might rose battle cries and song; men chanted for victory, drums beat, and horns wailed. The cry pounded against the city walls, louder than thunder.

"Idar protect us," Bailey whispered. She nocked her arrow.

Across the walls of Yintao, the other defenders—thousands of men and women who'd waited silently—now whispered their own prayers. They stared ahead, hands clutching their weapons. Some prayed to Xen Qae, others to the constellations, and some to the spirits of dead forebears. One man turned to flee, then another. The rest remained at their posts, staring, waiting.

A light gleamed above, and Okado looked up to see Shenlai the dragon flying high above the walls. Soldiers of Eloria pointed and cried out.

"Shenlai flies! The dragon of Qaelin blesses us."

Across the last mile, the enemy marched forth; they covered the land now, spreading into the horizon, an endless sea. Their cries rose.

"Death to Elorians!" the troops chanted. "The sun rises!"

Okado stared ahead. He saw him there, riding at the lead, a man in yellow robes astride a white horse. His banner rose high in the wind, a sunburst to lead his troops.

"Ferius," Okado whispered.

Across the distance, he thought that the monk stared at him, that their eyes met, and it seemed to Okado that his half-brother recognized him . . . and grinned.

Okado raised his bow in one hand, his sword in the other. He cried out for the city to hear—a cry for all the lands of darkness.

"Eloria!" His voice pealed across the walls and the army ahead. "Eloria, hear me! We are darkness. We are starlight. We will show the enemy no mercy, for no mercy would be shown us. Fight well, my brothers and sisters. Fight well for your city, for your empire, for all the lands of shadow. We are the night!"

The cries rose around him, shaking the walls, deafening, a cry of tens of thousands, a cry of millions across the darkness.

"We are the night!"

Okado nocked an arrow. Across the walls, thousands of archers tugged back their bowstrings. Below in the plains, Ferius raised a horn and blasted out a twisted shriek. With roars and banging drums and crackling torches, the soldiers of sunlight stormed toward the walls.

CHAPTER TWENTY-FIVE
A SILVER LIGHT

The enemy covered the land, stretching from horizon to walls, a tidal wave of malice. The city of Yintao shook.

Okado had fought in battles before; he had slain many Nayan warriors upon the plains, and he had slain bloodsun monks upon the riverbanks, and his body still bore the scars of those fights. Yet he had never seen an onslaught like this—myriads of demons shrieking for blood, their weapons firing, the world itself vanishing under the multitudes.

A dozen trebuchets twanged below. Boulders sailed through the air. Several crashed into the walls, chipping the bricks, scattering shards of stone. Others slammed into the battlements, knocking soldiers down into the city below; one boulder crashed only feet away from Okado, shattering a merlon and crushing men like a heart under a boot. Other boulders cleared the walls, and Okado heard screams, and when he glanced behind him, he saw the stones slam into buildings and crush nightwolves.

"Men, fire!" Okado shouted and loosed another arrow. He didn't have to aim. Wherever he shot, he hit an enemy. Men kept racing up from the city, bringing new quivers of arrows, yet Okado knew the arrows would run out before the Timandrians did. He fired on, taking out man after man.

"Where's Ferius?" Bailey shouted at his side, firing arrow after arrow. Her face was flushed, and enemy arrows thrust out from her shield. "Where's the bastard?"

Okado spat. "Hiding. Hiding at the back. The coward led the charge as some conqueror, then retreated once the bloodshed began."

"Then we'll have to kill every damn man between us and him. We—"

Bailey had no chance to finish her words. Creaks and thrums sounded below. The air screamed as ballistae—great cart-drawn crossbows—fired. Iron bolts flew through the air, longer than men, to smash into the walls. One hit a merlon feet away from Bailey, and dust flew and bricks shattered. She nearly fell from the wall; Okado had to reach out and grab her wrist. More bolts flew overhead to crush nightwolves in the streets below. Houses crumbled. Debris scattered and blood splashed.

"Hwachas!" rose a cry upon a guard tower. "Men of Yintao—fire death upon them!"

A hundred hwachas topped the walls—iron plates as tall as men, punched full of holes like a grate. Fire arrows filled each hole, bags of gunpowder tied behind their fletching. Men lit fuses and began to ignite the projectiles.

When Okado glanced at the nearest hwacha, he found its operators dead, enemy arrows in their chests. Ducking under an assault of more arrows, Okado raced toward the iron launcher.

"Bailey, you aim, I'll fire! Aim at their catapults."

She nodded, leaped down beside him, and grabbed a winch. She growled as she turned the wheel, aiming the iron plate—and the hundred arrows filling its holes—down toward the enemy.

"Fire!" she shouted.

Okado grabbed a fallen man's torch and waved the flame across the arrows' packs of gunpowder. Smoke billowed out. A hundred explosions crackled, nearly searing Okado's eyes. With screams and flame, the hundred arrows blasted out from the hwacha. Across the battlements, ten thousand more arrows fired.

Empires of Moth

Smoke and flame engulfed the walls, and the enemy screamed below.

When the smoke cleared and Okado dared to look over the battlements, he beheld hundreds—maybe thousands—of dead. The fire arrows had punched through armor like knives into mud.

"We've slain a drop in an ocean," Okado muttered.

As men around him began loading more fire arrows, the enemy rolled forth new terrors. Siege towers approached, a hundred feet tall. Wheels creaked below them, the spokes decorated with Elorian skulls. Armored mules tugged at their lead, arrows shattering against their steel. Atop each siege tower, men awaited, clad in plates, firing arrows at Yintao's battlements.

"Smash the wheels!" Okado shouted. "Slay the mules!"

He fired an arrow at one of the beasts, but it only shattered against the animal's armor.

"Okado!" Bailey ran along the walls and leaped over a dead man. "Help me!"

He saw her kneel by a toppled cannon. Shattered merlons lay around it, crushing dead gunners. Bailey knelt, grimacing as she tugged the cannon. An arrow slammed into her armor and snapped. Okado leaped over fallen bricks, knelt beside her, and helped her lift the bronze tube.

"Death to Elorians!" shouted the enemy in the siege towers. "Take this city!"

When Okado glanced up, he saw a dozen towers only feet from the walls. Arrows flew everywhere. One missile slammed into his shoulder, denting the armor, and Okado grunted; the tip nicked his flesh. Bailey was loading a cannonball into the muzzle. Okado lit the fuse, pulled Bailey down, and covered his ears.

Smoke blasted over them.

The cannon jerked back so violently it fell from the wall, crashing into the courtyard below.

295

Okado rose, the arrow thrusting out from his shoulder. The cannonball had torn through one siege tower; half its warriors had fallen. Yet the structure kept moving forward. Iron planks slammed down, snapping onto the battlements. Timandrian troops spilled out onto the wall, swords swinging.

Ignoring the pain in his shoulder, Okado drew his katana. Bailey hissed at his side, her longsword clutched in both hands.

The enemy surged toward them.

Okado's sword sang.

The enemy covered the walls like ants scurrying along a log. Men leaped at him, clad in metal plates, swinging their double-edged swords. Okado swung his shield in one hand, his katana in the other. He howled as he fought, a wolf's cry, his helm hiding his face. His sword sprayed blood into the courtyard below. His shield shoved against men, sending them toppling down. Blades crashed against his armor, denting the scales. One dagger pierced the steel and bit his flesh, and he roared and slew the man. He fought with animal fury, his brothers and sisters fighting around him.

Bailey stood always at his side, shouting as she fought. Her sword crashed through armor, severed limbs, shattered shields. She wore the armor of Eloria, but she fought like a demon of fire, cutting down her own people.

The swords rang. The arrows flew. Boulders sailed overhead, cannons fired, and the hwachas rained death upon the enemy. Yet still the enemy's catapults swung, and still siege towers moved forward. Ladders joined them, slamming against the walls of Yintao, and thousands of Timandrians began to climb.

Okado and Bailey raced from ladder to ladder. They fired arrows. They shoved down fallen bricks. At their sides, soldiers poured burning pots of oil and packs of gunpowder. Explosions rocked the walls, and the dead piled up—mountains of corpses rose below, yet more kept swarming. Living Timandrians raced

Empires of Moth

over the mounds of their dead, and more ladders rose, and more boulders slammed into the walls.

"Bailey, the city gates!" Okado shouted, the arrow broken in his shoulder, the dagger wound blazing on his chest. "They have a battering ram."

He raced along the wall toward the gatehouse, a structure of two towers, battlements, and an archway holding the city's doors. As he ran, a boulder slammed into one tower, raining bricks and men down into the city. Archers fired from the second tower, and cannons blazed. A trebuchet swung upon the plains, and a flaming barrel crashed against the gatehouse crenellations, scattering men.

Okado leaped onto the battlements above the doors, shield raised. Bailey ran at his side. Arrows slammed into their armor, and corpses lay around their feet. When Okado looked between two merlons, he saw the battering ram below. The pole swung on chains, its head shaped as a bear. The metal beast slammed into the doors again and again, denting the iron.

Bailey fired down arrows, picking out men. Okado grabbed a fallen brick and hurled it, hitting a man's helm. At his side, Elorians tugged ropes, raising a cauldron of boiling oil. The liquid sizzled down onto the enemy. Screams and steam rose. More dead Timandrians piled up.

"Shatter the ram!" Okado shouted. "Cannons, break those chains!" He gestured toward three men along the northern wall; they were firing a bronze cannon into a horde of enemy knights. "Cannons—to the gatehouse!"

As archers fired down, Okado cleared way for the cannon. He lit the fuse himself. The cannon ball blasted out with a trail of fire. It slammed into the battering ram's chains, shattering the links. The pole slammed against the earth and rolled, crushing men. More arrows rained and more oil spilled.

"We are the night!" he shouted, his bloody sword raised, his shield bristly with arrows. "Elorians, slay the enemy—we will stand!"

A hush fell upon the battle.

A chill crawled down Okado's back like a reptile.

He spun back toward the plains.

The enemy formations were parting, beasts and men pulling back to form a path. Catapults, ballistae, and even the towering siege engines rolled aside. The drums renewed their beat. Men slammed weapons against shields, a constant rhythm, and a chant rose among the ranks. In the distance, black smoke rose, a miasma like disease creeping forth.

"What devilry is this?" Okado said, voice hoarse and throat tight.

Bailey stood at his side, red sword lowered. Between splotches of her enemy's blood, her face paled.

"Idar save us," she whispered.

Above the smoke rose a great banner, ten feet wide, displaying a horned crimson beast upon a black field. Men moved within the cloud, clad in dark robes.

Bailey clasped Okado's hand. Her voice shook. "Mages. Okado, this is an evil we cannot fight."

He was already drawing an arrow. "Yet I will fight nonetheless."

He released his bowstring. His arrow sailed downward, pierced the black smoke, and shriveled in midair. It fell to the ground as ash. The dark mages stared up toward him, faces hidden in their hoods, and raised their hands.

Smoke coalesced, forming a demonic fist the size of a house . . . then drove forward.

At his side, Bailey screamed.

* * * * *

Empires of Moth

The Magerian curse blasted the gates like the fist of a god.

Bailey screamed.

The smoky hand shattered the doors below her. The battlements shook. One tower cracked and crashed down, burying soldiers beneath it. Smoke enveloped the wall and Bailey yowled in agony. The black fog clung to her armor like leeches, tugging at the steel, bending it, tearing the scales off like a man scaling a fish.

At her side, she saw the curse wrap around Okado.

"Enter the city!" shrieked a distant voice, tearing through Bailey's ears—the voice of Ferius, of her nightmares. "Slay everyone inside."

Her eyes watering, she tore off her armor. The curse raced across her shield; she tossed it aside too. When she gazed down, the smoke was clearing, and she saw Timandrian knights charge through the smashed gates. Their horses galloped, trampling bodies. Their lances thrust, impaling Elorian soldiers. A hundred horsemen or more charged; outside the city, hundreds more mustered to enter.

Clinging to the ruined battlements, Bailey grabbed Okado's arm. He had torn off his armor; it lay upon the wall, the smoke compacting it into a ball.

"To the wolves!" she said.

They raced down what remained of the gatehouse stairs, leaping over bodies and nearly slipping in blood. They burst into the courtyard inside the city and beheld knights smash into wolfriders. Blood sprayed and both beasts and men fell.

"Ayka!" Bailey shouted. "Ayka, to me!"

Through veils of blood and smoke, her silver nightwolf leaped. The animal's fangs shone, and her eyes were bright. Clad in only her leggings and tunic but still wielding a sword, Bailey leaped into the saddle.

"Fight them, Ayka!"

Her nightwolf leaped into the fray.

They crashed onto a stallion, and Bailey swung her sword down, screaming as she punched through the knight's armor. Ayka placed her paws upon the falling horse and leaped, clearing the animal, and crashed into a second knight. The man thudded onto the ground, and Ayka tore off his visor. Bailey finished the job, plunging her sword into the knight's face.

Around them, hundreds of wolves and horses crowded the courtyard. The collapsed gates lay beneath them. More Timandrians kept marching in.

The fight moved out of the courtyard and into the streets; they fought between homes and temples, atop roofs and inside halls. Bailey fought in a blind rage. Her wolf leaped, she swung her sword, and blood splashed her face. She jumped off her wolf only once, grabbed a new shield and scaled shirt off a corpse, and fought again. Everywhere she looked she saw the enemies: Ardish knights on horseback, fighters from her homeland; bloodsuns, warrior-monks of Sailith in crimson armor; Verilish barbarians, wrapped in furs and fighting upon bears; Nayan jungle warriors, chanting as they thrust their spears; even Sanian archers atop elephants, clad in beads, firing red arrows down into the battle.

My people, Bailey thought as she fought, her eyes damp as she killed. *These are my banners. These are my brothers and sisters. And yet I must kill them. I must stop their cruelty.* Astride her wolf, she let out a howl.

"I am Bailey!" she cried. "I was born in sunlight. I am a daughter of the day. Yet now I fight for the night." She stood in her stirrups, shouting for all to hear. "Hear me, my people—stop this madness! Fight against the poison of Sailith, against the lies of your leaders. Fight with me, with Bailey of Arden—fight for the nigh—"

Arrows whistled her way.

Two slammed into her shield.

Empires of Moth

Three more drove into her wolf.

Ayka howled in agony, and Bailey cried atop her, and more arrows flew. They slammed into Bailey's armor, and her nightwolf bolted. The wounded beast, arrows thrusting out of her flank, charged into the ranks of archers.

Ayka leaped, clawing and biting, tearing men apart. Archers fell dead beneath her. Bailey swung her sword, cutting into the troops.

Timandrian swordsmen rushed toward her.

Elorian soldiers raced to stand at her sides.

A thousand swords swung and more arrows flew. More of the projectiles drove into her wolf.

"Ayka!" Bailey cried as the wolf mewled. "Ayka, run! Flee!"

Blood matted silver fur. Ayka panted and her eyes grew hazy, but she still fought, tearing into the enemy.

"Ayka, please! Turn around. To safety!"

A knight charged forward, trampling over bodies, thrusting his lance.

Ayka leaped toward him.

"No!" Bailey cried, tears on her cheeks. "Ayka, back!"

But it was too late. Ayka sailed through the air. The lance thrust into the nightwolf, skewering her, emerging bloody from the other side.

The wolf bit, tearing open the knight's neck . . . then crashed down.

Bailey thudded onto the ground, weeping. "Ayka . . ."

She knelt by the dead wolf, stroking her fur, begging her to wake up. Her tears streamed.

Shouts rose ahead.

Bailey raised her head to see more troops march toward her.

She leaped up, screaming hoarsely, and stood before her wolf. She sliced the air.

301

"Come face me! I am a daughter of sunlight, and I fight for darkness. Come, soldiers of Sailith. Come taste my blade." She raised her sword and shield. She shouted a cry that rose from her toes and tore through her throat, the cry of an orphaned girl, of a woman in the dungeons of Sailith, of a soul who had killed and bled and would die under the stars. "We are the night!"

They charged toward her.

She swung her sword.

She killed and blood washed her.

All around, she saw them storm into the city—the multitudes of the day, an enemy they could not stop, a force too great for an empire. The torches blazed and it seemed to Bailey that the world spun again, that the sun rose upon Eloria. Houses fell and streets turned red with death. Pagodas collapsed, raining tiles. Behind her, she saw the enemy reach the second layer of walls, and another battering ram swung, and more gates smashed. The warriors of sunlight flowed inward, beating their drums, killing all in their path.

The screams of women and children rose behind her, and Bailey wept, for she knew that the people of Yintao lived beyond these second gates. And she knew that they were dying. The cries of babes rose upon the wind.

She swung down her sword, cleaving a man, and knew that it was lost . . . knew that this city would fall, that the night would burn, that she would burn with it.

Then I will die in a pillar of fire. Then I will die shouting and killing. I will not live to see this city fall. Even as she shouted for war, her eyes stung with tears. *Goodbye, Torin. Goodbye, Grandpapa. I love you all.*

An arrow flew and slammed into her shoulder.

A sword shattered her shield.

She fought with closed eyes, ready to die.

From the north, distant horns blared.

Empires of Moth

They are beautiful, Bailey thought, blood in her mouth. *They are the horns of afterlife, a keen of magic and starlight and an end to pain.*

"The gods answer!" rose a voice.

"Hope—hope in the north!"

"The stars shine!"

Bailey opened her eyes. Corpses and death sprawled around her, thousands of fallen, and still the distant horns blew. Those were no horns of Timandra; they were high, ethereal wails.

Bailey ran.

She ran among bodies, cutting the living down.

She jumped onto the stairs of a pagoda. She raced up, leaping over corpses, until she reached the top floor. She slew a Timandrian archer, dashed to the window, and leaned outside.

Her eyes watered.

"Hope," she whispered, tasting tears mixed with blood. "Hope rises in the north."

Across crumbling streets and shattered walls, she beheld the dark highlands of Qaelin. A silver army was flowing downhill toward the city, white banners billowing, bearing the diamond sigil. Myriads of soldiers ran as one, clad in bright armor and curving helms. They held spears and shields, and their snowy cloaks billowed. At their lead rode two nightwolves, and a dragon of pearly scales flew above, chanting the name of her empire.

"Leen! Leen!"

With light that nearly blinded Bailey, brighter than a thousand moons, the force of an empire swept toward the city.

CHAPTER TWENTY-SIX
A MEMORY OF DAY

Like a silver wave, they swept toward the city.

Their lanterns burned bright. Their trumpets sang. Thirty thousand soldiers of Leen, clad in flowing robes and bright breastplates, fell upon the hordes of sunlight. Their spears thrust. Their swords swung. Blood splattered their shields.

Suntai fought at their lead upon her nightwolf. She was a daughter of Qaelin fighting among the hosts of Leen, yet under this darkness, all Elorians fought as one. All were children of the night.

Hundreds of thousands of Timandrians surrounded the walls of the city. Countless more had smashed through the gates and now swarmed along the streets. Everywhere she looked, Suntai saw fallen walls, crushed towers, and the dead.

"Into the city!" she cried, sword raised high. "Into Yintao."

Her wolf raced. They swept down the hill. The steel arrows of Leen flew through the night. The wooden arrows of the enemy flew back, tearing into Leen's soldiers, sending men tumbling down. Suntai kept riding, arrows in his shield, her sword raised high.

Darkness and light crashed.

Timandrian soldiers in armor lashed spears and swords. Bears clawed and tigers bit. Steel clanged and blood filled the air. Suntai kept riding, trampling men down, carving a path. Above in the sky, Pirilin the dragon dipped and rose, crushing men between her jaws. The dragon's tail lashed, slamming into siege towers, scattering men.

Empires of Moth

"Into Yintao!" Suntai shouted.

The forces of Leen drove forward, a great spear upon the plains, shoving a wedge into the enemy's ranks. They burrowed forward, cutting men down, silver cloaks stained red, spears tearing into armor. They were few against many. They fought as one, a single beast that ever advanced, shields lining its flanks, spears driving forward like teeth.

Leaving a path of dead, they drove into the enemy like a blade into flesh, chanting as they reached the gates and entered the city of the dying.

* * * * *

Cam was fighting atop his nightwolf, swinging his sword at enemy soldiers, when he saw his best friend ahead.

After what seemed like hours of fighting, maybe entire turns, they had driven into the city. He rode down cobbled streets strewn with bodies, fallen bricks and tiles, and shattered weapons. Down every street, Elorians and Timandrians clashed blades, beasts leaped, and more bodies fell. Atop every roof, archers rained death. The lights of cannons and hwachas lit the sky, and several roofs burned.

Cam wasn't sure how many men he killed—three, maybe four. He swung his sword in a mad, blind fury, not knowing if he killed or maimed. His wolf bit and clawed. Linee sat ahead in the saddle, clad in armor, a helmet upon her head. She had no skill with the blade, but she had spent the journey south training with a bow, and now she fired arrow after arrow as they rode. Men fell down before them, pierced with iron.

They rode at the back; here was the wake of the battle, a place of blood and corpses. Countless lay dead around them. The vanguards fought ahead; Cam could see them down the streets, fighting at the fourth layer of walls. The great heroes and villains of the war—Suntai and Okado, Ferius himself, maybe even Bailey—would be fighting there, defending the inner city. Yet despite his wolf, and despite Linee firing her arrows, Cam was no hero, and whenever he tried to charge forth, he ended up trailing behind, fighting the rear lines. Here in third level, the stragglers battled it out in the blood and dirt, random skirmishes on every street corner.

He was moving across a toppled wall and scattered tiles, finally entering the fourth level, when he saw Hem's wide form.

The baker's boy, his best friend since childhood, sat upon a fallen chunk of battlements. Hem's back was facing them, but Cam recognized the broad shoulders, shaggy hair, and heavy arms that now lay drooping.

"Hem!" he cried out. "Hemstad Baker!"

The memories pounded through him. Songs and ale in The Shadowed Firkin tavern. Arguments about which knight slew which monster in ancient tales. Jokes about Bailey told in hushed whispers, then yelps when she found out and twisted their ears. Here he was—that stupid, lumbering baker—and he wouldn't even turn around.

"Hem, damn you! Can't you hear me?"

Sitting in the saddle ahead of Cam, Linee twisted around to face him. Under her helmet, her face was pale, her eyes huge and haunted. For once no tears filled them.

"Camlin . . . he's not answering."

Cam dug his heels into his nightwolf. The animal raced forward, leaped over a cloven shield and a legless corpse, and landed upon the shattered battlements where Hem sat. With a tug on the reins, Cam halted the nightwolf and dismounted. He knelt before his friend.

Darkness like smoke spread before his eyes.

Two arrows jutted out of Hem's chest, and one pierced his neck. His eyes were still open, staring at the sky, and it seemed to

Empires of Moth

Cam that his friend was smiling . . . a soft smile like a man seeing a single star between storm clouds, like a soul torn by fear and pain finally hearing a soothing song of harps. A young Elorian woman lay in his arms, her tangled hair hiding her face, a dagger buried in her chest. The two sat leaning against a fallen merlon like lovers watching the night skies . . . together, at peace.

"Oh, Camlin . . . I'm sorry." Linee approached him, the wind beating her cloak. "I'm so sorry."

Throat tight, unable to speak, Cam closed his friend's eyes. As the war raged across the city, he knelt here in this shadowy huddle, staring.

"This is a good place," Cam finally said, voice soft, barely a whisper. "He didn't look upon war when he died. He's facing the stars, and he's holding a friend." Something swollen and painful clogged his throat. "I only wish I could have been here with you, you lumpy loaf. I'm sorry. I'm sorry I was too late."

He felt Linee's hand on his shoulder. Cam lowered his head, and his shoulders shook, and he thought about those old songs, frothy ale, and days in the silly sunlight of their youth, and he wept.

"Goodbye, Hem." He held his friend's hand. "Goodbye."

CHAPTER TWENTY-SEVEN
THE BLOOD OF YINTAO

Down to half its size, charred and bloodied but raising the red flame banners high, Ilar's navy sailed upriver toward Qaelin's capital.

Torin stood upon the flagship, sword drawn and shield ready, and beheld a city of hope and ruin.

Ahead, the Yin River flowed into the city between two towers and crenelated walls. A battle had been fought here. One of the towers—the one guarding the western riverbank—had lost its crown of merlons, and holes peppered its eastern twin. Cracks filled the city walls, and corpses lay upon the riverbanks and floated in the water. Timandrian archers manned these crumbling battlements, shouting as they saw the Ilari fleet sail toward them. Through gaps in the fortifications, Torin could see the city within; it bustled with enemy soldiers, and the banners of Sailith rose from roofs. But Timandra had not yet claimed the entire city, it seemed. Deeper within Yintao the battle still raged; Torin heard cannons blazing and swords clanging.

"We arrive at Yintao's greatest hour of need," Koyee said, standing beside him at the prow. "The city still fights."

They sailed closer, approaching the mouth of the city. Across the riverside walls and towers, the Timandrian archers shouted and fired. Arrows fell upon the Ilari fleet. Across a hundred decks, Ilari cannons blasted. The rounds tore into the guard towers, shattering bricks and felling men. The fleet sailed on, leaving a wake of dust and blood.

The river led them into the first level of the city. Torin had seen maps of Yintao, one square within another. In those maps,

Empires of Moth

houses stood in neat rows and statues rose in squares. When he
looked around him, however, he saw nothing but devastation. The
houses burned or lay crumbled; the statues had fallen. Shattered
blades, cloven helms, and broken arrows lay among the corpses of
men, women, and animals. Timandrian troops marched upon
rubble, waving torches and firing arrows. Ilar's cannons blasted,
tearing into the enemy upon the riverbanks. The fleet sailed
deeper, arrows in their hulls.

Torin snapped an arrow that pierced his shield. "The river
should lead us to the city's fourth level. We'll have to move on
foot from there."

Koyee nodded. "The Eternal Palace lies behind the seventh
walls. I still hear battle ahead; Ferius has not yet taken Qaelin's
throne."

At the sound of the monk's name, Torin grimaced.

Yes, you wait here, Ferius, he thought. *I was a gardener and you
were a humble monk, two men from a village . . . now we meet in a great
capital, armies at our backs.* He remembered his duel with Ferius
back in the distant, fallen city of Pahmey. *Now we complete that old
fight.*

They sailed through a storm of arrows and another layer of
smashed walls. Now the full battle raged around them. Elorian
troops bearing the moonstar and diamond banners clashed against
the enemy. Thousands fought along the riverbanks, racing down
streets, climbing roofs, and charging upon horses and
nightwolves. The city rang with singing steel. Upon the Ilari decks,
archers fired and warriors sang for victory.

"The red flame burns!" the warriors cried upon the decks.
"We are the night!"

The ironclad ships sailed on, their oars moving like
centipede legs, their sails wide, the pagodas upon their decks
bristling with archers. Their cannons blasted, their drums beat,
and their horns blared. Thousands of Ilari warriors bellowed,

309

horrible to behold, demons clad in black and crimson steel, their helms twisted masks of bloodlust, their torches and swords bright.

Past several more smashed walls, they reached a bend in the river. Upon the curving bank, a boardwalk sent piers into the dark water. Beyond this port, the river crossed the eastern city, heading back into the plains. Ilar's ships had reached the end of their journey. Torin stood, sword raised and teeth bared, as the fleet sailed toward the docks.

Anchors dropped.

Warriors leaped into landing craft.

Upon the boardwalk, thousands of enemies awaited, firing arrows and brandishing swords.

"Stay near me, Koyee," Torin said, hand shaking around his hilt.

"Always."

They looked at each other and shared a tight, mirthless smile, then leaped into a rowboat. Hundreds of other landing craft sailed with them toward the city streets.

Screams, clanging steel, and blood covered the world.

As he emerged from the boat, rushing onto the boardwalk, the Battle of Pahmey returned to him. In his mind, he ran with his friends again—with Bailey, Cam, and Hem—racing into an unknown land. He had fought against Eloria then—against Koyee herself. Now he swung his sword with the people of the night, the people he'd been raised to fear, to hate, to slay. Now he fought with a woman he loved.

A year and a half ago, I watched Koyee's father burn. He raced along cobbled streets, Koyee and a thousand other soldiers at his side. *Now I fight with her to save the darkness.*

Soldiers of Arden—his old homeland—came racing toward him, bearing the raven banner, swordsmen and horsemen and archers in steel. Robed monks shouted orders from towers above. His people charged to kill, and Torin ran to meet them.

Empires of Moth

I am no longer Torin, a boy of sunlight. I am a man of Eloria.
Koyee shouted at his side. "We are the night!"

The dragon Tianlong swooped above, red beard fluttering, roar thundering. Ilari riders chanted atop panthers, raising banners and aiming lances.

With a song of blades, the armies slammed together.

* * * * *

She fought along the streets of Yintao, armor splashed with blood—a seasoned killer, a demon in red.

Two years ago, I was fishing upon the river in a forgotten village, Koyee thought, swung her sword, and severed an enemy's arm. *I've been fighting you since you killed my father, Ferius. And in this city, I will kill you.*

This was the battle of her life. She had sailed alone through darkness. She had lived among thieves in a graveyard. She had busked in city dregs. She had played her flute as a yezyana to lecherous, intoxicated men. She had slain soldiers upon the streets of Pahmey, sailed through death in the gauntlet of Sinyong, and thrashed through fever and nightmares in the bowels of a ship. She had fought starvation, armies, and disease . . . all to come here, to race toward the Eternal Palace, the center of her empire, perhaps the center of the night.

Here my battle ends. She thrust her sword, impaled a man, and raced forward. *I survived for this. Here will I meet him again . . . and here will the sun set or burn us all.*

Torin fought at her side. Thousands of shouting Ilari swung swords around them, some fighting on foot, others charging atop their panthers. They raced forward, past hall and pagoda, down street after street, and everywhere the enemy waited. The hosts of Timandra swarmed through the city. Tigers pounced toward them—some succumbed to swords or arrows, and others tore

311

men apart. Burly men in iron swung hammers from atop bears. Knights charged into the ranks of Ilar, leaving paths of dead. Clouds of dark magic blasted, tossing warriors aside like a broom scattering insects.

And still they fought on.

Trumpeting cries rose ahead. A barrage of arrows flew.

Ilari warriors shouted and fell. Panthers crumbled upon the cobblestones.

Ahead Koyee saw them—the elephants of Sania trampling through the city. Howdahs rose upon their backs—towers of wood and leather—and archers stood within them, warriors clad in beads, wood, and silver. Hundreds of the beasts moved through the city, armored and painted, stomping men. Their trunks rose in fury.

Koyee raised her shield. Arrows slammed into the steel. Around her, warriors fell from their panthers, clutching their chests. One man thumped down at her feet, an arrow thrusting through his visor. His panther bristled and made to flee.

Koyee grabbed the feline's bridle.

It burst into a run.

Koyee tugged, leaped, and landed in the saddle.

Wind whipped her face. The panther ran beneath her, leaping from corpse to corpse. A hundred other panther riders raced around her, calling battle cries and firing arrows. The elephants trumpeted and charged toward them, footfalls cracking flagstones and shaking the city.

"Fire at the howdahs!" Koyee shouted, grabbing the bow from across her back. "The towers on the elephants!"

She tugged back her bowstring. She fired.

Steel arrows fletched with red silk flew from the Ilari riders. From the elephants' backs, wooden arrows fletched with green feathers rained down.

Men and beasts fell.

Empires of Moth

Koyee rode on, shouting.

Her panther leaped toward one of the charging pachyderms. Arrows drove down, clattering against Koyee's shield and her panther's black helm. The feline drove its claws into the elephant's hide, scurrying onto its back. Through a storm of arrows, Koyee swung her sword.

Her blade severed the howdah's straps, and her panther bit, and the structure of wood and leather crumbled. Men shouted and fell. Her panther leaped off the elephant, sailed through the air, and landed on the back of another beast.

Koyee tumbled from the saddle, landing in another howdah. The elephant trumpeted and bucked beneath her. Sanian warriors—clad in wooden armor and strings of beads—drew curved blades. Koyee snarled as she cut them down. She leaped from the bloodied howdah, landed in her panther's saddle, and they hit the ground running.

Where was Torin? She looked around, seeking him, calling his name. She could not see him through the crowd.

"Torin! Torin, where are you?"

She did not know if he heard. Her panther kept running, choosing its own path; she could not control it. They crossed a courtyard, and her panther ran up a building wall as easily as a cat climbing a tree. Upon the roof, the feline paused. Koyee stared ahead.

"Stars of my forebears," she whispered, feeling the blood leave her face.

Below her in the streets, the battle raged. Ahead, she could see the seventh layer of walls. The enemy was crashing against them—climbing ladders, battering gates, and pummeling towers with dark magic. Behind those last walls lay the Eternal Palace—a city unto itself, a complex containing a hundred halls. The largest building Koyee had ever seen rose in its center, a pagoda she

313

thought could house a nation. Its roofs spread out, tiled red, and an idol of Xen Qae stood upon its crest.

The Hall of Harmony, she thought, recognizing it from paintings and tales. *The home of Qaelin's emperor.*

Thousands of Yintao's soldiers stood behind the seventh walls, awaiting the enemy.

"Too few," Koyee whispered. "Too few." She raised her voice to a roar and pointed her sword. "To the palace! Warriors of Ilar! To the Eternal Palace—we must not let it fall."

She looked below her, seeking him. Finally she saw Torin in a street, battling a swordsman, and she breathed a sigh of relief. Thousands of others fought around him.

"Torin!" she shouted. "Torin—with me! To the palace!"

He slew his opponent, raised his head, and nodded. With a swarm of Ilari warriors, he began to run north toward the seventh walls. Most of them raced afoot; others rode upon panthers.

Her own panther snarled beneath her, claws gripping the roof. Its sleek body bristled, fur rising and muscles ripping. Koyee stroked its head.

"Run fast, cat of the night," she whispered. "Leap through shadow."

With a hiss, the panther leaped from the roof. They vaulted through the air, and Koyee fired her bow, hitting a man on the street. They landed upon another roof, the panther's paws silent against the tiles, and dived again. They raced across the city. The enemy fought and died all around. Around her, she saw other panthers leaping from roof to roof, mere shadows.

As they made their way north, Koyee remembered her life a year ago, leaping from roof to roof in Pahmey, an urchin with bare feet, slaying soldiers in the streets below. She was still fighting that fight . . . the battle for her life, for her family, for the darkness.

314

Empires of Moth

They raced forward, a cloud covering the city, heading toward their last stand.

* * * * *

Ferius rode his horse up the stairs of a crumbling wall, stared from the battlements toward the inner city, and licked his lips.

"It falls like a ripe fruit into our hands."

All around him, Yintao blazed. His herd marched through the streets, carrying torches and lanterns, bringing light to the darkness. Towers fell. Dark magic knocked down walls. Everywhere he looked, the savages were falling, their feeble defenses burning in his fire.

Ahead, across the inferno, the Eternal Palace still stood, a puddle of darkness in the encroaching light like a cave untouched by dawn.

"Yet the fire of Sailith will burn there too," Ferius said, sucking in breath, already tasting the glory. "You wait there for me, my sister."

He saw her ahead. Koyee was riding one of the panthers, a demon of darkness. She leaped from roof to roof, firing arrows as she headed toward the palace. She was one among thousands, a distant creature in the night, but Ferius knew it was her.

The pain in his leg flared—the wound Koyee had given him in Pahmey, driving her sword into his flesh. Ferius clenched his fists. When he caught her, perhaps he would cut off her leg. Perhaps he would show less mercy and tear her flesh inch by inch, tugging and digging and sawing as she screamed, dragging her torture on for months, for years. She would be the only savage left alive.

"My lord!" rose a voice below. A bloodsun raced up the stairs, reached Ferius upon the battlements, and knelt. A crack cleaved his helm, revealing a bloody wound. "My lord Ferius, the savages are retreating into the last level. They are fighting like cornered beasts, my lord. They shattered our last siege towers and ladders, and they've slain the mages. We cannot break in."

Ferius sneered down at the man. "Then we will stack hills of bodies and climb over the walls."

"But my lord! Some of the men are losing heart. They are fleeing the seventh walls."

"Then we will cut them down." Ferius spurred his horse. The beast whinnied and raced down the wall. "Bloodsuns— follow."

He rode into a cobbled courtyard. A statue of the savages' deity lay smashed, and dead Elorians lay strewn around it. Hundreds of bloodsuns stood here, crossbows in hand, their lamps bright.

Ferius galloped down a boulevard between stone houses. His bloodsuns ran behind him, a red swarm flowing down the street like a clot down a vein. Elorian corpses lay all around— soldiers, women, and children. Ferius rode over the dead. One of the savages—a young girl with a smashed leg—was still alive and twitching. Ferius grinned as he ran her over, crushing her skull.

He reached a wide square. Ahead loomed the seventh walls of the city, splashed with blood, and Ferius beheld the most beautiful sight he'd ever seen.

Thousands lay dead here, hills of his glory and might. Timandrians and Elorians alike piled up outside the walls, pierced with arrows, slashed with swords, burned with oil, and crushed with stones.

"Our death will light the darkness," Ferius whispered, sucking in an enraptured breath. Here stank the true might of Sailith, purification through blood.

Thousands of his troops still lived, slamming against the walls and gates of the Eternal Palace. From the battlements, arrows flew down, cannons blasted, bubbling oil spilled, and

Empires of Moth

boulders tumbled. The defenders of Yintao were cornered, trapped within the heart of their city; they fought with their greatest passion.

"They will not surrender, my lord!" said the bloodsun with the cracked helm.

"Good," said Ferius. "Let them die in fear and agony, knowing their city falls."

More Timandrians surged toward the gates, wielding axes and hammers, only to be cut down. As a new volley of Elorian arrows rained, a few Timandrians turned to flee.

Ferius grinned and licked his lips. "Bloodsuns! Allow no cowardice. Keep them attacking those walls."

His bloodsuns raised their crossbows. Timandrian soldiers—men of Arden bearing the raven shields—came fleeing toward them, wounded and screaming. Arrows thrust out from a few; the burns of oil spread across others. The bloodsun bolts slammed into them, cutting them down.

"You will not flee the enemy!" Ferius shouted from atop his horse. "Back to the walls. Cut the gates with axes! Smash the bricks with hammers. Pile up your corpses so your comrades may climb."

The fleeing Timandrians screamed and fell. A few turned back toward the palace walls, only for Elorian arrows to fall upon them.

"Die at the walls, men of sunlight!" Ferius cried. "Die for Sailith. Die for the sun!"

They surged again, a swarm of ants crashing against stone. The Elorian arrows, boulders, and cannonballs tore them down. More men turned to flee, dragging broken limbs, clutching at shattered armor and gaping wounds.

"We must flee!" they cried. "We are hurt! We need healing. We—"

"Die upon the walls!" Ferius roared, hands raised, as his bloodsuns fired.

Crossbow darts tore into his fleeing men. They fell. Bloodsuns moved between them, crushing the survivors with maces.

"To the walls!" Ferius waved his lantern. "Flee and die in shame. Perish against the enemy walls and rise to sunlit glory."

Trapped between the Elorian arrows and his monks' bolts, the soldiers of sunlight died. They painted the square red. More bloodsuns moved through the city, herding more Timandrians toward the walls, driving wounded, terrified soldiers to the palace.

"My lord!" cried one knight, a warrior of Arden, his breastplate smashed and his arm lacerated. "They are slaying ten of our men for every one of theirs we kill."

Ferius smiled down at the groveling warrior. "That's why we brought ten men for every one of their demons. We will die in a great pyre of glory. Hand me your crossbow!"

Ferius leaned down from his horse, all but wrenched the knight's crossbow free, and aimed. He shot the knight in the neck, piercing his armor. He loaded another bolt and fired ahead, hitting a fleeing soldier.

"You will die against the walls or you will die in my fire." He laughed, tasting blood and flame on his lips. They kept driving against the palace, trampling one another, a writhing mass, crushing, slamming at the walls and gates, trapped between death and death. Their hills rose.

With death and glory, we liberate the night, Ferius thought, laughing even as an Elorian arrow slammed into his shoulder; the pain was beautiful, the blood intoxicating when he licked it off his fingers.

"For Sailith!" he shouted. "For the light of day. Leave none alive!"

Empires of Moth

CHAPTER TWENTY-EIGHT
THE RED MILE

Never had Emperor Jin wished more for limbs.

He sat upon his throne, desperate to be out there. He wanted to fight with his troops. He wanted to lunge at the enemy with sword and shield, to die for his empire if he must. Instead he lingered here upon a cushioned seat of gold and jewels, limbless, helpless.

"Let us fly out, Shenlai," he said, eyes stinging. "I can hear them from here. Oh, Shenlai, I can hear them dying."

The old blue dragon lay coiled around the throne, blinking sad eyes. "I am sworn to protect you, Jin. I cannot lead you into danger."

"But they're dying!" Jin said. He shook himself, tearing off his golden prosthetic limbs. He tried to hop across his throne, to fall to the floor, to crawl to the doors and emerge into the battle. Yet he only managed to hop against the dragon's scales, then fall back into his seat. "Please!"

A hundred soldiers stood in his hall, still and silent, awaiting the fire. Outside, the screams of the dying echoed. It had been two turns since Timandra had attacked, maybe three, and Jin had not slept and barely eaten. The din of war kept growing nearer— men shouting, steel clanging, buildings collapsing.

"If they break into this hall, Jin, we must fly away," Shenlai said softly.

Jin shook his head. "I will not abandon my people."

319

The dragon blinked, his eyes huge and damp, his lashes fanning Jin. "You cannot save them by dying. We will fly to distant lands."

Jin squared his jaw and glared at the dragon. "So long as another soul lives in this city, I will stay. I cannot fight. I cannot help. But I am Emperor of Qaelin. If my empire burns, I burn with it."

Tears rolled down the dragon's cheeks, but old Shenlai managed to smile. "For three thousand years, I've protected and advised the emperors of Qaelin. You, Jin, are the noblest among them . . . nobler than I."

Jin felt his own tears welling up. He leaned forward, pressing his cheek against the dragon's scales. "I love you, Shenlai. And I'm scared. But we'll be strong together."

The doors to the hall opened, and Jin started, sure that the enemy had made it into the palace grounds. But it was Empress Hikari of Ilar astride a panther, clad in lacquered black plates, a dripping sword in hand. She rode into the hall, ash and blood covering her face, the red flame of her empire upon her shield. Two bodyguards flanked her, their helmets' visors pulled down, shaped as cruel faces with bristly mustaches.

"Emperor Jin!" Hikari called, riding toward him across the mosaic floor. "They are too many. We're holding them back, but we cannot hold them back forever."

Jin gazed through the open doors of his hall. Outside in the courtyard, he could see his people. Women. Children. Elders. Mothers with crying babes. The city's residents crowded the squares, streets, and halls of the palace grounds, whimpering and praying as the seventh walls shook.

"If the enemy breaks in, they will slay everyone here," Jin said to the empress. "They will not distinguish between soldiers and civilians; they did not in Pahmey. Six layers of walls have fallen. The seventh must stand."

Empires of Moth

The empress reached his throne, her eyes blazing, her teeth bared. "Then we must evacuate them from this city; this would be their graveyard. My soldiers still control the port. A hundred of my ships await. Load your women and children into their hulls. My fleet will deliver them to safety."

Jin's eyes widened, for Empress Hikari was renowned for her cruelty in war. "Many times your ships raided the coasts of Qaelin. Now you will deliver our people to safety in your lands?"

Screams sounded outside and an explosion rocked the city—another catapult's boulder slamming into a tower. The empress did not remove her eyes from Jin. "We are no longer enemies, child. We are no longer Qaelin and Ilar. We are all children of Eloria."

Upon his throne, Jin straightened and peered across his hall. Outside, he saw the people huddle. Each one was a life. Each was a world entire.

"The port lies a mile from here," Jin said. "The Eternal Palace is surrounded. The enemy sweeps across every street between us and your ships."

The empress snarled and raised her sword, and her panther snarled beneath her. "Then we will cut our way through. We leave this place, Emperor Jin. You too. Summon what soldiers you can—many still guard your walls. The forces of Ilar fight with you; the soldiers of Leen will join us." She banged sword against shield. "We will carve a path through the enemy. A mile of sunlight? Let it be a mile of our glory, of Timandra's blood—a Red Mile, a road of shadow in the light."

* * * * *

He sat upon his nightwolf, loyal Refir, his dearest friend since his youth. His mate sat at his side again—fair Suntai clad in steel, her sword held before her. For long moons, Okado had ridden without her; now his pack, his life, and his courage were whole. *Suntai is with me again. Together we can face the light of day.*

Around him, a hundred other wolfriders stared at the gates, grim, silent, weapons raised. Behind him spread the hope of the night—the last survivors in this city, perhaps the last survivors in all Eloria.

"Beyond these gates lies the sun," Okado said. "Beyond these gates is our greatest test . . . the fall of the night or our path to life."

Suntai looked at him, and Okado could barely breathe, for in her indigo eyes, he saw their love, their past, the future they had dreamed of—babes around the campfire, a proud pack, a life of honor. As she looked upon him, she whispered words she had never dared utter, words their exile would have deemed weak, words that now filled him with strength.

"I love you, Okado, my mate." Upon her wolf, Suntai reached out and held his arm. "We fight together. We will save them."

He stared behind him. The survivors of Yintao spread across the courtyard, thousands of elders, mothers, and children. The warriors of Ilar stood to their right, armored in black and sitting astride panthers. The hosts of Leen stood to their left, men of pale steel and white cloaks, their spears tall, their shields bright. The hosts of Yintao still stood on the walls, firing their arrows and cannons upon the enemy outside.

"It will be we, the riders of Chanku, who lead the charge." Okado stared back at the gates. The bronze thudded and bent as the enemy attacked, slamming hammers and rams. "It will be Chanku that carves the Red Mile."

Suntai nodded. "For glory. For life. For death."

Okado clenched his fist around his sword's hilt. He rose in his stirrups. He raised his sword high and cried out for the city to hear.

322

Empires of Moth

"Eloria!" His voice rolled across the Eternal Palace. "Eloria, we ride! We ride to the port. We ride to life. We are the night!"

Guards upon the walls raised silver trumpets. They blared their keen, and the riders below banged swords against shields. Men tugged at chains, and the gates burst open.

To the sound of trumpets and howling wolves, Eloria raced into the swarms of sunlit warriors.

They were a shadow driving into drowning light.

They were a single spear piercing a beast the size of the world.

The Chanku Pack rode at the vanguard, swords swinging, wolves biting, cutting down the enemy. The Timandrians covered the city like worms over a corpse. Spears lashed at the wolfriders. Arrows pelted them. Knights in armor, elephants of war, and endless pikes tore into their ranks.

"Ride on!" Okado shouted as riders and wolves fell around him. "To the port! For the night, for death, for the children of darkness!"

Corpses paved their way. Blood painted them. The Red Mile stretched before them.

Behind the pack, the people of Yintao emerged from the gates, stepping onto the bloody boulevard. Mothers held babes to their breasts. Elders hobbled on canes. Children clung to one another, tears in their eyes. The Ilari rode to their right, slashing swords from atop their panthers. Leen's troops marched to the left, their helms blank masks, their silver spears thrusting. From both sides, the enemy surged like waves, crashing into the soldiers of Eloria, dying upon blade and fang and claw.

"Forward, Eloria!" Okado cried, riding at the lead. Arrows slammed against his armor, and one pierced his wolf's hide. "Carve a path of glory. Carve the Red Mile!"

They drove on, street by street, man by man. Soldiers of darkness fell. Demons of sunlight died, only for more to replace

323

them, an endless sunrise. They passed down boulevards, between shattered temples, over fallen walls.

And they died.

They died by the hundreds. Soon there were no separate clans of Elorian fighters—not three empires, just one army. They fought as one, died as one, their blood spilling together, a shield around their women and children, the living replacing the falling. With every step, they shed a life. And yet they moved onward, carving this path of flesh, until all the children of Yintao emerged from the Eternal Palace and the masts of ships rose ahead.

"The ships!" rose voices behind Okado. "The ships of Ilar!"

Okado pointed his sword. "Follow, children of Eloria."

The pack rode, trampling over Timandrian swordsmen, and turned onto a boulevard leading down to the port. Only two hundred yards now separated them from the water. The lamps of the ships beckoned, beacons in the darkness, hope for life.

Before the docks stood an army of Sailith warriors.

At their lead, clad in crimson armor, Ferius sat astride a white horse. The Lord of Light raised a lamp in one hand, a mace in the other. His warriors spread around him, sitting atop their own armored horses—demons of red armor and yellow cloaks, the rulers of sunlight.

"Hello, Okado!" Ferius shouted and laughed. "Yes, I know your name. At last, on your eve of death, we meet. Come to me, spawn of darkness. Come to die."

Okado stared down at this man, his half brother, the son of his mother and a Timandrian soldier . . . this man whose shame was so great he burned the night.

Okado turned his head to look at Suntai. She rode at his side, scales missing from her armor, her wounds dripping, but her was sword still high. Her eyes were still strong and full of love for him and the night.

Empires of Moth

"We ride together, my mate," she said. "We ride to meet him."

Okado reached over and touched her cheek, a pale cheek tattooed with lighting, smeared with soot. She smiled and a tear trailed down to his fingers.

He nodded. "Always, my Suntai, star of my heart. Always we ride together."

They turned back toward the monks and the ships behind them.

They roared their battle cries together.

The alpha pair led the charge, and behind them, hundreds of wolfriders—the remains of their pack—roared and followed in a thunder.

Eloria stormed down the boulevard. From the port below, the Timandrians surged. Horses galloped and nightwolves leaped. With swinging swords and maces, the hosts crashed together.

Okado was wounded. He had not slept or eaten for turns. His armor was chipped, his left arm was numb, and a vise of pain squeezed his head. Yet still he fought—the fight he had been born for, that he'd left his village for, that he'd spent years training for. It was the fight against the sunlight, against the shame of his blood.

The monks swarmed toward him, maces swinging. One mace shattered his shield. Another drove into his shoulder, and he roared and slew the man. Around him, he could barely see the city, only the sunlit demons crashing against him.

"Get the people into the ships!" Suntai called from somewhere within the fray. "We'll hold them back. Get everyone into the ships!"

The monks mobbed Okado, and his sword could barely scratch their armor. A mace slammed into Refir, and the wolf yowled but kept fighting. When Okado glanced to his left, he saw the first women and children race along a pier and enter a

325

rowboat. Thousands of Timandrians—hundreds of thousands—brandished their weapons, pressing toward the port.

I will hold them back.

He looked across the crowd of Timandrians, seeking him—the Demon of Daylight. Behind a dozen bloodsuns, he saw him. Ferius sat upon his horse, his arms raised, his lantern shining. He seemed like a man in rapture. He howled for sunlight and the murder of the night.

"Suntai!" Okado shouted. "Do you see him?"

She swung her sword at his side, severing a man's arm. She nodded. "I see him. We ride!"

With a yip, she spurred her wolf. Okado's wolf burst into a run too. The alpha mates sailed through the air, landed atop monks, and swung their swords. The enemy fell around them. Ferius still stood ahead, head tossed back, eyes closed.

"Into the boats!" somebody cried behind; Okado thought he recognized Bailey's voice. "Hurry—on board!"

He did not turn to look. His eyes remained on Ferius. He raced forward, sword hacking, his nightwolf biting and clawing. Suntai fought at his side, blood on her wolf's maw. They drove through the mob until they reached him.

"Ferius," Okado said. "You know my name, but do you know who I am?"

Atop his white horse, the monk stared, and a smile spread across his face. "Leader of a mongrel pack."

Refir bucked and clawed the air, and Okado sneered. "Do you know who I am?"

Ferius's smile spread into a grin. "My half-brother." He laughed, a sound like shattering bones. "The spawn of our harlot mother. She was a sinner, Okado. She was a filthy savage." He spat toward Suntai. "As is this harlot you parade as your mate."

Atop her wolf, Suntai raised her bow. She fired. Ferius swung his mace, knocking the arrow aside.

326

Empires of Moth

"You cannot stop me, creatures of darkness!" Ferius shrieked, voice rising as a storm. "I am sunfire."

As the wolves leaped, Ferius smashed his lantern against his chest.

Glass shattered, oil spilled, and Ferius burst into flame.

The two nightwolves yelped and pulled back. Okado shielded his eyes from the heat, and Suntai gasped. Their wolves growled and snapped their teeth, daring not approach. Ferius laughed, engulfed in flame, his horse burning, his shrieks rising.

"I am the sun!" cried the monk. "I am the light of Sailith and I banish your darkness."

His blazing horse screamed, an almost-human sound, and burst into a gallop. The nightwolves parted, allowing the burning animal to pass. As the horse raced toward the river, Ferius leaped from the saddle, a ball of flame, and crashed against Suntai.

"I will burn you all!" The shrieks rose like steam from a pot. "I light the darkness!"

"Suntai!" Okado shouted.

Refir yowled at the flames, too terrified to attack. Okado leaped from the saddle, reached into the fire, and tried to grab Ferius, to pull him off. His hands burned, and Okado shouted, grasping, tugging.

He could barely distinguish Okado from Suntai and her wolf; they were one ball of fire. Screams rose from within the inferno—Suntai's screams.

"My mate!" she cried. "My mate, get them to the ships, I— Okado! Okado, we will ride again. I love you. Goodbye—"

Her voice twisted into a scream . . . then fell silent.

His arms burned. Okado barely felt them. He grabbed something solid and tugged. With a ripping sound, he pulled the blazing monk off his mate.

327

Suntai and her wolf lay upon the ground, blackened, not moving. Before Okado, a demon from the underworld, Ferius blazed and laughed.

"The fire cannot burn me, my brother," said the living torch. "Do you see? Do you see the light? It will burn you too."

The monk advanced toward him, crackling arms held out.

Okado could barely hold his sword; his fingers were cracked and bleeding, the skin peeling off. With a hoarse cry, his lungs full of smoke, he swung the katana.

The blade slammed into the flaming creature and clanged against armor. From the inferno swung a mace, wreathed in fire. The flanged head drove into Okado's arm, shattering the bone with a snap. It flew again, landing on Okado's shoulder, driving him to his knees. A third blow smashed his hand, knocking his sword to the ground.

Bleeding and burnt, Okado looked up.

The demon stood above him. Through the flames, Ferius smiled. His flesh did not burn. He seemed a stone idol trapped in a burning star. The fire itself seemed to whisper.

"All the night will burn . . ."

The mace drove down like a comet.

Pain exploded against Okado's head.

He fell.

He lay on his side. Stars floated before his eyes, shadows and light, and he saw them there—the ships sailing away, the children of Eloria upon them.

We saved them. We die in fire, but we saved them, Suntai.

Broken, unable to breathe, he turned his head, and he saw her there. Her body was charred, but her face was still pure, her eyes open and brilliantly blue, almost alive. He crawled toward her. He reached out and held her hand.

"We ride now, Suntai," he whispered. "We ride upon the plains beyond the stars. Forever we'll ride together."

Empires of Moth

He could no longer feel the fire, no longer feel the mace driving down against his back. He smiled softly, holding his mate's hand, and saw only the stars. He rode upon Refir again, and she rode at his side, lights in the sky, children of eternal night.

CHAPTER TWENTY-NINE
BROKEN

Torin stood upon the *Red Flame*, flagship of Ilar's navy, watching the port burn.

A blaze engulfed the boardwalk, all-consuming, tearing through wolfriders and monks alike. The heat blasted him, and Torin winced, wanting to be there, to fight with the men, but most of the ships had already sailed downriver. Only three vessels remained in the port. The last of the rowboats were emerging from the blazing docks, charred and bleeding survivors upon them.

"Where are you?" Torin whispered, eyes burning in the heat.

He had seen none of his friends. With every rowboat that arrived, he scanned the people who climbed onto the ship. Mothers clutching babes. Elders on canes. Wounded soldiers. Crying children.

But no Koyee. Nobody else from Fairwool-by-Night.

"*Red Flame*, sail!" shouted Empress Hikari, flying above the ship upon her dragon. "Sail downriver."

Torin shouted up at her. "Wait! Wait—there's still room." He pointed at several rowboats emerging from the inferno, survivors upon them. "We can fit a few more onto this ship."

The empress swooped upon her dragon, nearly slamming into the masts, and nodded. "Three more rowboats, then sail downriver. Two more ships await survivors."

Torin turned away from the battle on the port. Stretching south along the river, he saw the lamps of a hundred Ilari ships.

Empires of Moth

Each vessel was crammed full of survivors, their hulls and decks crowded like coops.

"Are you on one of those ships, Koyee?" he whispered. "Are you safe, Bailey, Cam, Hem?"

He stared back at the city, wincing in the heat. The fires raged across the port. Farther back, pagodas blazed, walls crumbled, and Timandrian troops chanted in victory. Thousands of soldiers were streaming along the streets, heading toward the port; only a handful of Elorians now held back the tide. Smoke billowed across the battle and ash rained.

"We sail out!" cried the ship's captain, a beefy man clad in leather and steel. "Sailors—raise anchor. We sail!"

Torin raced across the deck, moving between survivors, and leaned over the railing. Three last rowboats were moving through the water, navigating between scraps of burning flotsam. In each boat, fifty-odd survivors crowded. As the *Red Flame*'s sails unfolded and she began floating downriver, the smaller vessels attached to her side like piglets to a sow. Survivors, most of them burnt and bleeding, began climbing rope ladders onto the deck.

Torin scanned the newcomers, daring to hope. As one group climbed aboard, he saw a tall woman among them, her head rising above the others. She wore tattered scales, scratches covered her skin, and soot painted her black. Two charred braids hung across her shoulders, and when she looked toward him, Torin saw brown eyes peering through dust and blood.

"Bailey," he whispered.

She saw him and froze.

His eyes watered.

"Bailey!" he shouted.

He ran toward her between Elorian survivors. He had not seen her—his dearest friend—in so long. When had they left the burning city of Pahmey? By Idar, it must have been almost half a year ago. She moved through the crowd toward him, tears etching

331

white lines down her cheeks. When Torin reached her, she crashed into his embrace, her body shaking, her fingers digging into his back. Her tears splashed him.

"Bailey," he whispered, holding her close, crushing her against him, never wanting to part from her again.

She laughed as she cried. "Oh, Winky." She touched his cheek. "You're still a babyface. You're all sooty and scruffy, but you're still my babyface."

He held her at arm's length, examining her for wounds. Blood and grime covered her, but she grinned, her teeth startlingly white in her blackened face. "Thank Idar you're all right, Bailey. I was so worried." He felt his eyes water again, and he knuckled them dry. "Have you seen anyone else? Have you seen Koyee?"

She stiffened and stared at him, and her smile vanished. Her eyes hardened, and for a heartbeat or two, she seemed almost heartbroken, then almost enraged. Then the moment was gone, and she blinked and nodded.

"I saw Koyee run into the palace. She vowed to fight alongside the emperor, to protect him on his way here. They were going to leave the palace last, only after all others were evacuated." She looked back toward the port; the last two ships were raising their anchors. "She'll catch the last ship."

But no warmth or hope filled her voice; it was as leaden and cruel as a cannonball. She might as well have added: *And if she doesn't, that's fine by me.*

The *Red Flame* sailed downriver, picking up speed and leaving the port behind. Enemy arrows flew overhead, launched from a guard tower along the river. A few tore through a sail, and people wailed and ducked below. Torin winced and grabbed Bailey's arm, about to tug her down, when a cry rose behind him.

"Torin! Bailey!"

Empires of Moth

He turned to see more survivors climb onto the deck from a second rowboat. A short, slim figure moved among them, worming his way through the crowd and calling to him.

Torin breathed a sigh of relief. "Cam!"

The young shepherd reached him, looking like a beaten alley cat; his armor was chipped, grime covered his face, and blood stained his gloves. Torin grabbed his friend and pulled him into a crushing embrace. Bailey joined them, her bitterness gone, wrapping her arms around the two and squeezing.

"Camlin Shepherd!" Torin said. "Thank Idar you're here. Are you hurt?" He examined his friend. "Where's Hem? Where's that big lump?"

Cam said nothing. He only stared, silent. Torin and Bailey were grinning and hopping with excitement, but the young shepherd only stood, his eyes dark, his face ashen.

Torin froze. His throat constricted.

"Cam . . ." Torin grabbed his friend's arms. "What . . . oh Idar."

Cam turned to gaze toward the distant port. The fire still burned, and ash fell like snow. "He was peaceful." Cam's voice was so soft Torin barely heard. "I don't think it hurt him. He held a woman in his arms, and he was gazing up at the stars." Cam turned back toward his friends. "The damn fool probably never saw it coming."

Bailey covered her mouth with both hands, eyes round and watery. Torin could not speak. He could not breathe. He could only stare at Cam . . . Cam who'd always been part of a pair . . . Cam and Hem, always together, the troublemakers of town . . . now only one. Now only silence.

Torin lowered his head. He held his friends, one in each arm, and they stood together. They watched the port grow smaller, the last ships leaving the flames.

333

A year ago, we left Fairwool-by-Night . . . four friends, four youths caught up in a war too big for us. His eyes burned and his chest shook. *We sail away from fire . . . three.*

A soft voice rose at his side. "Camlin?"

Torin turned his head. Through his tears, he saw a young Timandrian woman, ash and blood in her tangled blond hair, her face black with soot. It took him a moment to recognize her, and when he did, Torin reached out and held her hand, and he pulled her into their warmth.

"Linee," he said softly.

She clung to them, tears on her cheeks.

As they stood together, four children of sunlight in a fleet of darkness, Torin looked back at the city; they were now sailing past its last towers, emerging into the darkness of night.

Where are you, Koyee? he thought. *Where are you? I need you here with us.*

Darkness engulfed the *Red Flame* ship. Stars shone overhead. Torin stood upon the deck, holding his friends, watching Yintao burn. Upon the wind, he heard the victorious chants of daylight . . . and the fading song of the night.

Empires of Moth

CHAPTER THIRTY
KOYEE'S SONG

She stood in the palace doorway, her back to the throne, watching the last people of Yintao leave along the Red Mile.

Beyond the courtyard and halls of the palace grounds, a hundred soldiers of Yintao—the last remaining—stood upon the seventh walls, firing down at the enemy. A hundred more stood at the open gates, pikes raised, holding back the sunlit horde. Every moment, another man fell dead.

The rest of the Eternal Palace was deserted. Where once myriads had crowded—the survivors of the slaughter—now only dust, shattered blades and a few discarded dolls remained. They had all made their way to the port; as Koyee watched, the last survivor—an elderly woman holding her granddaughter—hurried out the gates, two soldiers protecting her.

Koyee spun around. She stared into the hall of the emperor. Jin sat strapped into a harness upon his dragon. Fifty soldiers stood around him, bearing katanas and shields emblazoned with Qaelin's moonstars.

"It's time, my emperor," Koyee said. "The last of your people have left. We leave too."

Jin nodded. "We leave. Shenlai! Do not fly high. We travel down the Red Mile like everyone. We stay with our soldiers. We will not soar safely as others die upon the ground."

Shenlai nodded, sadness in his crystal orbs. He uncoiled and began sliding forward, moving like a snake upon the hall's mosaic. Soldiers marched at his sides, helms hiding their faces, their swords raised.

335

Koyee glanced back at the courtyard outside. She winced. With most of the city's soldiers gone down the Red Mile, protecting the people of Yintao, the enemy was breaking in. Chanting and jeering, Timandrian soldiers burst through the gates and into the courtyards and streets of the Eternal Palace. Blood stained their swords, and they shouted for victory.

"We must hurry!" Koyee said. "Out!"

Shenlai increased speed, bursting out of the hall like iron from a cannon. The palace guards ran at his sides. Koyee ran with them, an arm's length from Jin who sat upon the dragon, strapped into his golden harness.

"Through the gates!" Koyee shouted. "Soldiers of Qaelin— cut down the enemy! Make for the port."

She grimaced as she ran. The enemy raced toward them. A part of her knew that it was too late, that she should have left earlier, that the last to leave would suffer the brunt of Timandra's wrath. Okado had begged her to flee sooner, but how could Koyee have abandoned her emperor, abandoned the last dragon of Qaelin, abandoned these brave palace guards who stood their ground? So she had stayed. And now she screamed as she ran toward the enemy, knowing she would die.

They raced across the palace grounds. They crossed a courtyard, ran around a temple, and skirted a statue of Xen Qae. Fifty yards from the gates, the enemy met them.

Koyee did not know how many Timandrians attacked— hundreds, maybe thousands. They kept flowing into the palace grounds, firing their arrows. Koyee screamed as arrows slammed into her armor. One scratched her thigh, and she nearly fell but righted herself and kept running. Timandrian soldiers ran toward her, hands bloodied, and she swung her sword. Her blade clashed against them. They thrust their own swords, denting her shield, and she shoved against them, pushing them back, not even trying

Empires of Moth

to slay them—there were too many to fight—just to break through.

"Push through them!" she shouted. "Get the emperor out the gates. To the port!"

She drove forward, shield held before her, shoving men down. They tumbled. Shenlai roared at her side, biting and whipping his tail, sending men flying. The palace guards thrust pikes, skewering men.

"Push them back!" Koyee shouted. "Don't bother killing them. Just shove with your shields. To the gates!"

Yet the enemy was too strong.

Two palace guards fell, pierced with swords.

Another five tumbled to her right.

Koyee screamed, hacked at a Timandrian's chest, and suffered a blow to her arm. Her blood spurted.

Another blow knocked her down; she fell hard on her tailbone, pinned between Shenlai and the enemy. More swords swung her way, and she raised her shield, her arm wet. The blows pounded against her, denting her shield, tearing her armor, spilling her blood.

"Fly, Shenlai!" she shouted. "Fly with the emperor."

She saw nothing but the enemies' leering eyes and hammering swords.

A blow shattered her shield, and blood dripped down her forehead.

She fell onto her back. Her sword fell from her hand. Smoke coiled above. She couldn't even see the stars.

A roar pierced the night.

Blue scales flashed.

Shenlai, last dragon of Qaelin, leaped into the air and slammed down ahead of Koyee, crushing Timandrians beneath him.

"Take the emperor!" the dragon cried. "Take Jin."

337

Koyee's head spun, but she managed to leap to her feet. She
was wounded, maybe dying, blood in her eyes. The Timandrians
roared and swords swung against scales. Koyee leaped, grabbed
Jin from his harness, and tore him free. She pulled the limbless
boy to her chest, arms wrapped around him. She had lost both
sword and shield, but she had the boy.

Shenlai roared his cry, a howl of ancient fury, a memory of
the mighty dragon he had been in older days. His long, scaly body
began to move forward, shoving Timandrians back like a plow
through dirt.

"Take Jin to safety!" the dragon said.

Koyee stood, holding the emperor. The dragon flailed,
shoving the Timandrians back, and formed a living wall. Koyee
and a few last palace guards stood at one side of the dragon, the
gates rising to their left. Behind Shenlai, the might of Timandra
roared and hacked. Scales and blood flew.

Koyee looked at the gates, seeing the Red Mile stretch down
to the last ship in port. She looked back at Shenlai.

"Shenlai . . ." Jin whispered, held to her breast. "Shenlai,
please . . ."

Koyee hissed, raised her chin, and placed Jin into the arms
of a palace guard—one of only five who still lived. "Take him to
the ship. Go! Now!"

The guard held the boy in his arms. He gave Koyee a stare
that lasted both a second and an eternity and then turned to run.
With his fellow guards, he raced down the boulevard toward the
last ship of Ilar.

Koyee remained in the courtyard. She reached down and
fished out her father's sword from blood. She raised the dripping
blade, leaped onto Shenlai's back, and stood facing countless
shouting Timandrians. They stretched across the courtyard. They
spread through the city. They crawled across all the lands of night.

Empires of Moth

They were a sea of fire, of hatred, of devilry. She faced them alone.

"I am Koyee!" she shouted, standing on Shenlai's back; the dragon was bleeding, many of his scales gone, arrows and swords buried in his flesh. "I am a daughter of darkness. I am a child of Eloria. You slay us. You burn us. But you cannot kill our honor. You cannot light our shadows." The clouds parted above, and moonlight fell upon her. She tossed back her head and cried for the city to hear. "Eloria! We are the night!"

Arrows flew her way.

One drove into her shoulder.

Another slammed into her leg.

Below her, Shenlai took flight.

She wobbled on the dragon's back. The enemy surged forward, and more arrows flew, thudding into the dragon. Swords sliced at Shenlai's belly. Yet still he rose higher, struggling for altitude like a hot air balloon with a guttering flame. Koyee wobbled and fell upon his back, reached out, and grabbed the harness Jin had sat in. She clung, bleeding and dizzy, as the dragon ascended.

Shenlai gained speed. They passed through smoke, rising higher than the palace walls. Shenlai was a long dragon, but his body was no wider than the back of a horse. Clinging on with one hand, Koyee gazed at the city below.

The armies of sunlight covered Yintao. They spilled across the palace and into the emperor's hall. They stood upon walls and roofs. They drove toward the port where the last ship of Ilar, cannons blazing and archers firing, made its way downriver. Around them lay countless corpses.

"After the ships, Shenlai!" Koyee pointed to the river; a hundred ships were sailing into the darkness.

They flew over the city streets. Shenlai dipped, his blood raining, losing altitude.

339

"Shenlai! Fly!"

The dragon blinked and strained, rising several feet higher. They flew toward a pagoda, and Koyee winced, sure the dragon would slam into the bricks. They managed to clear the tower, the dragon's tail thumping against its roof. Timandrian archers stood within, firing their bows. More arrows slammed into the dragon, and he whimpered, the sound of a creature too weary for screams.

"Fly, Shenlai, please," Koyee begged, clinging on as her own blood spilled. "For Jin."

The last dragon of Qaelin, full of arrows and shattered blades, flew across the burning streets. With a last roar, he gained speed and the city blurred below. Through fire and smoke and flying arrows, they cleared the last walls and burst out into the great darkness of the plains.

"There, Shenlai! To the river."

She pointed. The Yin River flowed south, lined with the lanterns of the fleeing ships. It would lead them to the southern coast, to the sea, to the island of Ilar . . . to safety. Torin waited upon one of those ships. Okado would be there too. Hope. Life. All of her friends and family were sailing on that river.

"Fly!"

Yet he could not. He had reached the end of his strength. With every breath, the dragon flew lower, until his tail skimmed along the riverbanks. Koyee tugged on the saddle as if she could lift him higher. For a moment, it seemed that Shenlai did rise higher again, but then he dipped, and his belly slammed against the earth.

Koyee grimaced, banging her teeth together. She clutched on with all her might as the dragon crashed, drove through rocks and dust, and finally lay still by the water.

Koyee lay for long moments upon the dragon's back. She blinked weakly, her vision blurry. She tilted her head back and saw the stars. Her hand loosened and slipped off the saddle. She rolled

Empires of Moth

off the dragon and lay upon the ground. Her head fell back, and she could see the last ship sail south, its lanterns growing distant, leaving her behind.

"Koyee . . ."

She blinked, pushed herself onto her elbows, and turned toward the sound. Was her mother calling her? Was this the voice of the afterworld?

"Koyee . . ."

She reached out and placed her hand in Shenlai's beard. The dragon had spoken, his voice barely a whisper. His eyelids were low upon his crystal orbs. Koyee's body felt wrong, too hurt, too thin, too dry. She crawled and wrapped both arms around the dragon's head. She whispered into his ear.

"I'm here, dearest dragon. I'm here."

He blinked, his long lashes brushing against her. "It's time, Koyee. It's my time to leave."

She shook her head, her tears falling upon him. "Don't leave me."

The dragon managed a smile, and his scales rubbed against her, smooth and cool. "For thousands of years have I flown across the night, and now I fly to the sky beyond. For thousands of years have I kept my secret. Now I must share these words with you."

"No . . ." Her tears flowed, and she howled and shook him and tugged his beard. "No, Shenlai! No. No. Please." She trembled. "You cannot leave us. You cannot go, dragon of Qaelin, sweet prince of the night."

"We all must go when our time comes, child. It is only when we leave too early that we may grieve. I have lingered. I have watched too many seasons come and go, too many turns of the moon, too many lives kindled and darkened. Watch over him, Koyee of the night. Watch over Jin . . . and watch over Eloria."

341

She trembled with sobs. She shook her head. "You will watch over us."

He rolled his head back and gazed at the stars. She lay against him, her cheek against his beard, her arms wrapped around him.

"Always, Koyee. I will always watch over you, my child, even as I fly where you cannot see."

She held him close. "I'm afraid."

"So are all in darkness." His eyes were but glowing, blue slits, his lashes low. "But there is hope."

Her tears rolled down his scales. She knew it was coming, the words she dreaded, the words that meant he would leave them.

"Speak, dragon of Qaelin," she whispered, trembling as she held him so tightly.

Shenlai smiled, and suddenly he no longer felt cold but warm and full of comfort. He whispered into her ear, his breath soft against her.

"Fix the clock and the world will turn again."

Like setting moons, his eyes closed. Their light dimmed and was gone.

Koyee shook silently and held him close. The distant lights of the ships faded over the horizon, and darkness fell upon her.

The story will continue in . . .

SECRETS OF MOTH

The Moth Saga, Book Three

NOVELS BY DANIEL ARENSON

Standalones
Firefly Island (2007)
The Gods of Dream (2010)
Flaming Dove (2010)

Misfit Heroes
Eye of the Wizard (2011)
Wand of the Witch (2012)

Song of Dragons
Blood of Requiem (2011)
Tears of Requiem (2011)
Light of Requiem (2011)

Dragonlore
A Dawn of Dragonfire (2012)
A Day of Dragon Blood (2012)
A Night of Dragon Wings (2013)

The Dragon War
A Legacy of Light (2013)
A Birthright of Blood (2013)
A Memory of Fire (2013)

The Moth Saga
Moth (2013)
Empires of Moth (2013)
Secrets of Moth (2014)

KEEP IN TOUCH

www.DanielArenson.com
Daniel@DanielArenson.com
Facebook.com/DanielArenson
Twitter.com/DanielArenson

CPSIA information can be obtained at www.ICGtesting.com
Printed in the USA
LVOW01s2003040514

384389LV00018B/1669/P